THE SECOND WE MET

MAYA HUGHES

Cover Design: Najla Qamber, Qamber Designs

Cover Image: Wander Aguiar

Editing: Tamara Mayata, Tex Thompson, Caitlin Marie Proofreading: Sarah Kellog Plocher

For Nicole, who has walked hundreds of miles with me and always shares a spark of her genius with every step.

CHAPTER 1
ELLE
JUNIOR YEAR - AUGUST

"I'd rather let Edward Scissorhands give me a manicure." My eyelids drooped. I threw the car into park, thanking God I was finally there. Outside my driver's side window, the bright and shiny brass sixty-six on the front of the house glinted in the afternoon sun.

"Now who's being dramatic? You two used to be so close."

"Who has a two-year class reunion?" I gathered up my road snacks from the passenger seat and shoved them into my frayed and battered, better-than-nothing tote bag. Mom had kept trying to convince me to buy a grown-up purse over the summer, but what good was a purse if you didn't have any money to put into it once you bought it?

"She was your best friend for seventeen years."

"Things change, Mom, and Alyssa has always done what's best for Alyssa." *Like my ex-boyfriend.* "So, I'm more than happy to not go. Plus, depending on how things go with the Huffington Award, I might not even be in the country when it rolls around."

She let out the long-suffering sigh reserved specifically for moms with difficult children. "I know you've worked so hard for that, but I just don't want you to lose touch with people who used to be so important in your life."

"Some people aren't worth having around, Mom. Not everyone is as awesome as you."

Her soft snort made me smile. "By the way, we'll get you the money for your tuition on the first of the month. You know how hard it's been."

"I'm glad I could help." The money I'd saved all last year for my tuition had gone to the late mortgage payments to stave off foreclosure on the house.

"Thanks, sweetie." It had taken us several weeks to convince my dad to take the money. If it saved the house, it was worth it, but that meant things would be tight—real tight.

The loan situation was a touchy topic. Apparently, bad credit and no credit were the best way to end up with not many options when it came to paying for college. My first two years had been paid for with scholarships, last semester I'd maxed out my student loans—which were racking up interest by the day—and now I was winging it.

"How's the hair holding up?"

I pulled a handful of my electric pink locks over my shoulder. "It's very pink."

"They don't call it Day-Glo pink for nothing. It'll last so long your grandkids will come out with pink hair." She laughed.

"Awesome. I need to get unpacked and then I'm off to the tutoring center."

"Honey, you're doing great work, but you need to make sure you're taking time for yourself. You've only got two years left, and they'll be over in a blink. At least try to enjoy them."

Now it was my turn to snort. "Frat parties, terrible beer, and being groped aren't exactly my ideas of fun." In the past two years on campus, I'd had more than my fill of bullshit stuff you're "supposed" to do, and I'd also had all the good I'd done since then rocketed back in my face. Maybe I just needed to work harder, or maybe it was me. Maybe I had a big neon sign above my head that only cheaters could see. I ran my hands over my face. Each blink felt like lifting twenty-pound weights.

"Well, when you sell it like that, you definitely don't want to miss out. Get some rest, study hard, and we'll see you for dinner soon."

"Next month, I've got a night off."

The gravitational pull of her eye roll on the other end of the line tugged at me from halfway across the city.

"I love you."

After hanging up with my mom, I tugged my phone out of the jury-rigged rubber band phone holder I'd constructed on my dashboard. Jules wouldn't be home for a few more hours, and my eyes weren't cooperating with the whole 'staying awake' thing.

I looked up at the houses lining the street and surveyed my new front door, which was right next to my car. Lucky me —prime parking spot.

I hefted one of the boxes from the back seat into my arms. The freshly painted steps and porch with planters didn't scream bargain-basement rent, but hey, I'd take it. Maybe the good deed gods were finally smiling on me. After catching Mitchell in bed with his 'totally not a threat' volunteer groupie two days ago, the last-minute scramble to find a place had begun. Most of the good apartments or townhouses in my price range were long gone, but Jules had a spot in the house she'd found at the last minute, and it was in a price range I could afford. Did I mention she's way too awesome to even be my friend?

The navy shutters and whitewashed porch made it look like any other house on the block. Well, maybe not the one across the street that looked like the porch was made of eighty percent splinters.

The door was unlocked, and I walked straight inside. Hardwood floors and white paint gave the place an airiness I hadn't expected. There was a lingering hoppy smell of beer, but what college dorm or apartment didn't have that?

Water drummed upstairs. Maybe Jules had gotten in early. I walked up the gleaming wood steps and peeked into the rooms. The one at the front of the house had a stripper pole. Yup, I was definitely in the right place. She hadn't even been able to wait to get it put up.

After leaving the one pole dancing class we'd attended with my body seventy-seven percent covered in bruises, I'd given anything to do with hard poles a hard pass (well, not everything...), but Jules had taken to it like a fish to water. She hadn't gone to any more classes, but damned if she hadn't run out and bought her own pole the next day.

This one looked bolted to the floor, though. When the hell had she had time to do that? I'd ask later. Now, I just wanted to unpack my sheets and pass out on my bed for the next seven hours.

"Jules, if I'm drooling on my pillow when you come out, just poke me with a stick before eight so I can get to the tutoring center."

The shower turned off as I dropped my stuff in a back room and tugged open the box's flaps. *Damnit.* I should've labeled these things like my mom had suggested before I packed them. It was the librarian in her coming out, and now I had to play a game of 'Where the hell would a sleep-deprived Elle have shoved her sheets?' With my luck, it would be the last freaking box I lugged into the house.

I headed out to get more of my stuff. One of the bedroom doors swung closed, but not all the way. I knocked and walked straight in. "You going to let me on your pole t—" But the words stalled in my throat like I'd taken a snowball to the face. It wasn't Jules in her long-sleeved shirt and jeans; rather, I was met with the sight of the tanned, glistening skin of a guy who'd been carved from marble like a Greek statue with water droplets falling from the tips of his hair.

Definitely not Jules. There was a naked man standing in the middle of the room, a towel draped over his head as he dried his hair.

My mouth hung open. My gaze dipped lower like a tractor beam had been attached to my eyes. I didn't know abs came in varieties above six-packs. He seemed to have them all, and that wasn't all he was packing.

"What the hell?!" He snatched the towel from his head and wrapped it around himself.

Damn, I was eye-fucking him into next week. Snapping myself out of it, the reality of the situation dawned on me: psycho naked guy in my house. I edged toward the doorway. "What the hell are you doing in my house?"

"Your house? This is my house." He tucked in the end of the towel.

No longer dick-matized, I shook my head. "No, it's not. I signed the lease earlier this week—sixty-six Aspen Drive."

He crossed his arms over his chest, muscles bulging and rippling. It had to be an optical illusion. No one was this cut. But any attraction I may have felt toward his body was killed by the smug look on his face. "This is sixty-nine Aspen Drive."

"No, I saw the numbers outside."

"Happen to check the numbers on either side of this house? They don't usually go sixty-seven, sixty-six, seventy-one. A screw was missing from the nine when they repainted."

His eyes swept up and down my body.

A shiver crept up my spine, licking at my skin. Maybe it was my drought of a dating life, or maybe I was deprived after tutoring at the center for underprivileged high school students all summer, but he was the kind of gorgeous that made you wonder if he weren't real-life CGI.

"But you're more than welcome to stay, especially if you're looking for some pole exercise."

And he killed it like a puppy with a hammer. My gaze snapped to his knowing, so-full-of-himself-he-might-float-away smirk. Cue the explosive rage, which was a hell of a lot better than soul-shriveling embarrassment.

I glared at him, and his face finally clicked into place. Phoenix "Nix" Russo, quarterback and pompous asshole. "Not on your life."

Storming down the steps, I whipped open the front door and touched the shiny numbers beside the door. Sure enough, the second digit had a freaking screw missing, making my complete and total embarrassment complete. The scarlet burn of it crept its way up my back, and my ears were probably glowing like Rudolph's nose.

Nix walked out with his jeans on, but it seemed someone couldn't find his way around a button fly. The expanse of skin from his shirtless chest stretched down...nearly all the way down. Even if I hadn't already seen all the goods, there wasn't much left to imagine. His self-satisfied little grin made me want to scream or punch something. I hated football players, hated assholes who thought they're a piece of heaven on earth, and I hated that I'd drooled over him—even for a split second. I stormed back inside.

"Need some help?" He leaned against the doorway as I picked up my box and shoved the stuff I'd dumped out while looking for my sheets back in.

Slamming the flaps closed, I glared at him. "No."

Standing there like he was God's gift to women, he stared at me with that grin that made my stomach flip and my fingers tingle to punch him all at once. Had I made a mistake? Yes. Did he need to be so smug about it, like I'd made his day by being a dumbass? No. Most of all, I was pissed off at how the damn butterfly wings in my stomach wouldn't stop. I'd been around hot guys before. Generally, they came in two varieties: complete-and-total douchebag and excels-at-hiding-that-he-is-a-complete-and-total douchebag. Guess which camp Phoenix too-cool-not-to-shorten-his-name-to-Nix fell into.

I brushed past him with my arms cradling my box, but he didn't actually move back, so it was less shoving him out of the way and more full-body contact topped off with the backs of my fingers grazing way too close to a part of his anatomy I'd been gawking at less than five minutes ago. "If you wanted a touch, all you had to do was ask."

"I'd rather cut my hand off," I ground out through gritted teeth before bursting free from the death wedge between him and the doorway.

"Have it your way." He walked behind me, following me out of his house.

"Nix, I love you! Are you going to get to the championship this year?" A fawning sycophant pounced on him the second we made it outside.

"I'll do my best. We're a solid team this year, and we're ready."

His pat, practiced answers turned my stomach. That scripted humility and noncommittal response—he was trained like a pro, and he wasn't even there yet. I welcomed the burn of anger. It was so much better than embarrassment, and I latched onto that. Nix was a total asshole, and the butterflies had just been sleep-deprivation-induced delirium.

Blowing my hair out of my face, I whipped my head around, squinting at the numbers on the other side of the street. Wouldn't you know it, the haunted-slash-murder house that looked like it was held together with duct tape and gum had a nice sixty-six spray-painted on the curb.

"Just freaking great," I grumbled under my breath as I crossed the street. A car horn blared, and I jumped back. I'd been so intent on not looking back at Nix that I might have neglected that kindergarten staple of looking both ways before crossing the street.

Charging up the rickety steps to my new place, my toe caught on a loose board and I banged into the front door.

"I'll be seeing you soon, neighbor," Nix called out from across the street.

Safely inside, I dropped the box and coughed at the plume of dust that shot up from the floor. "Perfect, just perfect." I closed my eyes and rested my head against the door. Talk about starting this year with a bang. Looking around the place, I could see exactly how Jules had gotten such a great deal on it. I braced for the floor to collapse under my feet with each step. *At least there is a roof over my head.* A piece of plaster rained down on me from above like jimmies on top of my craptastic sundae of a day. I shook out my hair and brushed the beige dust off the tip of my nose. Junior year was starting off in fine form.

Bracing myself, I went back outside and grabbed another box from my car, which was parked right in front of *his* house.

"Do you need some help, B and E?" Nix called out from his porch, leaning against the railing with a beer in his hand.

"Not from you." I stacked another box on top of the one in my arm and used my leg to heft them both higher. Picturing him with a beer gut in fifteen years lifted my spirits slightly.

"Don't be silly." He swung his body over the railing, and a solid thud landed behind me. *Showoff.* "Let me grab one. Those look heavy."

I swung the boxes away. "Touch them and die." It probably would've been a bit more convincing if the top box hadn't toppled out of my arms and fallen over, spilling out some of my volunteer stuff all over the sidewalk and street, namely a jumbo box of condoms.

Everyone who'd been hanging around to get some face time with Nix watched our little tug of war, which meant everyone was now one hundred percent locked onto the two hundred blue-foil-wrapped discs splayed everywhere.

"Busy semester for you," someone called out, and the please-open-a-portal-into-the-underworld feeling was back. Leaving the condoms, I rushed back across the street and into my house. I'd get the rest of my stuff after my shift later. Maybe the cover of night would be enough to tamp down my embarrassment.

At this point, I'd have napped on the mystery-stained couch if my sheets weren't in the box I'd brought in. No way was I going back out there unless absolutely necessary until the semester started.

Was it too late to find another place? Yes. We'd been lucky to find this death trap.

The hard thump of a knock stopped my embarrassment spiral from pulling me down into the depths of my clown freak-out at Becky Smith's ninth birthday. I tugged the front door open.

Nix stood there with his arms loaded with the discarded condoms. "You left these behind." He turned up the charm, flashing dimples and everything, looking like a shiny new toy on my ramshackle porch.

"She forgot some more," someone shouted across the street, the foil wrappers catching the later summer sun. Great, now I'd be known as the prostitute of Aspen Drive.

I glared at them and back at Nix. Grabbing the half-empty box off the floor, I held it out to him and let him dump the contents out.

"We're having a party—"

The rest of his sentence was cut off by me slamming the door in his face. Really? And make my humiliation totally complete? 'Hey guys, this is the chick who walked into the wrong house like a dumbass, gawked at me naked, and then exploded a condom factory all over the street.' No thanks.

I was sure he thought I'd be all over him after the way I

couldn't keep my eyes off him. I slapped my hand against my forehead. I knew all about guys like him. Arrogant. Hungry for the attention of anyone around them. All about the adoring fans and accolades and expecting every woman under retirement age to throw herself at them. Screw that!

Wouldn't you know it? My sheets were absolutely not in the box. Mystery stains and a balled-up sweatshirt would have to do.

The front door swung open and slammed shut sometime later. Jules pushed up her glasses with the back of her hand, her travel pole in its bag slung over her arm, backpack on her shoulders.

"Damn, you look like shit. I'll make brownies."

Her go-to solution for any situation was exactly what I needed right now.

She peered out the front window. "There are a ton of people out on the sidewalk blowing up condoms like balloons. What'd I miss?"

CHAPTER 2
NIX
A YEAR AND A HALF LATER

There were no sounds other than the blood pounding in my ears. The fans were on their feet in the stands, mouths open, yelling and screaming, but the noise didn't make it to me. I called out the play and my heart seemed to slow. Each beat was drawn out for seconds on end.

Fulton U flags, banners, and jerseys were a living, breathing tapestry covering the rows of the stadium. The band had taken up their spot in the student section of the stands, but no one played now. Their trumpets and other instruments were clutched in their hands as they waved them in the air.

Sweat rolled down my neck. The ball was snapped, and the pebbled leather smacked against my hands. Exhale. The line of scrimmage broke. The linemen from the other team rushed toward me, out for blood, their eyes trained on me, searching for the smallest opening. Big glowing numbers counted down to zero on the scoreboard on the other end of the field. One last play. One last time.

The Fulton U line held, and I spotted our wide receiver twenty yards away. He darted across the field, more determined to get open than he'd been all season. Keyton had been drilling his receiving for months until he could catch balls with his eyes closed.

Reece, one of the best players on our team, had at least three guys swarming him. In any other game, I'd have thrown it to him. No matter what, he came through in a pinch, but it was Keyton's time.

My fingers tightened on the ball. The leather dug into my fingers in a familiar pattern I'd memorized over the years. *Time to put it all on the line.* One. Last. Time. I pulled my arm back and whipped it forward, letting the ball loose. A twinge shot through my shoulder.

The second the ball left my hands, the roar of the stadium filled my head. Blocking it all out was easy when I powered up the laser-focus so I didn't let my team down. As I stared at the ball spiraling through the air, someone dug the remote out from between the couch cushions, cranked up the volume, and set it to ground-shaking level.

That's probably why I didn't see the hit coming. Someone slammed into me—a late hit after the ball was gone. I flew through the air just like the ball I'd released a second earlier. But I wasn't headed for the hands of our second best receiver. No, I went up and over, flipping through the air and my shoulder got drilled into the ground. The wind was knocked from my lungs. Every gasp felt like learning to breathe again. The burning ache punched at my chest and my shoulder throbbed.

"Stay down, Russo." Johannsen's bitter words didn't change the fact that this was the final play.

I could tell his body loomed over mine, even with my eyes closed. Losing was exactly what that dick deserved. Most other guys we played were cool, but the St. Francis U team was our biggest rival and it brought out the uberdick in most of them—Johannsen, in particular.

I forced my eyes open, Berk—who'd never let me down on a play where he was on the field was trying to pick himself up off the ground with three defensive linemen on his back.

His gaze darted to mine. The anger at the dirty play raw and bare on his face.

I gave him the best approximation of a smile. It would be okay. My gaze shot to the spiraling ball.

And there was silence. The ball sailed through the air, and the only bodies moving in the whole stadium were on the field. I kept my eye on it, unable to look away. A crush of bodies blocked my view. The pass slammed into Keyton's chest. His arms wrapped around it and he spun, darting for the end zone. The living, breathing animal that was our fans came alive again.

He pulled the ball in tight against his chest, pulled out some spin moves we hadn't seen all season, and ran it into the end zone. The entire stadium lost their minds. They'd be able to hear the sound from Jersey.

Berk, an offensive tackle, held out his hand to me and helped me up off the ground. My shoulder throbbed, but that didn't compare to the screams and shouts booming off every object in the stadium. Our team bench was cleared. Water bottles, towels, helmets, and jerseys were abandoned on the sidelines as everyone rushed the field to celebrate. I stood in the center of the chaos and stared into the stands, soaking it up. I looked downfield at my teammates piling on top of one another. Unsnapping my helmet, I pulled it off my head and committed every inch of it to memory.

Leaving this team behind wouldn't be easy, but nothing in life was permanent. We have to soak up what we can when we can.

————

WAS IT POSSIBLE TO PULL A MUSCLE FROM SMILING? BECAUSE I grinned at Johannsen as his team lined up to shake our hands under the falling confetti shot from cannons that lined the field.

"I'd have gotten you next year." He glared, squeezing my hand too hard, but it didn't hurt. I was untouchable right now.

"You won't get the chance." I was graduating and he still had another year to run the gauntlet. Hopefully, Berk and LJ would kick his ass next season right along with the rest of the Fulton U team.

We stayed out on the field for the post-game interviews and trophy ceremony.

After hundreds of games from the time I was seven, two surgeries, and more physical therapy sessions than I could count, I'd done it: a national championship, the first at Fulton U in nearly two decades. My dad barged down onto the field, practically throwing elbows to get to me, and tugged me in for a huge bear hug.

"Good job, son."

"Thanks, Dad." My grin could've been seen from a space shuttle.

"Wonderful game, Phoenix." My grandfather slipped through a gap in the sea of celebrating bodies.

"Gramps! You're here."

He wrapped his arms around me and patted me on the back. "I wouldn't have missed this for anything."

Dad grumbled something under his breath and shot a look at him.

Gramps held on to my shoulder, giving it a squeeze. "You played so well out there, better than I've ever seen before."

"It's the only time you've seen him before."

"I've seen him play." Gramps shot my dad a look. "Amazing display, and now that the season's over, you can come by the restaurant more."

"He has better things to do than hang around that sweaty, hot box."

Gramps rolled his eyes. "I'll see you soon. I need to get back before the dinner rush is over."

Dad crossed his arms over his chest. "Leaving already." It wasn't a question.

"The kitchen calls." Gramps tugged me closer again. "There's a chocolate chunk salted caramel surprise with your name on it." He let go of me and grinned before disappearing back into the swelling mass of shrieking teammates and fans on the field.

"He never sticks around." Dad stared after his retreating form.

"He's busy."

Dad scoffed and shook his head. "Great game, but it could've been cleaner. We can talk about that tonight."

Of course we would. Wasn't like I'd have a choice. Sometimes I swore I got even longer post-game breakdowns from him after a win than a loss.

"The whole team knows they're invited, right?"

"They'll be there." Like they ever turned down one of his invites. The storied history of Phil Russo...he was always generous with his praise of everyone on the team—except me —and they always took his advice like it was spoken through a beam of light shining down on them from heaven. None of them knew what it was like for that advice to be an endless stream of how you were continually not measuring up.

One of the reporters recognized him, and he started his own little press conference on the field. I was used to it by now.

The locker room was chaos piled on top of euphoria. Even though Coach would probably castrate anyone he found drinking, the smells of beer, Icy Hot, and athletic tape permeated the room. The championship trophy with confetti stuck to the wooden base sat in the middle of the space. My fellow seniors and I were going out on a hell of a high note.

"Is your dad sure he wants to host us tonight? I don't

think we're exactly upper crust material." LJ, my roommate and a safety who'd had my back on that field more times than I could count, rubbed his towel over his brown, curly hair.

I slipped my arms into my suit jacket. "You forget who he was before he was Phillip Russo. I've got a call to make, and then we can head over." Grabbing my bag out of my locker, I slung it over my head, wincing as it landed on my shoulder. It seemed my knee and shoulder wanted to be a matching set. *Figures.* I ran my hand over it and squeezed to alleviate the pressure.

"And why don't you look happy about this?" Reece, my fellow senior and best friend, stared at me with his eyebrows dipped down low like he was trying to figure out if I was having an aneurism.

"Tired, that's all. The adrenaline crash is real, but don't worry, I'll be good in a few."

"Hell yeah you will be! And you want to know why?" Berk jumped on the bench and started his own off-key and much too energetic rendition of "We are the Champions" for the seventh time.

I stared at them all through the slowly closing locker room door. Big smiles, towels snapping, and the kind of camaraderie that existed when you'd bled beside one another on the field. Damn, I'd miss them.

They spilled out of the stadium and we piled into my car. Berk pushed the buttons on the radio, cycling through stations until he found a song he liked, but LJ threw out his veto and it started all over again.

"Enough," I shouted and jammed my finger into the power button, blanketing us all in silence.

"Jeez, I liked that one." LJ sulked in the back.

My fingers tightened on the steering wheel. 'Do you want me to turn this car around?' was on the tip of my tongue, but going to this party on my own would be more of a punishment for me than for them.

We piled out of the car at the valet and headed to the restaurant to meet my dad, who was of course not at Gramps' place. As far as I could tell Dad hadn't set foot in there since my mom died.

I pushed through the doors with the guys behind me—and was blinded by the cascading wave of camera flashes.

Blinking to erase the spots dancing in front of my eyes, I was pulled into a bear hug.

"There he is, our national championship quarterback and future number one draft pick, and the rest of the first-round picks." Dad held out his arms, gesturing to the rest of the Trojans in his best Vanna White impersonation. "Let's get these boys some drinks." He clapped LJ on the back, and oversized glasses of beer appeared in everyone's hands like magic. "And there are more than enough ladies to keep you guys entertained for the evening."

I glanced behind me. LJ blanched as the women approached, looking like he was ready to run for cover. He took a step back, and even Berk kept his eyes trained on his glass.

The swarm began, but this party wasn't his normal booster schmooze session. It wasn't just former players and team donors along with the women. There were lots of guys in suits who looked suspiciously like agents, which would still technically be against the recruiting rules.

"Hey, Dad. What the hell is going on?"

He pulled me in for another hug. "Giving the guys a head start on recruiting. Gotta maximize those dollars."

My jaw ticked. "This could get them in trouble with the NCAA." And I was the team captain. Screwing the guys over at the eleventh hour was out of the question.

"Who do you think will trade to get the first pick for you? I know you want to stay in Philly, but going up to New England could launch your career," someone called out.

Laughter rippled through the room. Suits, lots of suits—

agents everywhere. It was like he'd put in a call with every agent in the entire country.

Business cards were slipped into my hand with every handshake.

"I feel like I'm on display at a meat market." Berk came up to me with his hands over his chest like he was hiding his imaginary boobs. "Is this what women feel like when they go out?" His eyes darted around the room.

LJ leaned over our shoulders. "Except with these guys, you wake up the next morning wondering what the hell you did and forty percent of your future potential earnings have evaporated."

Dad waved me over from across the room. After another round of introductions, he grabbed another drink.

"I'm headed to Tavola tomorrow," I told him. "You should stop by." With the season going the way it had and my classes, I hadn't been able to visit in way too long, since back when I had practically lived there.

Dad scoffed like he always did whenever I brought it up. "You know who I don't see here tonight to congratulate you on your win? Your grandfather. Never could pry the old man away from that place, no matter what." He took a gulp from his tumbler, the amber liquid swirling in his glass.

"It's Gramps' life's work."

Dad snorted. "You think I don't know that? I know that better than anyone."

"Don't start. It's awesome you've come to all my games, but he can't always swing that." My fingers tightened around the cold, metal fork.

"Try never." His face darkened before he drained his glass and wiped away the storm clouds. "Tonight isn't the night to discuss this. It's a celebration. You've got football in your blood. You've devoted your life to it. You play as well as you have been and you'll be an MVP in your rookie year next year, write your ticket to whatever you want to do." Dad shoved an hors d'oeuvre into his mouth and smiled for a picture, wrapping his arm around my shoulder. "Now, let's go over what went wrong and how you can make sure you don't make those same mistakes next time."

With a play-by-play notated on his iPad, which he'd had someone bring over, I was given excruciating details on how exactly my national championship win could've been even better. The veins in my neck throbbed and my blood pounded in my veins. I yanked at the tie around my neck. *Every fucking time.*

"Nix," my dad called out behind me.

I didn't stop—couldn't stop. Men in suits clapped me on the back and tried to get in a word, but those words stalled in their throats when they saw the look in my eyes. I'd paid my penance in blood and sweat out on the field for him. I'd run myself into the ground and kept coming back for more. If this wasn't enough for him, was there anything that would be?

I shoved open the doors to the restaurant, leaving my coat behind. The biting January weather sliced right through my sweater and blazer. I didn't know if they'd been warned or were just lightning quick, but the valet pulled my car up to the curb the second my shoes hit the pavement.

My dad had bought me the sleek black Mercedes S-Class when I'd won the high school state championship. If it hadn't been so damn cold, I'd have left it there and gotten it in the morning. I climbed inside and headed back to the house. Reece hadn't even made it. LJ, and Berk had been smart and ducked out over an hour ago, ready to get to the real party with their pockets stuffed with the cards of every agent under the sun.

There was sure to be a party in full, brain-melting swing when I got there. There always was, no matter how much none of us wanted to party.

Sometimes it was easier to go along with the tide than to fight against it. I'd learned that once again tonight with my dad. If you fought it, sometimes you drowned. That was me right now, flailing and flapping. Somehow I needed to figure out how to get him to see what he wanted for me and what I wanted were never going to be the same thing.

I'd left it all out on the gridiron.

———

THE FLOOR VIBRATED BENEATH ME, STRAIGHT THROUGH MY mattress. Sweltering heat from the party filled my room, and even with the window open, the stifling air stalled in my lungs. I flung the ball up and it nearly kissed the ceiling. Old scuff marks dotted the paint job. *There goes my security deposit.* Escaping the party hadn't been as easy as I'd hoped. Before, I'd never had any issues going with the flow of the celebrations that popped up in our house whether I wanted them there or not, but on this night, I needed a break.

I didn't want to kill anyone's fun, but right then all the noise and the people crowded my head, creating a simmering stew right along with my dad's words. 'Good job, son.' After all this time and all I'd accomplished, that was the best he could do. Even undeniable victory was wrapped in a shroud of criticism.

My arm whipped back. The pebbled surface of the ball dug into my fingers as I squeezed it harder, my blood pounding in my veins. Maybe it was because I'd had way too much to drink. Maybe it was because I'd yet to receive a 'Good job, son' without a hint of a 'but' in the distance. I launched the ball like I was back in the stadium. Instead of leaving a nice security-deposit-revoking hole in my wall, it burst through the screen on my window like a showgirl making her grand entrance. The metal mesh glittered in the moonlight, and the sound broke through the body-shaking rumble from downstairs.

There was a second shattering *pop* and I rushed to the

broken window, peering outside. The short, party-ending, *whoop-whoop* was accompanied by the flashing red and blue lights of a police car idled curbside. The splintered mosaic of what had once been his window had been blasted all over the ground. Shards of glass bounced across the sidewalk as the cop's head snapped up to my window. *Please not the township cops. Please not the township cops.*

I stared at the house across the street and two houses away. Not a sign of her, but I could practically hear the cackling from here. The cop climbed out of his car and stared up at me. His township badge glinted in the streetlights as he walked up to the porch with his gaze drilling into my skull.

The music downstairs came to a screeching halt, and people flowed out of the house and down the street like ants fleeing a can of Raid.

My own personal pain in the ass pushed her curtains aside and peered out at everyone like they were peasants who should've been dragged off her property. This was the eighth time she'd called the cops on us in four months. I had thought after last year, she would move out of her horror shack, but she'd been there glowering when we all came back from training camp. She dropped the curtain as someone knocked on my door.

The raised voices from downstairs filtered up through the open window, trying to stall the inevitable. The cop's clipped tone brooked no arguments. I ran my hands over my face. The perfect end to a perfect night.

Berk poked his head in. His shaggy hair fell into his eyes and his shirt was half on. The signatures of partygoers were scrawled across his skin, along with more than a few phone numbers.

"You've got a visitor." He braced his hands on the top of my doorjamb.

"Please tell me I'm drunk and it's a campus cop, not the township."

He clenched his teeth together and sucked in with a face filled with pity.

"Fuck."

"We just won the national championship—they've got to cut us a little slack." A couple of stragglers came out of the bathroom. The girls laughed and rushed by. He dropped his arms and jumped as one got a handful of his ass on her way downstairs.

"You weren't the one who humiliated the township police chief's son with a thirty-to-nothing loss at state back in high school, on top of the other thing."

Berk gave me a grim nod. "Also true. Should I escort you to the gallows?" He stepped back from my door and followed me downstairs.

"Are the cops here for you? Seriously, do they know who you are?" a guy called out, slurring every syllable.

A slow clap broke the gentle murmur of the crowd. I looked out over the sea of people and there was one that stuck out.

"What the hell is Johannsen doing here?" I hissed at Berk. My shoulder ached just at the sight of him.

"No idea. He walked in here like he was looking for someone and then the cops showed up."

This was not what I needed tonight.

His self-satisfied smirk made it hard to see straight. But I had bigger things to deal with.

"I'll take the fall." Another guy wearing a Trojans jersey pushed to the front of the crowd to pull an 'I volunteer as tribute' move. Damn, the temptation to nod and promise him a signed jersey darted across my mind. The cops had had a hard-on for me screwing up for a while now, but nah, I couldn't do that, even as much as it would make my life a hell of a lot easier right now.

The cop stood in the living room surrounded by red plastic cups, booze-soaked streamers, school flags, and way more FU-branded articles of clothing than I'd ever thought could be misplaced during one party.

"What do you have to say for yourself?" The look on his face told me there was nothing I could say to get out of this.

"Officer." I extended my hand. He stared down at it like I'd offered him a dead fish covered in thumbtacks, and then he slapped the silver handcuffs around my wrists and read me my rights. Everyone at the party chose that moment to start booing.

Well, my night was fucked. I wasn't going to pull the 'Do you know who my dad is?' card. Only assholes played that card, and no matter what our breaking-and-entering, condom-avalanche-triggering neighbor thought of me, I wasn't that guy.

LJ skidded into the living room. His eyes got so wide, I could almost hear his eyelids snapping back. He fumbled for his phone. "Do you want me to call your dad?"

The cop put my arms behind my back, tweaking my shoulder. "No! Do not call him. My wallet's upstairs. I'll call you if I need bail money. Just take the cash from my account."

I was walked down to the cop's car. He opened the back door and put his hand on top of my head, pushing me into the car. The scents of disinfectant and plastic invaded my nostrils. I supposed it was better than the alternative of beer-laced BO.

Berk and LJ stood at the top of the steps to our house, AKA the Brothel. That name, a holdover from when the house belonged to a frat, hadn't earned us any favors, especially not when the police chief's high school senior daughter had shown up on our doorstep, teetering on the edge of blackout drunk. He hadn't cared that we'd called the ambulance for her and hadn't served her one drop of alcohol. Nope, that had put a bullseye on our backs since almost six months ago, national football champions or not.

The cop car rolled down the street, and everyone craned

their necks to get a good look at who'd just been arrested. We drove past the house whose inhabitant had started it all. She poked her head out of her upstairs bedroom window. Her face disappeared as we rounded the corner, and I could've sworn there was a flicker of remorse. It was probably just the moonlight playing tricks, more likely the beginnings of a smile and a gleeful dance in her bedroom window like I'd seen her do a few times before.

Little did she know, this wasn't even the worst part of my night. Not by far.

CHAPTER 3
ELLE

The traffic getting home meant my normal thirty-minute drive took over ninety minutes. Screw me sideways for not having the college football schedule tattooed on my chest like everyone else in town.

By the tenth drunken rendition of the school fight song in near standstill traffic, I'd been ready to end things by slamming my head into the steering wheel. Was karma real? Wisps of my past life came wafting back, and they stank to high heaven.

My street was no better. People milled around in the middle of the road, and I had to park five blocks away from my house to find a spot.

I climbed out of my car and slammed the door three times before the latch caught. The last thing I needed was to come outside and find my battery had died because the door hadn't closed all the way—again. It wasn't like my interior lights even worked anymore, so how the hell did the freaking battery keep dying?

With every few feet closer to home, the bass pounded louder, but one was loudest of all: the fucking Brothel. Who named their house the Brothel, anyway? Asshole football players who had no respect for their neighbors, that's who.

The S-Class Mercedes I'd driven back in high school hadn't had these issues, but then again, this hunk of junk was all mine, though it was an insult to junk to call it such.

My shoulders ached. My feet ached. Hell, my eyeballs ached.

The tiredness I'd kept at bay for four years had seeped down deep into my bones. I was so close to graduation. All this hard work would pay off, and then what? *No time to think about that now. Just keep busy. Keep moving and doing good deeds. Win the Huffington Award and then figure things out.* The cash stipend that came with it would finally get me out from under the financial raincloud that had followed me everywhere since our middle-class life became anything but.

If I made it into the shower, it would be a miracle, but my clothes were rank. If I didn't make it into the shower, I'd be better off sleeping on the floor so I didn't have to wash my sheets the next day. How I'd gotten signed up for fried chicken duty, I'd never know, but the cooking gods were not smiling down on me.

My teeth rattled in my skull, and the pounding wasn't just from the headache trying to schedule a late-night appointment. It was one in the morning, and the party across the street wasn't showing any signs of stopping any time soon. I just wanted to sleep—in peace for once.

I tripped on the splintered wooden plank on our front porch. If I'd thought the landlord would actually do something, I'd have set a reminder to call him in the morning and add it to our list of three hundred other things that needed to be fixed, but if it weren't for him cashing our checks month after month, I'd have suspected he'd died.

Someone set off fireworks, my death grip on the strap of my bag slipped, and I punched myself in the face. *Son of a bitch!*

That was it. I was done. I wasn't putting up with this anymore. My phone was out and the speed dial pushed without a second thought. And it wasn't a text to my jerk of a neighbor for more of his fake promises to break up whatever bedlam was going on across the street. The cops arrived in record time like they'd been waiting for an excuse to enter the Brothel.

I slammed the door shut. Oh boohoo, their party would be over at only one AM. I was sure they'd survive.

After trudging up the steps, I was so tempted to flop onto my bed, but then I'd never get up—a lesson learned many times over the past three years. I put my hair up, grabbed my pajamas off the floor, and sniffed them. Eh, they'd do. Comfy flannel PJs that helped beat back the cold, my extra thick socks, and I was ready to go.

"Elle, you home?" Jules yelled from the bottom of the steps.

"No, it's not Elle. It's a polite robber who's come to steal your pajamas and a scalding hot shower."

"Okay, well you probably want to wash them first. Elle's been wearing them for over a week without washing them. Oh, and wash them before you bring them back."

It hadn't been a week. "It's only been…" I counted the number of days since I'd changed PJs on my fingers. *Yikes.*

"Exactly. Come down when you're done. I've got a surprise for you." I swear, she could've opened a phone sex line with that voice. Most people swore she was a pack-a-day smoker, but I'd seen her hiccup just drinking soda.

I chuckled and peeled off my clothes. The fried-food smell clung to everything. I'd need to do a double wash. Never again was I manning the fryer.

"Elle, look out your window." Jules' voice sounded like a siren wailing from downstairs.

I raced to the front of my room and leaned against the windowsill. My stomach plummeted. The gleaming silver of the handcuffs on Nix's wrists shone under the streetlights. He was on a perp walk out of his house. *Shit!*

They weren't supposed to arrest him, just get them to turn the music down. The car disappeared from sight, and I sagged against the window. Nothing I could do about it now. It wasn't even all their fault this time—okay, most of the time, but their partygoers always took up all the parking spots on the street, which meant I had to walk multiple blocks to get home, exhausted, alone, at night. There were also the almost nightly fireworks set off from their roof to celebrate every win since the Trojans had made the playoffs, the fact that half the street still called me Condom Queen after a year and a half, and the nonstop horn parade that rattled the windows in our house after every win.

A national championship was impressive no matter what, but did they have to be so damn loud? It was a weeknight. So, for the cops to pick him up, there had to be some shady stuff going on. A zing of vindication shot through me. What could it be for the golden boy? Letting underage kids drink at the party? Drugs? I'd thought he was a run-of-the-mill entitled asshole, but maybe he was a hell of a lot worse than that and I'd just done the world a favor.

I stared at my reflection in my sparkling and brand-new (unlike most everything else in this place) window. It had been repaired with hard-earned money—my money—after the FU Trojan's game of street football ended up with me sweeping up broken glass at one AM after getting off work. With that thought, my sympathy was well and truly gone, evaporated after being incinerated into the charred remains of my remorse. *Screw him and whatever he was mixed up in.*

I dragged myself into the shower and did the dance between the freezing cold air and the liquid fire pouring out of the showerhead. With my hair washed and my body bundled up like I was ready to climb Everest, I trudged downstairs. My bed called to me, but Jules' tease of a surprise got me to zombie walk down the steps.

She popped her head out of the kitchen and pushed up her horn-rimmed glasses with the back of her hand.

"What's all over your hands?" I yawned and steadied myself on the banister. It rocked and swayed.

"Come see. I saw this recipe on one of those time-lapse videos and I needed to try it. This is my fourth batch, and I think I finally got it right."

While some people saw a picture and needed to visit a hot vacation spot or needed to buy a new pair of shoes, Jules needed to figure out how to make anything she spotted in the wild. I wasn't complaining; I got to be her taste tester, and even her failures were better than I could manage on my best day in the kitchen.

It also helped battle against the freezing cold temperatures in the house. The oven kept at least the downstairs warmer than the ice-bath levels upstairs. It was so cold everywhere except the bathroom, which had lava pouring from the faucets. If we hadn't been actually paying rent, I'd have sworn we were inside a psychological experiment.

A wall of heat hit me and seeped into my skin as I crossed the threshold into the kitchen. The entire place smelled like cinnamon and sugar had been going at it all night long, and it hadn't been polite, nice-to-see-you banging. They'd had down-and-dirty, can't-walk-right-in-the-morning, need-a-cigarette sex, and their fried babies were lined up neatly on paper towels on the kitchen counter.

While I'd had my fill of food at the soup kitchen, it was forgotten once my eyes landed on the golden brown, crunchy goodness in front of me. Tears welled in my eyes at their crispy on the outside, soft and doughy on the inside beauty.

"Are those churros?" I turned to Jules and grabbed her shoulders before staring at her with my hand against my chest to hold back the surging emotions, or maybe it was just my PMS turning into a sweets-and-carbs craving.

"Yes?" She pushed the glasses up the bridge of her nose.

I pulled her in for a hug; there might've been a rib crack in there it was so tight.

"Elle, you're crushing me," she wheezed out with her arm pinned between us.

I let her go, and she stumbled back.

Her cinnamon sugar hand had left a print on her face.

"Does this mean you're a fan?" She laughed, wiping her cheek.

My earlier tiredness momentarily forgotten, I dropped my head down to the counter, sniffing their delectable aroma and nearly mainlining the cinnamon-and-sugar mixture beside the cooling desserts. The crispy, star-shaped sticks were perfection. The piping bag with the dough sat beside the pot with a thermometer sticking out of it. How many college students had an oil thermometer? There were people on campus who still couldn't do their own laundry. I should know—I had been one of them.

Horns blared down the street. I pushed back the kitchen curtains, looking across the street at the Brothel.

"Looks like the cops shutting them down didn't help things."

Jules stared out beside me, her nose-prints already smudged on the glass. "I think it's sweet they're celebrating their hard work." She'd taken the room facing their house once she'd found out who lived there. It wasn't that I didn't also have a view of their house, but hers was almost panoramic.

"Their hard work doesn't need to be broadcast across the entire campus."

"People just showed up. That seems to happen a lot. Remember that time people broke into their house to wheel the kegs in before their game was even over?" She dropped more dough into the pot and swirled around the crisp-ifying sticks in the crackling oil with a slotted spoon and tongs.

"They don't do much to discourage it." Parties like that had been mainstays back in high school. It didn't matter that we were all underage or that someone's parents should've been around. Houses were trashed. The world had been our oyster—but this was college. Some of us took our futures seriously.

She rolled a bunch of the churros in the mix on a tray, and my mouth watered. My stomach was practically lying spread eagle on the floor shouting, 'Take me!' Lifting them like a tortoise running in molasses, she put them onto a plate. Her lips quirked up, and she glanced at me out of the corner of her eye.

I probably looked like a dog eyeing up a T-bone, pacing in the kitchen, waiting for her to say when.

"I should probably let these cool a bit more. Wouldn't want you to burn your mouth." She waved her tongs back and forth in front of her.

My eyes narrowed.

She burst out laughing. "Go ahead, but when you burn the shit out of your tongue, it's not my fault." Jules had quite the potty mouth when she wanted to. It was probably for the laughs at the shocked looks on everyone's faces when she busted out a string of curses to make a sailor blush. Under her Easy-Bake Oven exterior was a hilarious, foul-mouthed, pole-dancing vixen who could rule the world, if she wanted—she just didn't know it yet.

I lunged for the plate with the words barely out of her mouth. My fingers wrapped around one. The oil on my fingers turned the coating into pure gold. I pulled it apart, nibbling on each ridge, biting my way down like an insane typewriter. I ate the first one with my mouth open, sucking in cool air to stop my tongue from catching on fire, but by the third, I pulled them apart like string cheese, holding each churro strand up in the air and dangling it into my mouth. The sugar rush hit me hard.

"You're the weirdest freaking eater I've ever seen." She laughed and threw me the roll of paper towels.

I caught it with my arms, keeping my hands far away. Oh no, those fingers covered in cinnamon sugar were not being sacrificed to the paper towel gods.

"You look like a sweet version of the Joker with churro dust smeared all over your face."

She pulled an upside down cupcake tin out of the freezer. It had dough piped over the backs of the cups.

"What are those?" My mouthful of churros muffled my words, but she was used to me talking with my mouth full of the stuff she baked.

"I'm going to try to make ice cream bowls."

I jerked back and sucked in a sharp breath, nearly choking on chewed churro. "Jules, why not just bend me over the kitchen table while you're at it? That's straight-up obscene. I knew you had a dirty mind from those letters you write, but this is probably illegal in twelve states."

She pointed her tongs at me and gave me a playful glare. "This is what I get for showing you. I'm never getting that drunk again."

Jules' freak flag flew high when she'd had a few drinks— or had the right muse. The one time I'd read one of her notes, it had taken a week for my cheeks to go back to their natural color. She still hadn't spilled who she was sending them to, but I'd get it out of her eventually.

With the kitchen shut down and my stomach full of melty vanilla ice cream and more cinnamon and sugar than most people consumed in a lifetime, we went upstairs.

"I don't know what I'll do without you next year." She flopped on my bed.

"You'll make new, non-snarky, non-sarcastic friends."

"But I like your snark. It's like a bitter, smelly shell over a funny, sweet treat."

I threw a pair of socks at her head.

"Those aren't even clean!"

She stuck out her tongue and retreated from my room as I pelted her with more socks. My earlier dead-on-my-feet feeling had been washed away by Jules, which meant thinking and overthinking. There was only one sure-fire, no-one-can-know way to help me sleep. Glancing around like anyone would be lurking in my room, I tugged open my bedside drawer and pulled out the glittery bottles of nail polish. Testing out the colors, I painted my nails with the neon pink glitter. The light from beside my bed caught the metallic flecks, and the kaleidoscope of color danced on my ceiling. Back in high school, I had gone for manicures every week, sitting for hours while laughing and sipping my arti-sanal coffee with my squad. It was a luxury I couldn't afford now, plus how would it look showing up to a homeless shelter or soup kitchen sporting a fresh French manicure?

"Elle." Jules' voice came from right outside my room.

I shoved my hands under the covers as she stepped into the doorway. "Yeah."

"Night. I'm out early in the morning and won't be back until after ten. Wouldn't want you to get worried and call the cops again."

"It was one time. Your phone was off for hours. You know I'm a worrier."

"I know. Thanks, Mom." She stuck out her tongue and pulled the door closed behind her.

I dragged my smudged nails out from under the blankets, grabbed some cotton balls from my dresser along with the nail polish remover, and wiped it all away.

I pulled the covers up to my chin. The cold had already gotten to my nose. As I laid my head on my pillow, Nix's eyes in the back of the police car flashed into my mind.

Why was I feeling bad for him? He and his teammates had made my life hell over the past year and a half. I was sure he was taking selfies with the cops at the police station and they'd drive him back home any minute. That was how it was for football players, especially winners like the Trojans. Athletes could always get away with murder, lying, and let's not forget cheating to their hearts' content. Some of us had fallen for that kind of act, hook, line, and sinker—but that was high school Elle. She was long gone now.

I refused to feel bad for Nix for one minute more. It wasn't like we'd be seeing each other outside of glares across the street from now until the end of the year. That was all we'd ever had.

Just how I liked it.

CHAPTER 4
NIX

"Don't they know you just won this school a national championship?" Berk threw his phone on the couch after reading over the final press release from the city police.

Dad had worked for nearly three months to keep the January incident out of the papers, but the day had finally arrived. I swore he had me under surveillance with how quickly he'd gotten to the police station back in January after the guys all swore they hadn't called him.

"I don't think the police chief cares after the incident with his daughter." I squeezed the bridge of my nose and leaned back in the beaten-down recliner in the living room. The pasta on my plate balanced on my knee would be enough to fill the pit in my stomach. The garlic bread perched on the edge had been made with my own homemade garlic butter. Everything was better with garlic butter.

"It's not our fault a drunk girl shows up on our doorstep, we turn her away, and her friends abandon her on our lawn. If we hadn't called the ambulance, who knows what the hell would've happened to her. He should've come and shaken our hands." Berk flopped down onto the couch cushion on the floor and picked up the game console controller, nudging his bag out of the way and stretching out his legs.

We'd given up on sitting on the couch, no one wanting to walk like a hunchback for the next few hours once they got up.

"I never thought I'd say it, but I'm done with house parties." LJ sat on the floor beside Berk, their backs against the couch, and picked up the other controller. "This place was like being locked in a closet and someone forcing you to smoke an entire case of cigars, only instead of cleaning up cigar butts, it's Solo cups, assorted mystery stains, and abandoned kegs."

"Returning the taps for all those kegs did pay for the new grill." Berk lifted an eyebrow and shrugged.

"The grill they busted when they jumped off the back deck." LJ jabbed at the buttons on the controller. "Oh, Alexis stopped by earlier today."

"She did?" Berk sat up straighter.

"What's the deal with her?" I shoved a forkful of food into my mouth. "You banging her or something?"

"What? Ew, no. That's gross, and don't ever say that again." Berk's face twisted like he'd just caught a whiff of a dumpster full of baby diapers roasting in summer. "It's not like that."

"Right, nothing sexual about a beautiful redhead who always shows up here asking for you."

"Exactly, nothing sexual." Berk curled his lip and spat out the words.

"You guys are staying here next year, right?" I stared down at the comments on the story. *'Entitled jerk…'*, *'Today's youth…'*, *'A program like Fulton shouldn't put up with things like this no matter who the person is.'*

"It won't be the same without you guys. Plus, this place is

a mess, and I'm sick and tired of cleaning up after every beer-soaked tsunami that hits it," LJ said with a shudder.

"But next year you'll be a senior and you can make the underclassmen do it for you." As I leaned back in the chair, the leather groaned beneath me.

"We could never be so cruel." LJ grinned and selected his avatar in the game.

Berk threw out his hand and grabbed LJ's arm. "Don't shut that idea down so quickly, man. This has some serious possibilities." He got a dreamy look in his eye that only meant trouble.

The front door opened then Reece slammed it shut so hard the floor shook. He walked in looking like a pitbull who'd eaten a wasp. Berk jerked his hand up from his side and popped Reece in the middle of the forehead with a Nerf dart.

He didn't even flinch.

"What the hell's up with you?" I shoved a forkful of pasta into my mouth.

"What the hell is Johannsen doing on our street?"

LJ hopped up and peered out the front window. "He's just sitting in his car halfway down the block."

"Do we need to go out there and see what he wants?" Berk pushed up off the floor.

"Calm down everyone. If he wants to be a weirdo stalker, let him. We don't need any more trouble." I held each of their gazes until they stood down and sat back in their spots. "And what the hell is up your ass?" I turned to Reece.

"Seph's driving me crazy." Reece dragged his fingers through his hair and turned to the room, staring like he hadn't realized we were even there. "Why won't she listen to reason?"

We all groaned and sat back in our chairs. Berk started up the race in his game, propping his feet up on his backpack, which never seemed to be more than twenty feet from him.

"Would you leave the poor girl alone? Maybe she doesn't want to live with you. Can't say I blame her. She wouldn't have any room for her clothes or shoes if she did." His attempt at mumbling under his breath was about as successful as his attempt at winning the race in the game. LJ rammed his car into Berk's on the screen, and it sat in a flaming heap at the bottom of an embankment.

"She's found a single in graduate student housing, and they're letting her move in now."

"That's perfect. You can go stay there instead of ear-banging us night after night." Berk covered his ears with his hands, rocking back and forth. "At least someone's getting some." He seriously needed some kind of grumble lesson, because that comment had been about as under his breath as a shout from the rooftops.

"You're one to talk—" Reece stopped midsentence and tilted his head, staring at Berk. "Actually, you haven't been running demolition practice in your room in quite some time. Lost your mojo?"

"Shut up, no." Berk took a bite of his candy. "Just haven't been feeling anyone lately."

LJ, Reece, and I exchanged looks.

"This wouldn't have anything to do with that letter you got a while ago, would it...?" LJ grinned, swaying from side to side.

"No, this doesn't have anything to do with her letters." Berk's shoulders hitched higher, and if he'd had a shell to duck into, we'd have been speaking to the air.

"Oh, *letters*—now it's more than one." Reece got up, practically floating closer, happy to have the attention off him and how hung up on Seph he was. "How many letters?" he teased.

"A few." Berk kept his eyes on the screen like we'd all disappear if he didn't look at us.

"How many's a few?"

"Ten."

"Ten secret sex notes." LJ again steered his car into Berk's onscreen. "Who knew you were such a reader?"

Berk glared at him. "They're not all sex notes." A splotchy red pattern raced its way up his neck. "I'm trying to figure out who's writing them. I thought they'd stop playing around and come out and tell me by now, but she seems perfectly content to just trade letters."

"You're writing back? What are you saying?" We all leaned in closer. The only note he'd let us read had left the three of us slack-jawed in the middle of the hallway. It had been pretty freaking hot. That he'd thought any of us would use those words to describe him, even as a joke, was beyond laughable.

"None of your business. Why's everyone staring at me? We've got a bigger situation to deal with—Nix's reputation rehab," Berk called out around a Twizzler shoved in his mouth.

And just like that, the spotlight swung back around, nearly burning out my retinas.

"Is that garlic bread?" Reece's fingers brushed the edge of the crispy crust.

I smacked his hand with my fork.

He hissed and shook his hand, sitting on the arm of the couch with his arms braced on his legs and his hands folded in front of him. "Sharing is caring."

"Go get your own. I made extra."

"How long have you known him?" LJ lifted an eyebrow at Reece. "You're more likely to convince him to streak across the end zone than share food."

"True. Back to your reputation rehab—your dad's still on that?"

"Once he gets something in his head, nothing short of a lobotomy is getting it out. He's giving me until the end of March to come up with something to 'redeem myself'."

LJ's lips pinched together and he nodded, pushing up off his legs. "How in the hell did ESPN even know you got arrested?"

"News travels fast. Someone takes a pic and that's all it takes for stuff to spread like wildfire." *Thanks a lot, Elle.*

LJ let out a low whistle. "Damn. What did he have in mind?"

"I don't know, and I don't want to know. My workload is crazy this semester. I banked on having lots of time without football eating my life, but this"—I shook my phone at them —"is going to seriously fuck up my semester."

"What if there was a way you could cram in a whole bunch at once? Like a goodwill binge." LJ tapped the controller against his leg.

"How'm I supposed to do that?"

"Weekends?"

I shook my head. "I have workouts every weekend, followed by PT for the shoulder. My dad wants to get these issues ironed out before the draft physicals. Also, I'd like to actually graduate." And I wanted to visit Gramps more at the restaurant. I hadn't been there since the summer, and I missed the kitchen madness, wanted to be a part of it again.

Reece's head popped up, and I could practically smell the heat off the lightbulb over his head. "There's a one-week build over spring break, building houses for families in need. They're doing twelve-hour days for six days. If that doesn't make you look like a saint, I don't know what will."

"I've seen that. Flyers are up all over campus." Berk talked around the licorice in his mouth. "I've heard there are some hot chicks there too, do-gooder types."

"Getting laid while building houses isn't exactly my idea of fun." I crunched on my buttery garlic bread. I might've overdone it. Who am I kidding? Is there such a thing as too much garlic or butter on toasted bread? I think not.

"A woman wielding a hammer and nails—it doesn't get

any sexier than that." Berk sucked in a breath and kissed his fingertips before flinging them into the air like a chef after tasting a delicious sauce.

"Don't let The Letter Girl hear you talking about other women like that. She might get jealous."

The scarlet flush was back like a neon sign on Berk's neck. He grumbled, "Driving me nuts," and tapped a button to un-pause his game.

I took the steps two at a time and went into my room. Turning on the computer, I searched for the build. It started on Monday. I left a message with Rick, the guy listed on the website, and asked if I could join in. It couldn't hurt to try to get out from under whatever master scheme my dad had all laid out back in his office, likely pinned up on his wall with strings spanning from picture to picture. This would show him I was being proactive in fixing my damaged reputation.

Classes were brutal this semester. Seemed the professors had forgotten about the national championship that had only happened a couple months ago—not that I wanted to coast. A business degree came in handy when it came to looking over big contracts and making sure I wasn't getting screwed over.

Cracking open my books, I hunkered down to work on some of the take-home midterms I needed to turn in. Economics equations and problem sets floated through my head for hours until my brain revolted. Massaging my eyeballs, I checked the time. *Shit!*

I'd convinced Dad that video chats were easier and would make me seem less eager to get a better deal with the pageant of agents I needed to meet over the next month. It also meant I didn't have to put on pants. Hanging out in my boxers and a suit jacket and tie, I sat through another boring call.

The coursework I still needed to finish for the semester sat mocking me on the far corner of my desk. I got changed and jumped to the bottom of the steps. A twinge shot through my knee, letting me know just how stupid that had been. "I'm headed to Tavola tonight."

"Bring us some of that thing with that sauce on it." Berk dropped his notebook and closed it before pressing his palms together and doing his best puppy dog eyes.

"You need to be a bit more specific."

"The one that makes me want to worship it as my new religion."

"The roasted pork loin with the balsamic reduction?"

"Yes! That's the one—and don't bring it back half-eaten this time."

"Beggars can't be choosers. It's my fee. Any other requests?" I walked into the kitchen and opened the fridge, trying to do some recon. "What the hell?" There wasn't a space open on the shelves. "Eat some of this stuff first, then I'll bring you guys more food."

LJ waved me off. "It's...um, fake."

"Fake?" I eyed the brown and white paper and Styrofoam containers.

"I had to fill it with empty takeout containers so Marisa wouldn't get any ideas about cooking."

I shuddered and shoved my keys in my pocket. "For the love of God, don't let her in there again."

"You're telling me." LJ shook his head and tapped on his phone.

I jogged out to my car.

Passing by the fun police house, I headed toward Tavola. My grandfather's restaurant had gotten a reputation over the years, but tonight was a special night. It was preview night.

Parking behind the building, I grabbed my supplies out of the trunk of the car. Bag in hand, I hopped out of the way as the back door swung open.

Gramps froze with a bag in his hand. A big grin spread across his face once he realized I wasn't a mugger. "Phoenix, I didn't know you were coming down tonight." He tossed the bag into the dumpster and pulled me in for a hug. How many restaurant owners threw out their own trash? Gramps saw something that needed to be done and jumped in without a second thought, not acting too good for even the dirtiest jobs.

"It's the first one since the season ended—of course I wasn't going to miss it."

He looped his arm around my shoulder and tugged me inside. "Look who I found outside," he yelled so loud I swore the pots and pans on the shelves rattled.

All the heads in the kitchen popped up.

"Phoenix!" There was a wave of my name being called out throughout the room, a few elbow-bumps and hugs without hands. No one wanted to have to go wash up again.

"Is there a spot for me?" I pulled my white coat out of my bag and put it on. Normally, I'd feel like a dick for wearing a chef's coat when I wasn't an actual chef, but the embroidered cursive writing on the chest made it all better: *Apprentice.* Never mind I'd been apprenticing since I was ten, but I'd take it.

"I've got an entire tray of carrots with your name on it."

Preview night was the one weeknight a month my grandfather closed down the dining room to paying patrons and let the chefs at Tavola try out new dishes. They could be anything from reimagined classics to off-the-wall new cuisine. My grandfather was a traditionalist, using recipes from his parents, but that didn't mean he didn't see the benefits of people innovating and coming up with different things. He'd stepped aside from the head chef role a few years back, so the menu was ever evolving.

There had been many new careers launched off a preview night dish, and it was also why so many of the chefs who'd worked for my grandfather were still here, or came by whenever they could. It was free to whoever wanted to taste the sometimes frighteningly inventive creations. First come, first served, and everyone always left satisfied.

It was my second home, and I'd been away way too long. I'd hung out there for hours on end as a kid when my dad was on the road. Every day after school, I'd come in and worked on my chopping skills. They'd probably just given me those tasks to keep me from stealing all the tiramisu, but I loved it. Noisy, organized chaos, the kitchen reminded me a lot of the football field, except there weren't three-hundred-pound linemen trying to detach my head from my body at every turn.

I massaged my shoulder. The scarring of the muscle sucked big time and made each throw during this season a miracle; the damage had been done.

"What's taking so long? You finally going to start coasting?"

"I'm moving so fast, you can't even see me, Gramps."

He let out a huffing laugh.

I washed my hands, rolled up my sleeves, took out my knives, and got to work dicing the catering tray full of carrots. It was grunt work, usually left for the newbies to the kitchen, but I didn't care. I was there, and man, my dicing skills were rusty.

I fell into that old familiar rhythm and worked my way through the entire tray, speeding up as the creaky wheels of my knifework came back to me. As I sliced through anything they put in front of me, everything clicked back into place, just like my shoulder every time I rolled it, only this didn't hurt.

In the kitchen, the world made sense. I'd do this PR thing for my dad. Maybe then he could see beyond the draft. Every next stage had his complete focus until I tackled it, and then there was always the next thing looming on the horizon, but once I was in the pros, there was nothing else, right? He'd finally be pleased by my accomplishments. That was a relief but also struck a spike of fear in my heart. What if I did all that and it was still never enough?

Shaking my head, I focused on the knife work and what I needed to do next. Choose an agent. Enter the draft. And pick the ball up again in the fall. Easy as pie.

So why did it feel like my life was a funhouse-mirror version of what I'd expected?

CHAPTER 5
ELLE

My car shuddered into the parking space. Every ride I made where something didn't fall off was a success in my book.

There were a healthy number of volunteers here already. They milled around like sleep-deprived zombies in the parking lot while we waited on the bus. Once I got to the site, I'd get the official list and make sure no one nailed their thumb to the frame of the house like last year. I probably should've gotten coffee for everyone first. I'd bring that up to Rick.

The spring break build was one of my favorites. It gave me a chance to rack up even more volunteer hours, was great publicity for Make It Home, and took place outdoors. After being cooped up in the student health center, high school libraries, and the tutoring center, not to mention the soup kitchen, it was a miracle I didn't burst into flames the second I stepped out into the early spring sun.

It wasn't even melt-your-face-off weather this time of year. I had a sweatshirt in my bag because early April mornings were still chilly, especially at six AM.

The glowing screen of my phone peeked out of the pocket

in my bag at my feet. I picked it up off the grass and stared at it. *Don't you dare.* I'd gone almost a month without checking out any of the HWITBA accounts, a new record for me.

Letting out a breath through my gritted teeth, I shoved my hand into my bag and pulled out my phone. I checked the social media accounts for He-Who-Is-The-Biggest-Asshole. *Oh, how's your spring break cleaning beaches in Nicaragua? Oh, and are you also surfing in almost every picture you post?* Well, I was building a house for families in need. It shouldn't have been a competition, I know, but Mitchell was also in the running for the Huffington Award, so I'd had a peek.

The comments made me want to scream.

How he was the best, most caring person they'd ever met.

Such an amazing guy.

How meeting him had restored people's faith in humanity.

At least I didn't have to worry about running into him on campus for the next week.

Those gushing comments about his character were barbs straight to my chest even now, and they brought back memories I thought I'd left behind almost two years ago right back into my face. The looks from everyone in the club we'd co-chaired after the word had gotten out that he'd cheated, the heated glares from everyone like *I'd* screwed up...

That was what I did.

James had turned me off football players since my senior year of high school, which was a damn shame because FU was a haven for athletic hotties.

But Mitchell? He had cracked open a barely healed wound. He'd known I'd been cheated on. He'd known how much James had hurt me and how long it had taken me to trust again then he'd cheated on me as well. Everyone else thought they were both so perfect, in different ways, the golden boy athlete and the humanitarian hottie.

Apparently, my radar was dialed to the cheating jerk

setting and I didn't know how to turn it off. It was safer to be alone.

Somehow, I'd gotten screwed over by two guys I'd thought couldn't have been more different, the football star and the philanthropist. It didn't seem to matter. They all got one look at me and went, *Yeah, sure, I'll fuck her over.* They were the stars in their realms in every way imaginable, and I'd been the perfect accessory—until James went off to college and accessorized with my former high school best friend on his dick and Mitchell decided to do exactly the same thing during his late-night sea turtle volunteer trip to South America.

I stuck my phone back in my bag, the curdled-milk feeling back. *Shake it off, Elle.* The long days meant I could eat whatever Jules had cooked when I got home without guilt, could drown my sorrows in a tray of still-warm chocolatey chocolate chunk cookies.

When we'd first roomed together her freshman year, she'd tried to sustain herself on celery and lettuce, and sharing a room with a rabbit was a hell of a lot less fun than it was to live with the baking goddess she'd let herself become. She had slowly come out of her shell with food and everything else, like that pole she'd put up in her bedroom. It was slow going, but she'd get there one pole dance at a time.

Dragging around two-by-fours and a nail gun all day meant lots of delicious carbs once I got home. She'd promised me all the edge pieces in the brownies she had going into the oven at exactly four PM today.

A girl in bright pink short shorts and a crop top bounded over to me. "Are there going to be drinks?"

"There's water and ice at the worksite, and I'll see if I can get us all some coffee for tomorrow."

"Not water, like, *drink* drinks." She smiled and shook her head like I was an idiot.

"We're building houses. What part of 'community build project' makes you think there's going to be an open bar?"

"On the flyers it said this would be a spring break adventure of a lifetime. How can you do that without booze?" She stared at me like I'd asked her to forgo air.

"How about building a home for someone in need who can't do it on their own? Seems like a pretty worthwhile and unforgettable adventure to me." I hoped my resting bitch face singed her perfectly tweezed eyebrows. "You don't have to come today. I'm sure you can book a last-minute flight to Cabo."

She let out a groan of disgust. "I can't. My dad took away my credit card. He said necessities only, but that bag was totally a necessity." The friends behind her backed her up, nodding along at their terrible luck with spending her father's money.

I stared back at her, letting the silence go from uncomfortable to excruciating—for her.

She tugged at the hem of her shorts. "Whatever, I'll go take a few selfies. Not like there's anything better to do."

Wonderful, a day of complaining and bitching was just what I needed right now.

"What's your name?"

"Krista." She bounced on the balls of her feet.

"Today is going to be hard work. You're going to get sweaty. It's going to be hot. You're going to be doing new things and you're going to be tired. I don't have time to hold your hand. Do not get on that bus if you're not willing to put up with some discomfort today."

She eyed me and looked back at her friends. Their faces had all dropped. *Please don't get on the bus.*

"I didn't think we'd really be building the stuff, more like painting or something."

"Painting comes later, as long as we've done our jobs right. This is about people's lives, people who don't have a roof over their heads and need this house." If I'd had more time to plan this thing out, we could've done ten houses in the same amount of time, but the funding had come through late, and by the time I'd plastered the campus with flyers, most people were already gone for the break.

"Maybe we'll get some good selfies." Her friend sounded as uneasy as they all looked.

Then Krista brightened, and I could see the little lightbulb over her head go off like a cartoon character. Oh, this would be good. "Maybe if my dad sees pictures of me doing good stuff, he'll see that I deserve the card back and then we can go away this summer." She held her friends' hands like they'd made a pact to end all pacts.

I gritted my teeth and hoped my college health insurance covered dental. How could someone be so out of touch with the needs of other people? Not seeing anything except how whatever they were doing impacted themselves and not the other people around them?

That could've been me. In so many ways, that had been me, and it freaked me out to see that mirror held up to my face. The inability to see beyond my own little bubble...my stomach twisted.

A squeal and rumble signaled the arrival of our ride, the luxurious and in-no-way-about-to-break-down-at-any-minute bright yellow school bus. *Glam life here I come.*

"Grab your stuff. We'll leave in five, and it's a thirty-minute drive to the build site." People picked up their bags, lunches, and whatever else they'd need throughout the day. The driver pulled up to the curb and flung open the rusted and creaking doors. Everyone filed onto the bus, which smelled like a field trip to a local farm, and I got a head count: thirty dead-assed, bleary-eyed college students ready to roll out. Leaving someone behind on the return trip was a serious pain in the ass, but I was thankful we had a better turnout than the previous year, when we'd barely been able to get a tiny house framed for the next group. All my work putting up flyers, sneaking into meetings held by other groups, and pushing the project in the study center had paid off.

I climbed the steps to the bus and sat in my seat. At least I'd gotten a semi-good sleep the night before since there weren't any parties raging until early morning. The Brothel had been quieter than usual. It had been splashed all over campus that Nix had been arrested, no charges or anything, but there'd been whispers of them serving booze to underage girls. In that case, super fuck them.

Still, that didn't mean I hadn't stayed up until two AM working on grant applications and trying to finish my term papers. Hopefully the bags under my eyes wouldn't turn into a full set of luggage before the end of the day. The ride over to the site would give me a chance to nap. I had one volunteer shift at the soup kitchen this week and that was it, no tutoring or barista shifts at Uncommon Grounds since the campus was closed for the break.

Getting on these old buses reminded me of elementary school trips to the aquarium or the zoo. Half the time the bus ride was more fun than the destination, but we were college students and it was way too early for excited squeals, except from Krista & Co.

"We can go, that's everyone," I called out to the driver.

I grabbed my sweatshirt from my bag and balled it up, resting my head against the window. I'd have slept standing up if I needed to. The bus's engine rumbled and the gears ground as the driver threw it into drive.

Someone thumped on the accordion doors, and the driver slammed on the brakes. I was thrown forward, slamming my hands against the back of the not-nearly-padded-enough seat in front of me.

Rick loved to invite people along at the last minute, which completely defeated my headcounts and the list he'd sent me the previous morning. I'd have to go over how important arriving on time was. People only tended to get more lax and show up later as the days wore on and the splinters set in. The doors opened again, and our late arrival climbed aboard.

A perfectly ruffled head of hair popped up at the top of the steps. We pulled onto the road and he held on to the seats, steadying himself, his forearms bunching with the sway of the bus. My brain fought to process the image as he walked onto the bus.

I was tired—too damn tired. I rubbed at my eyes, hoping a fever dream had taken me or I'd started hallucinating like Jules always warned I would.

The eyes. That nose. His mouth. *Error, does not compute. Abort mission.* Only no matter how many times I blinked, he was still there.

Nix.

He moved down the aisle, and his gaze collided with mine. Maybe it took his mind a second to piece it together just like it had for me. His eyes narrowed, and I swallowed past the lump in my throat. *Keep it together, Elle. You're fine.* It wasn't like he'd attempt homicide in a bus full of people. Then again, with who he was, they'd probably cover for him and gladly dig my shallow grave with their bare hands.

He broke the connection first. His gaze swept over the other people on the bus. Every eye was on him. The star quarterback. The campus hero. A lock for the first-round draft pick and an inconsiderate asshole of a neighbor who may or may not have been into some shady shit. I glanced out the window like I'd be able to jump from the moving bus then froze. Why the hell was I wanting to escape? I hadn't done anything wrong. Well, maybe I'd called the cops, but he was the one who'd gotten himself arrested. I resisted the urge to sink down in my seat.

My earlier words to Krista & Co. replayed in my head, mocking me. *"Don't get on the bus if you're not willing to be uncomfortable today."* Understatement of the century.

He made it to my row.

I'm not proud of it, but I did it. I scooted my ass to the far edge of the seat.

"Nice as ever, huh, B and E?" His lips welded together with a look of displeasure.

Why would he want to sit next to me anyway? He wouldn't. Still, that hadn't stopped me from sliding my butt across the worn, frayed seats to the edge, blocking even a flicker of doubt that I wanted him sitting nowhere near me.

"Find a seat. We're late."

Was it petty? Yes. Was it childish? Hell yes. Did I care? Not one little bit, but he clearly did as he rolled his eyes and kept on walking down the aisle. There were plenty of available seats from the shuffling and sighs from behind me. I wasn't going to turn around; nope, wasn't doing it. Krista & Co. had no problems with offering up a seat to him. I was sure that invitation came with much more intimate options as well.

Taking my sweatshirt, I balled it up again, punching my hand into it and wedging it in the corner between the window and the seat. I rested my head against it, but there was no way I'd get any sleep, not with Nix's heat vision on me. It wasn't in my head; I could feel his gaze sweeping over the side of my face from his seat three rows behind me.

Pretend he's not there. Pretend he won't be around power tools near the person who got him thrown in the paddy wagon. It seriously couldn't be the first time he'd ever been arrested. Drunk and disorderly was practically his middle name. I mean, not really, since he was always the one to come over to talk to me after noise complaint after noise complaint was logged, but —*ugh.* I folded my arms over my chest.

Best-case scenario: He'd leave after one day of for some reason thinking it'd be a boatload of fun like Krista. Worst-case scenario: I'd 'accidentally' fall off the roof and end up in a full-body cast for the rest of the semester.

CHAPTER 6
NIX

She Forrest-Gumped me.

I almost expected her to say *Can't sit here* with an Alabama drawl. Waking up after my alarm was bad enough, but I'd stayed for an entire night shift at Tavola. Gramps and I had stayed up late, prepping some of the meat for today. He always said if you weren't in the walk-in, you'd never know how things were going on the floor. He inventoried everything and could make recommendations to the chefs on what dishes they might try to keep things fresh. Also, I'd been promoted from chopping vegetables to soups. It felt good to flex my skills again after nearly nine months. Preseason training plus the full season hadn't left me any time to even breathe, and before this week, I'd been scrambling to catch up on everything I'd put off this semester.

If I could've chosen, I'd have been at the restaurant every day, getting back into the groove and learning how to make the new dishes everyone in the kitchen thought up. Stealing away for a meal here and there during the semester wasn't enough, but I didn't have a choice with the new training regimens and PT Dad pushed to keep me at the top of my game for the draft.

My shoulder killed after three hours of chopping and stirring, but it was a hell of a lot better knowing I wasn't going to face down three-hundred-pound linebackers ready to knock me into next week. No chance someone at Tavola would tackle me into the walk-in fridge—at least not as a regular occurrence, though Gramps had been known to get a bit rowdy from time to time.

I'd run into that kitchen when I was eight with my backpack slamming into my back and an apron in my hand. Stepping inside the tiled and stainless steel kitchen brought back all the old memories I never wanted to lose—Gramps ruffling my hair, the stern looks from the line cooks who thought I'd be a pain in the ass, making food that made people happy—but the crazy hours restaurant employees worked had slipped my mind.

My eyes were bleary, and I bit back a yawn. Dad had had me on three conference calls with agents last night. I'd nodded off about five minutes into the second one then woke up to my phone practically jumping across my desk with him calling my name in his irritated and exasperated voice and a piece of paper stuck to my face at almost midnight.

Rushing over to the volunteer meeting site, I'd leapt out of my car when I spotted the bus pulling out of the parking lot. Late on my first day—that wasn't going to go over well. Dad wanted me to check in on the place today and make sure it would make for a good photo op. I chaffed under his near constant badgering now that the season was over. Apparently, I'd been hit in the head a few times too many this season and it had made me think once I won a national championship, he'd let up. I did convince him to at least let me get a lay of the land first before he barged in with an entire press corps for my totally volunteer, in-no-way-made-freaking-mandatory-by-my-father community service.

I'd talk it over with the head guy when I got there and try

to keep things as low key as possible while also getting my dad off my back.

Being late was the least of my problems now. The pink-haired menace's glaring attention slammed straight into my chest the second I stepped into the aisle of the bus. Perfect. Maybe she was just hitching a ride to the nearest bus station for a trip out of town. If she was on this build, getting some good PR out of it would be a nightmare.

It was her fault I was in this mess in the first place. I found a little happiness in thinking maybe she was here for the same thing. Maybe she'd set fire to a toga party or run over the Trojan's mascot with her car, perhaps burned some bras in the name of feminism. I'd never seen someone so against a good party. Sure we got loud sometimes, but that's what college is about. With her funky light pink hairstyle, she needed to be careful—people might mistake her for someone who enjoyed having fun. She rested her head against a balled-up sweat-shirt, and I didn't look down at where her shirt had ridden up around her waist, totally didn't check out the tanned, smooth skin there. That would've been suicidal.

I wedged myself into my school bus seat and collapsed. The spring greenery was finally here after a long winter, but the freezing snap always tried a few last gasps before spring finally told it to GTFO.

The bus ride was quiet other than the squealing brakes our driver rode for the entire drive. That's what happens when you pack college students into a bus before eight AM. Our team rides to games had been the same, and no one gets rowdier than football players, just not at the ass crack of dawn.

Elle sat facing the front of the bus, not talking to anyone. The seats all around her were empty, like she projected a 'don't fuck with me' force field. I kind of wished I had that ability. Our paths had crossed a few times before on campus, usually with her doing everything but hissing at me before glaring and leaving. I had no idea what the hell I'd done to piss her off—joked with her to break the ice when she'd walked in on me naked? Returned her mountain of condoms? Invited her to a party at our house? Cardinal sins in her book, apparently. And then she went and called the cops on every party that sprung up at our house. We didn't even have to invite people over. They'd just show up with kegs, red cups, and thumping bass. Sometimes we even called the campus cops ourselves to get people out, but she'd escalated that by calling the city cops and getting me arrested, so screw her.

The seatback dipped as the guy behind me leaned over. His arm hair brushed the side of my neck, and I braced myself for the invasion of my space. He rattled off the stats for my entire collegiate career.

I closed my eyes and let out a deep breath. "Thanks for watching me out there." I wasn't a dick, no matter what Elle thought of me. What she thought didn't even matter.

After the tenth question about the draft, I smiled and didn't hold back my yawns anymore. *How do my tonsils look, dude?*

"Sorry. I had a long workout yesterday to get ready for draft camps."

The guy's face blanched. "I'm s-so sorry to bother you," he sputtered.

"Don't worry about it." A small twinge of guilt hit me, but he hadn't stopped talking for a solid ten minutes straight. Yes, I'd kept count, in between glances toward the front of the bus where Elle leaned her head against the window and slept. She wasn't faking, because her lips parted and her gentle—well, not so gentle, more like garbage-disposal-with-a-fork-stuck-in-it—snore made it the three rows back to where I sat. If it hadn't been her, I'd have appreciated that she didn't give a crap what anyone else thought, but it was her, so it annoyed the shit out of me.

I pulled my hat out of my lap and threw it on my head.

Crossing my arms over my chest, I rested my head against the seat and switched off my brain. After hours on the road on buses and planes, I'd trained myself to fall asleep anywhere necessary. Here was no exception. All I needed to do was get through the next six days without going anywhere near her. How hard could it be?

REAL FREAKING HARD, APPARENTLY. THE BUS RUMBLED INTO THE gravel parking lot. People stood around me. Opening my eyes, I massaged the side of my neck. These seats weren't made for football players; they were designed for underdeveloped third graders.

Elle shot forward in her seat and rubbed the side of her mouth with her hand. Damn, she really had been out, drool and everything. Her head whipped around so fast I jumped. Had I said that out loud?

Her eyes narrowed, but she didn't climb over the seats between us to strangle me, so I was going to go with no.

The collective eyes of everyone else on the trip bored into me. In front of a stadium full of people, it was no issue. Even parties at the Brothel I could handle; drunk people were never too interested in the answers you gave, just repeating the same question ten times and laughing like their jokes got funnier each time they said them. But with the season over, being around people I didn't know well meant the uncomfortable conversations cropped up more and more.

What team do you hope you get drafted to? No idea.

What city will you end up in? Who knows.

What are you going to do with your big paycheck? It's never been about the money.

I tugged my hat down farther like that hid anything from anyone. My knees banged off the seat back in front of me. I hissed, my bone hitting against the metal bars nicely hidden away under half an inch of padding. Maybe I should've brought my brace. Freaking twenty-two years old and my body was already breaking down.

Damn these buses were a hell of a lot smaller than I remembered from school. I had been maybe ten the last time I was on a bus like this. The team buses were the long-haul, charter types that had ports to charge our phones and personal TV screens on the back of each chair. Some of the guys had even snuck an Xbox on before Coach shut that down.

A sprawling lot was surrounded by parking spaces. There was lumber out in different configurations in various areas. Half-built frames were dotted around the space. Leaves on the trees swayed in the gentle breeze and provided some shade. At least it wasn't June. There wasn't much cover, so we'd bake under the sun by noon.

Ducking my head, I filed out after everyone else. Rick, the guy I'd spoken to on the phone, handed everyone matching nametags. He had a thick, blue plastic one with worn edges.

His well-rehearsed spiel meant to pump us up came tumbling out. "We've got five groups here this week working on a few different projects. These are houses we'll build here and then they'll be shipped off site. They're a cross between tiny homes and permanent structures, so it's easier to do it here and move them later."

Everyone stretched and nodded.

"We have smaller projects we might recruit people for as needed. Elle's done this before, so she can help if you have any questions. The construction expert volunteers will be over to check on everyone, show you what you need to do, and inspect your work. We appreciate everyone being here, but we're not trying to build death traps. When in doubt, ask someone for help. Let's get going and have some fun." He clapped his hands together and handed Elle his clipboard.

And the hole just got deeper. Of course she was the right-hand man—err, woman on this job. *I don't know what I did, but universe, I'm sorry, okay? Can we call a truce?*

"We'll be building the shell for one house and the interior on another as well as any additional features the houses might need, like ramps." She called out the orders, sending groups of people off to different areas to pick up their tools.

Feeling like the last kid picked for a game of kickball, I stood in the empty area waiting for my assignment.

She refused to look my way, slipped her pen into the top of the clipboard, and turned around.

Stepping forward, I took my hat off and dragged my fingers through my hair. "Elle, I didn't get an assignment."

Spinning on her heels like I'd catcalled her, she stared at me with her full, soft lips turned down. "You're not on my list."

Do you think I just like riding miniature school buses for fun? I bit back those words. "I called Rick on Friday. He said it was no problem."

Her lips tightened like she was trying to eat them, and she stared at the clipboard again. "Fine. Grab some gloves. You're on lumber duty." Was that a gleeful smile, or did she always wear that smirk when sentencing someone to hard labor?

"Can I be on lumber duty?" One of the girls from the bus rushed up to us.

"No," Elle bit out so sharply the poor girl jumped.

"No need to be so mean about it," she mumbled and slinked away, rejoining her girl squad.

"Are you always so charming, B and E?"

"There's a lot to get done this week and I don't have time to hold anyone's hand or break out the hose when you two are going at it behind the work shed."

"Way to jump nine hundred steps ahead. If there's anyone who'd be banging someone, it would probably be the woman who has enough condoms to last most people half a century —or are you all out of those? Been busy lately, huh?" All I wanted was a chill spring break, but she had to push buttons like she was manning a submarine.

"You're such a cocky asshole. And you know what? Yeah, I've been drowning in dudes. You haven't heard? Everyone on the block has had at least three rounds, but still nowhere near your man-whore levels, I'm sure."

"This man-whore doesn't kiss and tell." I puckered my lips, which were met with the cold, hard metal of a hammer shoved up to my mouth.

Could've been worse.

She could've used the claw end.

"Don't trip and fall over your ego and end up with a hole in your head." She dragged her hands down her face like the world was perched on her shoulders. "Listen, be careful and pay attention. We don't need anyone getting hurt and it screws up the work permits and stuff for the site. Wouldn't want to injure the campus golden boy." Her barely contained eye roll was all I got before she shoved a pair of work gloves at me. Her about-face from claws out to a hint of actual concern threatened me with whiplash. Was there ever someone more confusing and infuriating than Elle? Shaking my head, I got to work.

With my luck, I'd be knocked unconscious and that could be the story my dad ran in the paper to 'repair' my reputation.

CHAPTER 7
NIX

Drenched in sweat, I unlocked the front door. Why did it seem like I'd gotten five times the amount of shit to move around than everyone else? Probably because Elle cracked the whip the entire time. I opened the front door and stepped inside.

Heavy lifting was never a problem for me and it felt better to be doing it outside than in a gym or on the field, but damn was I aching. I rotated my shoulder as the front door closed behind me. The click in my rotator cuff never went away, and the doctors said it would only get worse over time, the soreness turning to pain in a few decades, and that was if I didn't screw it up even more. The upcoming season would be brutal.

Bypassing the couch, I kept myself from plopping down and passing out. I'd offered to buy a new one, but the guys had said no. Apparently the only thing they hated more than that couch was me throwing my money around. Walking into the kitchen, I skidded to a stop.

Marisa stood in the center in one of LJ's shirts and I prayed some boxers or something underneath. I'd forgotten she was here. She'd bunked here after a fire at her apartment a couple days ago. LJ had nearly lost his mind when she'd called him to come get her at two in the morning. We'd all let her borrow whatever she needed, and I'd offered to get her anything else we didn't have on hand, which had drawn a fire-poker glare from LJ. He'd been mother-henning her since she arrived.

"Hey, Marisa." I yawned and cracked my back.

"Hey, Nix. You're all sweaty. Keeping up your conditioning before the draft?" She closed a cabinet.

I threw my keys down on the table and looked at the state of the kitchen. Pots and pans out on the counters. Food in various stages of preparation. Mangled carrots. Raw chicken sitting next to grated cheese.

The blood drained out of my face and my skin went clammy despite being overheated. The horrifying terror of her scattered and erratic movements in front of the counters registered.

"What are you doing?" My voice was quiet, like when approaching a horse you don't want to spook.

Her head snapped up and she closed the fridge door. "I wanted to thank you guys for letting me crash here, so I thought I'd make dinner." She beamed. It was like walking in on a toddler who'd decided to make you a painting with the contents of their diaper.

I backed away, keeping my hands out in front of me like I'd walked in on a wild animal foraging in the kitchen, and shouted up the stairs, "LJ!"

He thudded down. "What?" He poked his head out over the banister, nearly banging the top of his head on the ceiling.

"She's cooking." I kept my eyes trained on Marisa. One false move and there'd be salmonella in our water and on every other surface in the house.

His eyes widened like I'd told him aliens had landed in the backyard. "No!" He jumped down the entire flight of stairs. "Hey, Ris, you said you were just coming down to get something to drink and study." He stood shoulder to shoulder with me like we were headed into battle.

"I know, but I felt so bad about hogging the covers and you sleeping on the floor, so I wanted to do something for everyone."

"But remember what happened last time you cooked?"

I clutched my stomach. We'd had a battle royale for who got to puke in the toilet. The rest of us had lined up along the bathtub like some seriously fucked-up watering hole. It hadn't been pretty.

"I didn't realize you were going to cook. I called in an order for pizza on my way home. It should be here soon." I slid my phone out of my pocket, hidden behind LJ, and used the app for the pizza place to order enough pizzas to fill the fridge for the rest of the week.

Her shoulders sank. "Oh." She stared out at the monstrosity of her meal prep. "I guess I can cook for everyone some other time." Sliding everything off the counter into one big container, she attempted to clean up. My cross-contamination radar went off like a Geiger counter at Chernobyl.

"We can do it," I shouted and moved into the kitchen.

She jumped.

"Don't worry about it," I insisted. "I left a mess in here anyway, and it's my turn." I plucked the sponge out of her hand.

The front door opened. Reece and Berk stood frozen in the doorway. They spotted Marisa in the kitchen with her hands on a pan as she moved to put it away. They looked at each other, then at her. Lunging forward, they both shouted, "No!"

ELLE

I COLLAPSED ON THE COUCH, MY BUTT BARELY HITTING THE cushions before my bag dropped and the contents spilled out all over the dented and splintered wood floor. Could it even be called a wood floor at this point? It seemed more like plywood held together with duct tape.

"Whatever." I rested my head against the back of the couch.

A successful day on the site. We'd gotten a lot done. Our posts to the Make It Home's social media accounts had gotten good responses. Maybe we could get some good donations to stretch our hard work even further.

My shoulders ached.

My feet ached.

My aches ached.

"Elle, you home?"

"No, it's Zoe, our ghost roommate."

"I'd believe it was a serial killer trying to lure me into a trap before I believed that." Jules snorted.

I closed my eyes and ran down my list of projects that were due. The final submissions for the Huffington Award had to be in at the end of the month. That didn't leave much time for the rest of the work I needed to get done, but the Peace Corps option didn't fill me with a yearning for exploration like it once had. With the Huffington Award stipend, I could finally pay off the last of my tuition, free my transcripts from registrar purgatory, graduate, and not be buried under the student loan cloud looming over my head. Until then, my life after May was a giant ball of who-the-hell-knows.

It was close. No time to slack now. I could rest when I was dead, hopefully holding the award high and shoving it in Mitchell's face.

The bang of a cabinet door brought me back to what exactly I was doing, and then the guilt crept in. Was that why I ran myself ragged with all this? To outdo Mitchell, get my degree, and crawl out from under some student debt with a two-year stint living in a hut somewhere? All about me. *Get a grip, Elle.* I was also helping people, so it balanced out.

"Where is Zoe?" I asked.

Cupcake tins and other baking tools clanked together. Jules was Pavlov, and I was her insanely hungry dog. "Your guess is as good as mine. No cops have shown up at the door to break any bad news to us, so I'm going to guess she's at her boyfriend's place," she called out from the kitchen.

Sugary, chocolatey smells tried to pull me off the couch as though the delicious tendrils could lift me up like a cartoon and carry me into the other room. With how my body ached, I'd have much preferred that to walking. "Which boyfriend?"

"Who knows? I can't keep track. There've been three in six months. If she weren't actually paying rent for her abandoned room here, I'd swear she was with these guys just for a free place to stay."

"She's been here no more than ten nights since she moved in in August."

"And three of those were when her parents came to visit." Jules came into the living room and pushed her glasses up with the back of her hand. This time they were covered in chocolate.

That perked me up. "Whatcha making?" I sat up and leaned closer. Her promise of brownies pushed my tiredness aside.

She switched the bowl to her other arm like I wouldn't know batter from a mile away. "Yours are heating up in the oven. Give them five minutes. These are for my philosophy study group."

"You're always baking for your classes." Was I whining? Hell yes I was. "That's mean. I'm so hungry." I stuck out my bottom lip, widened my eyes like a kitten begging for milk, and rubbed my stomach.

"You can lick the bowl when I'm finished and I'll bring you any leftovers."

"Yes!" I jumped up and followed her into the kitchen. "What about my brownies? You promised me brownies for all my good deeds."

"Always looking for the upside to exploit." She laughed.

My stomach soured. Was I?

"Don't worry, your batch is almost finished." Lifting the bowl, she held the whisk up until the mixture fell back into the bowl in thick, rich ribbons.

"How was your philosophy exam?" I followed her into the kitchen, some of my hunger beaten back.

"You do see all these dirty dishes and the mountain of baked goods, right?" She poured the batter into the zigzag pan that made every piece an edge piece and added extra chocolate chunks.

"That good, huh?"

"I don't know why I care. I don't even need this class to graduate."

"So why'd you take it?" I hopped up onto the counter and drummed my feet against the cabinets below.

Ducking her head, she ran the spatula around the bowl. "No reason." She held out the chocolate-coated bowl and spatula to me. "Here, you can have this."

Her diversionary tactic worked and I decided to let it slide for the time being, my hunger totally back. "How is it so good before you cook it?"

"It's probably the thrill of living on the edge with a risk of salmonella that gets your blood pumping." She stuck the brownie tray into the oven.

I stared into the glass bowl streaked with chocolate and shrugged. "That and the touch of love you whip into every batch."

"It's not love—it's blood, sweat, and tears." The corner of her mouth turned up, but the smile didn't reach her eyes. "My mom called."

Oh shit. "Don't answer her calls."

"Then there's the risk she'll come to find me herself." There was a sadness there that snuck in every so often. She didn't let it happen more than occasionally, but sometimes it hit so hard it could take your breath away. "There are some new recipes I want to try, so you're in for a mountain of sugar this week."

She wiped her hands on her apron and sat at the kitchen table. Her notebooks and textbooks were fanned out across our makeshift tablecloth. No one wanted to see what was under the table. If we were lucky, whatever growth had held on to the wood's surface throughout several bleach and disinfectant attempts wouldn't sprout legs and murder us in our sleep before we moved out at the end of the semester.

"Midterms that bad, huh?"

She ran her highlighter over an empty space on the edge of an index card. Ten others were tented on the table, folded, torn, and covered with highlighter marks. "I'm not worried about them."

"Then why the stress baking and note card decimation?"

"I didn't tell you this before because I know how much you hate them, but Berkley's in my philosophy class." She peered up at me over the top of her glasses.

Berkley? I don't know a B— "You mean Berk? As in one of the Trojans' Berk?" Mystery solved. So that was why she'd taken the not-needed-to-graduate philosophy class.

Her shoulders hitched higher. "Yeah, him."

"You're baking for him?"

Her head whipped up. "No, I'm not. I'm baking for my group and he just so happens to be in that group."

My issues with football players shouldn't have made her afraid to even mention his name. "Jules, I'm not your jailer. You don't have to cross to the other side of the road if you see them coming. I'd have thought you'd have mentioned it earlier."

"There's more." She shook her head like she was about to

spout pea soup from her lips. Her cheeks pinked up and she rearranged her pens neatly beside her notebook. "And it's been more than one."

"More?"

"He's the guy."

"What guy?" I tried to think back over any guys she'd talked about this year. There wasn't anyo— "He's the letter guy?" My screech ricocheted off the kitchen walls.

Her head snapped down in a sharp nod and her lips were pinched.

"And you kept this from me?"

"I figured it would peter out and there wasn't a reason to tell you."

"Holy crap." I pushed back the curtain on the window and peered out at the house that had been the bane of my existence for the past year and a half.

She plucked at the edge of her notebook.

"Are you going to tell him it's you? Right across the street from him…" I peered out the kitchen window.

Her head snapped up. "Never, and you can never tell him either." She splayed her hands on the table top.

I held my hands up in front of me with my fingers spread in surrender. "Why don't you—"

"No, Elle. Non-negotiable. You can't ever tell him." The sharp crack of her voice let me know there wasn't a hint of joking in her words.

"I won't ever tell. It's not like I'm hanging out with them or anything." I smirked to lighten the mood.

Her shoulders un-bunched and she sagged against the table. "That would be the day." She chuckled. "Elle hanging out with the Trojans."

"Well…" I cringed and my shoulders hitched up around my ears. "Nix did show up for the house build today."

Her head snapped up and she stared at me wide-eyed.

"Yes, I know. I felt the same way when he walked down the aisle of the bus."

"Does he still have all his limbs?" She pushed back her chair and checked on the batch of brownies on the cooling rack.

"He's fully intact, although his fan club will probably end up with at least a few broken fingernails if they don't pay attention while they're hammering. He laps up all the attention—it's disgusting." Not even her amazing-smelling food could keep me from scrunching up my face like someone had plopped down a week-old trout in the middle of the kitchen.

"Maybe he's just being nice. He can't help it if people fawn all over him."

"He encourages it." I'd seen it a million times with James back in high school, and Nix was cut from the same freaking cloth. *Oh no, don't pay attention to me. I'm just like everyone else, but I'm also always expecting everything I want to fall at my feet, no matter who gets hurt in the process.*

"For someone who says they don't care about him at all, you sure seem to know a lot about why he does what he does."

My eyes narrowed. I stuck my tongue out at her and chucked an oven mitt at her head.

She ducked my toss and grabbed her chest. "Shots fired. Baker down." She slumped against the counter before testing the brownies in the oven with a toothpick.

Maybe I could sleep through the next week and then I wouldn't have to deal with the Phoenix-Russo-sized bomb that had been dropped into my life. Did he look hot carrying all that lumber? Yes. Had it been just as hard for me to keep my eyes off him as it was for the Glitter Posse? Yes. Was tomorrow going to suck even more? Probably.

CHAPTER 8
NIX

Another day, another human zoo exhibit on display, namely me. My dad had arranged for a photographer to come to the site later in the week once we made it through a lot of the progress, so the sweat equity would be worth it, if only to get him off my case. Any number of agents he had me meet with never seemed to be enough for him. Although, I didn't know how to get it done without Elle showering me in an avalanche of rusty nails. It would confirm all the bullshit she thought about me, and as much as I didn't want to admit it, it bothered me what she thought. It did.

Rick waved me over. I put down the wood in the pile everyone else added to and dusted off my gloves. Sweat rolled down my back even with the spring temperatures in the cool range. Shifting hundreds of pounds of wood and marching tools back and forth had a way of ratcheting up temperatures even with a breeze.

"What's up?"

"I'm noticing some of the people are a bit distracted." He stared over my shoulder.

Turning my head, I tightened my lips. One of the guys tried to walk a two-by-four through a gap in the not-yet-completed wall that wasn't quite four and ended up flat on his back with the wood cracking him across the chest. The clothes the three who'd been in the open bar group from yesterday were wearing made their outfits from before look like they were headed to a convent. I hadn't thought shorts could get any shorter, and I had been wrong.

You'd think after going to school with me for the past four years, people would stop being so weird, but now that I'd been vaulted to the cusp of pro status, the weirdness had gotten worse. The only person who wasn't treating me differently was Elle. She hated me no matter what.

It was kind of comforting.

"Nix, let me get that for you." Krista leaned over, showing off her cleavage. I kept my eyes on the sky.

She handed me a box of screws when I'd asked for more nails.

"Thanks, Krista." I looked up and wiped the sweat off my forehead with my shoulder. It was hot as hell out here, not as bad as standing in the middle of a field at high noon with twenty pounds of gear on, but still no walk in the park.

I caught Elle's gaze. She glared at me, and I wasn't sure if the pounding in my head was from the sun or if she'd developed some kind of telepathic powers. Her scrutiny pissed me off. I wasn't up for leading girls on, but I might have laid it on a bit thick with Krista just to piss Elle off.

I gritted my teeth. She'd made up her mind from the second I caught her staring at my dick like it was a newly discovered prehistoric artifact. Whipping the towel around my waist and getting my jeans on as quickly as possible had been the only way to keep the blood flow that shot straight to my dick from embarrassing me. Once she figured out who I was, it was all over and her rampage began. Rumors about what had happened in the Brothel before we lived there were still floating around. While it had looked nice and shiny when we'd moved in, finding used condoms crammed into the sides of your drawers in the kitchen would make anyone pray for death.

Still, we weren't those guys, even if she'd decided in her head we were.

Our predecessors' reputation preceded us.

"I thought you might want to work on a project that'll help keep everyone else focused." Rick stared over my shoulder at the beauty pageant lineup going on behind me.

"That's probably a good idea, make sure no one nail-guns their heads together."

"Perfect, and I've got the perfect co-worker for you. She's a total pro at this and hasn't walked into any of the framed-out walls once since you've been here."

I let out a breath. "That would be great." The last thing I needed was the blame for another person ending up in the hospital being pinned on me.

"Elle?" He waved his hand over his head at her.

"Actually, maybe that's not—"

"What's up, Rick?" She wiped her hands on her cargo pants.

"I've found you the perfect partner for the ramp project." He gestured toward me, and Elle's jaw clenched. "We need specialty ramps made for the family that'll be living here. The specs for it are in the workshop area. If you could work on those, it would help a lot. I'm sure it'll be no problem for you two." Rick gave us both a wide grin. The guy crapped unicorns and spat rainbows.

"Great." Who knew you could growl out actual words. She stalked off, and I followed her.

"This wasn't a special request I put in or anything." I hoped to clear the air right there and then. I wanted absolutely nothing to do with power tools around her.

She tilted her head to the side, and the corner of her mouth turned up. "Sure you didn't."

"Why would I want to be trapped anywhere with you, B

and E?" I tended to stay away from people who'd probably enjoy seeing my balls ripped from my body.

"Stop calling me that." She brushed past me.

"That is what you did, right? Broke into my house?"

"The door was unlocked. I'm hardly a master burglar."

"Fine, I can call you Trespasser if you prefer."

"How about you call me nothing."

"Fine, where're the plans for these ramps, Nothing?"

"Are you five?" She threw her hands up and rounded on me. Her fists tightened and a vein stuck out on the side of her neck. I could practically hear the blood thrumming in her veins. Why did I take so much pleasure in her annoyance?

She glanced over my shoulder, spun back around, and walked to the workshop area like she had just been asked to dig her own grave.

Inside the makeshift wood shop, she crossed her arms over her chest. "We can get these done quickly and painlessly. No talking necessary."

"You took the words right out of my mouth." The less chatter the better, right? I'd had people in my ear for the past three months. Agents, terms, contracts, drills, doctor's visits, breakdowns of what teams had the best prospects next season —the talk about the future was starting to chafe.

The laughter and voices from outside filtered into our wooden prison. We worked in silence—complete freaking silence. Elle did her best cavewoman impersonation, pointing and grunting at me. With the third near miss of a finger with her hammer, I'd had enough.

"What's your problem?"

"There's no problem. Let's get back to work." She stared down at the wood like she could slice through it with her eyes.

"What's with this hate-boner you've got for me? If anything, I should be the one pissed off—you got me arrested!"

Her glare intensified peeling off a layer of skin. "You got yourself arrested."

"Bullshit. You got me arrested."

"I'm not the one supplying underage girls with booze and getting caught."

I chucked my hammer down on the table. "Is that what you think happened?"

"Campus cops never do anything about the noise complaints, over thirty since the beginning of the year. So, I called the city cops."

"You seriously think we were giving booze to underage kids?"

"Why else would they arrest you? Or was it drugs? Maybe fighting?"

I'd never wanted to shake someone more.

"None of that shit. A ball I threw accidentally burst through my bedroom window and broke the cop's window, and the city cops have had it out for us since the police chief's daughter tried to get into one of our parties, we turned her away, and her friends left her drunk and passed out on our lawn. We called the ambulance, and he didn't take too kindly to the fact that she was drunk and breaking the law."

Her mouth opened for a reply, but it stalled in her throat. "Oh." The wind was punched out of her sails.

"Yeah, 'oh', and maybe the campus cops never did anything about our parties because they know it's a college campus and people like to have fun."

"And some people like to sleep."

"Well, those people shouldn't rent houses on old frat row and expect to get a nice night's rest."

"Some people don't have a choice where they live and have to take what they can get. Some people care about not doing whatever the hell they want without regard for anyone else around them."

"You know nothing about me, but you've already decided

exactly who I am, and that's fine because I know exactly who you are." My blood pounded in my veins. I could barely see straight.

"And who am I?" She jammed her fists into her hips. Better that than wielding the nail gun with a grudge.

"You're one of those people who hates other people enjoying life because you can't do it yourself. Maybe it was sucked out of your body by a Dementor, but however it happened, seeing other people having fun drives you crazy because you're incapable of doing it."

"I have plenty of fun."

"I'm sure stirring your cauldron brings out the cackles."

"Maybe my idea of fun isn't blaring music and drunken antics at one in the morning when other people are trying to sleep or study without beer and a brain-blanking thump drowning out their ability to even think straight."

Crossing my arms over my chest, I leaned back against the wooden beam running down the center of the workshop. "Jealous?"

"Screw you. I'm not jealous." She scoffed and shoved her hands under her arms, which had the unfortunate side effect of making me one hundred percent aware of the great rack she had.

Her gaze followed mine and a scarlet flush crept up her neck, filling her cheeks.

"You sure seem to be. If people are having fun, they can't help it."

"I'm not into people being here for the selfies and pats on the back." Damn, that hit was a missile lobbed with uncanny accuracy, but she didn't know this whole thing came with a photo op for me.

My head jerked back and my eyebrows dipped. "Have I taken a selfie since I've been here?" I held my hands out to my sides with my fingers spread wide.

Was that a giant pulsing vein in her forehead? It looked like a giant pulsing vein in her forehead.

"I'm done." She stormed out of the workshop and straight for Rick. Shit, if she got me kicked off this project, my dad would be on my case double time. She barely stopped and said something to him. His head jerked back and he stared at me. I was so fucked.

He dug his hand into his pocket then pulled out a set of keys and cash from his wallet.

She snatched them from his grasp and stormed off.

Did she just rob him? Rick turned and walked in my direction. I backed into the workshop and picked up the level. We'd at least made it through half of a ramp frame. If I could finish that, maybe today would count for something.

"Elle said we were running low on water, so she's going to do a run to the store. Why don't you help? She's not going to be able to carry all of it on her own. She also didn't ask where I parked my car. Go catch up to her and let her know it's on the other side of the site."

I stifled the relieved breath that shot out of my lungs. So she hadn't ratted me out. At least there was that.

"I mentioned before that a photographer might be coming by to take some pictures at the end of the week—is that still okay with you? If not, I understand and I can cancel it."

"Not a problem. The more publicity we can get for the work we have going on here, the better."

"If we could keep this between us for now, I'd appreciate it." I looked after Elle, blazing her way across the site. "The timing might not work out and I don't want anyone to be disappointed."

"No problem. You'd better catch up before she walks halfway across the city."

I shook his hand and took off after her.

"Thanks, Nix." He waved and pointed me in the direction of his car.

What could I do about the unfortunate case of Elle hating my guts while still getting the reputation rehab I needed? She'd flip her shit if she found out, and I didn't want her to have the satisfaction of thinking she'd been right about me all along. Maybe I just needed to make nice and get her to ease the hell up. How hard could that be?

I followed the muttering and swearing to find Elle wandering the outskirts of the site, looking for Rick's car.

I cupped my hands over my mouth. "It's not over there."

Her head shot up and her eyes narrowed. If looks could kill, I'd have been talking to everyone through a Ouija board right about now.

"How do you know?" She stomped with each step.

"Rick told me where it was and said I needed to go along with you to help with the water run." I stuck my hands in my pockets and tried not to delight too much in the way her neck got all tight and red as she got closer.

"I don't need your help."

"That's not what Rick said, and if you don't want to spend the next hour looking for his car, I think you do need my help."

She stood toe to toe with me. There was no starry-eyed admiration like there was with most people I met. There was only a fiery, biting glare.

I'd learned early that there was a certain type of woman who was very good at making you think they didn't care about football at all but traded on the prestige of dating a QB when you weren't around. Elle was not that kind of woman.

I smiled big and wide. It shouldn't have felt so good to piss someone off, but I knew where I stood with Elle. No hidden agendas, no questions about the draft, only watching my back for booby traps and taking every chance I got to piss her off.

After I showed her where Rick's car was, she rushed forward and got in, nearly making it out of the parking spot before my fingers grabbed the door handle. "Going some-where without me?"

More muttering and grumbling. "Get in and let's get this over with." Her hands tightened around the steering wheel.

The latch on my door barely had a chance to click before she sped out of the parking lot, shifting gears like she was an F1 driver. I snapped my jaw shut as the car swung around a corner, hugging the curb.

"You can drive stick?" I pressed my hands against the dashboard, bracing myself as my life flashed before my eyes.

"No." She dropped her chin to her shoulder and stared. Her gaze whipped back to the windshield and she shifted again. The car sped up and her thighs moved up and down as she worked the clutch.

If my heart hadn't been trying to climb out of my throat, I'd have thought she looked damn sexy showing the gears who was boss. Then again, this was Elle I was talking about; such thoughts were a one-way ticket to castration.

I banged my watch against the glass as I reached out to brace myself when she took a corner like we were on a track.

"Can you not break another window please? Especially when you don't plan on paying for it." She talked like she was grinding glass with her teeth.

"What is it with you? Not pay for it? I think I've paid plenty. The city got their check."

"What about me, huh?" She took her eyes off the road for an uncomfortable amount of time. "After you broke my freaking window and never paid up, we had to pay for it. The landlord blamed us. Do you know how much that cost? I'm sure you have no idea since you're a big shot with unlimited funds, but some of us get stuck with the bill."

"I paid for that window."

"No, you didn't, and I got stuck eating peanut butter and jelly for a month so the freaking crickets and mosquitos didn't start setting up shop in our house."

"Your landlord was outside looking at the window and I gave him cash to cover it, over a thousand dollars."

Elle's eyes widened and her head whipped around to mine. "Sonofabitch." I'd never seen anyone's head lift clear off their head in a mini-atomic explosion, but I swore she was a split second from going nuclear. "That lying little snake weasel." She let a few more inventive combinations of insults fly. The wheels were turning, and I could only imagine the torture Elle was plotting in her head. At least I wasn't on the receiving end—this time.

She turned to me, and the rage in her eyes dialed down to a simmer. Her mouth opened and closed a couple times.

"I'm sorry." Those two words seemed so conflicted coming out of her mouth aimed at me. "He told us you denied any responsibility and said you hadn't done it." She squeezed the back of her neck. "And I believed him."

"What an asshole." That had started the real spiral of animosity. I hadn't hardly been able to believe she'd still continued to call the cops after I'd overpaid for her window to get fixed, and maybe part of me had let those parties get a little louder than they should've and stretch on a bit longer because I knew it got under her skin. Maybe the water balloon and water gun fights on our street that ended up on her small patch of lawn hadn't been the best way to smooth things over.

"You don't know the half of it." She ground her teeth.

Pulling into the grocery store like she was ready for the pit crew to swap out the tires and gas up the car, she hopped out and slammed the door.

I braced my hands on the open door and the seat then ducked my head between my knees, sucking in a deep breath. Air back in my lungs, I jogged after Elle.

Her fingers were white-knuckle tight around the shopping cart, and she wielded it through the aisles like a weapon. No one was safe, not even little old ladies, that guy in a scooter, or the shopping cart piled high with kids. Everyone jumped out of the way as she passed.

"I'm sorry about her. She's new to this planet and doesn't know how to act like a normal human being," I shouted out to anyone we blazed by who hadn't lost a toe already.

Charging into the aisle with the water, she grabbed the first case from the highest shelf. Her hand slipped off the edge and I dove for it, snagging it with one arm. I gritted my teeth as my shoulder ached at the awkward angle.

"Careful." I pulled it over her shoulder and used both hands to stack it in the cart.

"I had it," she grumbled.

"Next time, I'll let you get the concussion, then." I picked up another pack of water and added it to the pile. With a water-laden cart, I took over pushing toward the cashier. I wanted everyone there to keep their feet and knees intact. Snagging a few boxes of donuts and cookies to add to our haul, I skidded to a halt at the checkout lane.

"That stuff can't go on this card." She lifted her chin toward the snacks.

"Don't worry about it. I've got it."

She let out a sharp breath, and I could feel the eye roll through the back of my head. "Of course you do, Golden Boy." It sounded like the worst kind of backhanded compliment. Two steps forward and eight steps back.

CHAPTER 9
ELLE

Sleeping straight through my alarm should've been the first signal that it wasn't going to be a good day. I got dressed, grabbed my stuff, and rushed out of the house in less than ten minutes.

Hopping in my car, I rode the edge of the speed limit. Was taking the bus the mature thing to do? Sitting there with Nix and pretending our blowup hadn't happened? Yes, it was, and with anyone else, I'd have sucked it up, but this was Nix. So, was I mature? That was a big pile of hell no.

My engine rocked and clanked. Even with regular maintenance, there wasn't much to be done about taking care of a car older than me. How long did it take for a car to be considered vintage? Maybe it was secretly a collector's item. I threw it into park and the whole car shuddered.

Or maybe it was a pile of junk.

Buying a new car wasn't in the budget; it just wasn't. Hell, my tuition wasn't in the budget, but I tried to pick up as many paying shifts as I could, which meant I kept running into Mitchell as he walked into the community service center on campus. Without fail, it was like he had an alert out for when I was on my way to work, but avoiding that side of campus wasn't an option. I needed to work. It was a double-edged sword when the volunteer work was what I needed to finally pay off my tuition and have some money after graduation, but I also needed some of that money right now, a chicken-or-the-egg kind of problem. Plus, if I ended up in the Peace Corps, there wasn't much need to keep this hunk of junk going. I'd be gone for two years overseas in a country without running water and they'd help me pay off my student loans.

And here I was whining about my serviceable car.

Guilt and shame gnawed at my gut and I rested my head against the steering wheel. It was all I could do not to fall asleep there. The bus wouldn't arrive for another half an hour. If I got off my ass and got over to the ramp workshop, maybe I could get through the bulk of our work for the day before Nix got there on the bus and leave him to finish without guilt.

My head popped up at the low crunch of gravel in the parking area. Good, Rick was early; that meant I could get started and explain that I needed to be somewhere after our time on site and that's why I hadn't taken the bus—not because I was avoiding a certain QB who shall remain nameless. That somewhere I needed to be was not in a confined metal box with Nix. I threw open my door and stopped with one foot out of my car.

It wasn't Rick. It was a shiny, navy, brand-spanking-new Mercedes S-Class. My gaze darted to the driver. He stared at me through the passenger window.

Cursing under my breath, I reached into the back seat and grabbed my bag. I slammed my driver's side door. It took three tries, but I finally got it to latch.

The low purr of his engine cutting off and the smooth click of his door being closed were the only sounds other than the morning calls from the birds in the trees. I swore they were laughing at me. Nix's gravel-crunching steps got closer.

"Trying to get an early start?" he called out.

Turning, I resisted the urge to cross my arms over my chest. I let them hang at my sides.

He wasn't going to get to me today. His hair was still wet, falling in perfect tousled waves and brushing against his forehead. His gaze dropped to my legs.

My hands tightened around the strap of my backpack. It was laundry day, so the shorts I had on weren't exactly construction-site-friendly. *Don't you dare tug at the hems.* I clenched my fists at my sides. Since when was I so hyperaware of every aspect of my body?

"Seems you had the same idea."

There'd never been a grimmer nod than his.

"Let's get to work then." *And get this over with.* Did I mumble that or was it in my head? Either way, he followed behind me like we'd both been sentenced to the mines for hard labor for the next twelve hours.

I dropped my stuff on the work bench and picked up some tools. Shoving my hand into the front zipper of my bag, I cursed under my breath. That's what I got for leaving the house this tired.

"What happened?"

"Nothing, it's fine." I'd fill up on water and go get something during the lunch break. My stomach rumbled like a creature from the black lagoon.

The crinkling and rustle of paper behind me made my stomach growl louder. The heavenly scent of sausage and cheese drifted across the workshop like a cartoon scent trail, completely filling my nose. My mouth watered.

Lifting the hammer, I turned just in time for Nix to take the first bite of his breakfast sandwich. My stomach growled and I stared at the large bites he took, his jaw working up and down, dimples taunting me as much as the food in his hand. He picked up a box of nails and set them down beside the ramp. The muscles in his arms tightened and flexed.

I licked my lips. *Maybe I should go get some food before everyone else arrived.* I was hallucinating about Nix in a way that was not bordering on homicidal.

He glanced up at me with half the sandwich still stuck in his mouth. Taking it out, he licked his lips...full, strong lips... *Dude, get a freaking grip. Better yet, get some food.* Some people got hangry, and I'd apparently stumbled into another type of hunger to mask my grumbling stomach.

"Did you want some?"

I scrunched my face up. "No, thanks. I don't need your half-eaten sandwich."

Rolling his eyes, he walked over to his bag and tugged out another yellow-paper-wrapped bundle of joy.

"I brought three."

I wanted to say no. It was on the tip of my tongue to tell him no and suffer through it, but I couldn't. My body was not getting on the Nix hate train when breakfast meats were involved. "Sure, if you're not going to eat it."

"Nah, it's cool. I have some other stuff too, if you need it." He held out the sandwich like he was offering it up to a wild animal.

As I took it from his hand, our fingers brushed. I snatched mine back, careful to bring the sandwich with me, and slowly unwrapped it, not digging into it like a bear after honey like I wanted. Carefully unfolding the paper, I took the first bite, and it was the perfect mix of salty meat, cheese, and toasted bread.

"Glad you like it." He laughed and finished off the rest of his sandwich.

Covering my mouth with my hand, I mumbled through chewed food. "Thanks."

"Don't worry about it." Picking up a saw, he spun it in his hands, his biceps bunching under the soft cotton of his t-shirt. Football had been good to him. The strong muscles in his forearms stood out. He'd had twenty-three touchdown passes this season.

How did I know that? People had been screaming it while running down our street when he'd won the championship.

I set the paper down and picked up the bottom half of the English muffin. Scarfing it down, I used one hand to double measure the wood to make sure it didn't come up short. *Double sausage patties incoming.* I hadn't even known you could order these with two patties, but I'd never been more grateful for Nix's bottomless pit of a stomach. I stuck the pen behind my ear and picked up the egg. *Goodbye yolk!* I freed the egg whites from their gross chalky brother and ate what was left.

So good. It was probably full of at least ten pats of butter. That's why restaurant food always tastes so good. I marked the other pieces of wood. Lifting the other muffin to my mouth, I glanced to my side.

Nix stared at me with the hand saw mid-slice through the wood I'd measured.

"What?" I covered my full mouth.

"Do you always pick your food apart like that?"

I stared down at my breakfast massacre. "Maybe." I shoved the sausage patty into my face like he was going to steal it back. *Let him try and he'll pull back a nub.* I licked my fingers, not willing to sacrifice the salty goodness to a napkin.

Nix's gaze was on me even as he sawed through the wood. I could feel it. Could he feel it when I stared at him too? Could he feel it right now? Our eyes clashed and my sated stomach flipped. I turned around, gathering what I needed. A guy gives me some food and I've suddenly lost my mind.

We worked in silence, finishing the ramp Nix had almost completed the day before. There was a flicker of guilt that I'd bailed and given him such a hard time at the store. He had shared his sandwich with me, and Jules always said sharing food was a sign someone wasn't all bad. With the way she gave it away, she was practically Mother Teresa.

Burning the candle at both ends was catching up to me. With the shelter, my shifts at Uncommon Grounds, and tutoring sessions, I was limping toward the finish line of graduation in a marathon that had lasted for the past three and a half years. Most people were on spring break, jet-setting around the world. Cabo, Paris, Fiji—there wasn't a destination too spectacular, so why was Nix here? Why wasn't he in some exotic location, flaunting those abs I'd seen when he lifted his shirt to wipe the sweat off his face? He was hard to pin down, and that unsettled the hate-hate relationship we'd worked so hard on cultivating.

The bus's probably-not-safe-for-the-road brakes squealed, signaling the arrival of everyone else. I grabbed my water bottle and chugged half of it. Heading out to meet the new arrivals, I helped Rick get everyone assigned and set up.

Nix hung back, tugging his hat down over his eyes like that would be enough to deter the attention of everyone there. Jules was right—even when he attempted to be inconspicuous, he stood out. Broad shoulders, tapered waist, and an ass made for jeans and manual labor. Not that I was checking him out, but damn—that was a great ass. The earlier level of shit I'd given Krista & Co. came back to bite me.

I jammed the nail gun into the wood, leaving an indent before pulling the trigger. Back in the workshop with Nix, the few minutes' reprieve hadn't been enough. Everyone kept shooting him looks and talking about how big of a pro contract he'd get and what team he'd end up on. James had talked about going pro like it was a foregone conclusion, and I'd lapped that up along with everyone else in our high school. Never mind he'd attended a D3 college without a scholarship and no one from that school had ever gone pro. After seeing how real football players played, my fawning over him made me feel dumb even all these years later.

"Seems it's not just me who gets your horns. I'd have thought once your hanger wore off you'd be in a better mood." Nix laughed and picked up the saw.

Swinging around, I glared at him. "I wasn't hangry."

"My mistake. You weren't hangry—this is just your natural state."

My eyes narrowed, but my stomach was full. The rumble died down with the egg, cheese, and sausage—that he'd shared. "Not hangry, just don't feel like making small talk. We're here to do a job, not socialize." I should've been over it. James and then Mitchell...I mean, it wasn't like all my long-term relationships ended with me getting cheated on—or wait, that's exactly what it was. Swearing off relationships didn't mean those feelings didn't rear their head every so often. It was always a gnawing, ripping-open-an-old-wound feeling, and I hated it. *Don't be that stupid girl. You're stronger than that, stronger than them. Stop fixating on the fact that you're completely and totally the kind of girl guys have no issue cheating on.*

"What kind of good deed would it be if we weren't all trudging around whipping ourselves to prove how special our contributions are? God forbid people enjoy themselves while doing something good."

"I never said people can't have fun. I have fun."

"Could have fooled me." He could've at least had the decency to pretend to say it under his breath.

"Maybe our ideas of fun are completely different. Did you ever think that's possible? Oh, I forgot, you have a serious lack of empathy and no ability to put yourself in other people's shoes."

"What the hell kind of thing is that to say? One second we're cool and the next you're biting my damn head off. It's been like this since the second we met."

The back of my neck heated up as the flashes of Nix wearing nothing but a towel on his head played in my mind.

"One minute you're checking me out and the next you're flipping your shit."

I whipped around. "I have never checked you out." Okay, maybe a little. "Why are you even here?" Did I sound territorial? Yes, but that's what happens when someone gets under your skin, especially someone like Nix who I wanted to pretend could never do so.

The muscles in his neck strained. Was it with frustration? Good, at least I wasn't the only one pulling into that station. "Can't I want to do something nice? Can't I take the time to give back to a community that's given me so much? You're the one who can't put herself in other people's shoes. No wonder they still had spots for this project—apparently you have to be the right kind of person to help others or they get nothing but shit on by you." His words bounced off the wooden rafters of the workshop, and I stood there stunned into silence. He threw down the hammer and stalked off. "I'm going to get some water—*if* that's okay with you."

He walked through the open doorway and I slammed my eyes shut. Damnit, why'd he have to have an actual point? I ran my fingers through my hair. Guilt soured the breakfast meal he'd shared with me. I was an asshole and the one whose altruism had an agenda. He was there to help out of the kindness of his heart.

Nix came back with two bottles of water and slammed one down next to my stuff. Why'd he have to be so nice? Why couldn't he be the arrogant asshole I'd pegged him as since day one? Time to suck it up and make amends. How hard could that be?

CHAPTER 10
NIX

"I'm sorry," she mumbled beside me, picking up the water bottle I'd brought her.

Had I laid it on a bit thick about why I was here? Yes. She didn't know I was here for my reputation rehab. I could only imagine the roasting she'd give me over that. She didn't have any idea I hadn't signed up for this on my own. How'd I know? Because if she had, that would've been rubbed in my face from day one.

Everyone always thought they knew exactly who I was from the moment they met me.

Pro-football-player dad. Entitled prick. Went to private school and lived in a big house. Spoiled rich kid. Even in the kitchen when I'd visit my grandfather, everyone assumed I was there to be an asshole and make their lives miserable. At least at FU people just assumed I was a braindead jock with a libido in overdrive. In the grand scheme of things, it was probably the least terrible assumption. Usually people didn't assume I was out to get them, except for Elle, who'd had me pegged as all those things from the first day she moved in next door. One post-shower peep show and she'd decided to hate me with the fire of a thousand suns.

"I didn't hear you. Could you speak up?" I cupped my hand around my ear.

"I said I'm sorry." The words barely made it past her lips, like she was giving a forced apology in the principal's office to avoid getting detention.

This was a moment I couldn't let pass. It was like spotting a once-in-a-lifetime astrological event. "Why are you sorry?"

"I shouldn't have assumed you were here for any reason other than to help. I judged you based on previous experience with people who only volunteer to snap selfies." She cringed. Her shoulders were nearly jammed into her ears. "It's a great thing you're doing and more people should do it. You're right about my assumptions and that I'm an asshole."

Wow, that was an actual full-on apology. "I never said asshole."

"Not in so many words, but I'm sure it was on the tip of your tongue." The corner of her mouth quirked up. So there was a mildly soft center beneath her hard-ass façade.

"Maybe."

"Truce." She held out her hand.

I squinted at her offering and quickly assessed her for hidden weapons. "No."

Her face scrunched up. "What do you mean 'no'? That was a super gracious apology."

"We're not calling a truce. The war is over. I'm calling for an armistice."

She laughed, a big laugh with a bright smile to go along with it. It was a rainbow on a rainy day kind of wide. "Should I get out the full treatise or will a handshake be enough to mark the occasion?"

"A handshake will do it." I stuck my hand out.

She slid hers into mine. My fingers enveloped hers, and an electric warmth shot up my arm. Her soft fingers tickled the inside of my palm. Her smooth softness brushed against the callused pads of my fingers. My heart hammered in my chest, and I swore there was an orchestra outside ramping up to a crescendo.

A massive bang outside broke the connection and we jumped apart, snatching our hands back like we'd been burned. How long had we been shaking? Why hadn't she let go? Had she felt that same jolt that made my skin tingle? Was she trying to read my pulse and figure out if I was a liar? Okay, that last one was a bit paranoid. I cleared my throat and handed her a screwdriver.

She took it from my hand, careful not to touch me at all, and read through the checklist for finishing off our project. A bead of sweat raced down the curve of her neck and ran along her collarbone before disappearing under her tank top. I'd never wanted to be a bead of sweat more than I did right then.

She kept her head down but didn't snap at me while we worked together on the ramps and railings.

"Knock, knock." Rick thumped on the doorjamb, balancing a cooler in his arms. "Everyone else is taking a break. You guys want some ice cream?"

Elle dropped everything from her hands, and it clattered to the dusty wooden worktop. "Yes, you're a freaking saint." She hopped over to him and stuck her hand into the blue, plastic cooler. She pulled out two and I hung back. Rick ducked back out the door.

"Here you go." She held the white plastic-wrapped ice cream bar to me.

I took it from her hand and nodded my thanks.

As she opened hers, her shoulders shook in a dance like a little kid who'd chased down the ice cream truck and actually caught them.

Laughing, I ripped mine open as well.

She took bites, cracking the chocolate coating and eating it before touching the ice cream. Every bite covered her lips in more chocolate, the lips she kept licking before wrapping them around the ice cream bar once all the chocolate was gone...the lips that were so full and pink, glittering as her tongue swept over them once again...the lips that would have a starring role in my dreams that night.

Her gaze locked with mine and the corner of her mouth turned up. "You're dripping." She lifted her chin, and my eyes dropped to my hand.

It was covered in ice cream. Droplets of sweet, melted cream dripped to the floor. That jerked me out of the trance she'd put me in with the licks of her lips and tugs of her mouth on the frozen treat.

"Shit." I lifted the bar to my mouth and took huge bites, finishing it in less than a minute. Mistake—big mistake! A searing hot pain sliced through my brain. Blindly chucking the wooden stick into the trash, I squeezed my eyes shut and hissed.

A gentle touch landed on my back, running along my shoulders. "You okay?" Her low words and touch would've been enough to reset a bone.

My headache was forgotten in an instant.

Her hand paused over the raised scars wrapped around my shoulder. The thick bands of the healed tissue stuck out even under my t-shirt.

She jerked her hand back. "Sorry," she mumbled.

The loss of her touch hit me harder than it should've. "Brain freeze, and don't worry about it. It's an old injury."

"What happened?" Her gaze was riveted to my shoulder, and she interlocked her hands and bent her fingers back. "You don't have to tell me. That's personal. I'm sorry I asked."

I lifted my arm, rotating it and making a circle with my elbow. "Surgery to repair some muscle damage a few years ago."

"Was it an accident?" She stared at me intently. It was probably the first time she'd held my gaze with anything but anger. Any other time, she defaulted to the closed-off look in her eyes like a house being boarded up for a big storm raging off the coast.

A sharp blast of air shot out my nose. "Yeah, it's called a three-hundred-pound defensive linesman."

Her shoulders tightened and she lifted her chin in a half-nod of understanding. "Those types of on-the-field injuries suck."

What did she know about sports injuries? "You played?"

She laughed. "Cheerleading back in high school, but not the crazy acrobatic kind, so no, I've never experienced it before, but I've been around athletes." Her mouth tightened and a small crease appeared between her eyebrows.

"It's not pretty." How much longer could I keep pushing my luck? "Should we get back to work?" That was enough talk of the path I wasn't going down. I held out my hand, palm up, gesturing to the last of our projects for the day.

"One second." She grabbed her phone from her bag and unlocked the screen. "We could use some music."

"I didn't think it was allowed during our sentence." The corner of my mouth twitched.

Her eyes narrowed, but in a playful way I hadn't seen before. "The warden is feeling kind today." Classic 80s tunes floated through the air from her phone's speaker, and we hummed along to the melodies and lyrics everyone seemed to be able to sing along to. *Don't worry, Simple Minds, we won't forget about you.*

We worked side by side, the tension drained out of our tight space. Stilted words turned into full conversation and made the work we did that much faster.

"I can't believe you don't like *Some Kind of Wonderful*." She lobbed a rag at my head.

"It's ridiculous. If I had a badass best friend like Stix by my side the whole time, there's no way I'd be going after Lea Thompson's character."

"He didn't get it. He wanted the popular girl."

"Screw the popular girl. He was an idiot, and that movie should've been over in three seconds when he walked in on her playing the drums."

"Not all guys are that perceptive." She laughed.

Didn't I know it. LJ and Marisa had been doing their little dance for years now.

We finished almost all of the ramps then stood beside our cars. The bus had already taken off, so the flurry of activity was now a low rumble as people on site closed up shop.

"You did good work." The words fell from her mouth like droplets of water breaking free from a dam.

"So did you. Maybe tomorrow we can skip straight to being friends without the verbal daggers."

She popped open her car door and braced her hands between the roof and the open door. "Who said we're friends?" The twist of her lips did little to hide the humor glittering in her eyes.

"Who said we weren't?" I folded my hands on the hot metal of the top of my car.

She tipped her head back and climbed into hers. Her engine roared to life, knocking and clanking. "See you tomorrow, Golden Boy." With a two-finger salute, leaning out her window, she smiled at me—the first unsolicited, non-I'm-about-to-gleefully-hand-your-ass-to-you smile ever, plus a nickname. Or maybe she was trying to kill me with kindness. I stared after her clunker as she pulled out of the parking lot.

———

"WHEN DO WE GET MORE FOOD?" BERK CLUTCHED HIS STOMACH, rocking back and forth like he hadn't eaten in a week—with a Twizzler sticking out of his mouth.

"Go get some food, then. Why are you sitting here bitching at us?" Reece picked up the controller and started the game.

"Because I'm the annoying little brother of the group. It's in the job description."

"And what am I?" Reece's car jumped over two people in the barren post-apocalyptic scene on the screen.

"You're the wild older brother—at least you were until Seph." Berk swung his controller back and forth like he was actually driving his car. "LJ is the worrier, always freaking out that something bad will happen."

LJ crossed his arms over his chest and grumbled under his breath.

"And who am I?" I sat in my chair wedged in the corner.

"The dad," they all said in unison without looking up.

"Why the hell am I the dad?"

"You're the quarterback—of course you're the dad, making sure your little chicks are all lined up in a row. Plus, you're the only person I know other than my dad who reads the paper." LJ pointed at the newspapers sitting on the armrest of the chair.

"There's nothing wrong with reading the paper." I chucked them over my head into the gap between the wall and the back of the chair.

"Okay, Dad." Berk snorted.

"Real mature." Reece smirked.

"See, what did I say? I'm totally not the dad."

LJ clapped his hand on my shoulder as he passed. "Embrace it. Don't run from your destiny. Anyone want a beer?"

Three hands shot up. "Me too." Marisa's feet slapped against the wooden stairs.

She dropped the towel from her head to her shoulders.

"You've got super hearing when it comes to booze." LJ shook his head.

"Only when you're buying." She slapped his arm. The oversized T-shirt hung down to her thighs and LJ's flannel boxers peeked out from beneath it.

"Marisa, please, for the love of God, let me spot you some money to buy some new clothes." I reached into my pocket, grabbing my wallet.

She froze, scrunching her damp hair in the towel. "I'm fine. His stuff is actually super comfy. The money should be here soon from the insurance company, and I might get even more since Liv and I warned the landlord about the electrical shorts more than once. No more nightmares about being burned alive, so all in all things are awesome."

Everyone's eyes widened.

"And I'm going to get that drink now." She rushed out of the room and into the kitchen like a cartoon character. The guys gestured with arms flailing for LJ to follow after her. We'd learned our lesson about trusting her in there before.

I leaned back in my chair and my gaze shot to the window at the flash of pink across the street. It had been a mainstay of her look since we met at the beginning of junior year, even as her hair gotten longer. It seemed once Elle decided on something, short of a nuclear blast, she wasn't letting it go.

Standing, I kept my eyes trained on her as she turned and shouted something to her roommate at the top of the stairs on their porch. She'd changed clothes, nothing more than a different t-shirt and jeans, but I couldn't tear my eyes away. It wasn't often I got to just look at her. Where was she going? I was wiped after a long day of building. There weren't any classes today. Did she have a date? What did she do when she wasn't volunteering or calling the cops on us?

The need to answer those questions sat with me well into the night. My gaze kept darting outside to see if her car was back. As it inched closer to midnight, worry pawed at my gut like a restless dog looking for tummy rubs. The knocking rumble of her engine got me out of bed at just before midnight. I don't want to say I leapt out of bed, but I'd have probably made a convincing understudy for the Philadelphia Ballet.

I leaned against the window and stared out at the night sky like I wasn't being a creeper.

She didn't get out of her car. Her hands stayed on the steering wheel and she rested her head against it, staying there for so long the worry in my stomach turned into tendrils of fear.

I'd just pushed away from the window to head downstairs when her head popped up.

Much slower than when she'd left, she climbed out of her car. Her black t-shirt and jeans were stained with a kaleidoscope of colors. Every inch of her screamed dead on her feet. What had she been doing after the day we'd just had to make her look like that?

She slammed her door shut, and my fingers tightened on the windowsill. Rounding the front of her car, her head lifted.

Before I could take a dive, our eyes met. Her weary look changed, and not in the way I was used to from the many times our gazes had locked across the street. She lifted her hand and gave me a short wave and a smile. Her expression sparkled in the dim streetlights even though her weariness made me exhausted. I'd hefted a championship trophy over my head, but this felt like a win I'd never forget. My first completely unprompted smile from her lit me up like a damn Christmas tree.

She jogged up the steps to her place with a bit more energy than before. A small stumble at the front door and she glared at the porch like she was ready to dismantle it warped plank by warped plank. At least I wasn't the only one who'd gotten that stare. She disappeared inside, and I lay in my bed with my hands behind my head.

Why did I have to beat down the urge to run across the street and check on her? Why had I thought at all about where she was going tonight? We'd only begun our armistice, and the build was almost over; no sense in getting involved beyond that. Then again, there was nothing wrong with being a good neighbor...

CHAPTER 11
ELLE

I wiped the sweat running down my neck away with the FU Trojan towels Nix had brought the day before.

He'd held one out to me. "I got the team to send over a bunch they were going to throw out since they're redesigning them for next season." Uncertainty had filled his gaze as he'd gripped the towel in one hand.

Has the light always caught the gray flecks in his eyes like that? I'd shaken my head, willing the brain fog away.

"We'll get them a donation certificate." I'd taken the towel from him and stared down at it. "Thanks, Golden Boy." There had been no derision in the words this time. He was a good guy. Damnit, why couldn't he have been an asshole? That would've made my life so much easier.

The number of times I'd had to banish the thoughts of working beside him from my head when I lay in bed too exhausted to fall asleep right away had reached an annoying level. Every time I'd close my eyes, his mussed hair, razor-sharp jawline, and should-be-illegal smile invaded my mind.

But the week was over. I'd miss being outside, even if most of my build days had been spent in the shed with Nix. He'd held a mirror up to what a bitch I'd been. It seemed old habits die hard. Those old feelings of peering over my shoulder as people snickered at my misfortune turned my stomach. Shoving those feelings deep down and pretending they didn't exist kept me going just like it always did.

Krista and the Glitter Posse hadn't complained after the initial rundown from me. They'd gotten on the bus last after everyone else, sweaty and disheveled and laughing while snapping their pictures. One of the moms and her two daughters who'd get one of the modified houses showed up to put in a few hours on day three. The ramp for her youngest in a wheelchair had lit a fire under their asses, and her daughters had sat under the shade of one of the massive oaks on the property and laughed their way through princess chat with the Glitter Posse. Krista had shown off her bedazzled hammer and helped them drive a few nails into the wood. There were no complaints about sweat, the heat, or breaking nails. They'd even sung some of their favorite Disney princess songs with the girls and made it an even more special day for them. Their little kid smiles were freaking magical.

My judgmental bitch slap came right back around to me. I'd gone from cheerleading squad member of the queen bee posse back in high school to getting my hands dirty in college. I never wanted to be around people who'd be assholes. I wanted to do good things, and it didn't hurt that it changed the way people looked at me and treated me.

Which made me an even bigger asshole.

Shame pitted in my stomach at the thought that part of the reason I'd even dyed my hair initially was because it helped me stand out in pictures. My no-longer-as-bright-but-still-conspicuously-pink hair made me easy to spot while putting in all that good work. All this time, I'd hoped I'd changed, wanted nothing more than to change, but I was misjudging people left and right—especially Nix. The end of this week would also be the end of my time with him. We'd ended up with more than a truce. He wasn't anything like I'd expected, and that scared the shit out of me.

With this project finished, we could go back to being neighbors, but actual neighbors, not the call-campus-security-every-night kind. Okay, the kind I'd been before.

Rick clapped his hands and cupped them around his mouth to call us all over.

I put the tools back, and everyone else cleaned up their gear and stood in a semicircle around a beaming Rick.

"I want to thank everyone for an amazing week. I can't tell you how much your time and effort means to the families who'll get to live in these and use the special projects you've all worked so hard on."

Nix stood beside me and rocked his shoulder into mine. I nudged him back and crossed my arms over my chest, letting Rick do his wrap-up speech. Everyone clapped and dove into the traditional tray of soft-baked chocolate chip cookies we always got at the end of a build.

I grabbed a few and parked up at one of the wooden picnic tables in the setting sun.

"I'm totally doing this next spring break. You guys in?" Krista bubbled like she'd never bubbled before. She and the rest of the Glitter Posse flipped through their phones, laughing at the pictures they'd taken.

Maybe they'd be up for being coordinators next year. They could probably spread the word to a totally different part of the FU population we hadn't tapped into yet, maybe help promote this thing beyond the usuals.

Nix walked out of Rick's office trailer and shook his hand. Rick clapped him on the shoulder and headed back inside.

Dragging his hand through his hair, Nix's smile faltered for a second when he spotted me.

He didn't have to put up with me anymore. There'd probably be tire peel marks in the parking lot from his car now that the week was over.

I dropped my hands to my lap, the half-melted chocolate chips no longer holding the same appeal. The whole table and my bench popped up, lifting my feet off the ground.

My head shot up.

Nix slid onto the bench on the other side of the table.

"You going to eat those?" He pointed at the three fully intact cookies still on my napkin.

I pushed them toward him, unable to beat back my smile. "Go for it."

"Awesome. I'm starving." He was a bottomless pit.

"What were you talking to Rick about?"

He froze with the cookie halfway to his mouth. "Nothing, really. Just wanted to know more about volunteering after graduation."

"That's awesome. They can always use more help."

"What are you doing after graduation?" He licked the chocolate off his fingers and I tried not to stare. I mean, I totally did, but I tried not to.

"After graduation, you say? I don't understand the question."

"Caps, gowns, stupid long speeches by people we won't remember by the time we get to our cars." He listed out each wonderful staple of the pomp and circumstance waiting just around the corner for us. "You know, graduation."

"Nope, doesn't ring any bells." I shook my head and jumped up from the bench.

"You're leaving?" He rose halfway from his seat.

"We're finished and I'm beat. I've got a thing to go to later on tonight, so I'm going home to take a shower and squeeze in a nap."

"Oh." That almost sounded like disappointment in his voice. "A date?"

I want to say it was a laugh, but what came out was more like a delirious cackle that only strikes when you're stupid tired. "Maybe." Real smooth. I was Jif peanut butter

—that's how smooth I was. "I mean, yeah, I'm going on a date."

He laughed, shaking his head, and stood. "Don't hurt yourself. You almost ruptured something trying to come up with that lie." Balling up his trash, he sank it into the trashcan twenty feet away.

Weren't three cookies on that napkin...?

"Show off," I grumbled. "Who says I'm not going on a date?" Why was I following him? *Just get in your car and go pass out at home, Elle.*

"You—from the way you nearly fell over laughing when I asked if you were going on a date."

"Maybe I'm surprised you even have to ask. I'm on dates constantly—all the time, like almost daily. Remember that supersized box of condoms." I winked as I tugged on the handle of the driver's side door to my car and nearly pulled the damn thing off. Bumping it back in with my hip, I pushed it in and lifted gingerly until the lock disengaged.

"Interesting." Nix leaned his back against his car, crossed his arms over his chest, and kicked one ankle over the other, looking like a damn catalog model. He was stupid pretty like that, slightly sweaty, muscled, and mussed. "What was your favorite date out of the last ten?"

I froze with my door open, one foot inside and one on the gravel lot. "The movies?"

"Is that a question?" His goofy grin transformed his chiseled jaw into a dimpled tease.

Straightening my shoulders, I held his gaze. He was not going to take me down. "The movies."

He lifted his chin and pursed his lips together. "Which one?"

Damnit. I racked my brain trying to think of something current, something I'd seen a poster or commercial for in the last few months.

I hedged. "A Marvel movie." Lunging for that lifeline, I spat out the franchise I knew was still around.

"I love those. Which one was it? Was it Thor or Spiderman?"

"Spiderman. Gotta love Spidey." My attempt at a web-slinging motion probably looked like I was having some kind of unfortunate hand spasm.

"Those movies both came out last year." His pearly white grin should've made me want to glower and throw out a few choice words. But it didn't.

My mouth opened and closed. I slapped my hand into my forehead. Total fail. I threw my head back and laughed. The sound caught in my throat as I lifted my head and came face to face with Nix. He hadn't gone to his driver's side. He'd come to mine, putting us inches apart. I swallowed.

"But if you're up for a night out, I'd be more than happy to—"

I'm not a coward, I swear. I walked the halls of my high school with my head held high after James visited over Thanksgiving break with his new girlfriend on his arm. I pretended the snickering, pointing, and flat-out laughter didn't get to me. When I had to back out of the senior trip because we couldn't afford it anymore, I braved that like Cersei on her shame walk, but Nix asking me out on a date? I noped right out of that. Knocked him out of the way and closed my door before he could finish that sentence.

There may or may not have been peel-out marks in the gravel, and I didn't look in my rearview mirror. It was so much easier to say no when you didn't want something than when you did. And dating—hell, a date with Nix wasn't what I needed right then, or ever. My relationship track record would've made any sports fan cry. He didn't just have heart-breaker written all over him—it was scrawled up in the clouds by a skywriter, displayed in glowing neon above his ocean blue eyes and way-too-kind smile.

He was all my mistakes wrapped up into one bright, shiny package.

Not just any football player, but the star quarterback who'd just won a national championship and lived in a house nicknamed the Brothel.

Nice guy who did charity work.

And I was into him.

No matter how much I'd tried to deny it and used my anger and annoyance as a shield, I liked him. Do not pass go. Do not collect $200.

The last thing I needed to do was crawl across the college finish line with my heart trampled by the hordes of women scrambling for his attention.

Plus, I was leaving at the end of the semester for who knew where. Friends, I could do. More than that—not happening. The problem with my platonic plan became apparent as I pulled up in front of my house after driving around for a bit.

"Hey, neighbor! Getting ready for your date?" I jumped as the voice I'd thought I could outrun shot across the street.

The heads of a few other students walking down the side-walk turned to glance between us.

I lifted my hand overhead and waved before jogging up my steps. How the hell was I supposed to avoid him when he lived forty feet away?

CHAPTER 12
NIX

The tailored suit of the man sitting across from me was exactly like the suits of the four other agents I'd met with—tonight. It was my dad's version of speed dating. I'd rather be at home hanging with the guys, plus I was beat after the spring break build.

I rocked back in my chair, keeping my hands in my lap and nowhere near the stack of papers with a pen perched on top of them. Elle had smiled at me this afternoon when she'd walked out to her car. That smile and small wave were the reason I'd pretty much camped out on our front porch now that the weather had switched from flirting with spring to almost summer.

Every time I walked over there, she was gone. Heavenly smells came from the other side of the door, but the one treat I wanted was never there. She had to be the busiest person on campus.

"We'd love to bring you on board as one of our newest athletes. We always negotiate the best deals possible with an eye toward your career after you leave the field. I'm sure your father can attest to that."

"I'm sure he would." The song and dance grated on me

like a slow drip of water on the center of my forehead. Busting out of there as quickly as I could, I headed back home. I'd perfected the right amount of attention in a conversation to ensure a report wouldn't go back to my dad about how I didn't seem to be paying attention or interested.

Rubbing my eyes, I braced both hands on the wheel, fried and ready for bed. I kept driving for at least a block before her car registered. That wasn't just any car on the side of the road; it was Elle's, and it wasn't just a broken-down vehicle. She stood beside it looking under the hood. I threw my car into reverse and backed up, parking in front of hers.

She waved me off. "It's okay. I don't need any help," were the first words out of her mouth when my door opened.

Standing up, I walked around the back of the car.

"Seriously, I've got it."

Didn't she sound thrilled I'd stopped to help? Gumdrops and syrup practically poured out of her mouth. The space between her eyebrows was pinched tight. So she hadn't said no just because it was me; her guard was always up.

"Oh, hey Nix." Some of the tightness relaxed and she let out a sigh.

"Car trouble?"

She rolled her eyes. "It's on its last legs, and a defibrillator isn't going to work this time." She chucked the wrench at the remnants of the hunk of metal that may have at one point been considered a car. Wiping her hands on her pants, she let down the hood. She crossed her arms over her chest and stared at it like a teacher staring at a kid who'd let her down in class. The mumbling under her breath added to it. Turning, she ran her hands through her hair, spreading a streak of grease through her bright pink strands.

"Did you call for a tow?"

"My phone's dead."

"Dangerous thing when you're out on the road at night."

"Thanks, Dad."

I huffed in a totally-not-a-dad kind of way. "Did you need a ride somewhere?"

She spun on her heels and stared at me like she'd just remembered I was there. Wiping at the grease smudges on her face, she shook her head.

"I can walk. It's fine." She waved me off and wrenched open the passenger side door.

"Why walk when I'm offering you a ride?" I ducked down to look at her through the open driver's side window.

She was on her hands and knees inside, reaching into the back seat for her bag. The position also had the side effect of giving me a clear shot down the top of her V-neck shirt. Hints of her purple bra cupping the full softness of the breasts I'd been tortured by over spring break peeked out from under the gray fabric. I'd like to say I turned away and averted my eyes, but come on, they were spectacular. The gravitational pull of her cleavage was a thing of astronomical beauty.

My fingers tightened on the edge of the window. Visions of me running my hands over those smooth curves rushed through my mind.

Her head tilted to the side, and she followed my line of sight.

Letting out an annoyed hiss, she grabbed her bag and jumped out of the car. "Sure, I'll take the ride from you as payment for the show."

"I can't help it." I held up my hands in mock surrender. "They were right there. It's a reflex."

"A man-whore reflex."

Rounding the back of my car, I opened the door for her. "I'm no man-whore."

She slipped inside and I closed it. She turned in her seat the second I opened my door. "Tell that to half the girls on campus."

"They like to flirt—that's what they do. It's harmless."

She rolled her eyes. "Harmless to you as a guy, but it's an

indictment against every other woman out there who doesn't want to behave like that." She winced like even she'd heard how that sounded.

"They have fun their way. Take the Glitter Posse—so what if they like glitter and pink? Who are you to tell them how they should or shouldn't behave? Is there only one way a woman is meant to behave? That sounds pretty judgmental and condescending to me." I rested my arm on top of the steering wheel and stared at her over my shoulder.

She opened her mouth and snapped it shut. "Do you have to be so infuriatingly right all the time?" Her lips thinned and she sat back in her seat, staring out the front window.

I chuckled and started the car. "Where to, milady?"

She rattled off an address. After I plugged it into my phone, we were on our way.

"I'm not always a judgmental asshole, you know."

I lifted an eyebrow and bit my tongue so 'Could have fooled me' didn't come tumbling out. My balls enjoyed the close relationship they had with my body.

"But you're right—I misjudged them. I misjudged you." She ran her thumb over the back of her hand. "I can't help it sometimes. But you and them...you guys have always been more than upfront about who you are. You're honest and call me out when I'm being a jerk, so thank you."

A small thud occurred in my chest at the 'You're honest' comment. The photographer had come after Elle had pulled away that last day. We'd gotten some shots of me and Rick together at the build, a good fluff piece. Now I needed to figure out how to break that to Elle. Or maybe she'd never see it. *Honest...* Tightening my fingers around the steering wheel, I kept my eyes trained on the road. "You're welcome," I mumbled.

"Ruining people's fun isn't what I do. I'm fun. I laugh. I don't enjoy sucking the fun out of rooms."

More tongue-biting. "Then why have you called the

campus cops on our house dozens of times? Why not come over and tell us to turn it down?"

"Because I don't feel like wading through a sea of drunk people to find one of you to ask and have you say, 'Sure, no problem,' then the party keeps going for another three hours. If I called the cops, people scattered, and that was it. I'm exhausted, Nix. Some people don't get to stay up as late as they want and sleep in the next day. Some of us have jobs and responsibilities that make it necessary to get to bed before the crack of dawn."

The weariness of her as she'd walked back into her place over the past few nights flashed into my mind.

"What good does doing all that do if you burn yourself out? Give yourself time to enjoy your life."

Her back snapped straight against the seat. "I'm not going to burn out. The projects I work on are important to me. The soup kitchen, building houses, tutoring—those are people who need help, and some of us have to work to help pay for stuff." She squeezed the bridge of her nose. "Not to say you haven't worked hard or anything, and I don't really know your situation. The work you put in on the field and in the gym isn't nothing. It's been a long day and I'm snappy, so can we forget I said any of that?"

I made a tape rewind sound, and she laughed. It was a warm, husky sound that sent a shiver down my spine. "I can do that. Can you? How about we rewind things back to the beginning?"

Her eyes widened. "The beginning." She licked her lips.

"That first time we met." I smiled and drummed my fingers on the steering wheel.

Her mouth opened and closed.

"Are you actually speechless? Be still my heart."

She whacked my shoulder with her knuckles. "My hands still work."

I laughed. "I can see that. So, why were you so pissed that

day? If anyone should've been pissed, it was me for giving you that free show."

Her smile dropped like she'd just found out someone had already completed her crossword puzzle. She let out another weary sigh—I don't think she had any other kind—and ran her hand over her face. "I'd driven my hunk of junk a thousand miles from my summer community building project and had to be up for tutoring in the morning. This was after my housing plans for the last year fell through at the last minute and I scrambled to find something. I was irritable, run down, and really needed a night's rest."

"Most people are out partying, but you're out there killing yourself at all this volunteer work. When do you even study?"

She sucked in a sharp breath through her front teeth and squeezed the back of her neck. "I've gotten a few extensions here and there."

Does she ever sleep? It was nonstop with her, always trying to do better for other people, and I respected the hell out of her for it. If only she'd give herself a break every so often.

We pulled up in front of a run-down gray building. There were no signs on the front.

"Are you sure this is the right place?" I leaned over on the steering wheel and peered out the front window.

"Yup! Thanks for the ride." She flung the door open before the car came to a complete stop.

"Let me walk you in." I got out of the car. The shiny navy paint job reflected the mishmash of artisanal coffee shops and boarded-up buildings.

"I'll be fine." She walked backward with her bag over her shoulder, waving me off.

"Would you stop being so difficult and just let me do something nice for you without fighting for once?" Rounding the back of the car, I caught up to her.

We walked in the front of the building. People milled

around on the street, families, couples, men and women on their own. I glanced up at the small sign over the door: *Grace's Soup Kitchen*.

"You volunteer here?"

She peered over her shoulder. "No, I have an act as a lounge singer. Yes, I volunteer here."

"Okay, Mother Teresa."

She snorted.

"Elle, thank God you're here. We're shorthanded." A woman with gray frizzy hair up in a bun grabbed her arm and dragged her toward the kitchen.

"Thanks for the ride and walking me in," Elle called out over her shoulder.

"I can help."

The woman stopped so quickly, Elle banged straight into her, nearly knocking them both over.

They stared at me like I'd sprouted wings. "I can help. I know my way around a kitchen."

Grace shooed us both inside. We walked back into the commercial kitchen, and Grace handed us some aprons. The room was filled with the smells and sounds of a kitchen, and even though it wasn't Tavola, I was at ease there.

"If you two can peel and chop those vegetables, we can get them into the oven."

"On it." We rinsed the carrots and potatoes and set them out on the counter. There had to have been at least a hundred pounds there. I grabbed the knife and Elle picked up the peeler. Spinning the knife in my hand, I tested it out and checked the blade.

Letting the years of practice take over, I sliced whatever she handed me faster than she could peel. Switching back and forth between peeling and cutting, we slowed down only to dump what we'd finished into giant catering-sized trays, cover it all in olive oil, salt, and pepper, and shove it straight into the oven.

Service began and huge trays of food moved in and out of the kitchen, making the meals at Tavola look dainty in comparison. It was an industrial operation that moved even faster than my grandfather's restaurant. Things eventually slowed from the firehose-to-the-face speed to more of a trickle.

Dead on our feet, we sat on overturned empty industrial-sized tubs of ketchup, gulping down water like we had on the building site for a break. One thing about kitchens: they're never cold.

"Thanks for your help tonight." She nodded, and the corner of her mouth lifted.

I pointed at her. "Is that a smile? Don't worry, I won't tell anyone. You've got a hard-ass rep to uphold."

She laughed, a full-out, wide-smile laugh. "And don't worry, I won't let anyone know about your do-gooder streak. They might get the wrong idea about you."

"And what might that be?"

"That you're a really nice guy who gets shoved into a party boy jock box by people who are incredibly close-minded and don't like to change their preconceived notions— like me." She laughed and ran her fingers through her hair.

Her laugh reached down deep into me and sent my pulse skyrocketing.

She tilted her head to the side and smiled at me.

Cue a stampede in my chest that had never existed before. "I'm glad you're finally coming around."

CHAPTER 13
ELLE

The clank and clatter of the kitchen was only rivaled by the chatter from everyone calling out what they needed up front. A second wind I hadn't anticipated made the night's service zip by. As much as I didn't want to admit it, it may have had something to do with a certain football player who defied all my expectations.

Why'd he have to look so damn good slicing those veggies? The short sleeves of his t-shirt tightened around his biceps as he lifted the tub of dirty trays and dropped them off at the sink. One of the other volunteers nearly buckled trying to carry another one. A few people in the kitchen recognized Nix. He was all smiles and pitched in anywhere he saw someone struggling.

"Elle. Earth to Elle." Grace snapped in front of my face.

I jerked my head back and stared at her, wide-eyed. "Sorry." I licked my lips. "What did you say?"

"I said, if you bring any more hunky volunteers with you, we'll have even more people lining up next week."

"Stop objectifying the staff."

"At my age, I get a free pass." She laughed and patted my arm.

Other than a five-minute break when he checked his phone, he'd been grinding with the rest us through the meal nonstop.

"Did you need some help?" He hefted a large stainless steel bowl of peeled potatoes in his arms. Who knew a chef's coat could look so damn sexy stretched across the muscular body of a guy like Nix. "Elle?" He waved his hand in front of me.

"What? Yeah, that would be awesome."

He dumped all the potatoes in there and got to work mashing and not turning them into a fine purée. We grabbed our own plates, which Grace had set aside, and collapsed by the walk-in freezer.

"You know your way around the kitchen." I tugged on the sleeve of his coat.

"I've been working in kitchens since I was seven."

He laughed as my jaw dropped. "You?"

"Yes, me. There's more to me than this handsome face and phenomenal body." He flexed his biceps.

"There's also an incredibly large head." I shoveled mashed potatoes into my mouth.

"Good thing I have these broad shoulders to hold it up." More flexing.

"You're such a dork." I nudged him with my shoulder.

"I'm glad you finally noticed." He ate a few more forkfuls of food. "My grandfather owns a restaurant. My dad was always on the road, so I hung out there a lot, and once I started hovering my way through the dessert display cases, they put me to work."

"What about your mom?"

"She died before I turned one."

My plate nearly fell out of my hands. "I'm so sorry. I had no idea."

"Don't worry about it." He shrugged. "I don't remember her. It's always been this way."

I was always screwing up when it came to him, and he'd been nothing short of awesome. He hadn't had to help. He hadn't had to bring me there or stay the whole shift when I was sure he had much better things to do. My whole 'golden boy, perfect life' theory was blown out of the water and I hated being wrong, but with Nix, I didn't hate it nearly as much as usual.

"You've been doing all this for a while, then." I motioned to the kitchen, which was still bustling with activity as the cookers swapped out for the cleaners.

"Yeah, not as much more recently with football and stuff, but I'm getting back into it."

"You say football and stuff like it's not a big deal."

"In everyone else's mind it is."

"But it's not in yours? You're so above all the draft chatter." I chuckled and forked some chicken into my mouth.

A shadow passed over his eyes. "It is what it is." He stabbed at the string beans on his plate.

I stopped chewing, trying to figure out what the hell he was wrestling with inside his head. "While I'm sure I'm the last person you'd want to talk to under non-forced-proximity conditions, if you need to get something off your chest, I'm here."

"It's not forced proximity if I'm choosing to be here." And then he laid down the smolder. *Holy shit.* I'd thought it was only in movies, but there it was, in the flesh. I dropped my gaze to my plate and tried to keep the creeping heat racing up my neck from turning my cheeks into a cherry popsicle impersonation.

Our hips were glued together, not even brushing against one another, just settled against each other in a comfortable lean.

At least it had been comfortable until my body became hyperaware of just how hot he was. It wasn't like I didn't have eyes, but when you're working hard to hate someone and then finally decide you'll tolerate them, giving in to the hotness doesn't exactly help keep those walls up.

His dark brown hair skimmed across his forehead, not looking like it had been shoved into a hairnet for the past two hours. Damn him and his well-trained hair. He had a jaw you could slice celery against, and I swore his chest and arms should've been placed in a museum.

My gaze drifted back up to meet his, and the smile on his face clued me in to the fact that I'd been looking at him for a long time, an embarrassingly long amount of time that would get a guy arrested in some states.

I hopped up from my spot and dumped my plate in the trash. *Real smooth, Elle.*

Grace came back into the kitchen.

"If you need me to do—"

"Leave. That's what I need you to do. Go home, get some rest. You're banished for the next week. I don't want to see you here."

"But—"

"No buts. This isn't your full-time job. You've got schoolwork to do, an actual job, parties to get to." She leaned in close. "Guys to make out with."

I shot a look at Nix standing behind us, peeling off his chef's coat. I shouldn't have looked. I so shouldn't have looked. He was freaking edible.

"Nix, you two get out of here while there's still some time to enjoy your night. I usually have to push her out kicking and screaming, so it's your turn tonight."

He laughed. "I can handle that."

I lifted an eyebrow.

"There's an ice cream in it for you at T-Sweets."

"Sold!" I sprinted to the car like the hounds of hell were on my heels. The lights on Nix's car flashed and it chirped. I threw myself inside, my stomach already rumbling even though I'd had a full meal.

"Had I known that was all it took to get a smile out of you, I'd have brought you T-Sweets every day over spring break." He got in the car and turned it on.

"You think I can be bought by creamy, flavor-explosion, toppings-covered ice cream?" I folded my arms over my chest and pursed my lips.

"Pretty much." He grinned and pulled away from the curb.

"Lucky guess." I laughed, failing to keep the corners of my mouth downturned.

The fluorescent lights from the ice cream parlor cast a bright white glow like a beacon to anyone craving a late-night treat. There was usually a line wrapped around the side of the building and people stood, sat, or leaned anywhere they could once they picked up their goodies, but we were still on the tail end of spring break and most people weren't back yet. Cars pulled in and out of spots, and we nabbed one just as someone reversed in front of us.

We walked up to the window and placed our orders. Well, I told the girl behind the counter what I wanted, and Nix ordered enough food to feed an elementary school.

We sat on the curb outside, all the benches and tables being taken.

My mouth watered as I scooped up the first spoonful of my coffee ice cream sundae with chocolate fudge, sprinkles, and peanuts, topped with whipped cream and a cherry.

Nix got a banana split with cookie dough ice cream, whipped cream, and cherries, a soft pretzel, jalapeno poppers, and a milkshake.

"You're going to explode. You know that, right?"

"Haven't exploded yet. The season is over and my baked, boiled, and grilled chicken diet is done. I need to eat as much of this terrible food before my metabolism slows down, then I'm screwed."

"With the way you'll be training once the season starts, I

highly doubt your metabolism will be slowing down any time soon. They'll have you sweating blood by the time training camp is finished."

He sucked down the last of his milkshake, moving his straw around the bottom of the large cup.

My mouth hung open. *How in the hell...?*

He turned to me like he hadn't just chugged a gallon of ice cream through a straw. "You seem to know a lot about the football player lifestyle."

I shoveled more ice cream into my mouth and gave a noncommittal shrug. The perfect blend of thick chocolate, creamy coffee, and peanut crunch was more than enough to keep my mouth occupied. I didn't want to ruin tonight by talking about my ex.

He kept staring at me, waiting for a response.

I scooped another bite of ice cream into my mouth, not even trying to get the perfect balance of all the flavors, and was suddenly fascinated by the painted stripe work on the curb, picking at it with my fingers.

"Nix Russo?" A guy balancing his cup of ice cream and dragging his girlfriend behind him rushed over to Nix. "Holy crap, it's really you. Wow, can I get a picture?"

Nix was gracious and snapped pictures, signing a few things people thrust in his face, but his eyes locked with mine over the heads of the crowd. With a slight tilt of his head toward the car, he extricated himself from the people who acted like they hadn't seen him a hundred times walking across campus—not that I'd paid attention to that or anything.

———

"What's with the lights over at your place?" I stepped around the front of his car. There had been a few cases of laptops being stolen from unlocked townhouses a few months ago.

Nix glanced at his house. Flashlight beams arced across the front windows and shone out of the one at the top of the stairwell.

"Is someone breaking in?" My hand tightened on his arm.

His muscles flexed under my hold. "I'm not sure. Let's go check it out." His eyebrows were furrowed, but he looked more like a Scooby-Doo character going to investigate, not someone worried their house was being broken into.

"What do you mean go check it out? Are you going to be that guy in a horror movie?" I dug my heels in as he tugged me closer to the house.

"I'm sure it's nothing. The circuit breaker is probably out. Let's make sure the guys are okay."

"Dude, we need to call the cops."

He dropped his chin over his shoulder and stared at me.

My cheeks heated and I cringed. "Campus cops, not the city."

"We'll be fine." He climbed the steps and kept his arm wrapped around my waist, holding me beside him. I tried not to feel like I was about to be sacrificed to the burglars. Perhaps he'd throw me at them to knock them off balance. Maybe this had been his plan all along: lull me into a false sense of security and then chuck me at a robber the first chance he got.

The front door was cracked open, and my heart pounded in my throat.

Nix put his hand on the wood, and his arm tightened around me. I tried not to think about how good he smelled even after working in a kitchen all night, how his arm wrapped around my waist was like a solid wall, protecting me from everything else around me, and definitely not how much of my racing heart had nothing to do with the possible breaking and entering we were about to walk in on.

CHAPTER 14
NIX

A soft and chunky pop sliced through the eerie silence in the house. I hauled Elle against me and out of the way of direct fire. A Nerf dart hung in her hair. The hint of her strawberry shampoo lingered under the layered scent of the food we'd been making earlier. My stomach tightened, and it wasn't from hunger. *Down boy.* I was supposed to be playing it cool, not that she hadn't been running through my mind a hell of a lot for someone who'd only very recently professed not to hate me.

There was a lot going on in my life right now, complicated shit, but damn did I not care one bit when I was with her. Whether she got my blood pumping with some verbal sparring or her laugh that was halfway between a strained cough and a full-out wheeze, everything that came after didn't seem half as scary.

Her gaze shot to the blue and orange dart dangling from her strands.

"What the hell is going on?" she whispered, her eyes glancing over my shoulder.

"We've walked in on a battle the likes of which you've

never seen." I kept my voice low and serious and struggled to keep my lips tight and even.

Berk jumped down beside me from the top of the stairs. A blue bandanna was wrapped around his head, and there was smudged black paint under his eyes.

Elle jumped and her hands tightened on my chest. I shouldn't have been loving this closeness as much as I was. Her eyes widened with confusion and an edge of panic. Did I take advantage of this to hold on to her a bit tighter? Damn right I did.

"Where the hell have you been? We started without you. I'll cover you so you can get up to your room." Berk peered over his shoulder with his dart gun at the ready. "You brought reinforcements too—good man." He clapped me on the shoulder before his serious face slid back into place. "We're up against three. Freaking jerks said because we won the last few rounds on our own, they deserved the extra person. Now it's time to kick their asses."

I coughed to keep my laugh under wraps. Turning to Elle, I stared into her eyes. "When I say go, go." I grabbed her shoulders and stared into her wide, questioning gaze. "Run on three, two, one—go!" Wrapping my arm around her waist, I pulled her up the stairs. Someone shouted and darts flew past us. Diving to the top of the steps, I held her against me. We ducked into my room and I kicked the door shut behind us.

She pushed herself up off the floor and brushed her hair out of her face. Her chest rose and her cheeks were flushed. "What is happening here?"

I grinned. "You may or may not have stumbled into our monthly—well, semimonthly…actually, more like whenever-the-hell-we-want Nerf war."

"Stumbled into or was dragged into? You scared the crap out of me. I thought we were about to get shot." She shoved her hands against my chest, but the curve of her lips didn't lie.

Dragging the basket out of my closet, I chucked the clothes covering it over my shoulder and uncovered my arsenal. "Are you in?" I crouched down and peered at her.

She scrunched her lips up to the side and crossed her arms over her chest. "If I am, which one of those is mine?" Her knee brushed against my side. We'd been so close the entire night, the small touches and gentle brushes driving me out of my head. She didn't put that distance between us. Even now, the rough grain of her jeans rubbed against my body through my t-shirt.

I peered up at her. "You get your pick." Scooting the basket closer to her, I licked my lips.

She crouched beside me and her arm brushed against mine. We'd been working side by side all night, and every time she touched me, it felt like the first time. The deep tug in my gut only got more insistent with every instance of contact.

She reached into my stash and pulled one out. "How about this one?" She turned her head, her lips inches from mine.

Her eyes swam with something new that flickered under her lids, a look like the one she'd given me when we'd left the soup kitchen. It wasn't filled with annoyance or even that resigned-to-my-presence expression she sometimes wore. This was something more, and she wasn't hiding it anymore.

"Elle—"

My door banged open and she jerked back, landing flat on her ass but whipping the gun around to point straight at the door.

Damn, I think I'm in love.

I shook my head, blindsided by whatever the hell that was.

Berk held his hands up in the air. "Don't shoot! I'm on your team." He closed the door halfway and peeked out the crack. "We're getting decimated out there. Seph's going all tactical on us. Move it, people."

I loaded up my dart belt, gave Elle one, and even spread some of the paint we used under our eyes on the field under hers. She locked and loaded and glanced at herself in the mirror. Grabbing three extra dart clips off my belt, she shoved them into the pockets of her sweatshirt. A pop shot out from the gun as she checked to make sure the darts were ready to go.

"How many are we up against?" She leaned against the wall beside the door with her hand on the knob.

Berk stared at her slack-jawed, and the dart he'd been holding in his mouth hit the wood floor with a muted thud.

"Three." Did I have that dreamy sound in my voice? The way she handled that Nerf gun...why didn't she just kill me now? My dick strained against the seam of my jeans. I'd have a permanent imprint by the end of the night at the rate things were going.

She scoffed. "That's nothing." Lifting her finger, she closed Berk's mouth. "Let's do this."

"You look awesome," I blurted out like a kid announcing they had to pee. *Smooth. Real freaking smooth.*

She glanced over her shoulder and smiled wide. "You don't look so bad yourself."

"How do we know you've got the skills?" Berk tapped his gun against his chin.

"Three years running in the tutoring paintball championship at the end of every year." Then she pointed her gun at him and squeezed the trigger, hitting him straight between the eyes. "What do you think?"

Berk rubbed the spot and nodded.

"Now let's win this thing." Her competitive edge seemed to extend beyond being a do-gooder.

Turning off the switch beside her, she crouched down and

turned the door knob. She darted out, doing a full-on danger roll like she was in *Mission Impossible*.

I rushed after her. Berk grabbed my shirt while staring after Elle as she slid against the hallway wall. "Dude…"

"Don't even think about it. You'll never be able to recover the dart I shove so far up your ass if you even think about it."

"Nix's got a girlfriend. Nix's got a girlfriend," he whisper-sang while dancing on his knees.

A flash of pink reappeared in the doorway. "Are you ladies in here drinking lemonade? Let's do this."

"I'm ready to do it all right," Berk mumbled.

I slammed the heel of my hand into his chest and he toppled over, coughing.

"I'm on your team, dick." He rubbed the heel of his hand into the spot.

Following Elle out, we crept down the hall. There was a volley of darts as we hit the stairs. They'd gotten better since the last time we'd played. I'd have to find a way to recruit Seph, Reece's girlfriend, to our side.

Keyton shot to the bottom of the steps on his back and fired up at us. We returned fire, but he'd sacrificed himself and took out Berk…who then proceeded to put on his Oscar-winning performance of dying. He slow-motion fell down the stairs, hitting every step while holding on to the railing, howling and groaning the whole way.

At the bottom of the stairs, he grabbed Keyton's hand. "I'm so cold. Hold me, Key."

Keyton's shoulders shook and he wrapped his arms around himself like he might fly apart with his case of the giggles. He gasped for breath and held his side. "It hurts." Each word was on a half-laugh, half-choke.

Berk finally lay completely still, letting his mock death sink in with the required gravitas. Then his eyes shot open, staring right at Keyton. "You're laughing? I didn't think you knew how. Totally worth it. You want a drink?"

Keyton nodded, wiped the tears off his face, and held out his hand. Berk stood and clasped hands with him, tugging him up.

"Hurry up and finish this so we can drink! We'll be in the backyard so we don't get hit in the crossfire," Berk called out, ducking into the kitchen and turning the lights off. The house was once again bathed in darkness.

"Let's do this." Elle looked to me like we were about to go out Bonnie and Clyde style.

I slid down the steps on my back, shooting darts through the banister dowels. Reece and Seph retreated as Elle covered me and we both made it to the bottom of the steps.

Holding out my hand to wave Elle forward, I sucked in a sharp breath and my heart thundered in my veins.

She slipped her hand into mine. I stopped so quickly, she banged into my back.

"Why'd you stop? I can't see a thing!" she whisper-shouted.

"What can't she see?" Seph called out. "Are you two making out?"

"No," Elle shouted.

"We're retreating to starting positions. You have ninety seconds," Seph shouted, her voice getting more distant with each step.

Thirty sweaty minutes later, Elle leaned into me, her shoulder brushing against my chest. "I'm down to my last few darts. How's your ammo?"

My gaze was trained on her lips, shining in the barely there light from the basement window.

She nudged me.

"Right, I'm almost out too."

"Next time, I'm wearing pants with pockets. You can never have enough ammo."

Next time...so she planned on doing this again. It

shouldn't have made me half as happy as it did to hear her say that.

There might have been a bit more hands-on assistance throughout our game, a few stolen opportunities to shield Elle under my body when I thought I heard someone coming. She hadn't tried to knee me in the balls once, which I took as a good sign.

She might have also leaned into me a bit more than needed at least once. My fingers skated across the gap between her shirt and her jeans, and she didn't pull away.

Reece and Seph had us pinned down behind the pool table in the basement. They had the high ground in the reject stadium seating LJ had created down there with some old recliners he'd scored from sidewalk abandonment and some wooden pallets.

"I don't think we're making it out of this." Elle rested her back against the table, her breath coming out choppy after our dive-and-cover for our current safe haven. Another volley of darts showered us. Reece and Seph must have grabbed the extra ammo from Berk and Keyton.

Throwing myself in the way, I covered Elle. Her back slid off the polished wooden pool table and she toppled over. I wrapped my arms around her to cushion her fall and braced myself. Our weapons clattered to the floor and there was nothing but the adrenaline rush and the thundering of my heart.

She stared up at me in the dim light coming from the half-sized basement windows. The pale green glittered with a new emotion I hadn't seen in her eyes before.

The heat and softness of her body beneath me should've been why I got the hell up before I embarrassed the crap out of myself, but I couldn't move. Her chest rose and fell between us, pushing her breasts up against my chest. I wanted to touch them, wanted to wrap my fingers around them and toy with her nipples until she told me exactly how she liked to be touched. I had no doubt she wouldn't hold back.

She lifted her hand...a moment of hesitation...and then she slipped it to the back of my head. My hair slid through her fingers. The electric sparks of desire shot straight down my back, pulsing where our hips connected.

I bridged the gap between us, capturing her lips with mine. She tasted like vanilla with sprinkles on top. A shocked gasp shot from her lips and then she parted them, her tongue running along my bottom lip and sending a shiver down my spine.

This changed everything.

CHAPTER 15
ELLE

Nix unleashed his sexual artillery on me, starting with the light fire: a kiss that made me forget my name and want to beg for more. My fingers fisted his shirt against his back. His hips pinned mine to the ground, and I was half pissed they did and half relieved because if they hadn't, I'd have wrapped my legs around his body and ground myself against him.

What the hell was wrong with me? Why did he taste so good, like strawberries and chocolate? I ran my fingers through his silky strands. He nipped my bottom lip and we broke apart, panting like we'd just run a 5K.

I stared into his eyes, my chest rising and falling and trying to figure out how the hell that switch had been flipped. We'd been playing a game, finally having some fun, and here I was trying to ride him like a prized horse in the Kentucky Derby.

The pool table shook and our heads snapped up at the chunky plastic reload just above our heads. Reece leaned over with his barrel pointed right at us.

"We surrender." I slid my hands from Nix's chest and put them over my head.

Seph peered over the edge with her chin propped up on her hands. "What are you two doing down there?"

Were my cheeks on fire? Was steam coming out of my ears? Nix lifted off me and held out his hand to help me up.

I hesitated, not sure touching him wouldn't lead me straight to trying to climb him like a lumberjack.

"Thanks for the extra cardio, guys, but I should probably get going." Before anyone could say another word, I ducked my head and rushed out of there to escape the embarrassment, sprinting up the stairs.

"You guys finished yet? The food's ready," Berk called out from the door leading to the backyard.

I didn't even stop. I just kept going until I was back outside. The warm spring air didn't do much to cool me off or make it easier to breathe. The heavy press of Nix's body on top of mine had stirred things in me I'd never wanted to feel for someone like him.

Darting between the cars parked on the street, I headed over to my side of the road where it was safe and Nix-free.

Sleep—that was what I needed. I needed a good night's rest. I had a few days off. Although there was a mountain of coursework I'd been putting off and needed to finish, maybe I'd just sleep in and convince Jules to bake me treats so I didn't have to leave the house, because leaving the house would mean possibly running into Nix.

My foot caught on the busted freaking plank on our porch. I swore I'd strangle our landlord if he ever deigned to show up to our house. I didn't brace myself against the front door like I usually did, though. I barely stumbled at all because I wasn't walking up there alone.

Strong arms wrapped around my waist. Nix's warm, rough fingers skimmed across my skin, taking expert advantage of the gap that appeared between my jeans and my top, tugging me against him. Was I still kiss drunk? How had I missed him following after me?

"You okay?" He steadied me on my feet but kept his fingers against my hip.

I braced my hands against his chest. My heart rate spiked again and I kept my gaze trained on his chest, not that that was any better. The way the fabric molded to his body only made me want to peel it off—with my teeth. *What the hell?* This is what happens. I'd been warned. This is what happens when you enter a state of sex deprivation. It starts to make you go a little crazy.

Our kiss from earlier was running through my head like an 80s movie marathon. My grip tightened on his shirt, the soft cotton bunching under my fingers. Unable to stop myself, I lifted my head.

He stared into my eyes. In the dim light from inside my house, I saw the swirl of emotions in his eyes.

If someone had told me three weeks ago Nix Russo's arms would be wrapped around me and I wouldn't be looking for a way to nut-punch him, I'd have said they were crazy, but I wasn't looking for my opening to knee him in the groin. I wasn't trying to push him away. Instead, I was holding him close, not wanting him to let me go.

The thing I'd been fighting between us had evaporated with that kiss as a barrage of Nerf darts flew overhead. Now, I wanted more of those leave-me-breathless-and-forget-my-name kisses, and that scared the crap out of me. I didn't have much time for that fear to creep in.

In a breath, Nix had my back pressed against the door, his arms braced on either side of my head, his gaze dropping from my eyes to my lips. My body hummed with his close-ness, electric pulses pounding at each point of contact.

"You left before the food was ready." Had his voice dropped an octave? It was like chocolate syrup being poured all over me.

"We already ate." My voice came out breathy and barely a

whisper. "You're still hungry?" My throat was tight, and I swallowed past the fist-sized lump in my throat.

His gaze dropped to my lips. "I didn't get to say good night." Was his head getting closer or was mine?

His eyes were mesmerizing. The flecks of gold mixed in with a blue that reminded me of a sunny day on a camping trip. A whiff of him went straight to my head. He smelled like comfort food on a rainy afternoon and his own manly scent.

A minty coolness caressed my lips at his exhale. Had he popped a mint before coming after me? I wanted to taste his thin-mint lips.

I lifted my hand to the back of his neck and bridged the gap between us. The kiss was like being in free fall, and my eyes snapped open. No, we were in *actual* free fall.

Nix's eyes widened and he rolled us, breaking most of my fall with his body. We hit the floor with a thud and rattled the house. I was totally chalking that up to Nix and not the extra brownies I'd stolen from Jules' latest batch.

I can only attribute the maneuver to Nix's insane athletic ability.

"Oh my god, I'm so sorry! I didn't know you were out there." Jules yelped and covered her mouth with her hands. A purple envelope was pressed against her face.

"No worries, Jules." I grunted and rubbed the throbbing spot on my hip. "Nix, are you okay?"

He nodded, running his hand over his shoulder. "I've taken worse hits than that."

"I'm so fucking sorry," Jules blurted out. "Do you need ice or something? Or a mini chocolate raspberry torte? Chocolate makes everything better." She gave him a strained smile and looked three seconds away from bursting into tears.

Nix's head jerked up and his eyebrows scrunched down.

I pushed up off the floor and offered my hand to him. "We're fine. Seriously, no big deal. Not like I haven't taken a spill like that from the loose boards out there anyway. Where were you going?"

He chuckled and took my hand. My help probably assisted him a total of five percent, but at least I'd offered.

"Nowhere." Her gaze shot down to the purple envelope in her hand, which she snapped behind her back.

"Sure." I drew that word out to let her know secrets would be divulged or I'd have to break out the big guns, namely tequila. "In that case, we'll take you up on those tortes. We were actually going to head back to Nix's place. The guys made some food. You should come—if that's okay with you." I swung my head around to Nix. Here I was inviting people he didn't even know over to his house.

"Any friend of Elle's is a friend of mine, especially if they're bringing chocolate anything. Do you have enough?"

"I always make extra. There's plenty. If not those, I've also got chocolate chunk cookies, blondies, and old-fashioned sour cream donuts."

"Jesus, are you running a bakery out of this place?"

The tips of Jules' ears turned bright red. "I stress bake, and I've been a little stressed lately." She stared down at her sneakers, touching the toes of them together.

"Jules also makes a lot of desserts for Grace's when she can, so she tends to bake a lot."

"Your place is just filled with do-gooders. That's awesome, Jules. I'm sure any of it will be delicious, so bring anything you can spare and the guys will lap it up."

"I could send them over with you. I mean, I don't have to go. You don't have to invite me just for the desserts."

"Jules, stop. You're coming, and you're not getting out of this. It's all I can do to get her off the pole for a night..." I thumbed my finger at her.

Nix's eyes widened.

The scarlet creep from her ears blazed down to her cheeks. "She doesn't mean some dude's dick—not that you thought that, but that's not it. I'm not some super skank riding ten guys into the sunset every night. I pole dance." Now the fire engine red spread down her neck to her chest. "Not pole dancing as in stripping, but pole fitness. It's how I work out. I'm not a stripper." Jules' voice rose so high, I was surprised we could still hear it and dogs around the block weren't howling. "Not that anyone would've thought that." And she was back to shy Jules fascinated by the rainbow stitching of her high-tops.

"You say that, but you'd be an awesome pole dancer. Right, Nix?" I looked over my shoulder at him and saw his deer-in-the-middle-of-an-eight-lane-highway look.

"I feel like that's a trick question, so I'm going to slowly back out of the room and wait for you ladies on the porch." He did exactly that and gingerly closed the door behind him.

Jules slapped the heel of her hand into her forehead.

"I think that went well."

She glared at me over her shoulder with pursed lips. "I hate you. From the bottom of my heart, I hate you." She sighed. "An envelope came for you."

Huffing and dragging out all the boxes and trays of what she'd made that week, she set them out on the counter while I lifted the navy envelope from the table. As I ripped through the paper, the gold embossed announcement glinted on the front.

It was officially official: my invitation as a nominee for the Huffington Award.

"What should I bring? Berk liked the donuts at the study session, but I feel like the tortes are better." She stood in front of her creations like someone had asked her to choose between her children. A triangle of purple poked out of her back pocket.

"And what, my dear, is this?" I slapped the envelope in her back pocket and—well, her ass as I snatched the mysterious item.

"It's mine." She jumped up, trying to grab it from my hand.

"I know it's yours, but what is it?"

"A note."

"Do I need to open this and read it, or are you going to give me a bit more to work with here?"

"It's one of the notes and I was going to deliver it."

"Juicy. I need more details. How many have you written?"

"Thirty or so."

My mouth hung open. "You two have written thirty letters in four months? You've been dropping them off *all* this time and haven't clued me in?"

"It was embarrassing. Who'd do something like that? Anyway, I dropped off the second one and there was a note waiting for me. At first, I thought maybe it was them telling me to stay the hell away or stop it, but it wasn't. It was a reply, so we've kind of been trading letters."

"Oh my god that's so sweet, like something out of an old black-and-white movie." I pulled the note out of the envelope before she could stop me and scanned the page. Using my butt to ward her off, I devoured the note filled with positions I'd never heard of and a heaping helping of words you could see someone saying while lying beside you, brushing the hair back from your face, and looking at you like you're the only person in the world for them—if that even existed in the real world. I rushed around the kitchen evading Jules' grasp before she gave up on being gentle and tackled me to the floor. "Damn, girl, that was freaking intense. I take that back —not sweet at all. That was filthy." I fanned myself, laughing as she tugged it out of my grip and shoved it back into the envelope.

"It's just something silly." She shrugged and tucked the envelope into her notebook, which had a few other purple envelopes and folded pieces of paper between the sheets.

"They're not all like that. His replies are actually really sweet."

"Let me see." I made grabby hands for them.

"No, those are…private. He's a lot different than I thought he'd be, but it's fun."

"You're really not going to let me see?"

She shook her head, nearly giving herself whiplash.

"You suck, but if there's anyone who deserves some fun, it's you." I pulled her in for a hug and squeezed her.

"Enough with this mushy crap. Let's get this over with." She let go of me and pressed her lips together, scrunching them to one side.

"Don't worry, it'll be cool. There's nothing to worry about."

CHAPTER 16
ELLE

Campus was heating up. Summer and graduation were right around the corner, finals breathing down my neck. I wasn't making the dean's list this semester, but my craptastic GPA wouldn't matter if I got the Huffington Award. With a year off to figure things out, I could work my way into a position somewhere with that prestigious feather in my resume's cap. The Huffington Award wasn't just an award—it was a mic drop.

Everyone flowed out of the Founders Building and into the quad. Some classes were held out on the grass. There were other people laid out on blankets, studying or pretending to study while just working on their tans. Someone set up a volleyball net and hit the ball over. The grilling society was out at the first hint of summer weather. There wasn't a better place to grab a $1 burger, but the line was always insane.

"You should teach. You're so good."

"Tell that to your forehead." Jules stared straight ahead in her parka and snow pants. Maybe not full ski patrol, but it was close for an early May day. In my shorts and t-shirt, I felt like I belonged on a nudist beach next to her.

Jules had the maddening habit of always wearing long sleeves and pants no matter what. At the beach? A dark gray boatneck top with long sleeves and black pants. One hundred degrees outside? Long-sleeved black shirt and dark jeans. Surface of the sun? Navy turtleneck and dark gray snow pants. Everything she wore was too dark and had too much fabric.

"It's not that bad." Shifting my backpack to my other shoulder, I rubbed the barely there dent in my forehead and walked a little faster. At least the bruising from my fall had changed from an unearthly-looking green and purple to brown. My nose had been spared when I'd failed to execute the Rainbow and kissed the floor hard, so small miracles. There went my pole dancing future.

"It looks like you were trying to grow a unicorn horn out of your forehead."

"Still that bad, huh?" I poked at the spot.

She tilted her head. "No, now it just looks like you were making out with a guy with a seriously weird idea about erogenous zones. Speaking of which…" She slid closer to me. "How's Golden Boy?"

"No idea."

"Not one? So the making out on the porch and late-night phone calls—those are nothing?"

"We're hanging out." I shrugged and walked faster.

"And playing kissy face." She puckered her lips and made smacking sounds.

"We're not making out. We're friendly."

"Should I be expecting my own friendly make-out session then?" She batted her eyelashes at me.

"He's—" I ran my fingers through my hair. "It's compli-cated." Whenever I was around him, it was like the two sleepy brain cells I had left were shorting out.

"Complicated how many panties you're going through whenever you're around him. I've seen your laundry basket

—sky-freaking-high." Her laugh carried across the quad. A few people turned around, and she ducked her head.

"That's because our washing machine has been broken for the past three weeks."

"Excuses, excuses." She grinned and waved me off. "I've got class in five. I'll see you back at the house?"

"Later. I got another extension on my paper, so I've got to finish it or I'm screwed."

She ran one finger over the other, walking backward. "Get to it and make sure you're not daydreaming about Mr. Six-Pack."

I shook my head and watched her walk off. I'd finalized my Huffington Award submission and turned it in. Now, I just needed to make sure I graduated. Hit the books, buckle down, and study my ass off.

Keeping my head down, I raked my hands through my hair. One second I was headed back to the library, where I'd been studying and definitely not hiding for the past week, and the next I ran into a wall. Well, not an actual wall, but a human that might as well have been a wall.

Hands shot out and grabbed my arms, keeping me from adding another bruise to my body. I'd have known that chest anywhere. His muscles flexed as he took my entire bodyweight until I got my feet back under me. I kept my gaze trained on his chest. That was a much safer place to look.

"With a hit like that, you should try out for the team." There was a strained lightness in his voice, like he was putting a hell of a lot of work into it.

"Sorry, I didn't see you." I peered up, and all the reasons he terrified me came rushing forward, from the prickling of my skin to the way I wanted to sink into his eyes.

"When you try to run straight through me, I hope that's why." He squeezed the back of my neck. "I spotted your hair and called your name."

I opened my mouth and slammed it shut. We stood there like two performance artists personifying awkwardness.

"Listen—"

"Let—"

We started at the same time and laughed.

"You go first." He lifted his hand to me.

"No, you go ahead." I motioned for him to start.

"Are you headed back to your place?"

"Sure."

"Can I walk with you?"

"If you want." I shrugged, feeling like I'd just slid a note across my desk with 'Do you like me? Check yes or no' on it. The fluttery dance in my stomach made it hard to concentrate on putting one foot in front of the other.

"I want."

The happy dance inside me was complete with confetti, cake, and cannons.

He stepped to my side and rested his hand on the small of my back to navigate us through the masses of students criss-crossing campus.

People called out his name, gave him high fives, and tried to get him to stop, but even with all the distractions, there was never a question that his attention was focused on me. People pulled him over for pictures like he didn't walk across campus every day, but his gaze always found mine. I didn't mind the interruptions when he smiled at me over the heads of the people crowded around him to get selfies.

"Doesn't that get annoying?" I peered over at him.

The corner of his mouth lifted. "I was born into it. My dad's career meant whenever we were out in public, especially in the city, that was all I ever knew. I don't think we've had a meal outside of our house or my gramps' restaurant that didn't get interrupted at least once." He shrugged. "I guess it's always felt normal to me."

"The fans are lucky to have you." With all those people

swarmed around me, I'd snap someone's head off on day three.

He laughed. "This is a winning crowd reaction, but I've also seen the other side. Throw one interception and then see what people shout on the streets."

"Reassurances and hopeful wishes for the future?" I offered.

"Something like that." He smiled at me, and it felt like I was looking down from the crest of a rollercoaster. Excitement and nervousness bubbled inside me.

"Your dad's excited for you to follow in his footsteps?"

"More like unable to contain himself with finally having me go pro. He's been planning this since I was ten." His voice had a hollowness that didn't come with achieving a dream 99.99% of people couldn't even fathom touching, a sadness that didn't match his words.

I reached out, hesitating and biting my lip before taking his hand. He tightened his hold and looked at me with a level of uncertainty and vulnerability I'd never seen before. He was letting me in, letting me see a side of him I didn't think many people got to see, and I was there for him. I wanted to be there for him and to never let him go, a thought that rocked me to my core.

CHAPTER 17

NIX

She slipped her hand into mine. "Why don't you sound as excited about that as most people would assume?" Her words were as careful as a tiptoe in the middle of the night.

I stared at her, and it took everything in me not to haul her into my arms and kiss the crap out of her.

We stood at the end of our street.

"Do you want to go for a ride or something? Get some air?" She hadn't let go of my hand, and I didn't want whatever it was we were doing right now to end.

"Sure, let's go."

I pulled out into the light midafternoon traffic and followed Elle's directions, trying to figure out which shelter, soup kitchen, build project, or other volunteer activity she was taking me to. Instead, we stopped inside the parking garage under a stone and marble building I hadn't been to in years.

We went up in the elevator, and the smell reminded me of packed lunches, parent chaperones, and school bus excitement. She tugged me forward and got our wristbands under the constellation mockup overhead in the Franklin Institute.

"It's probably been fifteen years since I came here." I looked around the middle school and high school field trip staple and felt like I was a kid again. The Franklin Institute was a Philly mainstay. Exhibits moved in and out, but the replica of a heart, the skyline bike, and the electricity room had been around forever.

She stared up at the giant Ben Franklin statue. Her faded pink hair fell in gentle waves around her shoulders. It was longer than when we'd first met.

There was a tug in my chest to come clean with her about the project with Rick, about the story that would come out, and then she looked over at me and tugged me toward the electricity room where giant arcs flowed through cathode tubes and middle school kids ran all around us.

She turned, looked at me, and grabbed my hand, her fingers threading through mine, and that tug in my chest became a gravitational hold I couldn't escape and didn't want to. I'd do whatever else my dad wanted before the draft, but I'd tell him to kill that story, kill it dead.

"A lot's still the same. I have a membership from a city volunteer award I got last year. Sometimes I like to come here to clear my head."

A group of kids in matching t-shirts strode past us holding hands with their teachers in tow.

"Do they still have the giant heart?"

"Of course, although it's a tight fit."

We waited for a lull and climbed up into the heart. "You weren't kidding. I'm ninety percent sure they're going to need the jaws of life to get me out of here." I turned sideways and crouched to get through the left ventricle. "They should have a height limit on this thing."

She laughed behind me. The melodic sound of it bounced off the close confines of the blue and red walls.

Afterward, we grabbed a soft pretzel—well, four for me

and one for her—at the food cart and sat, staring up at the slow rotation of the model planets above.

"I've got trust issues," Elle blurted out just as I shoved a spicy-mustard-laden hunk of pretzel into my mouth. I jammed my fist up to my mouth as a cough racked my body, the spicy burn making my eyes water.

She shoved napkins at my face and patted my back. "Sorry to blurt that out like that." She stared at me, making sure she hadn't sent me to an early dough-and-condiment-induced grave.

"I'm good." I sucked down a gulp of soda. Clearing my throat, I motioned for her to go ahead.

"That probably wasn't the best way to start a conversation, blurting that out and then making you nearly choke to death." She half-smiled, half-snorted and scraped at the side of her finger.

"You can tell me anything you need to." I dropped my hand onto her leg and ran my thumb over her knee.

The corners of her mouth tugged up even higher, but she didn't look at me. I leaned back, giving her some space and pulling my hand back.

"Trust issues, right." She took a deep breath and stared out at the kids wandering in and out of the exhibits. "There was this guy I dated back in high school. We were high school royalty. I was a cheerleader. He was—he was a football player. Quarterback." Her lips tightened. "And he cheated on me."

"I'm sorry."

She shook her head. "It's not your fault, but it's definitely some baggage I should've left behind. I went to visit him at college. He was a year ahead of me and I walked in on him with someone else—my best friend. She was supposed to be up there visiting her new boyfriend. Turned out her new boyfriend was my current boyfriend. It was excruciatingly humiliating. Once people at my school found out, it was all snickers and laughter behind my back, people I thought were my friends... So when I started college, I decided I was finished with the superficial. Only genuine, good people need apply."

"That's when you started the volunteer work."

A small snort. "Exactly. Pretty selfish, huh?" Her lips pinched together. "Sophomore year, I was ready to wade back into things, date again. I found a guy, big into all the same groups I was in. He was involved in tons of projects and doing so much good. I figured I'd finally found a good one. He did a summer trip to South America, volunteering at an orphanage. There was a girl who'd been in all the pictures he posted online, but he swore I had nothing to worry about. I showed up early at the apartment we were supposed to be sharing and found him in bed with her."

I winced.

"Things sucked in a different way that time. He was such a nice guy, or so everyone kept telling me, so what exactly had I done to make him do that?"

"It wasn't your fault." I clenched my fist, seconds from hunting this guy down and kicking his ass for making her feel like the bad guy when he was the one who couldn't keep his dick in his pants.

"I knew that, but it sure as hell felt like everyone else didn't, and I got it stuck in my head that I'd show him and everyone else again. I'd win the Huffington Award and then people would see that I'm a good person. Plus, the mo—it's important for me to prove that I can do it."

"You've definitely been putting in the hours."

"You have no idea." She laughed. "But those wounds are still there. So when you showed up..."

I wanted to find the guys who'd hurt her and wreck them. Off the field, I wasn't someone who had to prove how tough he was by picking fights, but they'd hurt her. They'd wrecked her and made it hard for her to trust herself, let alone anyone else. I wanted to ram my fist down both their throats. "I was a walking talking reminder of two people who hurt you."

She peered up at me. "I shouldn't have taken everything out on you."

Her armor made so much more sense, as well as her intense dislike for me on sight. When wounds are raw, you're bound to lash out if someone pokes them, even if they don't know they're doing it. "I get it."

"That doesn't mean it's right, but I do have a severe aversion to liars, even when it comes to things that seem small." A muscle in her cheek clenched. "Even if it seems like no big deal, I can't have people in my life who lie to me."

"I get that, and I'll never do that." The words were out before I could stop them, before I could say the thing I'd just resolved never to say.

She nodded, but it was going to take more than my words to make her believe it.

"Your turn." She lifted her chin with her gaze trained on me.

"This is a you show me yours, I'll show you mine situation?"

"Something like that." The corners of her eyes creased with a small smile. "Don't leave me out here dangling by myself."

A tightness in my chest that had been there for a long time squeezed the air from my lungs. Steeling myself, I let out a shaky breath. "I've never wanted to play football." Out of the corner of my eye, I saw her straighten and turn to me. Those were words I'd never said to another person. "When I was little, I never even played catch with my dad in the backyard or anything. He was always gone. The kitchen was where I felt most comfortable, but my dad played football, so I kind of came into it by osmosis.

"When I was young, going to the locker rooms and practice was just as natural as sitting on the counters at Tavola, my grandfather's restaurant. Dad didn't have time to push me when he was playing. Travel and practices took up a lot of his time, and then one day it was like a flip switched. Even before he retired, he was there pushing me to be a football player.

"I was just happy to have him around, so I was cool with doing whatever it took to keep his attention. I brought up maybe not playing back in high school, and he stopped talking to me for a week. That was that. I never brought it up again. After every practice, he'd run me through even more drills. Every game, win or loss, needed a full debrief—he even recorded all my games so we could go through my mistakes frame by frame, and now... I thought if I won the national championship, he'd finally tell me he was proud of me." Shaking my head, I rested my forearms on my legs. "How stupid am I? Doing all this for Daddy's approval." I glanced over at her.

She shook her head and reached out, taking my hand. "Not stupid. You trusted someone you should've been able to trust with your absolute faith." She paused for a moment. "You don't want to go pro?"

"I don't think I have a choice." I squinted over at her.

"You always have a choice."

"It's all I've ever known."

The slow strokes of her thumb on my arm halted, a question in her eyes.

"Is it what you want?"

"Sometimes I close my eyes and try to see something beyond that."

"What do you see when you think of your future?"

"The pain and how my body will betray me. It'll be with me forever. Even with the best physical therapy money can buy, I've got injuries that'll only get worse as I get older. My dad's broken down. He hides it well, but I've seen how it's wrecked him. I'd like to have a life where I'm not dreading getting older because I'm destroying my body out on the field for even more money. I see myself taking over for my grandfather, following in his footsteps."

"It's hard to know what life has in store for us." Her slow strokes began again, tickling the hair on my arm. The way she stripped me down without even trying, getting me to talk about things I hadn't said out loud made my throat tight. She licked her lips. "Don't do what you think other people expect you to do if it's not what you want."

"What do you want?"

She licked her lips and her gaze dropped to my hands. "To find something I love so much I could never walk away from it…to find something that'll make me happy."

You make me happy. I choked back those words. "Thanks for being someone I can talk to."

"That's what friends are for, right?"

"Is that what we are?" My gaze collided with hers. The flicker that lit me up like a house on Christmas Eve pulsed between us.

Her lips parted. Pink. Full. Hers. "Yeah." It didn't sound convincing to me.

I scooted my chair closer, the blue metal scraping across the floor between us. "Is that all we are?"

She licked her lips and her gaze dropped to mine. Her pulse raced against the back of my hand.

Dropping my hand on top of hers, I made a Nix-Elle sandwich, twining my fingers through hers.

"What else would we be?" The words were so low I could barely hear them.

"I'm crazy about you, B and E, and you're not like anyone I've ever met before." *I can't say I want you to be my girlfriend because you'll probably turn into The Flash, bolting out of here with a fire streak behind you.*

She squeezed my hand. "I can say the exact same thing." Her smile wasn't restrained and tentative like it usually was. It was wide and bright, and I needed to taste her again.

Tugging her forward until she was almost on my lap, I attacked her lips with a pent-up hunger that had been burning in me since that first kiss. She was just as hungry, giving as good as she got.

A loud throat clearing broke us apart. With flushed lips that matched her hair, Elle stared at me wide-eyed. We both turned our heads, wincing at the ticked-off chaperone and mini-me troop behind her. She tapped her foot and we bolted, our laughter bouncing off the elevator walls as the doors closed behind us.

"I don't go around kissing just anyone, you know." I leaned against the wall.

"You mean I'm special?" Elle pressed her fingers against her chest, doing her best Southern debutante impersonation.

"You have no idea."

CHAPTER 18
NIX

'd been summoned—again—only this time it wasn't to our house, but to the stadium. The clock was ticking down and Dad was no longer amused by how long I'd put off this decision. Graduation was less than a month away.

Security let me in with little more than a wave. I weaved my way through the underbelly of the stadium and stepped into the locker room. It didn't smell anything like our campus locker room. There was nothing more than the lingering smell of Icy Hot in the air, but it had more of a new car smell. Symmetrical vacuum lines ran across the green and silver carpet. Every locker was three times the size of the ones we had at FU.

Coming in here this time was different. It wasn't my dad's old locker room; it was one that could be mine...but that didn't send thrills of anticipation through me. As nice as it was with flat-screen TVs, padded bench seats, and solid wood lockers, this wasn't the place for me.

"You're here." My dad stalked out of one of the side doors. The slight limp in his gait was nothing compared to the large ice pack bandaged to his arm.

"Dad."

To have me meet him here was breaking all kinds of recruiting rules, but he was the great Phillip Russo who didn't care what anyone said, not even the commissioner.

"Threw a few balls out there—not as easy as it used to be." He went back out the doorway he'd come in through.

I guessed that meant I was supposed to follow him.

He lowered himself into a swirling whirlpool of water. The sharp smell of the topical muscle ointments blanketed the room. It was like my room back home after every game and practice. Some of the physical therapists, conditioning specialists, and other team staff came into the room, and a few guys from the team showed up. The game wasn't until that night, but when you needed to work those kinks out to be one hundred percent, you showed up early.

"All this is waiting for you, son." Dad spread one arm out all the way. The other only moved as far as he could with the bandage and ice pack restriction on his arm. To him this was about the glory of the field. He had a grin on his face like he was giving me the keys to the castle. For so long, this had been exactly what I'd wanted: sweating it out beside my old man as he ran me through practice drills on the field, grinning like an idiot as he coached me from the sidelines and became a fixture in my life. After way too long without an ounce of his attention, I'd lapped it up, basked in it, and had never been happier—but once all the warm, shiny feelings wore off, all that was left was his scrutiny and unending disappointment. Nothing was ever good enough.

But here, in a room soaked with Icy Hot and painkillers, all I saw were guys holding it together for one more minute on the field. Knee braces. Long deep scars from surgery. The nail gun pattern on shoulders and knees from pins being inserted. They gave it their all out there through blood, sweat, and pain. My surgery paled in comparison to what they went through to stay on the field.

"A ring just like this is in your future."

He rested his elbow on the edge of the tub and held up his fist. The bulky gold- and diamond-encrusted ring didn't make me want to rush to the gym and get ready for next season.

To top off our highly-against-regulation time in the stadium, Dad brought me around to the team doctor. One of the linemen walked out, lifting and dropping his ice-pack-covered and Ace-bandage-wrapped shoulder. Sympathetic pain throbbed in my own.

I held my head high. "I wanted to talk to you about the volunteer project thing."

"The story's ready to go."

"I need you to kill it."

"It's PR gold—why would I kill it?"

Of course he wouldn't just do it because I asked. "There are a few other things I'm working on that'll be a better fit, more focused on the sport." I'd figure a project out later, but I didn't want Elle to find out about this. Ever since we'd left the Franklin, guilt had been riding me hard. Thinking about fucking things up with her sent a panicked streak through my chest like nothing else. Slowly, I was winning her over, and I didn't want to erase all that.

"What kind of things?" He leaned over the edge of the soaking tub.

"Phillip." An older man with salt and pepper hair clapped Dad on the back.

"Frank." He shook the man's hand.

"Your dad said you've been complaining about your shoulder. Let's go talk." Frank dropped his hand onto my shoulder and led me into his office. Dad followed behind. The doctor put on a white coat over his team t-shirt and looped a stethoscope around his neck then wheeled his stool closer to me. My dad kicked one of his feet in front of the other and leaned against the wall. So much for doctor-patient confidentiality.

"Yeah, I've tweaked it a few times this season. Took a few hits too many."

"No problem. Don't worry about it. I can set you up with a few muscle relaxers and painkillers before games and practices and you won't feel a thing."

Not feeling pain didn't mean I wasn't doing damage... "Won't that make it worse?"

"I've been a team doctor for long enough to know if you don't play, you don't get paid. I give my patients what they need."

"But what about the damage it does?"

"That damage hurts a hell of a lot less once the paycheck rolls in. Believe me." He clapped me on the shoulder and laughed like it was the most natural thing in the world.

Dad walked me outside to my car. The solid hitch in his gait only got more pronounced with each passing year. "Nothing to worry about. The docs keep you healthy enough to play, even if you're hurting. Play through the pain and bask in all the glory." He looked up at the stadium like it was the gates of heaven.

"Our team doctor told me I'll probably need to get this worked on."

A short, loud blast of air shot out of my dad's nose. "Your team doc was trying to keep you scared to show off too much this season. They've got nothing left once you're gone, and if you're breaking records left and right, it doesn't give them any room to grow."

There was a zero percent chance of that being true. Plus, the team still had LJ, Berk, and Keyton, guys who were all set to be strong draft picks, but arguing with Dad when he was like this was a one-way ticket to Lecture-Ville. "Permanent damage isn't what I want, Dad."

"I've been doing this for longer than you've been alive, son, and I know what it takes to make it in this business. Now, about making sure you're on the right track with the publicity ahead of the draft, I've got a few things in the works."

"About that—why don't we hold off? Maybe do it closer to the big day?" I still hadn't told Elle. One kiss from her hadn't been enough. It never would be. She was finally letting me get closer, and I hadn't realized how much I wanted that. If my face was splashed all over the internet with what had happened over spring break, she'd remove my balls.

"Don't worry about it. I've got it all handled."

"So, the story's not coming out yet?"

"I handed that off to my assistant, but don't worry. We'll get it all taken care of."

"Thanks." I nodded and got into my car.

———

SIZZLES AND POPS FROM THE PANS MELDED WITH THE CALLS FROM everyone behind their stations across the restaurant. The bustle of a kitchen was so different from the commotion of a locker room or gym, but also more of the same—people working to create something others could enjoy. Here, though, it was my fingertips in danger, not my entire body ready to be pummeled into the ground.

"If you cut those any slower, we're bumping you back to the dishes." Gramps clapped me on the back and stared over my shoulder.

"Sorry, Chef. I'm a little rusty." I got back to work, trying and failing to keep my mind on not slicing off any fingers. Cramming my thumb into my mouth, I backed away from my station.

"Lost your touch, huh?" He chucked all my chopping into the garbage and someone else got to disinfecting my station.

"I'm a bit out of it."

"No shit. Grab a plate and get out of here—*one* plate. Please leave some food for the customers."

"Actually, do you mind if I take some for a friend?"

Gramps' knife clattered to the stainless steel worktop. "The boy who would snap at anyone coming near his plate is willingly giving away food? Or is this just a ploy to get me to give you more?" He arched an eyebrow and gave me the stern look that had always made me spill growing up. He was a prickly old man, but that was what made him Gramps. He ran his kitchen like a tight ship, sometimes pushing harder than the coach ever did on the field, but in here, it never felt like work.

"Seriously."

"In that case, you'd better bring her here when you get a chance. I'd like to meet the girl who's gotten Phoenix Russo to part with even a morsel of food."

I ducked my head as he loaded up the container with chicken in a creamy sauce and grilled vegetables then stacked a smaller box with a dessert on top. "Thanks, Gramps."

The lead weights I'd carried deep in my stomach since leaving the stadium had been lifted with some kickass food and even better company at the restaurant, and that mood brightened as I jogged across the street to Elle's with a shot of excitement at her finally seeing a place that had meant so much to me growing up. Gramps would love her, and she'd love Tavola. I'd introduce her to everyone and maybe take her on an extended tour of the walk-in.

She'd been quiet all day, not a single call or text, which was out of step with our new norm after the kiss. Her schedule was more jam-packed than mine, but even when her replies came at two AM, she always got back to me. I always made sure there was a spot open in front of her house, some-times jogging out there to convince whoever it was to move their car. I didn't want her walking into her place so late from blocks away.

And I might have happened to check from my window to make sure she got home safe. The last thing she needed was me keeping her up all night, so I gave her the hours she needed as I bided my time for the days, weeks, and months ahead, and more. That little wave she'd give me from the porch even when she was dead on her feet felt better than anything had in a long time.

I knocked on her door and rocked back on my heels with my sweaty palms shoved in my pockets, eager to pull her into my arms and kiss the face I'd only seen from across the street for the past seventy-two hours.

"You're a fucking liar." She waved a paper in front of my face.

I jerked my head back and looked at the crumpled pages held in her hand. My stomach dropped. My picture was plastered all over the flyers for a new build session they were running.

"Rick asked me to help with one last session this semester since there has been a lot of interest after you got involved. He told me all about the photographer who came by after the last day and the little interview you did."

Shit. I should've told her, and now it was too late.

"I can explain."

"Explain what? How you were only there for some bullshit reputation rehab session?"

Ding ding ding. Nail on the freaking head.

Anger radiated off her and she released the pages from her hand. The paper fluttered to the ground.

"Yes." I scrubbed my hands down the sides of my face. "But it wasn't like that. The PR thing was my dad's idea. I was trying to find the right time to tell you."

"All your big speeches about being there just because and jumping all over my case for misjudging you and I was right all along. You only cared about your football career."

"No, you weren't right about way more than why I was there."

There was a flicker in her gaze as she fisted her hands at

her sides. "You're a fucking liar. I asked you point blank why you were there, more than once, and you lied to my face."

Her words hit like a kick to the chest. "Maybe I did, but what does it matter why I was there? Do you want to know why I didn't tell you there'd be a story written about this?"

"Because you're a lying asshole who's only out to do things that make you look good?"

"I knew you'd react like this, knew you'd freak out and blow this whole thing out of proportion. We had a great time together. We've been having a good time." I stepped closer, hating the anger burning in her eyes.

She crossed her arms over her chest.

"You said it yourself—Rick's getting more interest in the projects, and the story hasn't even run yet. Isn't that a good thing?"

"Don't change the subject. This is about you going behind my back because you were wrong. This is about you doing this for the wrong reasons."

"And what does it matter? If the work gets done and people are helped, what does it matter why people are there? And what about you? Why are you doing all this? Why were you out there? To win an award? To get back at some old boyfriend? To settle a score and prove to people that you're a good person?"

"This isn't about me." Her words were like a shot from a nail gun.

"It is about you. If I'd told you why I was there, what would you have done?"

"Told you to get lost."

"Exactly, and the good that'll be done by the next group wouldn't be there. That's five more families who'll get a house who wouldn't have otherwise."

"It doesn't matter."

"Well, it should. You call me a liar, but you're lying to yourself. You know who I am. You're one of the few people who do." The anger and distrust in her eyes was slicing straight through my chest.

She crossed her arms. "Leave."

"If there were no Huffington Award, if there weren't a single bit of recognition for what you do, you'd have stopped a long time ago. You think I'm all about ego and being seen— maybe that's because you see the same thing in yourself, only I'm not martyring myself over it."

She staggered back like I'd hit her, and I knew those barbs had smacked her straight in the chest the way I'd aimed them, but now I wished I'd pulled a few punches. The thing was, she'd made up her mind about me long ago, and all the progress we'd made would be wiped away because I wasn't the right kind of person she needed to help.

"I'm a good person. Maybe I let shitty parties go on too long and don't snap at people who enjoy what I do and compliment me about it, but that doesn't mean you get to raise the good person award high over your head and tell everyone else to fuck off." I stormed off her porch and back across the street.

I could've sworn there was a low call of my name, but I didn't feel like dealing with any fans right now. Staring out my bedroom window, I checked out Elle's house. It was totally dark. Truce over.

CHAPTER 19
ELLE

"And then he turned it around on me like *I* was the problem, like there was something wrong with me for being pissed at him. Can you believe that?"

I rocked back on Jules' chair.

She stared at me with her hands wrapped around the shiny brass pole in the center of her bedroom.

"Yeah, I do believe it, and I've believed it all three times you've told me." Wrapping her hands around the pole, she held herself out perpendicular from the floor and slowly spun around.

"It hasn't been that many times."

She lifted an eyebrow as both feet landed back on the ground.

"You're right—it was five. I forgot the two times on the way to and from class yesterday."

"I'm not wrong here."

Jules' gaze slid from mine.

"Are you serious?"

"Is it shitty he didn't tell you they were doing some big story about the build? Maybe, but you'd have lost it if he had."

"No, I wouldn't have."

She crossed her arms and pursed her lips.

"Okay, maybe I would've lost it on him." I flopped down on her bed and stared up at the ceiling.

"Maybe? You'd have bitched him out eight ways from Sunday. You'd probably have tried to persuade Rick not to even let him stay, and you probably would've let the air out of his tires."

"You're overreacting."

"You have the cops on speed dial. You can't blame him for being freaked out to tell you anything."

Jules' vision board was stuck to the ceiling above the bed. Cutouts of pictures and destinations and their signature dishes merged into a collage that was completely and totally her, all bright and sunny with accompanying treats to try. "He scares me, Jules." The way my heart raced every time he got close to me. The way I hadn't been able to stop thinking about that kiss since his lips left mine. The way I couldn't trust any of those feelings because I was number one supreme at getting my teeth kicked in by love.

"Why's he scary?" She lay down beside me and turned her head to stare at the side of my face.

I turned and met her gaze. "Because I like him." I stared back up at the ceiling.

"Why's that scary? He gave you a ride when your car broke down. He helped at Grace's. He seems nice."

"So did James and Mitchell."

"You can't write a guy off because of one mistake."

"And what happens when he breaks my heart and I still want him? What then?"

"*If* he breaks your heart."

"I wish I had your confidence. If there's one thing my track record tells me, it's that it's only a matter of time."

"A couple wrong choices don't really amount to a track record."

"I chose a guy who was as far from James as possible. Mitchell wasn't an arrogant showboater. He wasn't big into his looks. He was visiting orphanages in South America. And then I find him in bed with a girl... It was like a shot-for-shot remake of my senior year of high school, complete with the big tub of cookies you made for me. I'm still pissed I dropped them." I hoped they'd attracted rats to the apartment I'd planned to share with him.

"You made up for it by eating that double batch I brought for move-in day." She nudged me with her elbow.

"After all that time, I thought I was good, thought I was over what happened in high school, but to have it happen twice, back to back...that's the universe telling me something." Telling me I'm not someone anyone will ever want to be faithful to. I resisted the urge to curl into a ball. Seeing Mitchell wandering around campus like he was a saint made me want to puke. At least I'd kick his ass when it came to the Huffington Award.

"It's not." She held my hand. "Do you know why I made this?" She pointed up at her collage on the ceiling.

"To keep a running list of all the awesome places you want to go to?"

"That's part of it, but also to remind me that there's a shit ton of goodness out there. Sometimes it feels like all we see is the bad. That's the magnifying glass we hold up to everything, and sometimes that glass is so focused I can feel it burning me, heating up my skin and making me want to run and hide. So, I lie in my bed and use this to remind me. It doesn't always work, and some days I want to rip it down, but some days it helps me smile."

Tears shimmered in her eyes and she tilted her head to look at me. I squeezed her hand and smiled.

"Now that you know you've been a shit, what are you going to do about it?"

"Nothing."

THE SECOND WE MET   163

She shot up. "What do you mean, nothing?"

I shrugged. "I'm sure he doesn't want to hear from me. I'm sure he's got an entire swarm of girls all over him as we speak and has probably forgotten all about it."

"You're wrong, and you're a coward." She had the disapproving mom stare down pat.

"Why do you have to be so sage and wise?"

She dusted off her shoulder. "I'm kind of a big deal."

I smiled at her and the momentary splash of intense confidence she totally deserved. "You totally are."

She snorted dismissively. "Whatever. Come on." She smacked my leg. "Let's go. Some time on the pole will help you think. Get up." She tugged on my arm. "I need you to spot me while I try the Allegra, and you can do the Rainbow."

"Isn't that the one where I banged my forehead on the pole and had a bruise for a week?"

"It'll be fine. You're better now than you were before. You'll be fine."

STANDING OUTSIDE ON THE THUMPING SIDEWALK, I STARED UP AT the house I'd only recently stopped praying to be knocked down in some freak sinkhole eruption. Two days and this was all I had. Jules had been wrong. Nothing had come to me, short of blurting out my apology. It was too bad that by the time I'd finally gotten the balls to do it, there was a party in full Brothel swing going on.

Rick's frantic call earlier in the afternoon asking for help with handling the deluge of volunteers who wanted to help after Nix's story ran meant I'd put aside the stack of schoolwork I had and pitched in to sort through all the corporate inquiries along with other people asking if Nix or the rest of the FU football players were going to be there. One seven-hundred-word story featuring a football player would have

Rick's group swimming in volunteers and corporate sponsors for the next six to eight months.

I read the article complete with pictures not just from the photographer, but also taken by other volunteers. Krista & Co. were in a bunch and I was, of course, scowling in the back glaring. Not exactly a welcoming face, but every word in the story was all about the great work the group had done and how much it helped the community.

Make It Home was scrambling to get all the materials for three more groups to come in. That meant twelve new houses for people who didn't currently have them. The publicity had done something neither of us had been able to do before. I couldn't stay mad about him lying to me after seeing the good it was doing and also couldn't figure out how to pull my foot out of my ass. It was so far up there, my shoelaces were tickling my tonsils.

Some people laughed as they walked down the sidewalk and froze when they spotted me at the bottom of the stairs at the Brothel. Their gazes bounced from me to the house and back to me.

My reputation preceded me. I held up my hands. "I'm not calling the cops."

The two girls and three guys didn't seem at all convinced.

"See, look, I'm going in. Not here to break it up." Taking a deep breath, I climbed the steps, trying to smother the jumping beans going crazy in my stomach.

A thumping wall of sound hit me as I reached the top of the steps.

I pushed the door fully open, and the music rang in my ears. Old-school pop hammered inside my skull, and the overwhelming beer and sweat cloud rushed over me.

Girls danced with their arms up over their heads, screaming out the lyrics to the songs and sloshing beer all over the place. Guys danced behind them with red plastic cups filled to the brim.

Pushing through the crowds, I looked for anyone I knew. I might not have recognized anyone, but they sure recognized me. The partygoers' expressions were split between fear and anger.

I tried to keep my lips from tightening with a hint of a smile. Maybe if they thought I was having fun, they wouldn't hoist me up into the air and pitch me back outside. I searched the entire house and didn't see the guys who actually lived there. Looking through the kitchen, I spotted the back door leading out into the backyard. There was a big sign on it with *Do Not Enter* scrawled out in large red letters.

Dodging a keg stand, I slipped outside—literally slipping on a puddle of beer and bracing myself on the wooden staircase leading to the neatly cut grass.

From inside the kitchen, someone called out behind me. "You're not allowed out there."

All the heads of the seven people outside swung around to me. "You can't—" Marisa piped up, but she cut herself off when she spotted me. In the darkened backyard, all eyes were on me, and then they were on Nix, and back to me.

I closed the door behind me and walked down the wooden stairs, not a creak or groan to them. They were solid, not like the rickety driftwood our house across the street was made of. I focused on that and not the fourteen eyes tracking my every move.

Crossing the grass, I stopped behind the ring of chairs tucked away from all the madness inside.

I folded my hands in front of me. "Nix, can I talk to you?"

The muscles in his cheeks tightened. "Guys, can you give us a minute?" He stared at me, even and cool, detached. I'd never seen him look at me like that, and it turned my stomach.

Everyone got up, except for Berk. He sat perched on the edge of the lawn chair with a Twizzler between his teeth. Nix shot him a disapproving look and LJ grabbed his arm, dragging him toward the house with everyone else.

The back door closed, and I rocked from foot to foot.

Nix held out his hand, offering me the floor. "You wanted to talk, so talk."

I swallowed, trying to buy myself time. My plan didn't exactly extend beyond finding him in the party house. "Everything you said...you're right." I wrapped my arms around my waist. "But it really hurt me that after everything I told you, you didn't come clean. Maybe I'd have been an asshole if you told me that first day, but after the Franklin Institute? It hurt."

He leaned forward, gestured to the empty seat across from him, and then rested his forearms on his knees, hands clasped.

I sat on the seat, perched on the edge, ready to make a fast getaway.

He stared at the grass between us and let out a deep breath. "I shouldn't have lied to you. I know that wasn't cool, but we were finally starting to not hate each other and I didn't want to ruin it. My dad is on this kick to make sure my image is perfect for the draft. I told him not to run that story, but he's never listened to me. Not sure why I expected him to do it now." He peered up at me with disappointment heavy in his eyes.

My fingers tightened around the front of the chair. "You didn't want him to use the story?"

He shook his head with a noise of disgust. "No, but that doesn't mean I couldn't have told you, doesn't mean I shouldn't have told you, especially after the things you told me about what you've gone through. Lying to you..." He made a growl of frustration. "I know all about how much that hurts, and I didn't want you to think I was using you or the work we did at Make It Home. I'd just gotten you to see I wasn't an asshole."

"I'm sorry you felt you had to keep it from me, and you were totally right about how I would have, and did, react. The story has Rick up to his eyeballs in volunteers, and there are even some donation and sponsorship ideas being thrown around. So, thank you for bringing the spotlight to what Rick's doing over there. It'll make a world of difference to him and the people he can help. Thank you." I drummed my fingers on the seat on either side of me, nervous under his exacting gaze.

"Looks like we both screwed things up."

"I'm happy to take the bulk of the blame."

He let out an amused huff. "I'm not going to fight you for it."

The secluded nook in the backyard might as well have been an island away from everyone else.

His jaw clenched and he set down his beer. "We had something good, didn't we?" He stood up, and I lifted my chin to stare him in the eyes.

My throat tightened. "Had? As in, in the past?"

"Only if you want it to be." The hoarse whisper sent a shiver down my spine.

The words caught in my throat, and I shook my head.

"Good." He took my hand. The rough pads of his fingers unfurled the aching need I'd wrapped up tight and locked away.

I found my voice, and the words came out as a hungry whisper. "What now?"

"Let me show you." He walked us back through the kitchen, and everyone moved out of his way. Determination burned in his gaze and in the clench of his jaw, which had nothing to do with anger.

The same burning need ping-ponged inside me. He kept me close as we walked through the living room, shifting and holding my hand against his back as the crush of bodies got even thicker.

We burst free from the throngs of people and thumping music. Outside, the warm spring air felt cool after leaving the writhing mass of partygoers. My ears adjusted to the volume crash, and it sounded like the whole world was underwater.

Nix didn't slow his steps until we got to my front door. His gaze skirted up my body, tender and hungry all at once. I squeezed my thighs together against the heady throb between my legs. He held on to me like he was afraid to let go, but that was all I wanted—to let go with him.

I fumbled for my keys, trying to remember how locks worked. My fingers shook and his hand enveloped mine, steadying it.

He pressed a soft kiss against the back of my neck, and my knees nearly gave out.

I pushed open the front door and dropped my chin to my shoulder, looking at him behind me.

"What now?"

CHAPTER 20
ELLE

The door slammed closed behind us. Light from the street was the only thing illuminating the entryway. People laughed outside. The house was whisper quiet. It was only us, secluded in a cocoon of darkness. Every breath crackled with anticipation. Every creak of the floorboard sent a shiver through my body. Each creak a step closer. His body blocked out the little bit of light from outside.

"Elle." The keen longing of my name on his lips was the only warning I got before he bridged the gap between us. His hands were in my hair, on my face, everywhere I wanted them and nowhere near close to where I needed them.

His lips crashed down on mine, demanding repayment for the teasing I hadn't even realized I'd been doing. Only weeks ago, we'd called a truce, and now I wanted nothing more than all of him. Every touch. Every taste. Every temptation I'd never stopped needing. The backs of his fingers ran along the gap between my shirt and my jeans.

My hands bunched in his shirt. The soft cotton dragged up over the hard surface of his abs.

He moved forward with his arm wrapped around my

waist, lifting me off the floor. My back pressed against the wall and the solid muscles of his chest.

I ripped his shirt up and over his head.

He shoved my jeans down over my ass and palmed it, squeezing and lifting me off my feet. I clenched my thighs together at the ache brought on by the bulge at the front of his jeans. He dropped kisses onto my bare shoulder.

"Are we taking the scenic route?" I chuckled and my head rolled back as he nipped and sucked on the spot where my neck and shoulder met.

"I'm not going to let you rush me, Elle. I've been waiting for this for too long." He let go of me and peeled my top off, dangling it from his fingers before letting it drift to the floor.

"How long?"

A flicker flashed across his eyes. He sank to his knees and tugged my jeans the rest of the way down. "Probably since the first time I saw you dancing in your bedroom window when you first moved in." Staring up at me, he ran his hands up and down my thighs, sliding them between and skimming across the purple fabric covering my heated pussy.

"That was at the beginning of junior year." I shuddered. The ache between my thighs became a cascading inferno as he began his sexual torture.

His lips turned down. "I know. Can you even imagine how pissed I was the first time you called campus police on us?" He unbuttoned his jeans. Each pop of his button fly sent another throbbing ache straight to my clit. My greedy need made it hard to think.

"Your house was so loud, I could barely see straight." I stuck my hands on my hips.

"You could've come over. No one would've turned you away." His fingers danced along the frilly edge of the cup of my bra, backing me up each step of the way to my bedroom.

"Maybe I didn't want to be just another pretty face in the

sea of FU Trojan groupies." I sucked in a sharp breath, my stomach coiling around the building pleasure, the old embers of our anger sparking the heat between us even hotter.

He ran the backs of his fingers along my cheek. "You were never just another pretty face, Elle. Never." He slipped his hand to the back of my neck and captured my lips in a kiss that demanded nothing more than my complete surrender.

I fell into him, my hands plastered against him. His heart hammered under my touch, each thump driving my need for him even higher.

Taking the steps two at a time, he wrapped his arms tighter around me.

He stood at the top of the staircase, his cock bouncing against my ass. Without a word from me, he shouldered his way into my bedroom.

"How'd you—"

"You think I haven't been paying attention?" He smiled at me, his ocean-blue eyes glinting with mischief and desire all rolled into one. He kicked the door closed.

His hand traveled up my bare back, exploring the new expanse of skin naked to his touch. My body rippled with an unfettered pleasure, and the hungry edge of need grew with each unrushed stroke as he moved like he had all the time in the world.

"Nix." It came out high and reedy like a whine from a kid being teased with a piece of candy, only he wasn't candy—he was the whole freaking cake, and I was just getting licks of frosting. I wanted a slice.

"Don't rush me." His lips never left mine. Nipping, licking, lathing. His skills on the field weren't the only ones that were head and shoulders above the rest. His tongue danced with mine, giving me a prelude to what was to come.

Wrapping his arm tighter around my waist, he walked us backward. He turned and sat me on the edge of my dresser. A couple bottles beside me rattled and clinked together. The cool mirror against my back sent goose bumps breaking out all over my body.

He crouched and slipped his hands down my waist. His fingers spanned the width and tugged me forward against him. Kissing me until my head swam, he slipped his hands lower. His fingers slid under the elastic of my pink- and purple-striped boy shorts. Our eyes met, a clash of fiery desire. My breath caught and I stared at him, unable to break this connection between us, a tether that sent me sky high and kept me grounded at the same time, hyperaware of every racing beat of my heart and determined touch of his fingers.

With one smooth tug, he lifted me and yanked my underwear down over my hips. His hands squeezed my ass, palming it. The rough pads of his fingers sent shivers of pleasure pulsing through my body.

Spreading my thighs apart, he ran his strong hands along my sensitive skin. I moaned at the whisper of his breath against my clit, the heat building to an unbearable crescendo in anticipation of his lips on me. My heart pounded and the entire world became centered on his hands, his gaze, his mouth.

His fingers sank into the flesh of my thighs. Leaning forward, I stared at the decadent sight in front of me. He was chocolate chunk cookies on top of a brownie sundae. The corner of his mouth lifted, and I sucked in a shuddering breath.

I wasn't prepared. I'd thought I was, but I sure as hell wasn't. Nix ran his tongue along my pussy, equal parts leisurely to drive me crazy and precise to hit all the right buttons. I couldn't stop myself from bucking against his mouth. He held on to me, pinning me against the dresser top. My heels banged against the wooden drawers below, drumming out a rhythm of pleasure.

I threw my head back and sank my fingers into his hair.

My legs trembled and I tried to close them against the sexual onslaught. It was too much and not enough all at once. Nix plunged two fingers into me. My walls clamped around them and fireworks exploded in front of my eyes.

They could probably hear me coming halfway across campus. While I was still in the clouds, Nix lifted me off the dresser.

Snagging a condom from his wallet, he rolled it on with his hands on mine the entire time. He covered me with his body. The warm wall of muscle descended on top of me.

"I guess I was wrong." I lifted my hands to the sides of his face and pulled him closer. Our lips mashed together in a fevered pitch, and the minutes-long reprieve from the driving, pounding need to have him inside me evaporated.

I hooked my legs around his waist. My foot dug into his ass as I tried to pull him in closer.

Goose bumps rose on my skin at the brush of his cock against my soaking wet entrance. The broad tip tapped against my clit, and my hips shot off the bed. I reached down between us and positioned him against the seam of my pussy.

He rested his forehead against mine. "Eager much?" The strained smile and growl to his voice told me he was hanging on by a thread, possibly one thinner than mine.

"Shut up. We could always go back downstairs and finish those—" Before the sentence was out of my mouth, he thrusted his hips and the thick head of his cock pushed inside me, stretching me to my limit. I sucked in a sharp breath and rolled my hips. Every nerve ending received special attention from his overpowering invasion. My toes curled and my back shot off the bed.

I hitched my legs higher and he sank in even deeper. He shuddered on top of me and I held on tighter as his grinding thrusts rubbed my clit, stealing my breath away with each push and pull. I dug my fingers into his back and my entire body seized, paralyzed by the rocketing orgasm ripping through me.

His hips slammed into me and his cock expanded, sending another shudder through me as he groaned out his release against the side of my neck.

CHAPTER 21
NIX

There wasn't anything sweeter than Elle. One round melded into two. I wrapped my hands around her hips, fingers sinking into her flesh, and slammed into her again. Releasing my grip with one hand, I slipped it between us and found her clit. Circling it with my finger, I kept up my thrusts. The hot wetness of her threatened to consume me.

It was too much and not enough all at once. Her muscles tightened and her core squeezed me in a blissfully excruciating hold. The pleasure shot to my toes. My name on her lips was more than I could bear. Under me she writhed and jerked, her walls clamping even tighter, and I couldn't hold back anymore.

Turning nearly inside out, I held her close, needing to feel every part of her. Stars danced in front of my eyes and I tried to remember how to breathe. In a sweat-covered haze, I collapsed on top of her smooth softness like I'd just run in a ninety-yard touchdown.

The feel of her body beneath me made me never want to move, but I didn't want to crush her. Rolling to my side, I took her with me, keeping her pressed against my chest. My head swam and even now, every stroke of her fingers down my skin sent more blood straight to my dick like a boxer who refused to get KO'ed. *Down boy or I'm headed straight for a coronary.* My heart pounding like a rookie on his first day of practice, I brushed back the streaks of pink hair plastered to the skin of her forehead.

I stared into her eyes. The hooded exhaustion in them mirrored my own, along with the unbridled hunger that meant we'd both spend the rest of the night satisfying one another until sleep overcame us.

"That was unexpected." She chuckled.

"It's your fault for doing what you did."

"What did I do? Look at you?"

"Exactly." I kissed the tip of her nose.

Holding her in my arms, I stared down at her and ran my fingers along her collarbone. I'd never be full of her. This one moment was etched bone deep, and I didn't want it to end.

That scared the shit out of me.

Dragging my arm from under her shoulder, I got up and disposed of the condom.

She spread out on her bed, propping her head up on her hand. "While you're up, there's still half a tray of Jules' heart-stopping-good brownies down in the kitchen." There was a mischievous curl to her lips.

"Your wish is my command." I bowed and grabbed my jeans off the floor, throwing them on and going back downstairs to retrieve the treat for Elle. I was sure they'd taste even better when I ate the chocolate off her skin.

Taking a plate out of the cabinet, I sliced two giant brownies for us before heading back upstairs. Her roommate probably wouldn't appreciate coming back to a completely empty pan after her hard work.

Leaning back, I peered down at Elle. Her eyes were closed. I smiled at the low, gentle cadence of her snore. Kissing the top of her head, I pulled the blanket over the two of us and shifted down lower in the bed. "Night, Elle."

———

ELLE GRUMBLED IN HER SLEEP, NOT A MUMBLE OR TALKING EVEN, but a steady gripe session under her breath like she was one second away from pushing someone off her front porch. This felt more right than anything had in a long time, maybe as much as walking back into Tavola, like something had been missing and I hadn't realized it—only with Elle, it was someone.

After nearly two years living across the street from one another, there hadn't been more than glares and verbal barbs exchanged between us until a month ago. Now, I wasn't sure what happened next.

What I wanted to happen was to never leave this bedroom again. Well, maybe except for regular trips down to the kitchen to see what Jules had baked. We could both be fork-lifted out of the house at the end of the semester.

I brushed back the hair from Elle's face and she grumbled, burrowing deeper into my side. Grabbing my phone, I checked the time and groaned, dropping my head back onto the pillow.

An angry, red glowing reminder of a meeting I had coming up blinked on my screen.

Sliding my arm out from under her head, I kissed her on the cheek. Her eyes fluttered open as the bed dipped with my departure.

I grabbed my clothes up off the floor and threw them on.

"You're leaving." She sat up and didn't do that thing girls sometimes do when they cover themselves up, like in movies where the dude has the sheet at his waist while she has it chastely tucked up around her neck. Elle stayed bare and stretched her arms overhead, trying to torture me or maybe make me tackle her back into the pillows.

"I have to meet with my dad. What are you up to today?"

"Tutoring, working on my end-of-year papers, and eating whatever's wafting up here from the kitchen. I have a shift at Uncommon Grounds later tonight."

Like my nose was linked to Elle's words, a delicious buttery smell poured into the room like a blanket of sugary bliss. She put on some clothes and followed me downstairs.

Jules sat at the kitchen table, chewing on the arm of her glasses.

"You two are going to have heart attacks by the end of the semester." I slid on my shoes.

Elle hopped up on the counter. "She's a stickler for giving almost all of it away—sometimes too much of it. It'll stay in the house for like two days max then she ships it all out like wayward orphans looking for a good home."

"The baking is relaxing, but having all that extra food around makes me antsy."

"I'm more than happy to take anything you're looking to unload off your hands, and I might even share it with some of the guys."

"Perfect." Jules hopped up, grabbed a baker's box, and loaded it up with three different types of cupcakes, more brownies, and chocolate tarts. "Berk seemed to like those last time I made them, so I added in some extra." Her gaze was trained on the box like it might disappear at any second.

"I'm sure he'll appreciate it."

———

A PURPLE ENVELOPE STUCK OUT OF THE MAILBOX AT OUR FRONT door. I glanced up and down the quiet street. No one was up this early—well, except the baker across the street. I held on to the letter and opened the front door.

Berk froze on the steps, shoving something into his back pocket.

"Where have you been, young man? Out all night?" He came the rest of the way down with his mock dad voice on.

"Nowhere."

"Nowhere, huh? Wouldn't have anything to do with a certain pink-haired harasser across the street, now, would it?" He stood at the bottom of the steps, resting against the banister with a self-satisfied grin on his face.

"I might've spent some time with Elle."

"Elle and Nix, sitting in a tree…" he sing-songed.

"But if you're going to give me a hard time about it, I don't have to hand over this stuff her roommate baked."

He froze, snatched the box from my arms, and rushed into the kitchen, starting a pot of coffee. He opened the lid on the box and shoved his head inside, inhaling so loudly I thought he'd have a cupcake or brownie attached to his face when he pulled it out.

"How does she do it?" He picked up one of the treats and shoved it into his mouth. "I swear she's laced this stuff with something. It's insane. It's Pavlovian now. Every time I see their house, my mouth starts watering."

Pouring a cup of coffee, he took bites from the brownie. After dumping half a cup of milk and five sugars into his coffee, he leaned against the counter.

"On that note, I've got something else for you." I waved the envelope in front of my face.

He dropped the food onto the counter and reached for it. Glancing at his chocolate-covered hands, he licked them clean and wiped them on his sweats before snatching the letter from my grasp.

He rushed past me and back upstairs, leaving his piping hot cup of coffee on the counter.

"Shut the hell up!" LJ called out from the living room.

Berk's steps thundered above before his door slammed shut.

I poured myself a cup of coffee.

"What the hell is going on with him?" LJ jerked his thumb at the doorway, standing up straight, every bone in his back cracking along the way.

"He got another letter."

"Who knew he was so into reading." He yawned and rubbed at his eyes.

"I'm thinking the subject matter is probably a lot different than in class."

LJ picked up Berk's abandoned mug and took a sip. There's always that split second when someone realizes they've made a mistake. LJ's eyes bulged and he rushed to the sink, spraying a fine coffee-colored mist into the basin.

He wiped his mouth with the back of his hand. "Did he pour insulin directly into his coffee or what?"

I didn't even try to hide my laughter. "That's what you get for trying to steal his drink. You're sleeping on the couch? What happened to your bed buddy?"

"I got bumped."

"She brought a guy home?"

LJ shot me a steel-melting glare. "No." That word was sharp as a punch.

I held up my hands in surrender.

"Liv, her roommate, needed a place to crash, so I gave them the bedroom."

"How chivalrous."

"Not like I can tell her no."

"Not like you ever could."

He rolled his eyes. "She's my best friend."

"Is that all she is?"

"We've known each other since we were eight."

"You're not eight anymore."

"Not this again." He kept his gaze trained on the mug in front of his face.

"You two are always all over each other."

"Fighting."

"Flirting."

"Annoying the shit out of each other."

"Foreplay."

"Been there, done that, did not get the t-shirt."

I lowered my voice. "If you two actually dated, you never said anything about that."

He shrugged. "What's there to tell? There was an attempt, but we decided we'd be better as friends."

"We?"

He chewed on the side of his lip. "She."

"So all this bullshit about better as friends and all that— you're just biding your time?"

His gaze drifted to the floor above our heads. "We almost didn't make it out the last time we tried and failed. Risking her... I'd rather have her as a friend than lose her altogether, so I'm good with this." The unspoken 'for now' hung in the air between us.

The house came alive with footsteps and doors opening and closing above us. Coffee was the universal alarm clock. Stumbling down the steps like zombies, Marisa, Liv, Reece, and Seph emerged.

Marisa and Liv went over some paperwork from their landlord and insurance company, and the rest of us tried to slowly join the land of the living.

Berk showed back up with flushed cheeks to reclaim his now cold cup of coffee.

"Do we need to invest in a bigger table?" Reece said from behind Seph, who was perched on his lap with her hands wrapped around her mug, sniffing the sweet aroma she was now hooked on.

"In a few months, half of you are abandoning us, so we'll

have plenty of room then." Berk leaned against the wall with a look of seriousness that didn't match his words.

"We'll be around," I offered.

"Don't make promises you can't keep." His smile was less teasing and more haunted. "You two have no idea where you'll be drafted. It's cool, though—enjoy it while we're all here together."

Things would never be the same once Reece and I graduated. We couldn't let moments like this pass us by. I leaned back against the counter and stared out the slatted blinds at the front of the house and at the falling-apart porch of sixty-six Aspen Drive. Sometimes you have to grab life with both hands and never let it go, and I planned on starting that today.

"I almost forgot. Is there a reason Johannsen is outside with a guitar serenading some chick outside her window?" Berk jerked his thumb toward the front door.

The whole table jumped up at once, even the people who had no idea what was going on. We piled out onto the porch and stared slack jawed at Johannsen, strumming a guitar standing on the small patch of grass outside a house a few doors down from us.

"I guess now we know why he was hanging around on our street." LJ craned his neck.

"He's not half bad." Marisa laughed.

"Whose house is that?" Seph leaned over on the railing trying to get a better look at the house.

"That's Willa's house. I don't know who else lives there though." Marisa sipped her coffee with a huge ass smile.

"Willa." The name rolled around my head. It was familiar. Maybe she'd come to some of our parties. Meeting hundreds of people on and off the field didn't make it hard to place people.

Berk shot forward. "Willa as in Willa Goodwin?"

All the guys eyes widened. "Brick's sister?" I glanced up

and down the street like he'd come rolling down the center in a tank at any moment.

"Damn, I hadn't planned on witnessing a murder this semester, but here we are." Berk shook his head and took another sip of his coffee.

CHAPTER 22
ELLE

"That's awesome, Mom."

"Your father is so excited. At his age, he wasn't sure he'd find anything."

"I knew he would." After nearly eighteen months without work, he'd finally found a position.

"And once he gets that first check, it's going straight to you."

"Don't worry about it. I've got my job here, and I'm making it through okay." The struggle would only make Dad feel worse. When I'd been home for a visit over the summer, he'd barely been able to look me in the eye, and on my way out, he slipped me a twenty for gas. It killed him not to be able to help me, and I didn't want to bring back that feeling. The unpaid-bill mountain was high and treacherous. I'd figure out my problems on my own, and the Huffington Award would solve 99% of them, giving me the breathing room I needed for a one-year hibernation after graduation.

"Dinner is burning, so let me get to that, but I wanted to tell you and let you know I love you."

"Love you too, Mom."

"We'll see you at graduation."

If I make it. I walked out of the tutoring session barely able to keep my eyes open. That's what happens when you get sexed into next week by a guy who has the stamina of a race-horse. There wasn't a damn thing that was selfish about Nix in or out of the bedroom. I'd been so damn wrong about him, and it scared me to think how things could've gone. It also scared the crap out of me to think where things were going.

We'd stayed over at each other's places almost every night. It wasn't like it was far, just across the street, but every time I made the walk over, nerves rumbled in my stomach. Watching him jog across to my side made me giddy and want to do a happy dance before opening the door.

While on campus, I'd stopped by the dean's office to make sure they'd received my award application, and I might have snuck a peek at the other nominations. Of course, Mitchell's name was there on the list, but his projects were nowhere near as extensive for the semester. He was my only real competition. Now I needed to make sure I actually graduated so I'd be eligible.

Dead on my feet, I tugged my key out of the lock then slammed the door behind me with visions of my bed dancing in front of me.

As I walked past the kitchen, something soft bounced off my head. I stopped, backing up and looking down at the bright yellow sponge that had hit me and was now sitting on the floor.

Jules glared from the kitchen doorway. "Could you please let me know when Nix is going to be staying here?"

"Why?" I stretched my arms over my head, my back cracking like a new pack of Kit Kats.

"I came out of my room naked like a bridge troll foraging for food and ran straight into him."

"Stop it." I glared at her. "You weren't naked. Your pole outfit is badass."

"You know I don't show my arms or legs out in public."

"The short shorts and crop top were cute."

"I wanted to crawl into a hole dug twenty feet beneath another hole and die. I'm surprised he didn't run screaming from the house."

I snorted. "You're always hiding the goods. You need to let the girls loose every so often." I lifted my hand toward her chest.

She smacked my hand away. "If you nip flick me, you'll pull back a nub."

I held up my hands in surrender. "Touchy, touchy. Always ruining all the fun."

"I'm not the one trying to feel up my roommate."

"All I'm saying is, you're awesome and beautiful. Stop being so self-conscious."

"Like you'd even know anything about that." She scoffed and spun around, her long, thick, black ponytail swishing with each step.

"You don't think I get self-conscious?"

"It's not the same, Miss Size Four," she threw over her shoulder like I'd never wanted to crawl out of my own skin, size notwithstanding.

"You're not much bigger than me. You've got curves for days, and you pole dance. That's most guys' wet dream."

Her gaze narrowed. "I don't need your pity." She spun around and disappeared into the kitchen.

Nope, she wasn't getting away. Not this time. "Who said anything about pity?"

"Whatever." She wrenched open the cabinet so hard, the craptastic hinge we kept fixing ourselves came loose. "See, I'm the Hulk." She braced her hands on the counter, her knuckles white around the edges.

"We've been trying to get that fixed forever. This isn't normal Jules frustration. What's going on?"

"Nothing, I'm fine." She wiped at her face and worked on fixing the hinge.

"You're not pulling that with me. What's the deal? Spill, or I'll march right across the street and tell a certain football player—"

"My mom wants me to come home this summer." She kept her head down, the words falling to the cheap linoleum like wet rags. "Laura is getting married—" Her throat worked up and down. "To Chad, and she wants me to be her maid of honor."

The blood drained from my face.

She lifted her head with tears and resignation in her eyes.

"Fuck no, you're not going. Nope, especially not to run after that witch and her fuckboy fiancé. Nope. Not happening. I forbid it." After the shortest Christmas break visit known to man, I had thought I'd have to buy all the booze in three states to get her through that chapter of her life.

"You forbid it." She wiped at the corner of her eye. "They're my family, right? If you had a sister, you'd want to be there for her."

"I'd also hope she wasn't a huge cu—"

"Come on, even I draw the line there." She let out a watery laugh. "The wedding's next spring. My mom wants me to help them go dress shopping. 'Stop being such a child, Julia. It's water under the bridge.'" The false cheeriness was a parody of her mom's voice. "'Helping us prepare for the big day will make it all better by the time the wedding arrives, and choosing your dress now means you can work on fitting into it by next year.'" It was a voice so smooth and light it almost made the viciousness of the words lash that much deeper.

"You know I'm solidly in the camp of leaving shitty people in your wake, even if they're family. Don't go. I'm begging you."

"She's my mom, and my dad would want me to be there for them."

"Don't let her manipulate you with that shit."

"They're all I have."

"They're not. You have me."

"And you're graduating. Next year, I'll be in this place all by myself. Who even knows where Zoe is."

"You won't be on your own. I'll be around."

She swung her head around. "Do you even know what you're doing after graduation? You could be in Micronesia for all we know."

"Or a third semester senior. I've put off every single paper for this semester. I'm a little screwed."

"Maybe instead of racking up even more volunteer hours that you don't even need, you should get to finishing those papers. The award ceremony is in three weeks. You're fine. Slow down and think about what you're going to do after graduation."

"I was supposed to be the one handing out advice."

"Glass houses, Elle. Glass houses."

"Please don't help Laura with her wedding. Please don't let them drag you down."

Jules sighed. "Maybe it won't be so bad."

"He's your ex and cheated on you with your sister—I don't think that can be not bad."

"I can push through this and come out the other side. I'm ready to stop feeling like this, like I'm the sister who should be living under the stairs."

"Then don't go. We can hang out, help me figure out my life and stay here this summer. No matter what, I'll be here through August. Don't go home. Stay here and we can go to the Burger Festival in June and Booze at the Zoo in July. It'll be the best summer ever. Maybe you can walk straight up to Berk and tell him who he's been trading letters with."

She was shaking her head before I could finish the sentence. "Not happening."

"Why not?"

"I can't deal with another person staring at me with that intense look of disappointment that makes a part of you die."

"And you think he'd look at you that way? No freaking way. He'll be doing backflips, especially once he sees what you can do on the pole."

She tugged at her long-sleeved shirt. "I can't chance it."

"So you're never going to tell him who you are? Never meet up and do half the things in those letters?"

"Sometimes the fantasy is better than reality. I'm sure he's got a picture of who I am in his head and I'd bet a lot of money it looks nothing like me."

"How do you know? For all you know, he's picturing the librarian over at Harbin."

Her head jerked up and she scrunched her face. "She's, like, seventy."

"Hey, don't judge his preferences."

She lobbed a kitchen towel at me.

"All I'm saying is you're more likely to regret never saying anything versus going for it."

"I'm better with the fantasy than taking that chance on a crushing reality. I've had more than my fair share already." She grabbed her computer and fled the kitchen like it was on fire.

Shaking my head, I turned off the oven. My phone rang, and I slipped it out of my pocket.

That light giddy feeling was back. "Hey."

"What are you baking?"

I spun around and glanced out the kitchen windows at the front of the house. Nix leaned against the railing of his porch across the road. I pulled up the blinds.

"That would be an abomination no one should ever allow to happen. Jules and I were talking."

"What are you doing tonight?" His voice was like a caress and washed away some of my tiredness.

"I have a couple papers I need to finish and get turned in."

"So, I can't come over right now?" His forearms were braced on the edge of the railing, the intensity of his look already set to panty-destroying.

I groaned. "I have to get these done, but I might be finished by ten."

"Ten? Am I just a booty call? You're summoning me to service you in the dead of night."

I smiled at the laughter in his voice. "If you're not up for the invitation—"

"I never said that. I'll let you get some work in then all bets are off. I'm knocking at ten on the dot, so you'd better be ready." The hungry growl of his voice sent me into overdrive.

"I'll leave the door unlocked."

"Don't tempt me. Get to work, B and E. I'm coming for you in two hours."

"I'll be ready."

"You'd better be."

CHAPTER 23
NIX

"Are you paying attention?"

I dropped my pen onto the notepad in front of me. "Sorry, what did you say?"

"I said, the news story about that house building thing went over well. I'm working on a few other things to get your profile even higher. Didn't you say you went to some soup kitchen or something?"

"Tagged along with a friend, but I'm not going to turn that into some publicity thing. I did it because I wanted to."

"Everything can be used to our advantage. We have endorsements lined up for you after your first year. I've made some calls, and Philly looks like they're set to pick you up. The quarterback right now is doing well, but it's only a matter of time before his shoulder gives out and then it's your chance. He's been spending more time taped up and wrapped up in the offseason. Even with that surgery and throwing reform, the clock is ticking on him."

The quick, dismissive way he talked about another guy's career failing settled in my stomach like a rock.

"As long as you step out onto the field and get a few

completions in the next season, you'll be good. We can start local and move into national sponsors."

"Isn't that getting ahead of ourselves?"

"We'd be even more ahead if you'd finally choose an agent. The clock is ticking. Once the draft is over, you'll start training camp. You need to come out strong there so there's no doubt that once the QB has his first bad hit, you'll get off the bench."

My stomach soured, and the rising of that nauseated feeling that overtook me when the slow-motion hits happened around me. The sickening crunch of their helmet against mine, the gasping panic when I hit the ground and the air was forced out of my lungs—this conversation felt just like that.

My palms tingled and I flexed my hands.

"What if—" I licked my lips, all the blood leaving my head. I took a deep breath and tried to get a handle on the feelings threatening to overwhelm me. "What if I didn't— what happens if I get injured?" I licked my dry lips again.

He waved those words away. "You'll be fine. Sure, you'll take some hits, but who hasn't? You get back up like you always have. You put in the work and you'll get a ring just like mine." He flashed the ring he seemed to wear almost every time he left the house.

"Did Mom like watching you play?"

He got as still as a statue. It was almost like he stopped breathing, the blood stopped pumping through his veins, and everything shut down.

We didn't talk about my mom—ever. Dad went radio silent any time I tried. I talked about her more with Gramps than I ever did with my father.

He cleared his throat. "No, your mom didn't like to watch me play."

"Why not?"

"She didn't like to see the hits, especially after the first time I tore my ACL."

"What did she do while you were playing?"

"She studied." His throat tightened. "She wanted to be a doctor. She was in medical school when she got pregnant with you."

"I never knew that."

"She decided not to keep going after you were born." Every word was tight like a rubber band being plucked.

A dream dead because of me.

"Never think for a second she regretted it." He dropped his hand on top of mine, a softness in his eyes unlike any I'd seen before. "Even if she'd known she'd only have two hundred and thirty-seven days with you after you were born, she'd have made the same choices. She loved every second she was with you and never doubted she'd made the right choice for herself."

It got hard to breathe, and a prickling sensation danced just under my eyes. I blinked to keep the welling emotions at bay. "What else did she like doing?"

I had my opening and wasn't going to let it pass by. There were no pictures of my mom up in the house. Sometimes it seemed like my dad wanted to wipe her away completely. His track record with women wasn't exactly stellar. The only saving grace was that he hadn't paraded them through the house as I was growing up, but other than that it had just been him, me, and Gramps.

"She liked to cook, was always over at Tavola helping Gramps. She was on her way back from there when it happened." His lips thinned into a line and the shutters were closed again. "Enough of that. Let's get back to work." He shook his head like that was enough to wash away the past, but it was more than he'd ever said about her before. Maybe there was a glimmer of hope there.

Leaving the house, it was like a little piece of my mom came with me, a piece of her I'd never known before: she'd liked being in the kitchen with Gramps just like I did. I'd look around the kitchen next time I was there and imagine her in front of the ovens or dragging something out of the fridge.

She'd changed her plans and decided not to become a doctor. That had to have been a hard decision, one not made lightly. Dad said she'd never regretted it, and I sure hoped she hadn't. He'd never told me about where my mom's accident had taken place. It had happened when she was leaving the restaurant—was that why Dad hated it? It wasn't like Gramps or anyone else could've known, but maybe that was part of why he'd always resented it.

————

THE DRIVE BACK TO MY PLACE SEEMED TO STRETCH ON FOREVER. I wanted to tell Elle. Since I'd stepped outside of my house, that had been the main thought on my mind: to let her know everything my dad had told me. I wanted to share this part of my history I hadn't even known existed. Stopping by Tavola, I picked up some food and promised Gramps I'd be by later that week.

"Nix!" someone called out. Usually, I was happy to say hi to someone who recognized me, but not right now. Still, like my programming couldn't be overridden, I turned and smiled at the two women in matching pale blue tops with Greek letter patches sewn onto the front.

"Have you thought about what team you'd like to be drafted to?"

The same noncommittal answers I'd given a thousand times poured from my lips. They got closer with each passing second. Every time I tried to skirt around them, they blocked my path, working in unison like some sorority homing beacon.

A rumble and pop followed by squealing brakes filled me with equal parts dread and excitement. Elle's car was a calling card from three city blocks away, but me being Nix the football star never seemed to appeal to her. It was a scarlet letter that meant I had to work doubly hard to get her to let her guard down, and now that she had, I wasn't taking that lightly.

The metal-on-metal grating of her door closing rang out. I turned and she got closer, her eyes widening as she spotted me, a small smile just for me, but the shields were engaged when she glanced around me at the baby blue bloodhounds on my heels.

"What's up?" She shot an uneasy look over my shoulder. While the current situation was innocent, we hadn't exactly set any ground rules about what we were.

"I brought you some food." I held out the boxes to her.

"Aww, isn't that sweet? Is she your tutor or something? Cleaning lady maybe?"

I clenched my teeth so I didn't spit out the words on the tip of my tongue that were itching to be spewed at them. I settled for a glare, and both of their gazes dropped to the ground.

Elle's scowl over my shoulder nearly singed my eyebrows off. "Thanks for this. I'll need it while I'm up until who knows when. I've just been told they need me to run the blood drive tomorrow, so that's what I'll be doing tonight."

"I can help with the planning. What time is it at? Where is it?"

She dragged her hands over her face and squeezed the bridge of her nose. "It starts at noon in the old gym. It's a disaster, and I'm trying to clean it up. Thanks for the offer, but I'll figure it out. I'm sure you have better things to do." She tugged at the strap of her backpack and marched up the steps to her house.

"I'm serious. Let me help." I chased after her and stepped

over the shitty lifted floorboards of Elle's porch. LJ and I had come over to nail it down over the weekend, but already they were popping up again. If the whole thing didn't collapse before the end of the semester, it would be a miracle. "At least take the food."

She stood in the doorway, her gaze drifting over my shoulder. "I don't want to interrupt your fan club meeting. They might like it better."

My lips thinned. "I didn't get it for them. I got it for you. It's from my grandfather's restaurant. He asked me to bring you by sometime. I know you're busy, but I'd like you to meet him."

Her gaze softened and she stared down at my full hands. "I'd like that, and thank you for the food." She reached for the boxes.

I held on to them and shifted my hands so they covered hers. "I can help you get things ready."

"I'm not—I've got it." On her tiptoes, she peered over my shoulder. "They're still here."

As I stepped in closer, the box creaked between us. "They can stand out there for the next year for all I care. Let me help you." I ran kisses along her jaw, featherlight against her skin. She tasted sweet against my lips.

Her eyes fluttered closed. "If you come in here, we both know I'll get nothing done." She licked her lips. "It'll start with looks over books, then touches, and before we know it, I'll be under you for the rest of the night."

"You say that like it's a bad thing." I stepped closer, lowering my lips to hers.

"They'd probably storm my house if I let you in before they get their autograph or picture, or send in rescuers because they'd figure I was holding you against your will." Her lips turned up and mischief glinted in her eyes. "I've got it, but thanks for the offer. I mean it, and thank you for the food." She jiggled the box, using it to put some space between us.

"Tomorrow—I'll be there."

Her lips parted and I took the opening, tugging away her to-go box shield. I slipped my other hand behind her against the small of her back and pulled her against me, delving deep into her mouth.

There were sharp gasps from the sidewalk. *Good.* I wanted them to see this and know there was no way in hell they were getting anything from me.

Elle's body relaxed into my hold, and my hungry caress was met with her eager, soft touch. She tasted like every dessert I'd been denied throughout every season of football I'd played.

She broke away and kept her gaze trained on the center of my chest.

"Are you sure you don't want some help?"

Her hand settled over my heart and she peered up at me. "After that?" The corner of her mouth quirked up. "I have no doubt I'd get absolutely nothing done if you did."

"Not nothing." I braced my hand on the doorway and leaned in closer.

"Oh no you don't. Get back to your fan club." She lifted her chin toward the sidewalk, but there wasn't any anger in her eyes this time. "And I'll get to work."

"See you tomorrow." I stepped back, keeping my gaze trained on her before turning and jogging down the steps.

"You don't have to come," she called out after me.

I turned and looked over my shoulder. "I know."

She smiled and closed the door.

"Nix, you're going to be at the blood drive?"

I swung around, having totally forgotten about the sidewalk stalkers. "Yeah, I am. You two should come." Elle would get as many donations as she needed and wouldn't have to worry about getting the word out. "Actually, tell all your friends—blood drive tomorrow, and I'll be there."

"We'll tell everyone," they shouted after me.

Maybe so many donors would show up, Elle would get to leave early for a change. There's no such thing as too many people at an event like this, right?

CHAPTER 24
ELLE

"This is an unmitigated freaking disaster." I stared at the completely overrun basketball court. We'd only scheduled for a couple dozen beds, and there were over three hundred people swarming all over the place. People hadn't read any of the requirements for donating, so the intake volunteers were questioning ten people for every one that was actually eligible.

"What the hell is going on?" One of the harried volunteers had sweat rolling down his face. He'd had to run out to buy more water and juice for the people who had been able to donate after the horde took over the after-donation table.

"I have no idea." I tried to close my ears to the babbling around me, but one conversation in particular got through.

"Where's Nix?"

"I don't know. Is the rest of the team coming?"

"I hope Reece shows up. God, he's hot."

"He's got a girlfriend now."

"How is that even possible?"

I was 3.8 seconds from losing my shit. "Where did all these people come from?"

Someone set up a wireless speaker, and music blared from

the other end of the space. I stomped over to that side, and behind me, everyone started cheering.

Turning, I stared at Nix striding onto the lacquered wood court, and I slowly pieced together how this day had gone completely to shit.

"He's here—break out the kegs," someone shouted from one of the side doors they'd propped open, letting out the air conditioning, which we needed to keep the people who'd just donated blood from passing out.

Nix was glad-handing with people like he was running for office. The music was cranked up, and the pungent smell of beer overwhelmed the latex and medical-grade plastic that mingled with the lingering sweat in the gym.

My blood pounded in my veins. I couldn't move a muscle because that would mean causing someone bodily harm, one person in particular. All the freaking doubts I'd had, all the reservations were thrust straight in my face as he waved to me from behind his wall of hangers-on and adoring fans.

Beside me, a volunteer sighed. "Elle, this really isn't conducive to the work we need to be doing. One of the techs was just sprayed with beer."

I was so damn exhausted, blinking back the angry tears I flat-out refused to let spill. "This wasn't what I had planned for today. I have no idea what happened." I had one now, though, as all the bitching and moaning from people before his arrival filled in the gaps.

"We have to wrap up early. It's not safe to have people bounding all over the place."

Someone raced down the side of the court and threw a basketball into the hoop as it was lowered from the ceiling.

"I completely understand, and I'm sorry for this. Could we get you to come back? I can make sure nothing like this ever happens again." Burying Nix under this gym would probably solve the problem.

"We're slammed at the end of the school year, so I'm not sure."

"I understand. Thanks anyway, and I hope you were able to get some good donations in."

"Only about a third of what we normally do, but every little bit helps, right?" Her helpless shrug matched the hold I was trying to get on myself. This event had been thrust onto my lap at the last minute, but it would've been a great last-minute addition to my resume for the Huffington Award. Instead, it had caused me additional stress as well as wasting the organization's time, potentially even costing lives if there was a blood shortage in a crisis.

"Hey, there you are." Nix jogged over to me in his Trojans t-shirt and jeans. Girls all around the gym craned their necks, checking him out.

I balled up my fists at my sides upon hearing the light, carefree tone of his voice.

"Great turnout, huh?" He held out his arms like he was freaking Caesar surveying the construction of the aqueducts.

"Did you do this?" I bit out through gritted teeth. My attempt at keeping my voice even went up in flames like whatever had been brewing between us.

His smile faltered. "I didn't think this many people would show up, but yeah. Isn't that what you needed? More bodies? Look at how many people are here." He dropped his hands to my shoulders and turned me around. Oh, I saw the fruits of his efforts all right: people knocking over tables and chairs, the blood drive techs packing up their equipment, red plastic cups in half the hands of the people there. Who knew if they were even twenty-one.

I whipped around. Nix took a step back, his eyes wide. "I can see just fine. I see this whole day down the freaking drain. Maybe I should've just handed over the planning to you, then I could've finished the paper I needed to write last night. Instead, I get a front-row seat to another FU party."

"You said you were worried about turnout." He held his hands up, palms out, but that gesture of surrender just pissed me off even more. It was the same way he always said the parties appeared in their house like there was nothing they might have done to encourage it.

"I didn't sleep last night. I put off two papers that are due tomorrow to get everything ready here."

"And I offered to help."

"This is what I get when you help." My hand swept out toward the people who seemed to have nothing better to do than hang out and fuck around. Angry tears burned in my eyes, and that pissed me off even more. I refused to cry in front of anyone. I took a shuddering breath and glared at him. The tired, can-barely-keep-my-eyes-open feeling amplified my anger, tingeing it with deliriousness. My tank was on E, and I couldn't deal with this right now.

"You turned the blood drive into one of your goddamn parties, Nix. They can't even work under these conditions." My finger shot out, pointing at the volunteers taking down the privacy screens they'd had up for people donating, the beds that were already empty and being taken down. "They couldn't even get the pitiful amounts of blood they usually get because of all the assholes you apparently invited to hang out, gawking and waiting for your arrival." The tears stung my eyes, but I slammed my lips shut and breathed through my nose. "You think an appearance by you is all this thing needed to be better? It would've been better if you'd never come at all. Do you understand how serious this is? The blood is needed—we're literally talking life or death, here. This might cost people their lives, and I was the one in charge of the drive. Now, excuse me, I've got to help them get packed up and maybe, just maybe, I can salvage another spot for them before the end of the year."

"Let me help."

He reached out from me, but I jerked my arms back out of

reach. "*No*. You've done enough. If you want to help, keep your fan club out of our way."

He stared after me from the other side of the gym with a stunned expression on his face, but that didn't last long. Soon the party moved around him, swallowing him in a crowd of adoring fans.

Good. Let them stay over there, far, far away from me.

———

IT HAD BEEN ALMOST THREE DAYS SINCE THE BLOOD DRIVE, AND I swore, if I could've spit nails, Nix would have been pinned to the nearest wall. I'd cut back on my volunteer hours, because what good was winning the Huffington Award if I didn't actually graduate? Deadlines breathed down my neck like a horny freshman standing outside the girls' locker room.

Even worse, I hadn't heard from Nix—not that I wanted to, but I figured he would've at least sent a text or something to apologize for the fiasco he'd caused. But no, nothing. This time it was all freaking him. At the end of the whole thing, someone had lobbed a basketball halfway across the court and nearly taken out the refrigeration unit holding the blood.

I hadn't expected radio silence from Nix, but maybe it was for the best. We'd had a flirtation, a fling. It was hot, toe-curling sex, quiet nights looking at one another over our piles of books, but better to not have things go any further when I couldn't trust my feelings when it came to him. He'd made me all lightheaded and irrational. That wasn't what I needed.

Huffington Award. Graduate. Stipend. Peace Corps? That last one was a nebulous cloud hanging over the end of the year. Then what? I'd focused on this next milestone for so long, but the yawning expanse of after college terrified me. At least the stipend would give me some time to figure it all out.

"I thought you could use some study fuel." A plate of

chocolate chunk brownies slid into view, scraping across the wood grain of my desk.

"You don't have to keep feeding me, you know."

"I know." Jules flopped down on my bed and propped herself up on her arms.

"Something on your mind?" I picked out the chocolate chunks.

Her mouth opened and closed. She scrunched her lips up to one side. "No. Did you want to go out to dinner?"

"I can't. I've got a shift at Uncommon Grounds, but we can use my employee discount to snag some of the quiche before I start."

She clenched her fist and shoved it down. "Yes, and I can grab a salad from Archie's." She nudged her glasses up with her knuckle. "Let me know when you're ready to go."

I licked the chocolate off my fingers and checked the time. "Now?"

"Let me grab my wallet." She grabbed the edge of the doorway and swung back in. "You never said how the blood drive went—success?"

My eyes narrowed, and I may have growled.

"That good, huh?" She laughed.

We made it to Uncommon Grounds and I ordered our food—two quiches and a chicken wrap—then grabbed us a table. Jules came back with the food she'd ordered: a salad with dressing on the side and a water.

I lifted an eyebrow. "Way to make me feel like a glutton."

She waved off my look. "I'm eating quiche, too, unless you didn't order one for me." She eyed the counter behind me. "Plus, I had French toast this morning, and there are still brownies at home."

Someone behind the counter called out my name, and I picked up our food.

"Do you think Zoe will come back?" Jules split her quiche down the center, letting the steam escape.

"How do we know she hasn't been coming back? Maybe she's got an invisibility cloak." I sipped on my drink.

"It's going to suck being in the house all alone next year."

"You won't be alone. You can get new roommates. Hell, rent out Zoe's room and pocket the cash. It's not like she'll even know."

"I'm serious. Maybe I'll move into a single on campus or something."

"And leave behind the luxury of our little shack? What about baking?"

"Maybe I don't need to bake as much."

"Your head would explode if you couldn't."

Her frown deepened and she nodded.

"Are you going to tell me what the deal is or do I have to torture it out of you? I can do things with kitchen utensils that would make anyone break. Ever seen a spatula snapped in half?"

"You're a monster. You know that?" Her gaze darted to the table.

"Spill."

She licked her lips and peeked around the edge of the booth. "The notes." Swirling ice in her glass was apparently now a new wonder of the modern world. "Berk wants to meet me."

"What's the problem?"

Her eyes widened and she sat back in her seat before hunching over and hissing across the table. "He's freaking perfect, that's what's the problem."

"No one's perfect."

"He's damn near close. The notes have changed. It's not all Dear Penthouse letters like you think it is. He's different than I thought he'd be."

"Different how?" I leaned in.

"Just different. I didn't think he'd care after the first

couple, but then we started talking more, about ourselves." She picked at the label on her water bottle.

"Again, what's the problem?"

"His cock cleavage could sink a thousand ships."

I choked on my soda. "Cock cleavage?"

"That V-thing only super-hot guys get. It's like a giant arrow pointing toward their junk like, *You're in for a treat, ladies.*"

"Wow, I never knew that had a name."

"I mean, I don't think it's the technical medical name for it or anything."

I tilted my head. "You don't say."

She chucked a cube of ice at me. "Anyway, he wants to meet, but I'm not okay with that."

"Then don't meet with him." I shrugged.

"But I really want to."

"You just said you weren't okay with it."

"I'm not, but I want to."

My quiche was no longer at mouth-melting levels.

Jules scooted her salad closer to her and dove in with gusto.

"Is this a booty-call type of situation? I've seen some of your scribbles on those notes."

"It started that way, all hot and heavy, but somehow other things have been slipping in. In the last letter, there was only one mention of my pussy."

And there went the chicken down my windpipe. Dropping my food, I bent over, trying to keep myself from asphyxiating on chicken and cheese.

Wheezing, I choked out. "What a romantic?"

"He really is." She got a dreamy look in her eyes. "Way more than I expected."

"I don't suppose you're going to maybe tell him who you are any time soon?"

Her eyes got wide like I'd asked to see naked pictures of her.

There was a commotion toward the entrance of Uncommon Grounds. I peered around the edge of our booth and scowled. Fucking Trojans, always making a mess wherever they went.

CHAPTER 25
NIX

Who doesn't love a steaming cup of coffee as a nice refresher after a workout? Earlier, I'd wormed out of someone behind the counter that Elle had a shift tonight. I'd thought the place would be quiet, but it was jam-packed. I scanned the coffee shop.

Elle's faded pink hair disappeared from view the second our gazes collided.

I headed straight for the table, not deterred by any of the waves from other people in the coffee shop.

"Hey, Nix." Jules peered over the top of her cup with both hands wrapped around it.

Elle shot her a look meant for a traitor.

"Elle…" She was beautiful as always, and the speeches I'd worked on flew out of my head like a fumbled ball. I hadn't wanted to talk to her until I'd fixed everything.

She brushed right past me and walked behind the counter.

"Go ahead." Jules nudged me with her elbow and gave my arm a reassuring squeeze before walking off.

"Can I talk to you?"

"No." She tied an apron around her waist. "Can I help whoever's next?"

Someone walked up behind me. I turned around. "What did you want? I'll pay."

The girl's eyed widened and her gaze bounced from me to Elle. "Double mocha iced coffee. Extra whipped cream."

Turning back around, I gave Elle the order.

She didn't move. Her arms were crossed over her chest like she'd had a run-in with Medusa.

"I didn't think about the logistics of the whole blood drive thing and how a whole lot of uninvited people could screw that up. I—"

She grabbed a cup and made the drink with a ruthless efficiency and attention to detail.

Leaning over the counter, she handed the cup around me to the girl standing beside me, staring at our little display like it was her new favorite show.

"I wanted to make it up to you."

"Next." Elle looked right through me.

Waving the next person forward, I got their order. "Meghan, here, will take a double espresso."

"Coming right up." If she wasn't careful, she'd crack a tooth.

"Elle…" I covered her hand with mine, and she snatched it back.

"No, Nix. No. You can't just keep barging into my life."

"I fucked up. I was only trying to help, but I did it the wrong way. I know that now, but I want to make it up to you and get even more blood donations than you'd have ever gotten before. Just let me try."

The look of skepticism was palpable. Her mouth opened and closed. "How?" There was a wariness to her that I hated seeing.

"With another blood drive."

"It's not even going to be worth it. For the numbers we pull in, I'm sure they're not going to give us another slot before everyone leaves for the summer."

"What if it was? What if there were over three hundred people who could give? And they were all cleared ahead of time and met all the requirements?"

Her eyebrows dipped in confusion.

"After that day, I went and checked on all the things people need to do before they can donate, and I asked my coach if we could do it at the stadium with all the players there. I got the yes from everyone on the team and the facilities crew, and we're at your disposal. You have the full run of the facility and any of the concessions to have enough food for the volunteers and people giving blood."

"We could call it Give on the Gridiron." Her eyes lit up.

"The entire FU Trojans machine is behind you, whatever you need. I know this is all my fault. I'm used to—well, I'm used to just showing up to things like that. My dad's always got me doing that kind of stuff, and I've never had to think about the logistics. I know how important this is to you and how much work you put into everything, and I don't want people to have to be hurt because of my mistake."

"Um, excuse me." There was a tap on my back. "Can I have my coffee?"

"Sorry, let me make that." Elle made the drink in record time and handed it back to the girl standing beside me with her gaze bouncing between me and Elle.

I ordered three more drinks for other people before the line died down.

"Why didn't you call or text?" Elle wiped down the counter.

"Words weren't enough. I didn't want to tell you I was sorry—I wanted to *show* you I was sorry. It took me some time to get them to agree to let me use the field and make sure I could do this for you. That's why I waited. The final okay came down from the facilities guys earlier today and I knocked on your door before coming here to tell you, but you weren't home."

"Are you serious about all this?" She peered up at me with an uncertainty in her eyes that stabbed me straight through the heart. Her trust was hard won, and I wasn't going to mess it up again.

"I'm a constant fuckup around you, something about always trying to impress you and failing miserably."

"You're trying to impress me?" She stood up straight with a question in her eyes.

"Damn, it's even worse than I thought if you can't even tell."

"Did you order already?" someone asked behind me.

"I'll let you get back to work. Come to the stadium tomorrow at seven and we can go over everything you'll need. We can make this the best event in FU history."

"In the morning?"

"Bright and early." I backed away from counter and ducked out before she could tell me no. I headed back to the house, determined to show her how much this meant to me, how much *she* meant to me.

CHAPTER 26
ELLE

The lights on the field flooded the space as the blood drive stretched into the third hour. Music played on the far end of the end zone where there was a touchdown game set up. Nix hadn't been lying when he'd said the whole team was at my disposal. Berk, LJ, Reece, and the rest of the players had gone door to door in a lot of the dorms and off-campus housing to find volunteers.

Sponsors came out of the woodwork in the few days following the announcement. There was food, drinks, prizes, t-shirts, and more. It was part carnival, part good deed, and everyone was having so much fun. The might of the FU machine behind anything changed the scale in a huge way.

What other projects could benefit from this level of visibility?

"Holy shit, this is the coolest event you've ever put together." Jules stared up at the stadium lights and pushed her glasses up her nose.

"It's the first time I've had a literal stadium of people ready to do my bidding."

"I take it this means Nix is out of the doghouse." The corner of her mouth lifted.

"On his way there."

Berk bounded up beside me. "Elle, Nix said to check with you on where we should put these t-shirts."

Jules' eyes bulged and she froze like we wouldn't be able to see her anymore if she didn't move.

"They can go by the far exit so people can pick them up on the way out."

Berk shouted across the field to the guys holding the massive boxes of folded shirts.

"You remember my roommate, Jules, the baker."

Berk's eyes widened and he stepped closer to her. "I could eat your treats any day of the week."

"You should probably buy me dinner first." A stuttering laugh broke free from her mouth and scarlet blush traced a trail up her neck.

"If you keep baking like that, I'll keep you as fed as you need—truckloads' worth, if need be."

Jules' smile died a lopsided death and she crossed her arms over her chest. "Thanks."

"It was nice meeting you." He held out his hand, and Jules offered hers like he was a bear looking for a meal. Berk rushed back across the field to grab a box of shirts that had fallen and busted open.

"Fucking truckloads." Jules shook her head and looked after him.

"He didn't mean anything by it. Seriously."

"Spare me, Elle."

"Go talk to him. Tell him about the letters."

"After that? Are you serious? Why not just tie myself to the field goal naked and give everyone a chance to experience my embarrassment?"

"If you don't tell him, you'll never know."

"I've never had my heart carved out of my chest with a rusty spoon, but I'm pretty sure it would suck. My timeslot to donate blood is about to start. I'll see you later." Jules hustled to the intake area.

"Elle." The coordinator strode across the field toward me.

"Are things going okay? I know it's a bit of madness, but I thought with things cordoned off, it would keep that away from the donors."

"This is the most amazing drive we've ever run. We've never had turnout like this from a school of this size. It might actually be the biggest single day donation we've ever had. I can't thank you enough. Going into summer once all the schools are finished, it's rough for us, but this will do so much good." She pulled me in for a huge, bone-creaking hug.

"It was a group effort. Nix Russo is the one who got everyone ready to work. So many people put in the hours to make this happen."

"And we are so grateful. I need to get back to my station, but I wanted to say thank you. Tell Phoenix I said thank you as well." She waved and headed back to the donation area.

"I will."

People walked around the stadium with their *Give on the Gridiron* t-shirts, eating popcorn and hot dogs. Laughter and music surrounded me. It was a sea of people who'd never have found this without the work Nix had put in. The need to see him overwhelmed me.

Rushing from the field, I asked everyone I passed if they'd seen him. LJ looked up from his face-painting and pointed in the direction of one of the tunnels.

Nix came out of one of the doors with a couple other guys, all balancing large boxes. "These are the stress ball footballs. They ran out over in the donor area, so take them there," he directed the others before spotting me. "Go ahead guys, I'll catch up." He turned to me. "Is everything okay?"

The words stalled in my throat. Leaning over the box between us, I reached up with both hands and cradled his face, attacking his lips like I'd wanted to since the last time I touched them.

His box hit the floor with a thud and he wrapped his arms

around me, matching my hungry kisses with starved ones of his own. Fumbling behind him, he shifted us into the open doorway and into the darkened room.

"I've missed this," he whispered against my lips.

"Me too."

His fingers tightened around the hair at the base of my neck. Tilting my head to the side, he ran his lips over my skin, sending shivers down my spine.

One second we were standing in the middle of the pitch-black room and the next the whole world tilted. I landed against Nix's solid chest.

"Are you okay?" I tried to push myself up.

He tightened his hold around me. "The stress balls, sweatpants, and t-shirts cushioned my fall."

"Thank you for today." I peppered his jaw with kisses.

"Thank you for letting me do this for you." The outline of his erection pressed against the front of my mound. *Just one inch higher…*

He wrapped his hands around my waist and lifted me, perfecting the angle.

I shuddered and ground my hips against him. Someone walked by the door, but we didn't stop—couldn't stop.

His hands cupped my ass, dragging me harder against him. The texture of his jeans added extra sensation against my clit. I was on fire for him through two layers of clothes.

My short gasps and his low groans were the only sounds in the room other than the fabric friction.

"We should get back out there." I raked my teeth along the side of his neck.

"You're probably right." His hips shot up and I wanted to scream in frustration that he wasn't inside me, but I didn't want to break from the thrumming pleasure rushing all over my body.

"In a second."

"In a minute." His tongue danced with mine in time to the

rhythm of our hips. Laughter rang out in the hallway behind the door, but I couldn't stop. If someone came in, there wasn't anything that would stop me from dry-humping Nix into next week.

He slipped a hand under the waistband of my pants and palmed my ass, squeezing me even tighter against him, and that was all I needed. The urgent throb met a blinding spark of release.

Nix groaned under me and ran his hand up my back, hugging me to his chest. Our panting breaths were punctuated by voices from the other side of the door.

Resting his forehead against mine, he kissed me, his lips tickling mine. "I think I'm going to have to borrow a pair of these sweatpants."

CHAPTER 27
ELLE

Did I walk out of a supply closet looking like I'd had my world rocked like a high school student hiding in their parents' basement? Yes, yes, I did.

Finger-combing my hair, I laughed as Nix followed me out in gray sweatpants with *Fulton U* printed down the side.

It wasn't fair how much sexier he looked in those damn pants. They hung low on his trim hips, and it took all my willpower not to tug them down and push him back into the closet.

"You keep looking at me like that and I'll have to tape my dick down with athletic tape."

"I didn't do anything." My innocent look wasn't working on him.

"Only a few more hours until this is finished and then we get to properly make up." He picked up the previously abandoned box of stress balls and we walked back out to the field.

A reporter came by, took our pictures, and did a short interview about the blood drive and the possibility of it continuing in the future, suggesting maybe I could continue organizing the event in the coming years.

Tired but more energetic than I'd ever been after something like this, I sighed when we finally got back to our street. There was a silent promise in our quick, quiet steps in the Brothel, like one word spoken might screw things up and invite interruptions neither of us were ready to tolerate right now.

With my hand in his, we took the stairs two at a time, and Nix closed his bedroom door.

My hands flew straight for his waistband and his to the sides of my face, cradling my cheeks and skimming his thumbs along my jaw. "Do you think today went okay?"

"More than okay. You did good. Scratch that—you did freaking stellar." I snaked my hands under his shirt and up his back before pulling his shirt up over his head. The combination of that sleepy bedhead look, bare chest, and gray sweatpants was a walking wet dream come to life.

"I'm glad you liked it."

I wrapped my arms around him and rested my cheek against his chest. His heartbeat drummed against the side of my face. "It was better than I ever could've imagined. Thank you for all you did and getting everyone on board. Thank you for being someone I can count on."

He hugged me tighter and skimmed his hand up and down my back, the other cupping the back of my head.

Gently leaning me back, he stared into my eyes. "I always want to be that for you. You can count on me."

I nodded. The mood in the room shifted from hungry to something else. Another type of warmth crept over me, and I stood there, staring into his eyes, wanting so much for this moment to never pass, for things to always feel this good, to always be in his arms.

The tightness in my chest squeezed at my heart, and I broke the connection between us. I wanted it so much. I wanted him so much, wanted to be everything I had sworn I would never get to experience, everything I'd been sure no one would ever want to experience with me. Squeezing my eyes, I knew I needed to stop myself from heading down a rabbit hole with no end in sight. He said that now, but what happened when he left? What happened when the school year ended?

"Do they have someone who does this type of stuff for the team?"

"Community events type stuff?" Nix toyed with the hair at the base of my neck, wrapping it around his finger. "I don't know. I could ask. It seems like it would be a good way to capitalize on the team's popularity."

"Hmm." I took his hand and led him toward the bed. Why was the physical so much easier?

He sat down and corralled me between his legs, lifting my shirt and peppering my stomach and chest with kisses.

The frantic sex I'd envisioned when we left the supply closet gave way to something different in his bed, slow and languid with a connection that made it hard to breathe. Nix settled above me with deep, powerful thrusts, grinding at the end of each to tease my clit and draw out a seemingly unending orgasm. I was still tightly wrapped up in him, his name an uncresting wave that built and built until I could barely breathe.

With sweat dotting my skin, I stared up at the ceiling, waiting for the feeling to return to my body.

"Elle, I l—" He swallowed his words. His body was rigid against my back. "Will you to come to dinner with me?"

I turned to him and rested my head on his chest, letting out a little laugh. "You have to ask? Of course I will."

"Good."

Running my fingers along his stomach, I drifted off to sleep feeling more content than I had in a long time.

———

"FINALLY. I WAS BEGINNING TO WONDER IF YOU'D BEEN LYING TO me all this time." A tall man whose quick movements spoke of a man much younger than the wrinkles on his skin indicated came up to Nix and hugged him before turning his open arms toward me.

"Gramps, this is Elle." Nix grinned super wide as his grandfather cupped both my shoulders.

"Did he actually bring you the meal I sent with him?"

I looked to Nix and smiled. "He did, but I think there might have been a few bites missing."

"Hey, I was good. I didn't touch it."

His grandfather tsked and shook his head. "Because of this, I think he should make the food this evening."

My eyebrows shot up. "You cook?"

"I dabble." Nix tapped the bag on his arm.

"Dabble—*psh*. After all I've taught you, you'd better be better than that. Tonight, it's time for you to surprise us. You know what's in the back. I'll get your friend a drink and then we'll be there."

Nix headed into the kitchen.

"Thank you for having me here, Mr. Russo."

He scoffed. "Call me Patrick. Red or white?"

"White. Thank you, Patrick."

He poured me a healthy glass and handed it over. "If he hasn't cooked for you, you're in for a treat with Phoenix in the kitchen."

"I'd imagine he wasn't able to come by often during the season."

"No, but he's been back more often lately. It's nice to have him here. He always loved the kitchen." His grandfather's pride shined brightly in his voice.

We went into the kitchen and Nix sliced some meat, sprinkling seasoning on it. Patrick pulled out a stool for me, and I hopped up on it.

"I'll leave you two. I'm going to help with the service. Phoenix, don't eat my portion."

"If you're not back here in an hour, old man, maybe I will."

"I can help." I set down my glass of wine.

"You're a guest—no helping. See that she stays put."

Nix saluted with the knife in his hand and nudged my wine toward me.

"This is how you were so good with the vegetables at Grace's."

"A few years of chopping duty in here"—he motioned to the stainless steel countertops, orderly prep stations, and people bustling around—"will do that to you."

"What are you making?" I wrapped my fingers around the front edge of the stool between my legs and shook my shoulders in anticipation.

"It's a surprise."

"Just like you." I took a sip of my wine.

"You've been full of your own surprises too."

"But none as delicious as this." I leaned over the seasoned vegetable mixture and inhaled.

His eyes raked over me. "I wouldn't say that."

The flush that had nothing to do with the steaming kitchen was back. I bit my bottom lip and took another sip of my wine, keeping my eyes off him. Not a great way to make a first impression, jumping his bones in his grandfather's restaurant.

Nix working in this environment was a thing of beauty. I'd never seen him play, but if he was half as fluid on the field as he was in the kitchen, it was no wonder he was set to be a number-one draft pick.

"Can I come watch you play next season?"

His chopping faltered and he nearly took the tip of a finger off.

"Or not. Don't feel like you have to invite me or anything.

I know…" My words died in my throat, and all the promises he'd made me felt like a hollow pit in my stomach. Maybe he didn't want me to come see him when he was playing. Maybe he'd be laughing it up in a hotel room crawling with football groupies by the time training camp was over. A panicked breath caught in my throat.

"Elle." He stepped in front of me with his hand on my neck and his thumb running along the side of my face in what I'd discovered was his favorite 'I need your attention' move. "Wherever I am next year…" He traced his thumb along my bottom lip, breaking all kinds of kitchen sanitation rules. "I want to see you as much as I can. I know you don't know where you're going to be either, but we'll make it work." His soft eyes stared into mine with so much sincerity it made my chest hurt. That just-tasted-wasabi feeling shot through my nose, and I tugged my chin away from his hold to get a grip on myself.

"We can work it out." I nodded, keeping my gaze trained on my legs.

"We can do more than that." He planted a kiss on the top of my head, and I squeezed my eyes shut.

Don't you dare lose it, Elle. Fortifying myself with another gulp of wine, I slapped on a bright smile and went back to Nix-watching.

A little while later, he presented a plate of baked shrimp scampi, wiping the edge of the plate with a kitchen towel. A beautiful mix of colors wove themselves together on the plate that smelled even better than it looked.

My gaze shot from him to the juicy meat and perfect vegetables. "You're a freaking magician."

He laughed and tossed the towel over his shoulder. "We reserve that for the bakers. That's true magic. Jules could command an army with the stuff she makes." He leaned in close and glanced over his shoulder. "Don't tell anyone, but her stuff is five times better than anyone's here." He held out a fork to me.

"She'd be happy to hear it." I froze mid-bite. "Do you know if Berk is dating anyone?"

Nix's head shot back and his eyebrows dipped. "Not that I know of. I mean, there was this one girl who came by pretty regularly, but I haven't seen her in a while. He's been trading notes with someone recently, and that seems to be occupying a lot of his time. Why?"

Jules cutting me off from all edge brownies and baking me into a pie flashed through my mind. "No reason. It seems like you guys have a lot of visitors."

"More like nosey neighbors. Reece is all loved up with Seph, LJ and Marisa are constantly bickering, and Berk's doing his best hermit impersonation, so the Brothel madness has died down."

I took a bite, and the meat melted on my tongue. The flavors combined together in my mouth into heavenly bite after heavenly bite. I may have grabbed hold of the counter at one point so I didn't fall off the chair.

With every bit of strength I had, I kept myself from licking the plate clean, savoring each morsel.

"What do you think?"

"Not too bad." I shrugged my shoulders.

"Then you won't mind if I just clear this away for you..." He grabbed the edge of my plate, and I whacked him with my fork.

"Back off."

He grinned and slowly slid it across the counter as I scooped up the last bites and shoveled them into my mouth as quickly as possible.

"Not too bad, huh?"

"I was hungry." I held up my hand over my completely stuffed mouth.

"I'm glad you liked it." He took our plates to the stack of others being washed.

"Usually he eats all the food himself." His grandfather chuckled and brought me another glass of wine.

"Sorry we ate without you."

He waved his hand. "Don't worry. He set some aside for me. Once the floor gets busy, there's never any time to sit down, but it always feels good to see how happy it all makes the diners. He hasn't cooked like this in a long time." Pride filled his voice.

"Hey, Gramps, taking a break?"

Patrick scoffed. "Never. The meal was wonderful. You haven't lost your touch."

Nix beamed with a smile so wide it could be seen from space.

"It's good to have you here. You've got to come as much as you can before the draft. Who knows where you might end up."

"I'll always end up back here as long as you have a place for me."

"Always, Phoenix." He hugged Nix and clapped him on the back. "Now what was this I heard about desserts even better than mine here at the restaurant?" His gaze swung to mine and my eyes widened.

CHAPTER 28
NIX

"Pass the syrup," Berk shouted, nearly climbing on top of the table and knocking his backpack off the back of his chair.

"Calm down! It's coming." I waved my hands toward him, giving the people around the Tavola dining room a placating smile. Even with the brunch crowd packed in, Berk's voice carried.

Rubbing his hands together, Berk licked his lips. "An IV drip of this stuff wouldn't be enough for me."

"Would you like a side of diabetes with your breakfast?" LJ passed the small pitcher of syrup to Berk.

He drenched his pancakes, his sweet tooth in overload.

"Shouldn't we have waited for the others?" Seph toyed with the edge of her napkin.

Reece wrapped his arm around her shoulder. "Remember those teeth marks in the back of my hand when I tried to take a cookie from the Tupperware? Getting between Berk and a mountain of sugar is hazardous to everyone's health."

"There's going to be none left for anyone else." Seph touched the handle of the syrup container. Berk growled and dragged it away while keeping his eyes locked on her, ready to fend off any attempt to remove it from his hold.

"Jeez, sorry. They're your arteries, I guess." Seph unrolled her napkin and settled it on her lap, unlike the other heathens at the table.

The front door opened, and Elle's pink streak broke through the people near the entrance waiting to be seated.

She walked over and I pulled her in, kissing her, ignoring the whistles from the guys.

"Looks like Nix is getting his sugar already." LJ laughed.

"What are you, eighty?" Berk shook his head.

Settling my hand on the small of her back, I guided her toward the table. "The jackass crew couldn't wait and we ordered already."

A small smile like she was only smiling for me broke out across her lips. "Don't worry about it. Jules was stress baking and needed a muffin taste tester this morning, so I'm not super hungry."

"It's Jules, queen of the sugar rush," Berk called out, dragging a chair over beside him at the table. "There's an open seat here, and tell me what I need to do to get another batch of those cinnamon rolls." He pressed his palms together.

She paused and grasped her purse tightly like she was afraid she might be mugged at any second.

"I swear I don't bite—at least not without consent." He chomped his teeth. "Seriously, I'll do anything for those rolls. Do I need to get down on my knees and beg?"

Jules slid into the chair beside him, holding herself tight like a snapping dog was perched beside her. "Anything, huh?" She relaxed a little and set her bag down on the table. "How do you feel about marriage?"

His eyes bulged and he choked on the pancake he'd shoved into his mouth. A muffled "*What?*" was nearly swallowed up by his coughing.

"It was a joke. Don't hurt yourself." Jules' deadpan voice was accompanied by an eye roll.

"She *will* need a date to her sister's wedding. Maybe it should be you."

Jules shot a glare at Elle then her gaze collided with mine and she softened her expression. "She's joking. I don't need a date." Those words were spoken through gritted teeth.

Elle swanned over to her and sat in the chair beside her. "I think it's a great idea, Jules. Seems like a fair trade to me."

"Sorry, everyone, Elle must've hit her head on the way over here. She's not thinking clearly. Can I see a menu?"

Even more food arrived at the table, and everyone dug in while discussing plans for the rest of the year and training camps for the Trojans in the pros or for their senior year.

"Not sure yet, but if I do go, I won't find out about my placement until the week after graduation." Elle's face pinched for a second before her gaze flitted to mine and relaxed a bit.

"Don't sound so thrilled about it. Elle's got it in her head that she has to join the Peace Corps if she doesn't win."

"But if you do win, you stay?"

"It's not a big deal. I haven't decided yet. If I win the Huffington Award, I'll be able to stay. I'll live off the stipend for a year and figure out what I'll do next. If I don't, that's sort of the only life plan I have in place."

I dipped my head and ran my hand over her leg. "But we wouldn't get to see each other." *Did that come out as a little needy?*

Her startled look told me it might have, along with at least a little whiny. "At this point, I'm a lock for the Huffington Award. I spoke to my assistant dean and he said my application was the most impressive he'd ever seen."

"I really hope you win it." The thought of going through everything that was coming my way without Elle by my side only made the unknown that much scarier.

"Me too." She ran her hand over mine.

I left my hand on her leg with a happiness glowing in my chest that eclipsed a comeback touchdown. The server dropped off a stack of blueberry waffles in front of me with a side of bacon.

"Those look so good. Maybe I should order some."

I cut off a piece and held it out to her on my fork. "Here, try some of mine and see if you like them."

A fork clattered to a plate.

"Thanks for the syrup shower," Jules grumbled.

"Did you just offer her food?" LJ leaned across Marisa.

"It's not that big a deal." I met his gaze, praying he'd drop it and chill the hell out.

"You nearly tackled me for the last butterscotch cookie the other day." Marisa's playful glare made LJ laugh.

"It was a choice between that and the soup you made."

All the guys at the table shuddered.

"Would you stop being such babies? It wasn't that bad."

"You've built up an immunity to your own cooking, Ris. It's like Rasputin ingesting poison daily for years."

"Did you just compare my cooking to poison?"

LJ shrugged. "I mean…we've actually sent it out to be tested for crimes against the Geneva Convention, so…" He held his hands out palm up.

"You never complained before." She smacked his shoulder.

"Probably because my vocal chords had been melted away."

Marisa speared a perfectly cut waffle square and lifted her fork, looking over at LJ. "It's really that bad?"

He rushed to tell her it wasn't, which meant we'd all have to try to choke down some Marisa concoction that weekend. I knew I'd better stock up on Pepto and Tums.

I held up my fork to Elle and she took a bite. Her lips wrapped around the fork. Hell, I'd have fed her the rest of my waffles bite by bite just to watch her pink lips get shiny with syrup, ready for me to kiss them clean.

"Those are delicious."

"Here, take the rest." People three tables over whipped around at my gunshot-loud voice. "I mean, if you want."

She laughed and scooted my plate closer. "How about we share them?"

Sitting next to Elle, sharing the best blueberry waffles covered in syrup and whipped cream, was the best breakfast I'd ever had. The words I'd wanted to say to her for so long burned a pattern on my heart, and they were in the shape of her name.

I rested my arm on the back of her chair and she leaned into me, laughing along with everyone else at the verbal sparring going on between LJ and Marisa. Seemed someone was a blanket hog, but neither was fessing up, even though Marisa's roommate had left our house a couple weeks ago and one of them could've slept on the couch or the floor. No one wanted to rock their friendship boat, which seemed to be teetering on the edge of something neither would walk away from unscathed. Either way, the longer they shared a bed, the bigger the explosion, no matter how many times they tried to pretend it was just like old times, but last I'd checked, neither of them were in middle school anymore.

Elle threw back her head, laughing. The smooth lines of her neck called out to my fingers. It was the same spot I'd run my lips along while tangled in the sheets with her and where I whispered her name each time I was pressed up against and inside her.

"Nix." She looked to me with a hungry amusement. "Berk's talking to you."

"What did you say?"

"I said, which one of us is going to get one of your friends-and-family season passes next year?"

"Who said you jokers were either?" I laughed.

Berk blinked and his head jerked back.

"Kidding. I'm kidding."

He let out a *pfft* and shook his shoulders. "Like I don't know that. Whatever, man. It doesn't matter." He stabbed at his plate.

"You can both have one. My dad won't need one—he'll weasel his way onto the sidelines and watch from there."

"At least you won't need a prostate exam with how far up your ass he is."

"His own personal meat puppet."

Reece's face scrunched up. "And now I'm done with my food. That's the most disgusting visual ever described."

"How's everyone doing?" Gramps stopped by the table.

I got up and hugged him. "What are you doing here? Weren't you in last night?"

He scoffed. "Who else will be here if I'm not?"

An abundance of servers, customers, and chefs bustled behind him. "You're a regular one-man show."

"I worry, that's all. Is everything here that you need?"

"Of course. Come and sit with us."

"No, I need to get back in there. Those Eggs Benedict aren't going to plate themselves."

"I'm sure they'd make it out to the table without your help."

He grinned. "I know, but that doesn't mean I don't enjoy it. Ah, is this the Jules you said makes desserts better than my own?"

Jules practically sprayed her mouthful of water all over Berk with wide eyes, shaking her head. "I'd never say that. No. Definitely not. No way."

"She's being modest. They're amazing. Everyone?" Elle held her hands out for consensus, and the table agreed.

"They're just being nice," Jules insisted.

Gramps grinned. "Well, we can always use someone good

around here. The world needs as much sweetness as we can get. The check is taken care of. You kids have a great day."

"Gramps, you didn't have to do that."

He shot me a 'no shit' look and disappeared back into the kitchen.

Everyone threw down some money for a tip and we headed outside.

"My dad's rung his bell, so I'm headed over there. Are you two headed back to your place?"

Jules stood beside the person-height glass window in front of Tavola, pretending not to see our PDA.

"I'll see you at my place later?" After however long my dad kept me in his office, I'd need an Elle injection to revive my day.

"My shift at Uncommon Grounds ends at seven."

"I'll be there then to pick you up and maybe score some stale donuts."

She motioned me closer, crooking her finger and glancing over her shoulder. "I'll save a couple for you under the counter."

"The perks of dating a barista." I kissed her quickly. She tasted like sweetness and coffee.

"More like a coffee burner." She grinned and linked arms with Jules. "See you tonight."

The drive to my dads was like it always was: way too long and over too quickly all at the same time.

As I walked into his office, Dad closed a drawer and rested his hands on the top of his desk. "Spending time at the restaurant again?"

I paused in front of it. "How'd you know?"

"You think after all this time I don't know the smells of my father's kitchen?"

"Would it hurt you to go by now and then?"

"More important things are going on. Speaking of which,

there's an award ceremony at your school happening next week. You've been invited and you need to be there."

He held out an envelope. The Fulton U Pre-Commencement Recognition Ceremony invitations raised blue embossing shone on the front of it.

"If I was invited, you'd think they'd send this to me."

"I was meeting with the university president and he passed it along."

"We only have a few weeks left until the end of the year. Stop meddling. Everything will be fine." I rested my hands on the back of a leather armchair.

He stood from his seat and rounded the large wooden desk. "It will be fine *because* I meddled."

"Ever think what you'd do with yourself if you didn't have my life to arrange anymore? No more behind-the-scenes talks and meetings?" I tugged my phone out of my pocket. The level of disappointment at seeing it was a phantom buzz and not a message from Elle, even though I'd just seen her, told me everything I needed to know about this thing with her, and it didn't scare me nearly as much as it should have.

Linking his hands behind his head, he sat in the other chair in front of his desk. "We won't have to find out, will we? Who's the girl?"

"What girl?"

"The one who's got you checking your phone like an eager puppy. She's distracting you."

"I'm not distracted."

"Haven't I told you how important it is to be careful with women right now?"

"She's not like that."

He crossed his arms over his chest. The unspoken 'They're all like that' hung in the air between us.

"She's big into charity work, volunteering. She's at soup kitchens, community build projects, tutoring, *and* she's got a job. If anything, I have to schedule time to see her. She's going to get this big prestigious award from the university for doing all that community service. She's not some football groupie."

There was a strange flicker in his gaze, but then it was gone and he was back to all business. "I'm flying to LA tonight. I wanted to go over everything before I left."

Relief that we weren't going to keep harping on the Elle train made me latch onto any lifeline. "Maybe you should go look for a girlfriend, someone to keep you occupied, less worried about my life and a little more focused on your own."

"Your mom's gone."

"I know she is…but it's been almost 22 years."

"She's gone." His split-second faraway look was replaced by the determined one he always took on when he was ready to lay out one of his big plans. "Now let's go over those videos."

He pushed up out of the chair, banging his knee. A pop shot through the room and he grimaced before dragging out an indexed binder, dimming the lights, and flicking on his presentation that glowed on the projector screen on the far wall.

If I made it out of there before graduation, it would be a miracle.

CHAPTER 29
ELLE

"I can bury you in places out in Jersey where they'll never find your body." Jules shook her whisk at me, sending batter splattering on the floor.

"What's the big deal? All I did was throw out there that maybe you could use a date to your sister's wedding."

"To Berk. Berkeley Vaughn. Are you kidding me? I'm the fat girl with the baked goods. He's not thinking about twirling me around the dance floor any time soon."

"You're always putting yourself down."

"Better I do it instead of anyone else."

"I never knew you were such a freaking bully."

"Oh please, my threats of murdering you are *mostly* for laughs."

"I wasn't talking about me."

"Who the hell do I bully?"

"Yourself."

"I learned from the best." Her half-laugh didn't do anything to cover the age-old wounds. "Anyway, it's better to toughen up since I'll be going to the engagement party this summer." She kept her gaze trained directly ahead.

"There's nothing I can do to talk you out of this, is there?"

"Short of a lobotomy, no. It's a long weekend, and my mom made it clear that she'd find it difficult to pay for my last year of school if I didn't play the role of best little sister in the world."

"Would you be super offended if I ran her over with my car?"

"The spell she's cast would probably break your car before it got anywhere near her. Anyway, it'll give me a chance to hunt down those Peter Rabbit books in the house."

"A, that's offensive to actual witches, and B, don't let your mom know you're still looking for them."

"Oh, I know. She'd gift them to Laura as a wedding present the second she got a whiff that I still wanted them. Anyway, on to less depressing topics. Three weeks until graduation—how's the job search going?"

"Definitely not less depressing. Every application has been rejected or disappeared into a black hole. I had to get the companies where I applied to ask for my transcripts directly because the registrar won't even release them to me until I pay the last five grand I owe for the semester, and my GPA doesn't exactly scream hire me, even for some of the nonprofits. They either don't have the funding to take someone else on or they want someone who's done more than arrange some events. They want data people or business people. I'm over here with my humanities degree with my pants down."

"What about something outside of that world? Like event planning or something like that?"

"Why in the hell would you think I'd be an event planner type of person? Do I look slick and coiffed with nails and hair to match?"

"No, but why would you think you'd need to be? The blood drive, everything else you organize—it seems like it would be a good fit for you."

"Right, and everyone would take me so seriously if I started picking out flower arrangements and tablecloths."

"Who the hell gives a flying fuck what anyone thinks about you?"

I lifted an eyebrow and stared right at her.

Her gaze dipped and her shoulders popped up. "Touché, but if you need a job and you don't want to get shipped off to Burma or somewhere else, why not look into it?" She flicked her nails against each other.

"If I say I will, will you drop it and give me a cookie?"

"What are you, five?"

I held up four fingers. "Almost." I smirked. "Can I take a nap and you handle my shift for me, *Weekend at Bernie's* style?" I slumped over in the chair in our kitchen.

"While my pole dancing has toned muscles I didn't even know I had, I don't have time to hook up a pulley system to move your body around behind the counter at work."

"You ruin all my fun."

"Don't I know it."

Closing my books after a few hours, I jammed what I needed into my bag and headed to Uncommon Grounds. Switching off with the shift ahead of me, I wrapped my apron around my neck and manned my spot behind the counter.

The door opened and my not-too-bad, actually-kind-of-great day withered like a flower on a severed vine. Mitchell sauntered in with his arm around a brunette—not the girl he'd cheated on me with.

"Elle." His mock surprise given the fact that he'd seen me walk into this coffee shop at least ten times in the past month made it clear to me that this asshole hadn't turned over a new leaf at all. Come to show off his new girlfriend? How nice of him.

"Mitchell, what can I get you?" I wasn't going to let him get to me.

"I'll take a medium organic coffee with almond milk and a vegan biscotti, and I brought my own cup. What would you like, babe?"

"I'll have the same."

"Coming right up." I grabbed the cups from him and turned to make the most pretentious cup of coffee known to man.

"I'm glad they got rid of the plastic straws. I sent a petition around last month to make that happen." He preened for his newest conquest.

I happily corrected him. "Actually, the board made a decision a couple of months ago, but it took a while to find a supplier since everyone else is switching to paper right now too."

His face froze and his gaze darted to New Girl before he recovered. "Well, I'm sure my petition got them to move things along. Same with getting in the almond milk. *Fresh milk*—I mean, it's a horror show, environmentally speaking."

Had I ever been this holier-than-thou? Was I this sanctimonious and annoying in different ways? Had I been acting like this with Nix and everyone else I'd worked with before? Holy crap, it was a miracle I still had all my teeth.

"So, you're going for the Huffington Award too?" He leaned against the counter like he had all the time in the world.

"Yes." I poured the almond milk into their cups.

He put a hand to his chest and bowed his head, ever so humbly. "You know I'm also nominated."

"Of course you are."

"I've done more than eighty projects over the past four years. I'm pretty sure we both know how things are going to work out." He glanced at his girlfriend, who simpered appropriately.

"Here are your drinks. Have a great day." I slid the cups across the counter to him.

"No hard feelings, right, Elle?" He leaned forward and tried to give me his best sympathetic look. "Are you doing any better? You look tired. If you ever need someone to talk to…"

"Actually…" I leaned over the counter closer to him. "You've got a booger."

He snapped up straight and grabbed a handful of napkins, rubbing them against his nose.

"Have a great day. Bye."

———

"WEREN'T YOU FINISHED AN HOUR AGO?" ONE OF THE GUYS from the shift after me wiped down the tables.

After the shift from hell, I'd been looking forward to Nix's smiling face. I checked the clock on the wall behind the register.

"Someone's supposed to be picking me up, but my phone died and I forgot my charger at home." I closed my notebook. I should've brought my laptop, or just, you know, gone home, but I'd already waited long enough to not give it fifteen more minutes.

Seeing Mitchell had brought up all kinds of feelings I'd tried my best to avoid. It had made me feel like the same dumb high school girl fawning all over the star football player, only I'd diverted that attention to the star good guy. Stupid girl. So stupid. What a track record.

Why was I still waiting for Nix to come? Had I told him the wrong time? I checked the clock on the wall again: nearly eight. My leg bounced up and down and I craned my neck to look out the coffee shop windows.

What was the worst that would happen? Nix showed up and I wasn't there? He'd come to my place after. Staying minute after minute made me feel more and more stupid, even though I knew standing me up wasn't in his character. It was stupidity mixed with anxiety. What if something had happened to him? Maybe his ridiculously expensive car had broken down and there wasn't a kind enough person to stop and offer a ride like he had when I needed help.

Maybe heading home to see his dad had gone on longer than he'd expected. *Just walk home, Elle. This is starting to look pathetic.* Lifting my bag, I slung it over my shoulder and got up from my seat. I'd fish some of Jules' salted caramel chocolate chunk cookie dough out of the freezer and nurse it when I got home.

The handle was ripped out of my hand as the door flew open. Sweat pouring down his face and panting, Nix stood in front of me with wild eyes. "You're still here—thank goodness. I'm so sorry. My dad practically locked me in his office all day." He squeeze-hugged me against his chest. His heart pounded like he'd run all the way there.

"There was some homework I needed to catch up on. No problem."

"I tried to call, but your phone wasn't working. I figured you were ignoring me."

"It died."

He chuckled. "You're the worst at charging your phone."

"I know."

"Let me make it up to you." He pushed the door open and led me outside, taking my bag off my arm. "Maybe I can finish your paper for you? Or fix your busted doorbell?"

"There are a number of ways you can make it up to me... with your hands." I cupped one of his in mine, drawing us closer together.

His pupils dilated and he licked his lips.

"With your mouth." I ran my thumb along his bottom lip. Leaning in, I whispered in his ear. "And with this." I dropped my hand between us and my fingers brushed against the straining erection pressing against the zipper of his jeans.

"Let's go." We rushed out of Uncommon Grounds, my feet barely touching the ground as Nix spirited me away to his car.

He pulled my door open so quickly, I figured I'd see screws from the hinges clattering to the ground. As we sat at a light, he drummed his fingers on the steering wheel.

I ran my hand across his thigh, and he grinned over at me.

The light turned green and he pulled out into the intersection. I sucked in a breath and my hand tightened on his thigh so hard he winced.

My eyes widened. The navy blue car was a blur behind him as they ran their light. A shower of glass showered over me and my head whipped back. Then, darkness.

CHAPTER 30
NIX

"You were incredibly lucky." The doctor stood at the foot of my bed. "But you need to keep your arm in that sling for at least a week. Our scans showed no fractures. There's some intense swelling right now, but that's to be expected. It also looks like there's some muscle damage, but I don't believe it's from the accident."

Scratchy white sheets bunched under my legs as I shifted. At least they didn't crinkle like the paper on the beds in the ER. Machines were lined up on the other side of the room, unplugged and soundless. Those could've been hooked up to me now, but they weren't. Other than my swollen shoulder, a couple cuts on my neck, and a bruise from my seatbelt, I was okay and had been cleared to leave.

Antiseptic, fluorescent lights and the almost-below-freezing temperatures reminded me of my surgery back in high school—not the headspace I wanted to find myself in again.

Elle's limp figure beside me in the car had nearly made me lose it when the paramedics arrived. Blood poured down her face like a horror movie. Holding her in my arms as we waited for the ambulance had been the scariest four minutes of my life. I'd never been happier for the med school and hospital on campus.

The low throb hadn't been much more than a normal day for me before they shot me up with some drugs at the hospital. If anything, right now, I finally remembered what it felt like when it didn't hurt.

"I'm a football player." I stared down at my arm cradled against my stomach in the bright white sling.

"A lot of damage for someone so young."

"Comes with the territory." I shrugged and winced at the precise dart of pain that zinged down my arm. "Can I see my girlfriend now?" We hadn't officially put that label on things, but if anything, this showed me I sure as hell wanted to. Elle would probably freak the hell out if she heard me call her that, but desperate times call for desperate measures.

"Sure, she's just been discharged as well."

The knot in my stomach wouldn't loosen until I'd seen her. The mental picture of the fear in her eyes just before the impact of the crash sent a shiver down my spine. We'd been lucky. If I'd pulled out into the intersection a split second sooner, we'd have been hit full on.

"Phoenix." My dad's booming voice rocked and rattled the curtain-covered windows in the hallway. His unmistakable form turned the corner and made a beeline straight for me.

"Dad, what are you doing here? I thought you were headed to LA."

"We were backing away from the gate and I told them to let me off."

"And they were cool with that?"

"It was either let me off or I was pulling the emergency slide."

My throat tightened. Somewhere deep down where I didn't want to admit it existed, I could never be sure Dad would care enough about me to change any plan he'd made.

He must've been scared to get a call saying something had happened to me in a car accident after my mom.

"Sorry about your trip. I'm fine, a little banged up, but no big deal."

He tugged me into a back-breaking hug.

I winced and hugged him back. It was the first one I'd gotten that didn't come with a whispered correction to a throw I'd made or a play I'd run.

"You're okay." He seemed to be saying it more to reassure himself than tell me.

"I'm good. My shoulder's tweaked, but it'll be good to go with some rest."

He let go and held on to both of my shoulders, staring at me. "We'll get you to a team doctor. They'll give you anything you need for that. We've got to have you out and mobile for the draft. If this gets out, it could push you down a few spots. Take that sling off. That's all we need, someone seeing you with it on and having it cause an even bigger issue."

He might as well have kicked me in the chest. Without fail, it was the first place his mind laser-focused on after making sure I wasn't on death's door—how this would affect my draft number, if a team would try to lowball me out of a few million to scoop up a deal. Who gave a fuck? All I wanted to do was see Elle and go home.

"The doctor said to keep it on."

"Some hospital hack who doesn't know what this can do to your career before it even starts. You're not leaving with it on." He said it in his 'My word is final' voice.

Shaking my head, I grabbed my chart from the end of the bed and slammed it into his chest. "You go tell the doctor his entire medical degree means nothing because you said so."

I charged out of the room. Getting into a fight with my dad in a hospital hallway wasn't on my list of things to do.

My dad called after me but stopped when he ran into my doctor, demanding everything in my file from that afternoon.

I shook my head, cradled my arm against my chest, and walked away.

Jamming my finger into the exit button, I walked into the discharge area. It was filled with people in various states of being patched up, all waiting for their numbers to be called.

A pink-haired blur plowed into my side, and relief washed over me like a cool drink of water after a midday practice.

Elle's hands wrapped around me, her fingers tangling in the fabric of my sling. "They wouldn't let me come back because I wasn't family. I was freaking out and about three seconds from launching myself over the nurses' station to go look for you. I woke up in the bed and had no idea where you were or if you were okay!"

I held her tight with my free arm. "Good thing I came out when I did. Are you okay?"

"Just a couple of cuts on my forehead—apparently they bleed like a mother. Two cuts, two stitches, a ruined uniform, and your clothes are ruined too." She pointed to the blood stains all over the collar and front of my shirt.

I brushed back her hair from her forehead. The small white bandages were taped to her skin. "You're really okay?"

"Fine. They thought I had a concussion for a bit, but now they think I probably passed out from the blood."

"From blood loss?" My heart squeezed.

She blushed. "No, from the blood itself. I'm not exactly great with seeing it."

"Is anyone?"

"I was pretty much ten seconds from passing out during both blood drives."

"You were great at hiding it." And so much more. The gaps in her wall were getting bigger, but it was still there and holding on strong.

She tilted her head and stared into my eyes. "How are you?" Her fingertips traced the edges of my bruises and cuts.

"Other than my arm, I'm all good. Doc said I need to rest up for a bit and it'll be fine. The damage—the damage I've got doesn't have anything to do with the crash. They'll know more once the swelling goes down. I'm sure I'll have a full battery of tests at all the appointments my dad is probably setting up right now."

"He's here?" She craned her neck, looking behind her.

"Yes, it's a long story—actually, it's a short one, but I don't want to talk about it right now. Let's get out of here."

"We've got to do any final discharge stuff, and they'll probably want me to leave a kidney behind as collateral for the bill." She cringed and squeezed her eyes shut.

"Are you hurting?"

"No, but this wasn't an expense I'd counted on for this semester."

"Don't worry about it."

"Phoenix." My dad's baritone cut through the murmur of the discharge area. "We need to talk."

Turning us around, I kept Elle pressed against my side. "We've talked enough already, Dad. I'm taking my girlfriend home. I'm going home to rest."

My dad's gaze bounced from me to Elle. I kept my arm tight around her.

"This can wait. I'm tired, and I think one six-hour-long one-sided conversation per day is my limit. We were discharged, so you can take care of the details. After all, that's what you love to do. We're leaving."

"I'll need to talk to you about this." His pointed stare at Elle and the blink-and-you'll-miss-it tightening of her hold against my back made my blood boil.

"Don't you always." Without another word, I walked her out of there and got her into a taxi.

She cuddled against me in the back of the car with her arm resting on my stomach, her fingers picking at one of the drops of blood there.

"That was scary."

"It was. I can't believe someone would be so irresponsible to blow through a red light like that."

"I meant the part where you called me your girlfriend." She laughed and looked up at me.

"Pretty scary stuff, huh?"

"Maybe not as scary as I once thought it was." She nestled deeper into my side, and the throb in my shoulder melted away.

The taxi pulled up to the front of her house.

"Can we stay at yours tonight?" She threaded her fingers through mine. "Jules is away tonight and it'll be too quiet."

"Of course. Do you want to go get some clothes?"

"If it's okay, I can wear yours to sleep in." The uncertainty in her eyes made my heart ache for how little trust she had that I'd be cool with whatever she wanted to do.

"You have no idea how much I want to see you sleeping in one of my shirts."

With my arm over her shoulder and her fingers interlocked with mine, we crossed the street and headed into my place.

"What are you doing getting home so late? And did you get out of a taxi?" Reece drummed on a notebook while sitting on the floor in front of the TV.

"We got into a car accident after I picked Elle up from work."

Like seagulls calling for another piece of funnel cake, the entire house came alive with people popping up from every direction. We were swarmed.

"Are you sure you wouldn't rather go to your place?" I whispered into the side of Elle's hair as we said we were perfectly fine for the nine hundredth time.

"No, I like having people around that care this much."

I nodded. "As you can all see, we're okay, but we are tired, so we're headed to bed."

"No nookie while you're recovering." LJ wagged his finger and tapped his foot.

"Says who?"

Berk chimed in before shoving a cookie into his mouth. "Doctor's orders."

"Night everyone."

Closing the door behind me, I flicked on the light. Elle lay down on my bed and crossed her hand over her stomach.

I could have stood and watched her forever. Even a little bruised and in blood-speckled clothes, she was breathtaking in the kind of way that made never seeing a sunset or the ocean again absolutely okay with me as long as I got to see her.

"You coming to bed?" She patted the spot beside her.

"I'll get you some clothes to change into and you can take a shower. The airbags did a number on my nose, and every breath is filled with a gunpowder smell."

She sat up. "I thought I was losing it. What the hell makes it smell like that?"

"It's the shells they use to deploy the airbag." I grabbed some shorts with a drawstring and a t-shirt.

"How do you know all this?" She walked over to me, teasing me with her swaying walk, the curve of her ass that fit my hand perfectly.

I shrugged. "No idea. I'll get you a towel."

"Who's going to wash my back and make sure I don't get water on my head?" Her chin dipped and she looked up at me, turning the tease up to a ten.

"It's probably not the best idea tonight." I gestured to the discarded sling on my dresser.

"Don't worry, I'll do all the work." Like I was going to say no to that.

She pushed me toward the bed until I fell backward. Unbuckling my jeans, I wanted to tell her she should sleep and rest before we even thought about it, but those words were a pipe dream lost to the wind when she whipped her shirt up and over her head.

Snatching a condom from the drawer beside my bed, I teased the tips of her bare breasts, skimming my fingers over her marred flesh. I pushed up onto my elbows, grimacing at the ache in my shoulder.

"Mine don't hurt." She pushed me back and rolled on the condom. It took everything in me not to come right then. Her fingers felt so good stroking up and down my length, sending shivers of pleasure shooting along my spine. Any pain was long forgotten under her entrancing gaze, riveted to mine and focused on me.

She lifted onto her knees and sank down onto me. The tight warmth enveloped me, but I fought to keep my eyes open as she sat on top of me looking like every fantasy I could hope for, so real and so her and every dream I'd ever had rolled into one.

CHAPTER 31
ELLE

I sank lower, relishing moving down onto every inch of him. He filled and stretched me, lighting the fuse of pleasure coursing through me. My ass settled against the tops of Nix's thighs, and he stared at me like I was the eighth wonder of the world.

He had the uncanny ability to always make me feel like I was the center of his universe. His eyes sliced through my walls like a hot knife through butter and overwhelmed me.

I ducked my head, because it was too much for today, too much all at once—the accident, not knowing where the hell he was, rushing over to him and not wanting to let go then him dropping the G-word bomb on me.

There were too many emotions wrapped up in what had happened tonight. Even the way he was looking at me made my chest tight. I dropped down and kissed him, closing my eyes.

He held on to my hips as I moved, rocking and grinding while keeping as much of a connection between us as possible.

My orgasm came too quickly and not fast enough. I wanted to reach that peak right along with him, wanting us to

250 MAYA HUGHES

live in this moment for as long as possible. The sparks of pleasure grew and spread down my legs and to my toes.

His hands braced against my back, hugging me close like he never wanted to let me go, and his mouth sucking on that spot on my neck sent my back arching as a strangled cry burst free from my lips.

He squeezed my ass and groaned into my ear, expanding inside me and filling the latex between us.

Our shower was fast and sloppy, spilling water out of the too-small-for-two-people bathtub and onto the floor. We fell into bed, and I barely got the t-shirt over my head.

Nix's still-dripping hair, flannel pajama pants, and bare chest made him look more delicious than any man had any business looking.

Curled up against him, it felt like all the things that would usually keep me up at night couldn't touch me. Overdue tuition. What the hell came next in my life. Cheating exes. Disapproving fathers. Jerky neighbors who couldn't ever turn down the volume of their parties. With Nix's heart drumming against my cheek, I could sleep and dream without the worries I always carried with me.

He was my own personal worry stone, only when I rubbed him, I got a much bigger surprise. His gentle snores ushered me into sleep and whatever tomorrow would bring.

"AND ANOTHER ONE." I WANTED TO CHUCK MY COMPUTER across the room, but I didn't exactly have the budget to replace it.

"Another what?" Jules came down the steps and flopped onto the couch beside me.

"Another rejection." I was overqualified to work minimum wage and underqualified to get an office job—or any job, according to everyone I'd applied with. I squeezed my head in my hands, wincing as I hit the small cut on my forehead. At least the bruising was now just a light yellow.

"What happens if you don't get the Huffington Award?"

"I'll just have to hang around here." I hoped my smile didn't look as brittle as it felt. I'd have to find work wherever I could to get the money together so they'd release my transcripts and I could get something else. Peace Corps, nonprofits—all of them wanted that annoying little piece of paper.

"Don't even tempt me. Being all alone in this house by myself next year..."

"You can get new roommates, and there's always Zoe."

"I wonder if she'll come to move out her stuff." Jules tapped her chin.

"If not, we can always sell it."

"There is this blowtorch I've been eyeing all semester."

"A blowtorch?"

"My crème brûlée game would be upped to the next level."

"I didn't know there were crème brûlée levels."

"No need to use the broiler like a savage." She shook her head with disgust. "How many more job applications do you have out?"

"A few. I haven't been keeping track." Actually, I knew it was three, and they were for jobs where I'd be hard-pressed to make enough to live and eat and save to pay off my balance for the semester if I didn't win. My dean had assured me my application was strong, and the only thing I could do was wait it out. "It'll work out. I'm just freaking out in the moment is all. No baking today?"

"You act like I bake every day."

I lifted an eyebrow and looked at her sideways.

"Fine, I usually do, but finals are going well, so I'm not losing my shit right at this moment."

"Dean's list?"

"Maybe." Her cheeks flushed and she looked away. "Fine, I'm a nerd! Sue me."

"I'd say you're more of a dork rather than a nerd. Aren't nerds usually big into like comics and sci-fi and stuff?"

"I know my way around a few different star franchises."

"Star franchises?"

"Come on, Elle. Star Trek, Star Wars."

"Right, I totally knew what you were talking about—I was just checking to see if you did."

"How are things going with Prince Charming?"

"Good?"

"That's a hedge if I've ever heard one. What's the wrinkle?"

"Nothing, and that's kind of why I feel that way. He makes me happy. He's gorgeous and so sweet it makes my teeth hurt."

"And he's awesome in bed," she added.

I looked at her like *Wtf?*

"Our walls aren't that thick. I can hear Nix doing the Lord's work in there."

My mouth opened and closed. "I don't think that's what that means."

"It does for me."

I laughed at her matter-of-fact, singsong voice.

"Anyway, he's got an amazing future and he's graduating cum laude."

"And...what's the problem?"

"No one is that perfect."

She shrugged. "Maybe he is."

"If he is then it's only a matter of time before he realizes how screwed up I am."

"You're nowhere near as screwed up as you think."

"When I'm with him, it's like nothing can touch me. I feel like I'm giggling like an idiot and nothing else matters."

"And that's a problem...why?"

"It feels eerily similar to how I was with the other two, even beyond how it was with them."

"Maybe you're someone who goes all in with a relationship and you've finally found someone who deserves that from you."

"Or I'm a terrible judge of character and the other shoe will drop, only this time it's going to knock out my head and my heart at the same time."

"If you keep looking for the cracks, eventually you'll find them."

"You're probably right."

"Of course I am. I'm your wise old owl of a friend." She pushed up her glasses with her finger and jutted out her top teeth like a nerd character come to life.

I lobbed a pillow at her head, sending her hair flying across her face.

She blew it out of her eyes. "Next time, you should lie down and I'll charge for the advice."

A knock forced us to declare a truce in our half-assed pillow fight.

Jules opened the door and leaned against it. "Elle, it's for you."

"Actually, I wanted to talk to you." Berk stepped into the house with his hands shoved into his pockets. He glanced around, probably hoping the place didn't crash down around his ears. I didn't blame him. After Nix had told me he'd paid our landlord for that window they'd smashed, I'd put in a complaint with the city over his complete lack of concern for our safety in this place, not that they'd done anything about it yet.

Jules' eyes widened and she glanced from me to the open door.

"Me?" Her squeak was so high I was surprised it didn't shatter the lenses of her glasses.

"Yeah, I have a special occasion coming up and wanted to know if maybe you'd be able to make a cake for me."

"Me?"

"Unless it's the Keebler elves making all the awesome stuff you bring over to the house."

"It's me. What did you need?"

"A layer cake. It's this recipe." He handed her a printout. "I've searched all over for a bakery to make it, but on short notice with graduation season, no one can get it done."

"Any decoration?" She sounded like a bubble machine was about to carry her away.

"Do you have rainbow jimmies?" He shifted from foot to foot like it was impossible for him to sit still.

"Of course. Is this for one of the guys?" She beamed at him. "Do you need me to write anything on it?"

"Nah, not for the guys, and you can put 'Happy birthday, Alexis'. She's going to freak when she tastes this. I've told her all about your stuff and she's really excited."

My eyes slammed shut and I dropped my chin to my chest. It was like watching someone get punched full on in the face.

"I—" Jules cleared her throat. "I can do that, for sure." She covered the crack in her voice well. "When did you need it by?"

Standing, I gingerly walked toward them. The floorboards squeaked and creaked under my feet, each one like a new splinter in Jules' heart. Berk was oblivious, but the way her fingers gripped the edge of the paper and the slight tremor rumbling through her made me want to pull her into a hug and order a gallon of ice cream.

He pulled out his phone and glanced at the screen. "Tomorrow at four?"

She nodded, like she didn't trust her voice.

"You're the best." He squeezed her in a hug with her arms trapped down at her sides. "Tell me how much it is and I'll get the money to you—or did you need me to pay in advance?"

She shook her head and forced a smile.

"You're a lifesaver." He waved to me and popped back out the door.

Jules stood staring at the closed door for so long I was afraid to move.

Lifting her hand, she wiped at her cheek.

"Jules..." I dropped my hand onto her shoulder, and she jumped.

She grinned at me, a kind of sad, deranged expression, and rubbed at her eyes under her glasses. "I'm fine." An exhale of breath that was meant to sound light and carefree sounded anything but. "No big deal, I'm just baking a cake for Berk's girlfriend or something." She shrugged.

"Jules..." I reached for her, but she stepped away, crossing her arms over her chest.

My mouth opened and closed, and the helplessness killed me.

"Why'd you keep pushing me at him?" Her voice cracked, and the corners of her mouth tightened. "Oh my god, I'm the other woman!"

"Maybe it's new." I covered my mouth with my hand, tears burning in my eyes at her pain. "Has he ever mentioned anyone when you've written to each other?"

"In our sex letters? You think he'd mention having a girl-friend?" She flung her arms out.

"You said they'd moved beyond sex stuff."

"They have." She stared after the closed door. "I thought we were getting to know each other, but I guess he got bored."

She shrugged like she didn't care, but the wobble in her lip and the look in her eyes were unmistakable.

"Don't say that." I grasped for anything, absolutely anything to make this less shitty. "Maybe she's just a friend."

Jules shot me an 'are you freaking kidding me' look. "Let me go get the stuff together for this thing." She scanned down the paper. "She's got good taste. It's an awesome Milk Bar recipe."

"Do you want me to help?"

She wiped her nose with the back of her hand. "It's better I do this myself. Don't you have work?"

"Shit." If I wanted to make rent I did, not that I doubted Jules would spot me, but I also wanted to be there for her. "You sure you don't want me to stay?"

"I'll be okay. It's not the first time something like this has happened, and it won't be the last. At least I didn't have to look at the pity in his eyes as he sawed my heart out of my chest."

CHAPTER 32

NIX

S weat dripped off the tip of my nose. Gripping the ball in my right hand, my fingers found the familiar groove of the laces against the pebbled skin. I shouted out the play and looked for my open receiver.

Reece was taking the meandering route through the defenders. His draft position was secure. He shouldn't have even been out there on the field, and the same went for me. A flash of blue streaked across the field. Keyton had been practicing in the offseason. He broke free from the defenders, finding a perfect pocket for me to sink the ball into.

I let it fly, wincing at the pain in my arm. Looking up into the stands, I stared at my dad talking to a few different agents and recruitment teams. I almost expected him to jog onto the field and lift my upper lip, showing off my teeth to them like a prized horse.

Elle was coming over after her shift. I wanted to pick her up, but I didn't want to be late again. She'd said she'd be fine. The easy way she walked into our house and I walked into hers made me happier than it should have. Three months ago, she'd have removed my balls with pliers if I'd crossed on the sidewalk in front of her house and now there wasn't a night I didn't sleep with her head resting against my chest, running my fingers through her hair.

She always smelled so good, like the color of her hair tricked my brain into thinking of anything sweet, though she'd probably have killed me if I ever called her sweet. As much as she still pretended to be prickly, I saw the real her, the vulnerable and unsure Elle who was just as afraid of getting hurt as anyone else.

I lifted my hand to my shoulder to massage it but pulled my helmet off instead. Rubbing my shoulder after a throw would result in at least a three-hour rundown lecture after practice, AKA the final showcase.

"Thanks, man." Keyton jogged over to me. "I wouldn't have gotten those guys to look twice at me if you hadn't shown up today."

"Don't worry about it. You'll kick ass next year and wow them even more."

He tugged on the front of his jersey, jerking his pads down. "Ah, I don't know. This season's been so awesome because of you and Reece. Once you're gone, I don't what we'll do."

"You'll survive, and if you want this, don't let anything get in your way. You've got the skills. Now you just need to trust them." I tapped the center of his chest. "Did the guys talk to you about moving into the Brothel next year?"

"LJ and Berk mentioned it, but I wasn't sure." His eyes dropped to the pristinely cut grass.

"Reece and I are moving out no matter what. I'm sure they don't want to split the rent two ways."

"They said someone else already said yes. Marisa?"

Well, that would be interesting. "She's staying there already."

"Cool, I've never lived with a woman before."

"Not even your mom?"

"Nah, she died when I was little."

"No shit. Mine too. Looks like we're both in the club and didn't even know it."

He let out a short huff. "I guess so."

"Living with Marisa will be no big deal. Other than the weekly manicures and tampon runs, you'll be fine." My eyes widened. "But seriously, under absolutely no freaking circumstances do you let her cook, or eat anything she's cooked."

His eyebrow lifted.

"I'm not kidding. Nothing. Not toast. Not a bagel or a muffin. *Nothing*, or you'll be praying to the porcelain gods for who knows how long."

"Good to know."

"And we've found most of the leftover remnants from the old frat and cleared them out by now."

"Remnants?"

I shuddered. "Latex doesn't exactly break down as quickly as you'd think. Even with the new paint job and cleanings the landlord did, let's just say there were...stragglers."

"Maybe I should look for another place. I'm not much of a partier, and I don't want the guys to feel weird about it."

I clapped both my hands onto his shoulders. "Trust me, they're not big into partying either. It's a great house. The landlord fixes anything we need." Unlike Elle's asshole of a landlord. "It's a great location and the price is good. Do you know which room you'd be in?"

The tips of his ears reddened. "They said yours."

"Great. Come by after you have a shower and check it out. Seriously, I'm glad it's you they've got moving in there. Those two need someone responsible to keep them in line."

His chest puffed up at that compliment as he smiled wide.

"I've got to go talk to my dad. I'll catch up with you, and if I don't see you, just head to the house."

"Thanks, Nix." He jogged toward the locker rooms.

My dad droned on and on and I stood there, letting my

mind wander to better things, Elle-shaped things that felt so good pressed up against me. All the layers of padding and protection came in handy. I clasped my hands in front of my crotch.

"And not only is Phoenix an asset on the field, he's an asset off of it as well, and there are so many ways he can bring a positive spotlight to a team in these days when so much negativity has taken hold."

Dad had his speech down pat. I nodded at all the right spots, smiling and going along with it all. It was easier this way, and frankly, I didn't give a shit. Maybe once I finally played my first season, I'd blow out my shoulder and all his aspirations for me would die right along with his attention. Then I'd be free from a dream that had never been mine.

That thought blindsided me, ramming into my head like that car through the intersection.

That wasn't what I wanted.

I wanted to play. I'd always wanted to play...right? But, the idea of getting hurt like that...didn't scare me like I'd thought it would. A career-ending injury to stop all the madness didn't send shivers down my spine or fill me with a clawing dread. What the hell did that mean?

"Nix."

I shook myself out of those thoughts. "Yeah, Dad." I walked up to his side.

"Anything you'd like to say?" He looked at me out of the corner of his eye.

"No, I'm good. Nice meeting you all, and I look forward to seeing you at the draft."

Everyone dispersed, and Dad kept his hand on my shoulder. The message was clear: *Stay put.*

"That was a missed opportunity to stand out. You've been distracted." He stared straight ahead.

"I've been taking the meetings and calls whenever you've

asked." I shook his hand off my shoulder. "Stop trying to control everything in my life."

Rushing into the locker room, I showered, changed, and looked around the blue- and gold-painted space one last time. This was it.

I pulled up in front of my house, greeted by the smiling face and soft lips of the only woman I'd ever pictured a future with. The urge to tell her was almost undeniable. I wanted to drag her to the rooftop garden of the student center and shout it to the whole campus.

"You're still sweating."

I brushed back her hair from her face. "It was a tough workout. Being back on the field felt weird." I tucked her under my arm as we walked into the house.

"Good weird or bad weird?"

I shrugged. "Just weird knowing it was the last time I'd suit up on the field with those guys."

She rested her hand on the center of my chest and looked up at me. "I'm glad you got to do it one more time."

"Me too. Closing this chapter was going to happen whether I wanted it to or not, so it was nice to go out on a positive." I looked around the living room, the posters hung on the wall, Berk's textbooks and snacks all over the table.

"It was here and gone in a blink. Now the real world. Well, real for some. I don't think we can count pro football as the 'real' world." She curled her fingers in air quotes.

"What about you? The real world beckons."

"Don't remind me. At least with me winning the Huffington Award some doors will open up and I can breathe a little. Then I can make a decision."

"It's a lock? They told you?" I sat in my char and tugged her down onto my lap with her legs draped over the side. "I knew you'd win!"

"Nothing's official yet, but my dean said he's never had a better application, so I can't imagine it going any other way."

For once she was glowing with happiness without any tired shadows around the edges.

"You worked hard for it." I ran my hands over her thighs, gently squeezing.

"Is anyone else here?" She leaned in closer and cupped my head against her chest, absently running her fingers through my hair.

"I don't think so, but—"

The front door flew open. "And if he's feeling generous, he might leave his chair behind."

A cavalcade of football players came storming inside, laughing and breaking the momentary tranquility of me and my girl.

Elle spun around on my lap, facing the door with the unfortunate side effect of rubbing me just right through my sweatpants. She lifted her butt to stand, and I grabbed onto her hips.

"This is all your fault, so you have to suffer with me." I ground myself against her as I whispered in her ear, letting the results of her teasing torture us both.

She let out a yelp and shuddered.

"Which chair?" I called out.

"The one you're sitting in." The guys piled into the room, taking over the formerly quiet space and filling it with Yuengling, chips, and video games.

"Maybe. I might leave it behind, but it's also got some good memories." I tightened my grip on her hips. The subtle throbbing sent rippling waves of pleasure through me, and it affected Elle too judging by the way her fingers tightened on the wide leather armrests of the recliner.

"This isn't fair," she whisper-yelled at me.

"It's not fair you gave it to me in the first place."

"Not like I can help it."

"And I can't help my reaction to you. Looks like we're stuck here."

Elle's eyelids fluttered and she shot up off my lap, grabbing my hand and tugging me forward with more strength than I'd ever imagined she had.

Rushing to the stairs, she nearly collided with LJ bringing out a pan of buffalo chicken dip.

"Nix needs to show me something upstairs," she blurted out then yanked me up the steps behind her.

"I'm sure he does," Berk called out after us.

Inside my room, she slammed the door shut. "Naked, now." She whipped her shirt up and over her head. "I'm going to make you pay for that little stunt down there."

Grinning, I kicked off my shoes. "I can't wait."

CHAPTER 33

ELLE

"Elle." Mitchell stood beside me as we waited in the wings of the stage before taking our seats in the neatly arranged rows behind the podium the deans and the president of the university would stand at to give us our awards. "Good to see you here."

"Wish I could say the same." There wasn't any need to play nice. He was an asshole and that was that. A few people peered out at the audience, shielding their eyes from the bright lights of the stage.

His smirk was as self-satisfied as ever. "No need to get snarky. We're both here for the same reason."

I hated that he was right. We were there to stand up on the stage and have people applaud our good deeds.

Nix came up behind me and rested his hand on my arm. Mitchell's eyes widened as his Adam's apple bobbed.

"Hey, Elle. I was looking for you." He stared into my eyes like we'd been apart for years—not hours—with a yearning and happiness that made my toes tingle.

Mitchell cleared his throat, drawing Nix's attention.

Breaking the connection between us, Nix stepped to my side and turned to Mitchell.

THE SECOND WE MET   265

"Sorry, I didn't see you there. Phoenix Russo." Nix extended his hand. "And you are?"

"This is Mitchell Frank. I told you about him." I looked at Nix over my shoulder.

He scrunched his eyebrows together like he was scanning the recesses of his mind for even the slightest mention of someone with that name. I could've kissed him. "You dated?"

Mitchell tugged at his tight collar. "We dated for nearly a year."

"A whole year? Elle hasn't really mentioned you much at all. I guess it wasn't that big of a deal." Translation, *he* wasn't much of a big deal.

"We worked on the Fulton Filanthropists together. This year, I'm heading it up solo, and we've raised over five thousand dollars for charity."

"Elle, didn't your Give on the Gridiron event raise that in the first hour with the signed jerseys?" Nix looked at me, and the delighted glint in his eye made it hard to keep my hands off him.

"I think it was by the third hour. Things were a little disorganized at the start." The struggle to keep a wide, gloating grin off my face failed miserably. I loved this man. The fleeting thought stuck in my chest, and my heart sped up. *I love him.*

"I'm sure next year you'll top that in no time." He draped his arm over my shoulder.

"The dean's waving us over. Let's see what he needs." I pressed my hand against Nix's chest. "Bye, Mitchell." Mitchell stared after us slack-jawed. I shouldn't have let it make me so damn happy, but it did.

"Now's your time to shine, B and E." Nix kissed me on my temple as we stood offstage, waiting to walk out to our seats.

The awards droned on for what seemed like hours, but I kept my face neutral, trying not to be blinded by the lights hanging in the rafters. With Nix beside me, it wasn't so terrible sitting in front of a couple hundred people in the audience. His small finger strokes to my pinky were enough to keep my mind off the fact that the stack of award note cards didn't seem to be getting smaller.

A room-shaking round of applause broke out for Nix as he stepped up to receive his award for sportsmanship. There might've been an airhorn or two smuggled into the much more subdued ceremony.

He sat back down beside me and winked.

They moved from sports to community service. At least I'd be put out of my misery before they gave out the academic awards.

"This year, we have three awards for the work our exemplary students have done in the community. First, the Brennan Award goes to Mitchell Frank."

His stunned expression was a sight to behold. The Brennan and Grayson awards were pretty plaques to shove in a drawer. They didn't come with the prestige and financial award like the Huffington, but who the hell could've done more than Mitchell other than me? Who the hell had come in second place? Whoever it was, I'd thank them after the ceremony for the look on his face alone.

My legs bounced up and down, and I slipped my hands to the edge of my seat. There wasn't anyone else who'd been as visible in our area. The Huffington was mine! With the award and the money, I could take the summer and figure out what I wanted to do. The Peace Corps wasn't what I wanted. Maybe I'd get Nix to find out who I could talk to with the team about more community work there.

Nix mouthed, "You've got this," and gave me a wide grin.

Maybe I'd see where he got drafted and follow him like a lovesick puppy. That didn't make me want to run away screaming like I'd have thought it would.

"And for the Grayson Award..." The university president

read through his spiel, but I couldn't even hear him. I'd done it! I looked around to see who else I'd seen at the events who might be in the running. "Elle Masterson."

My head jerked back and my stomach plummeted. What? There had to be a mistake. I hadn't won the Grayson; I'd won the Huffington.

They were calling me too early.

Only, they weren't.

The air in my lungs shrunk to a pea-sized spot and I couldn't feel my lips. Every waking hour for nearly two years, I'd busted my ass for this award. I'd sacrificed my social life, sleep, and sometimes my sanity. A pre-sob shudder reverberated in my chest, and the petering applause of the audience crackled in my ears like shattering glass.

On numb legs, I stood and walked forward to claim the award—my shiny, new, second-place award. I shook the hand of the university president and posed for a picture from the photographer in front of the auditorium full of people. I'd peeked at the results that day in the dean's office—there hadn't been anyone who'd done more than me, and no one could've swooped in with such a short amount of time to fill with events they'd organized. Mitchell sitting behind me with his even smaller plaque was a testament to that. I'd raised money. I'd ladled out soup and chopped vegetables until it took days for the feeling in my fingertips to come back.

Had the winner discovered a cure for a fatal disease?

Sitting back in my chair, I stared at the plaque. Nix sat beside me, trying to get my attention, but the rabbit hole I'd fallen down was way too deep for me to come up and face him right then.

It wouldn't have physically been possible for me to do more than I'd done. I had three settings: burnout, just past burnout, and careening into burnout.

The only thing I'd done for myself in the past two years was the time I'd spent with Nix, late nights snuggled up beside him in bed as he stroked his fingers down my side, sending ticklish zings down my spine. All I wanted to do was crawl under the covers with him and not come out until he made this numbness go away.

"Our final award for community work is one I'm especially proud to present. This nominee was a late entrant, but with all the work he's done lately, it was hard to overlook the contributions he's made to the community on top of the exceptional spotlight already on him out on the field. This year's Huffington Award winner is Phoenix Russo."

I've heard people say when something big happens in life, the entire world slows down, and I swore I could've seen a hummingbird's wings flapping in front of my face.

Nix stared at me wide-eyed as everyone in the audience clapped and cheered.

"Phoenix was a major part of a recent community service project building homes for families in need, and the story brought massive attention to the cause. He also started the first of what we hope will be many campus-wide blood drives. It was the largest ever for a campus our size, according to the Red Cross."

The scene in front of me got blurry like a funhouse mirror had been slipped in front of my eyes.

Like a zombie, Nix walked over and stood beside the president as he rattled off all the accomplishments Nix had achieved in addition to his incredibly busy football schedule, things like giving out meals at a local soup kitchen. The audience swooned and clapped, murmuring about how surprisingly good he was.

Betrayal was something I'd tasted before. I'd been burned by the raw, searing pain that comes along with it, but I'd never had anyone serve it up quite like Nix. I'd never had someone rip open my chest and ladle scalding mounds of it straight onto my heart.

Dropping my plaque, I bolted from the stage. My attempts at keeping it together were like a bucket against a tidal wave.

A hand wrapped around my arm and spun me around.

Nix stood there in his suit with his perfect hair and the award still in his hand. "Elle, I don't know what the hell is going on."

I shoved both hands against his chest. "No!" My voice echoed off the rafters on the side of the stage, and more than a few heads turned in our direction.

The rest of the winners filed off the stage and posed for pictures with their families and friends.

"You don't get to lie to me about this. You don't get to use me like this and then try to pretend you don't know what's happening." Angry tears burned in my eyes.

"There are no lies. I don't know what's happening. I was supposed to get the sports award and that's it. I never applied for this. This was yours. I never wanted it." He was frantic, trying to get me to meet his gaze.

"All your caring and surprises were a freaking cover—for what? What benefit can this have? You know how much this meant to me." There was no stopping the tears now. "You knew I needed this grant to help me figure things out."

He reached for my arms, but I jumped back.

"And that's exactly why I'd never do this." His gaze jumped from mine to over my shoulder. "But I know who might've."

I turned to follow his gaze. A tall, broad man with the same eyes as Nix stood near the stage, a man I'd met once before at the hospital.

"My dad…" Nix took a deep breath and shook his head. "My dad did this."

"Right, your dad just magically won you the award I've told you all about."

"Yes. That's the only thing that explains it, and if you need the money from this, I'll give it to you. I don't want it."

"I don't want your charity. You know it's not just the money I needed from this award, and I'm sure that would be blazed all over the cover of *Sports Illustrated* too: 'Selfless athlete assists indigent college student.' Shove it."

"I'm telling you the truth."

"No, you're a liar. That's all you've ever been."

"Would you just listen? Elle, I love you."

"Liar."

He hung his head and shook it. "You've been waiting for this, haven't you?" He stared at me with tears in his eyes. "Waiting for a reason to end this, a slip-up to justify cutting me loose..."

The slow shake of my head was like a match strike in his eyes. I covered my ears with my hands.

His fingers wrapped around my arms and he stared into my gaze with a pleading that sliced me to my core. "I love you. Tell me you don't feel the same about me. Forget what you're trying to come up with in your head to use to push me away and believe me." He pressed his lips against my forehead.

Tears flowed down my cheeks, and I squeezed my eyes shut. I wanted to believe him. I wanted it so badly it made it hard to think straight, but I'd been down this path before, ignoring things because I wanted to believe someone loved me as much as I loved them. I loved Nix, and he'd lied. He'd been using me to help his reputation.

I'd faced this before, and I couldn't let myself believe what wasn't really there. The ticking clock on this had started the second I'd slept with him; that was how it always went. "No."

I broke the hold he had on me and backed up.

His lips tightened and he nodded. "I don't have anything else I can say, Elle. You're so worried about being hurt that you can't even see that you're hurting the people around you.

I love you and would never hurt you like this. No matter what you think, know that's true."

I stared past him to the bright lights of the stage and other award winners taking pictures and laughing together.

Would he have really stolen my award, knowing how much I'd worked for it, how much I needed it?

My head was spinning. None of this made sense.

His body rigid, Nix walked past me with a slow gait like he was waiting for me to change my mind, waiting for me to tell him all was forgiven, but the words stalled in my throat like my car going up a hill. As much as this hurt, it would be okay. Better for us to end now rather than in a year when I walked in on him in a hotel room with some other woman, or five years from now when I walked into our bedroom with him balls deep in someone else.

The future I hadn't even let myself admit was floating through my head evaporated in a puff of smoke.

I walked outside, and it was already dark. There was no one else around, everyone having run off to their celebratory dinners or parties. I was there…alone.

"Elle."

I'd made the right choice, hadn't I? Nix and I had always been this weird picture people kept trying to figure out. He'd have been gone in no time anyway.

"Elle." Fingers wrapped around my elbow.

Turning, I came face to face with Jules. "What are you doing here?"

She looked at me with concern swimming in her eyes. "Nix called me."

His name burst a dam I'd been holding back, a swelling tide breaking through the last lines of defense. I threw my arms around her and collapsed.

Her soothing pats on my back as she rocked me back and forth only made the tears and choking sobs rack me harder.

We folded onto the curb outside the theater I didn't even remember leaving, and she brushed her fingers down the back of my head, telling me how it would be okay, only it wouldn't.

It couldn't be after what had just happened.

When my hiccupping tears turned to sniffles, Jules peeled me off her shoulder and took both my hands in hers.

"What happened?"

The story came pouring out of me like water from a busted fire hydrant.

Jules held my hands and brushed a tear off my cheek.

"And I let him walk away. No..." I shook my head. "I shoved him away, but it was bound to happen eventually, right?" I looked at her, waiting for that Jules support she always gave me.

"Elle, you're my best friend, and I love you." Her lips tightened and she took a deep, shuddering breath. "But why don't you think you deserve someone to love you?"

Her aim was far too accurate for that kind of solid gut punch, and I tried to tug my hands away from her.

She held tight. "No, don't run away from this. I'm not going to let you push me away too. Have you not seen the way that guy looks at you? They fixed our freaking porch— that was way too much work to just be some PR stunt or an attempt to get laid. He cares about you, Elle, even when there are no points to score. Why else would he have called me? He wants to make sure you're okay. He loves you."

Those words were too hard to bear. If it was true and he did love me, I'd just broken the best thing that had ever happened to me, and I had no idea how to get it back.

CHAPTER 34

NIX

Wrecked. I figured after having defensive linemen out for my blood, fighting tooth and nail to separate my head from my shoulders, I'd known some serious pain—but those hits were like a paper cut compared to this. I'd take non-stop hits from Johannsen on concrete, if it eased this pain even a little bit. My nostrils flared like someone had just opened a jar of Icy Hot right under my nose. The pinprick tightness centered between my eyes.

What have I done? I left. Numb, I stumbled off the curb and braced my arm against a parking sign, trying and failing to catch my breath. I'd had the wind knocked out of me a lot over the years, but it had never felt like this. The burning sting made me think I'd never take a full breath again. She'd robbed me of more than the air in my lungs.

My heart was hers fully and completely, but she'd never trusted that. She'd never trusted me, and I couldn't live teetering on the precipice of a world where she wasn't mine. Better to do this now before my soul was bound to hers completely and being separated from her was like ripping off a limb.

Part of me understood her initial freak-out, even if she should've known underneath it, something was off here.

Why had they called my name? Why would they have even thought to give that award to me? I hadn't done anything Elle had talked about when it came to prepping her application.

Anger was in an on-the-field brawl with a yawning sadness inside me. I clutched my phone in my hand, torn between rushing right back into the theater to beg Elle to believe me and finding my father so I could wrap my fingers around his neck. My phone buzzed in my hand. I glanced behind me, hope that it was Elle burning like a cruel mistress.

Of course it wasn't Elle.

———

THE SLOW-MOTION RUN THEY DO IN MOVIES? I THOUGHT THAT was just for dramatic effect, but every step I took inside that hospital was like stepping on freshly poured cement. For the second time in two weeks, I was back there, only this time it was more serious.

My stomach slammed into the reception desk and I braced my hands on top. "We're here to see Patrick Russo. He was brought in a couple hours ago."

The receptionist in her bright purple scrubs tapped on her keyboard like we were annoying passengers at an airline check-in desk, trying to purposely inconvenience her, not family waiting to know whether our loved one was breathing his last breaths.

Her response was long and drawn out, each syllable stretched for maximum frustration. We took the steps, Dad lagging two levels behind me, his hand braced on his knee. I burst onto the floor, nearly taking out a doctor walking with a clipboard.

With wild eyes, I raced down the hall to his room. A

doctor closed a chart and shook Gramps' hand. He looked smaller, almost swallowed up by the huge bed and the tubes running from his arms and chest. The dark circles under his eyes and the slight shake to his hand as he dropped it back to the bed sent panic rushing through me.

Gramps turned to me and gave me his trademark smirk. In his eyes, he still had that same mixture of determination and mischief. My anxiety dipped from a twelve to a ten.

The doctor—who looked way too young to be a surgeon—offered his hand. "You must be his grandson Phoenix. Patrick's been bragging about you since they brought him up here."

I shook my head to focus on the doctor's words. Shouldn't he have had distinguished gray hairs on his temples? He looked barely older than me.

"Yes." I reached out and shook his hand.

"You've got a strong grandfather. The surgery will be standard business. The bypass shouldn't give us any problems, but he'll have to take some time to rest, keep the stress levels down."

"When's the surgery?" Under my suit jacket and tie, sweat beaded on the nape of my neck.

The doctor's calm and cool demeanor didn't do anything to stop the crazy pounding in my chest.

He lifted the sleeve of his lab coat. "In about forty-five minutes. The nurse will be here to prep you in five." Tapping the edge of Gramps' bed, he smiled at me, and I wanted to throw him across the room. If it wasn't serious, why did he need surgery today? And if it was serious enough to need surgery today, why were they waiting? Did he have forty-five minutes?

"Calm down, Phoenix. I'm fine."

"You're in a hospital attached to eighty different monitors —I hardly think you're fine." I hugged him, careful of everything attached to him.

He flicked his hand away like this was no bigger deal than slicing off a bit of his finger in the kitchen.

Dad intercepted the doctor outside, his voice seeming to vibrate the floor.

"What happened?" My fingers skimmed the freezing cold bedrail.

"Everyone was overreacting in the kitchen, saying I didn't look so good."

"Yeah, obviously a total overreaction—they're about to wheel you into heart surgery in less than an hour."

"I'd have been fine."

"You'd have been dead."

"I've lived a long time, almost eighty years—it was bound to catch up to me."

"What was?"

"All that good food." He laughed, setting off a cough, and some of the monitors beeped wildly.

"Mr. Russo, how are you doing in there?" A nurse walked in, the kind of walk you did not to alarm someone, but to still get to where you needed to go quickly.

"It's my grandson's fault." He looked at her with big puppy dog eyes, and she shot me a censorious look. I swallowed past the lump in my throat, and the corner of my mouth lifted. Even in a hospital bed, he was still sharp as ever. How much longer would I have with him? Being on the road, training camp…even if I was still in town, how much of that little bit of time we might have left would I be missing out on?

"I'll be back in here in five minutes with the razor and shaving cream. Be prepared."

I blinked at him. "They're shaving your chest?"

"No, my crotch. The doctors thread a catheter up through my groin—"

"Nope, I don't need the play-by-play. As long as you'll be okay."

"Pops." Dad stood in the doorway of the room like a visitor waiting for an invitation.

"Phillip."

"How are you feeling?"

"Fine. Phoenix is going to help the nurses prepare me for the surgery, maybe hold one of my legs so they can really get in there."

"Dad, be serious." My dad strode into the room, his gaze bouncing wildly from one machine to another.

Gramps scoffed. "Why start now?"

"The nurse was pretty cute—maybe you could get her number." I winked at him and peered out the open doorway.

Gramps rubbed his chin. "Maybe I could. Perhaps she likes a silver fox." He ran a hand through his full head of hair.

"And the doctor said you need to take it easy, so that means less shifts at the restaurant. Let someone else handle things for a while." I picked up his hand.

Every bone stood out against his thin skin. Since when had Gramps gotten so old?

"It's my life's work." Gramps crossed his arms over his chest, doing his best annoyed teenager look.

"For once, put something else above it. It's your health we're talking about here." Dad braced his hands on the rail of the hospital bed.

"I didn't think you'd care either way."

"I can help out, Gramps."

My dad's head snapped up, his eyes wide.

"You know how much you like my basil ricotta gnocchi. I don't mind coming in and doing whatever I can."

Dad scowled. "You don't have time for that place."

"I'll make time for Gramps."

An assertive knock on the door cut off his next words. "Excuse me, gentlemen, I need to get Mr. Russo ready for surgery. The family waiting room is down the hall to the left."

Dad stormed out past the nurse holding her supplies in

her hand. I kissed Gramps on his cheek and gave him another hug.

"See you on the other side, old man." Leaving the room, I followed the disappearing figure of my dad down the hall and into the waiting room.

"You will not step foot in that kitchen to the detriment of your career." Dad broke off his pacing to point his finger straight at my chest.

"Gramps needs our help."

"He doesn't need anything but that precious restaurant."

"What the hell is your problem? He's your dad and he's about to go into surgery. This might be the last time we see him, and you didn't even say goodbye." The words I'd kept buried deep down since we got that phone call came charging forward like a linebacker finding his pocket.

"Did you know your grandfather never came to one of my games?" Dad stood with his back to me.

"Growing up?"

He braced his hands on his hips. "No, not just growing up. I mean never. Not once did he ever take a day or a night off to come watch me play."

"Are you seriously pissed about that right now?" I guess we were going to be one of those families—not the kind that came together in a crisis, but one that lost it on each other. I was already teetering on the edge, and the previous anger shoved down by worry was percolating, cresting on the edge of explosion.

Dad's lips twisted. "The old man will probably die just to spite me."

"You're unbelievable. It's about you, isn't it? It's always about you." I balled up my fists and tried to keep the thundering blood in my veins from drowning out the rest of the world. "You interfered with the Huffington Award, didn't you?" My words shot out like nails, ripping through the air.

He looked at me like I'd asked if the sky was blue. "Of course."

"Why?"

"With how well the charity stories were going, it would've been stupid not to capitalize on that. I talked to Sam and he mentioned the blood drive, which you failed to tell me about, and how good that looked for the school."

"Because it wasn't about any of this. I did that for Elle."

"She'll be fine." He waved it away like she didn't matter in the looming behemoth of my future prospects.

I clenched my fists at my sides. "What the hell did my mom ever see in you?"

The thunderclouds of his anger whipped across his eyes. "What kind of fucked up thing is that to say?"

"No worse than what you just did. All you care about is creating this perfect picture for you to pitch to the highest bidder to make even more money. It's not about the money— it's never been about the money to me."

"All I want is for you to have the best future you can. The opportunities out there for you…they're even better than the ones I had."

"And I don't care." I held my arms out wide. "I don't give a shit about any of this. All I wanted was for—"

"I took steps to make sure you don't screw up your future. You've worked so hard to get here. One mess up—one bad day can bring all that crashing down."

"You think I don't know that? It's a mantra you've beaten into my head every day, before every game, watching every tape of every play I've ever made, only ever pointing out my mistakes."

"I made sure you've had a life most people would dream of, and I was there to support you every step of the way."

"You were there pushing me into every step."

"And if I hadn't, what were you going to do? Kick around

your grandfather's restaurant? Throw away your football career to become a *cook*?"

"Maybe! What if I did? What if hanging out with Gramps and making food people love was what I wanted?"

"You're my son, goddammit!" He jammed his finger into the center of his chest. "And I've done the best I can to give you everything I never had. He was setting up Tavola and didn't have time for silly things like watching me play football. I played my ass off out on that field, hoping maybe one day he'd see that I'd made it and be proud of me, and I made a promise to myself that I'd never do the same to my son." He stared into my eyes.

"Dad, you weren't there. Mom was gone and you were on the road. I practically lived at Tavola. It was my home."

"You had a home—our home."

"As long as I did everything *you* wanted, right? As long as I went along with *your* plans, did what *you* asked. When you asked me to jump, I said how fucking high. That's the kind of home I had. That's how you showed your love—by making me pursue *your* dream."

"I've never done anything like that. I wanted you to shine and I wanted to be there to hold that light on you so everyone else could see it, not just because you were my son, but because I knew you had the talent. I knew you had it in you— that greatness."

"You wanted your do-over. I was an extension of you, a way to sweep up all those endorsement deals you never got, all the championships you should've won. I'm not you. I never wanted to be you, and I'm sick and tired of the people I care about always having conditions on their love.

"Gramps is the only one who's ever not given a damn about anything other than me being happy. This is my fault, though. I let you run my life. I went along with whatever you wanted, no questions asked, and let you think you could pull shady things like this and get away with it."

Dad's eyebrows dropped.

"I've been scared. Scared of what might happen if I told you no. Scared of what my life would look like if I did what I actually want to do. Scared I'd lose you. But I'm not scared anymore." Tears burned in my eyes. "I'm not going to let you railroad me into a life I don't want."

Dad stormed out of the room, the door groaning and banging against the wall in the hallway.

I had the thought that I might have just lost the last family I had left.

CHAPTER 35
ELLE

The clock on my bedside table ticked, echoing inside my head. Had it always been this loud? Or was this the first moment of silence I'd allowed myself in who knows how long? I wrapped my arms tighter around my legs and buried my face in my knees.

Darkness filled my room. How long had it been? Hours? Days? Weeks? No, not weeks. Graduation was only a few days away—or was it tomorrow? Everything ran together since the pieces of tape I've been using to hold myself together had been peeled away.

My tears had run dry, tears for what happened to me now, for how I was meant to drag myself into whatever came next, and tears for how I'd hurt Nix. At every turn, I'd let my past wrap its long, slender fingers around the neck of our future.

I'd tried to call, so many calls over so many hours. Each call and text went unanswered. I had my answer. This time, there was no coming back from how I'd hurt him, how I'd hurt myself.

This was my fault—had been since the first day I'd moved into that house. I'd let my issues grow into a tangled wall of thorns, so sharp and wide it was a miracle anyone would try to traverse it, but he had. He'd put up with everything I dished out and didn't let me get away with any of my old tricks when it came to pushing people away and protecting myself.

Only this time, the protection had backfired, and he was gone. I'd dragged myself across the street probably looking like I'd been hit by a car and knocked on his door. No answer.

I'd dragged myself back to my bedroom and had stayed in bed since.

"Elle…" Jules' gentle knock and the creaking of my door sounded like a jet engine taking off in my room.

The bed dipped, but I kept my head where it had been for so long that even the cramp in my neck had given up.

"I brought you some chocolate chunk cookies." Her voice was low, and even that was like a roar to my ears.

I buried my head deeper.

"No response for a chocolate chunk? Now you're scaring me." Her strained laugh didn't do anything to help the hollow pit in my chest. "A letter came for you."

"I don't want to see it." At this point, only bad news and junk mail landed in our mailbox, official letters from the university and crappy credit card offers.

"It's from the registrar."

Resigned to my fate, I took it from her hand, slipping it from her grip like a dirty tissue. I ripped it open: an official note saying the tuition deadline for the semester had passed. I could walk with my class, but I wouldn't be able to graduate. The worry and fear that had mounted throughout the semester before the award ceremony were dulled by the chunk of my heart that was now missing. The one thing I'd been trying to avoid had occurred, slamming straight into my face, but it paled in comparison to losing Nix.

———

THE DAYS MELDED INTO ONE CONTINUOUS SESSION OF JULES knocking on my door, trying to get me to come out, and, when I couldn't, bringing me some food and brushing my hair. Nix still hadn't returned my calls, not that I could blame him. And then, I couldn't hide anymore.

My parents had called from the road; they'd be arriving in a couple hours. I'd have to smile for all the pictures and wear my cap and gown knowing I wasn't graduating. If I told them the truth, it would crush them. Dad was only just back on his feet at work, and I couldn't deliver the blow of me not being able to graduate because of money. Adding another helping to this disappointment stew wasn't going to help anyone. Walking across the stage with the rest of my class, I'd pretend everything was okay for my parents.

The front door slammed shut so hard it rattled the floor then a set of footsteps raced up the steps. The bathroom door banged open and the shower turned on. Not a word.

Unfolding myself from the fetal position, I padded out of my bedroom.

Zoe's bedroom door was open a crack.

Pushing it open, I peered inside. She had a towel wrapped around herself and smacked her bed, sending a cloud of dust all over. Grabbing her discarded socks, she wiped down the dust on her desk and dresser. She picked up her bag off the floor and scattered her books all over the newly cleaned desktop.

Clutching the towel tighter around herself, she rushed forward, nearly knocking into me.

"Hey…"

"Elle," I supplied.

"Right, hey, Elle. Did you need the shower? I just turned it on. I'll be super quick." She bolted into the bathroom, taking the quickest shower known to man.

I glanced between the open doorway and the bathroom across the hall. Was she really here? It had seriously been a thought in the back of my head that Jules had made Zoe up as a ploy to help me afford this place, going so far as getting someone to pretend to be her on move-in day and throwing some furniture into the room.

The water shut off and she stepped out of the bathroom.

Someone knocked at the front door, and I bent to check who it was through the window.

Zoe grinned. "Perfect timing." She sprinted down the steps and opened the door for a middle-aged couple dressed in business wear like they were getting ready for a corporate takeover. Throwing her arms around them, she invited them in.

"Mom, Dad, I'm so happy you're here. I was just grabbing a shower. Stay down here and I'll run up and get changed." She showed them into our living room.

"This is where you've been living?"

"Well, the allowance you gave me this year made it hard to find anything better, but I love this place so much and my roommates are amazing." She beamed so brightly I was nearly blinded from a whole floor away. "Make yourselves comfortable. I'll be right back."

She darted back up the steps and winked at me before closing her door.

I stood at the top of the stairs, in awe of her balls. The front door opened again.

"Ready to graduate, biatch—oh!" Jules yelped as she spotted our strange visitors.

I laughed, covering my mouth. It felt weird, like getting on a bike again after years away. I rested my head against the wall and closed my eyes.

"Why the hell didn't you tell me we had people over? And who the hell are they?" Jules hissed at me as she tiptoed up the stairs.

"They're Zoe's parents."

"Zoe?"

As if conjured by our words, she breezed out of her room like a quick-change artist in a sundress with her cap in hand and her robe over her arm. "See you two at graduation," she called out on her way back down the stairs.

"What the hell?" Jules and I bent to watch her disappear out the front door with her parents.

"If you weren't here, I'd have thought I hallucinated the whole thing."

"She just showed up?" Jules nudged Zoe's door open, looking inside her room.

"Out of the blue. Rushed in here minutes before her parents knocked on the door."

"She lives," she whispered like an ancient prophecy had been fulfilled.

I huffed.

"There were a couple letters for you on the floor down there." Jules held them out to me.

A potent cocktail of fear and longing ricocheted inside my chest. My head shot up, the blood rushing to my brain and black spots dancing in front of my eyes. I lunged for the envelopes in her hand, ripping through the less official-looking one. It was a cream square envelope with a hospital return address on the back flap. *What in the hell?* My name was scrawled across the front, a single sheet of paper inside.

You deserve this.
- Nix

Did he mean my pain? The torture I'd been putting myself through? I wanted to curl up into a ball and disappear. Being cheated on didn't compare to this. That was a pain all its own, but this was a living, breathing creature digging deep inside me and tearing me apart. I squeezed my eyes shut, and the well of tears I'd thought had long gone dry found a new source. They poured down my cheeks and made it hard to breathe.

"Open the other one." She nudged the fallen envelope toward me.

With trembling hands, I slipped my finger under the unsealed corner of the envelope. Flattening the tri-folded sheets of paper, I sucked in a shaky breath. Through watery eyes, I scanned the document, searching for the words I'd hoped to see over and over with every request for something I could do to get the hold released.

Block removed. Tuition paid in full.

Behind the short, perfunctory memo was a full copy of my transcript.

Degrees awarded:

B.A. in English

And today's date.

A sob caught in my throat. He'd done this for me.

After everything, after the things I'd said to him and how I'd treated him, Nix had saved my future. I didn't deserve him, and it would only be a matter of time before the love I had for him wouldn't measure up and he'd realize every way I was lacking then I'd have to watch him walk away.

Wrapping my arms around myself, it was all I could do to hold myself together. I laid on my bed. Curling up on my side, I clutched his letter against my chest and rocked back and forth.

Jules ran her hand over my back, and I wished it were the type of cure that solved all problems like it had back in elementary school, wished she could give me a cookie and a back rub, telling me it was all going to be all right and me believing her because I knew it was true.

Now, though, I knew the real cost of mistakes. There weren't any do-overs like in kickball. I didn't get to say the pitch was a bad call and ask for another.

A bit later, with Jules' help, I dragged myself back out of bed, took a shower, and got dressed. The least I could do was attempt to function in front of my parents. I didn't need to add to their worry on top of everything else crumbling around me.

They showed up at our door, knocking and snapping a picture of me as soon as I opened it wearing my cap and gown.

"Sweetheart, look at you." Mom pulled me into her arms for a hug, and it was all I could do to maintain my composure. Forcing a big, wide smile, I let her fuss over me.

"You look good, kid." Dad hugged me and squeezed me tight. "I'm sorry I let you down."

Pinching my lips tight, I shook my head. "You didn't." I patted his back. "Everything's great. I'm graduating, right?" I pushed back the welling tide that had my eyes prickling and made it so I had to let out a deep breath through my mouth. I was graduating because of Nix.

"I'm so proud of you." Dad squeezed my shoulders and released me back to Mom's fussing and fixing, dealing with the imaginary smudges that can only be removed by a mother's spit, the stray hair that's always in the way for every picture.

Standing in front of our house, we took more pictures: just me and Mom, me and Dad, Jules and me, Mom and Dad and me with Jules serving as our photographer.

In more than one picture, Mom called me out for not looking into the camera. Instead, my gaze drifted to the house across the street. It was quiet. The guys were in the business school, which meant their graduation had been earlier. The philosophy department was relegated to the last slot of the day.

Fake it till you make it, right? I'd fake it like I wasn't broken inside in a way I had no idea how to fix. I'd been running from love for so long, and I'd have to keep running—away from his soft eyes, his strong arms, and the way his soul sang to mine. I'd wear this fake smile as long as I had to, because there was no coming back from Nix.

There was only an expanse of desolation in front of me. He'd given me everything I'd worked so hard for, and it all dimmed in comparison to what it was like trying to go on without him.

CHAPTER 36
NIX

"We brought you this." Reece stepped forward with his fingers twined with Seph's.

I winced at the alcohol-on-an-open-wound pain radiating through my chest.

He handed over my cap and gown. Graduation would come and go, not that there would be anyone there to watch me walk, not that I even wanted to stand up in front of crowds of people who thought they knew me because they'd seen me throw a ball across a field for the past four seasons.

"We figured you paid for it. You should at least get to wear it."

"How's your Gramps doing?" Berk sat beside me and crossed his arms.

"We're just waiting for him to wake up." I dragged my hands down my face.

"Has Elle been here?" Reece craned his neck like she might be pressed up against the wall and would pop out from behind one of the chairs like a street magician.

"No, she's not here."

"Do you need one of us to call her? Or go get her?" Berk grabbed his phone. "I have her roommate's number, I think."

I shook my head. "No."

"Seriously, we can go get her."

"I said no." My words were a shot in the hushed tones of the room. Everyone stared at me like I'd lost it. Little did they know, I'd lost it a while ago.

"We can wait with you." LJ sat in one of the chairs. Marisa sat beside him and gave me a small smile.

"You don't have to." I shook my head. "I'm sure you've got graduation parties and stuff to get to."

"Nah, we're good here." Berk patted me on the back. "Anyone want some candy from the vending machine?" He popped up, and everyone laughed. It was the first ray of lightness that broke through the intense cloud cover on my life.

Gramps was in the clear, though the surgery had been rough with an even larger blockage than they'd antici-pated. After sleeping on the miniature furniture in the hospital for three days, I'd dragged myself back home once he woke up and pretty much banished me, saying I smelled rank.

Dad had stayed too, but we hadn't spoken for two days once he came back into the waiting room. We took up our spots on opposite sides of the space, making it unbearably uncomfortable for anyone else who tried to grab a seat. The other waiting rooms didn't have the same simmering tension and unbridled animosity clogging the air like the blockages clogging Gramps' arteries.

My only break from the antiseptic and fluorescent limbo I was in had been when I went onto campus and did what needed to be done. No matter what happened with Elle, I knew she shouldn't be trapped in some bullshit limbo not able to properly move on with her life because my dad had screwed her over.

I'd slipped the envelopes under her door then Jules had opened it. She'd tried to convince me to come in, but the thread I was holding it together with was fraying more and more by the second.

Collapsing into my bed, I'd slept long enough to remember I was human and then headed back to the hospital. Dad took up his spot in the corner of the room and let his ominous presence do all the talking since his mouth wouldn't, even when Gramps made me promise to go check on the restaurant. Dad didn't say a thing when Gramps asked me to get the new menus printed and gave me a list of things to make sure had been ordered, not piping up even when he asked if I'd stay through the preview night dinner service while he was in the hospital.

On autopilot, I got to the restaurant, and everyone swarmed me, needing to know what was going on. I gave everyone the rundown and they got to work, just like they knew he'd want. With all the dishes ready to go, everyone started sitting down at the large family-style setup we'd created, transforming the restaurant into an extension of the family they'd all become.

"Sorry, we're closed for a private event," someone said through a small crack in the door, ready to close it on whoever couldn't read the three signs posted and didn't know the neighborhood tradition of preview night.

But the pale pink flutter of hair through the closing gap between the door and the frame had me getting out of my seat. She wedged her face into the small space, and our gazes collided.

"I know, but I wanted to talk to Nix." Her words carried and died on my name, a swallowed sound like it was hard to push it out.

I crossed the distance between us. It might as well have been the Grand Canyon. Every step reverberated through my body.

Her voice sounded like one I hadn't heard in years, not

less than a week. I felt like I'd lived a thousand lifetimes since standing with her in the wings of the theater.

"She can come in." I patted one of the new guys on the shoulder and pulled the door open, letting her in.

She ducked her head and stepped inside. "I just found out about your grandfather. With everything that happened with graduation, my parents were here and I...well, I thought you were avoiding me. Not that you had a reason to, because you didn't do anything wrong. That was self-centered to think it would have anything to do with me—you know, you not being home, not taking my calls...and now I'm rambling." Her gaze landed on every square inch of the place except where I stood.

I wanted her to look at me. Close up, with nothing between us, I wanted her to see me, to finally see me and how much I loved her, how much I needed her, even when I wished I didn't. Even when I told myself I shouldn't, the way my heart was making a dash for the end zone from the fifty-yard line, I didn't know if I'd ever be able to.

I held out my arm, motioning for her to follow me back into the kitchen. Holding the door open for her, I let her walk inside.

The door swung shut behind her, and I pretended everyone on the other side of the room didn't have their eyes trained on us through the slowly closing gap. Restaurants were second only to hair salons for the amount of gossip that swirled around.

I crossed my arms over my chest, balling up my fingers against my sides to keep from reaching out to her. The muscles in my shoulder resisted the extra pressure.

Her cheeks were flushed like she'd run from wherever she was coming from. The soft pinkness of her lips was just as I remembered, just as I'd memorized staring down at her night after night. With everything that had happened over the past few days, I'd been so close to calling her. Breaking down in the moments I left the waiting room or my grandfather's room, I wanted to bury my head in her stomach and let her wrap her arms around me and tell me she loved me and it would all be okay. But I couldn't, not if she'd never trust me. Giving her all of me while she held some of herself back would eat away at me.

"You wanted to talk." I kept my voice level, swallowing past the lump in my throat.

She took a deep breath, sucking it in through her pursed lips. "I'm so sorry about your grandfather. I just heard and... and I wanted to say that to you. I know how much he means to you, and he was always so kind to me."

At least she cared enough to come here. She looked as worn down as I felt, but it wasn't like all the times I'd seen her dragging herself home before. If anything, all that should have been over now that graduation had come and gone. "Was that all?"

"Thank you," she blurted out. Her lips tightened and her voice wobbled. "Thank you for what you did with my tuition. I'll pay you back, but thank you. You didn't have to do it. I don't even know why you did it, but thank you."

"You don't know why I did it?"

Her words fanned the glowing ember sitting in the bottom of my chest, the doubt. Would it always be there? Even after everything I'd said, did she still not know?

"You don't know why I did it?" My pointed repetition drew her attention, and her gaze shot to mine.

"I get that you didn't plot behind my back with the Huffington Award, and I know you were telling the truth. I knew even then, but I'm not good with trusting myself. So, I wanted to tell you that in person. I know that isn't something you'd have done behind my back. You've been who you are from the beginning, and that's the same kind, loyal, and patient guy I met the first time I saw you." Her voice cracked. "But I blinded myself to that. My own hang-ups and bad experiences stopped me from believing everything we could've been." She wiped her nose with the back of her hand. "I'm sorry. I wanted to be the girl who could be everything you wanted and needed. I wanted to give that to you, so much, and I'm sorry I'm even here talking about this when your grandfather's in the hospital, but I didn't know if or when you were leaving town and I didn't want to leave without saying that to you."

"You ripped my heart out, Elle."

She stared at the floor between us and nodded. "I know."

The sides of my eyes prickled with tears.

"I know. If it means anything to you, I ripped my own heart out. I thought…" She took another deep breath, steeling herself for the words to come. "I thought if I didn't ever let myself love you, I couldn't be hurt again." She brushed at the tears trailing down her cheeks. "But I was wrong."

She looked up at me with the sawing pain I'd felt in my chest reflected in her eyes.

"And there's nothing I can do to make up for how I treated you."

I tipped my chin to the side and held her gaze. "There is one thing."

CHAPTER 37
ELLE

The knot in my stomach tightened with each passing second. Pretending everything was just fine in front of my parents for the past two days had put me on the razor's edge, and the way Nix was looking at me now turned the knot in my stomach into a fist. It was hard to look at him. His jaw was so tight I could see each shift of his tendons.

I shouldn't have come, maybe just sent a letter or carrier pigeon when I was on the other side of the globe. With my diploma, the Peace Corps had given me the final approval to head off on a two-year stint in Burma, 8119 miles away from Philly, away from Nix—although in this moment, I wished I were already that far away.

I hadn't been sure exactly what kind of reception I'd get from Nix when I saw him, but I hadn't expected this kind of cold detachment. I'd failed. He was surrounded by his restaurant family, and I was intruding. That had been made abundantly clear.

Was I a hair's breadth away from ugly crying?

He had his arms crossed over his chest. His button-down shirt stretched over his body in all the right places. I missed him. I missed the warmth in his eyes and the way he put everyone around him at ease. I hadn't thought he had this kind of stone-cold look in him. Maybe it was one he saved for the field.

My stomach plummeted. I was receiving—and deserved —the same look he gave his opponents.

"There is one thing."

His words filled me with a flicker of hope.

He stepped closer, nearly toe to toe with me. "Did you ever love me?" His words felt clinical, like an exit interview question.

"How could I not? You have an entire city ready to throw you a parade whenever you leave your house. I love you and that's why I couldn't trust you—because it's not just you I didn't trust, it was me. The two times before when I thought I was in love? They're peewee football compared to how I feel about you. You're the pros, Nix, and if I couldn't handle my heart being broken back then, there is no way I'd be able to deal when things fell apart with you. It was a preemptive strike, but all I did was blow myself up. So that's me being completely and totally honest. I love you."

His silence was so loud it hurt. It was like two hands squeezing my chest.

His face was an impassive mask, and I'd lost him. Of all the things I'd lost, losing him hit me the hardest because it was my own stupid hang-ups that had gotten in the way.

"You're busy, and I'm sorry for barging in here and ruining your evening. I'll let you get back to it. Please tell your grandfather I hope he's back in the kitchen soon, and I —" I turned and blinked back the tears I refused to let fall until I was back outside.

"Stop." That one word sliced through my rambling, soon-to-be-blubbering mess.

"Nix?" The pain of his rejection crushed me. I'd have to make it through, and maybe someday I'd find something to fill the hollow space in my chest where my heart had been. I backed away from him.

His arms shot out and he held on to me.

My pulse throbbed in my arms as his grip tightened.

"I needed to know." His voice covered me like a thick, heavy blanket. Staring up into his eyes, I saw they brimmed with unshed tears that matched the ones drying on my cheeks. His Adam's apple bobbed up and down. "I needed to know this wasn't one-sided."

After everything I'd learned about trust, I didn't trust my ears. I couldn't, and any response died in my throat because hope was a cruel jokester and I couldn't handle that right now when the glue hadn't even dried on the parts of me I'd tried to stick together.

"I needed to know." He sank his fingers into my hair, his palm resting against my cheek and nearly lifting me off my feet as his mouth crashed down on mine. I couldn't move, couldn't breathe, and then, like a movie slipped into fast-forward, I scrambled to get even closer to him.

I wrapped my arms around his back and tilted my head, parting my lips and letting him inside—into my mouth, my heart, and anywhere else he'd have me.

"It was killing me thinking you didn't love me too."

"I've loved you for a long time, so long I didn't let myself believe it."

Tears burned in my eyes, but this time I didn't try to hold them back. They were tears of joy born out of a trial by fire of my own making.

Nix kissed away my tears and cupped the back of my head while our tongues danced, each swipe of his lips rekindling the embers of desire that had been drowned out since the last time we touched.

He broke off our kiss. Our matching panting breaths were the only sounds over the gentle din of chatter from the other side of the door. Resting his forehead against mine, he gazed into my eyes, and I wanted to kick my own ass three ways to Sunday. Love shined in his eyes like a lighthouse beacon in a stormy night.

"What will you do now that you've graduated?"

"I got my Peace Corps assignment."

"Where?" The word was rough and tight.

"Burma."

"8000 miles away."

My eyes widened. "How'd you know?"

"I researched everywhere on your list when you told me before and checked out some flight schedules. Thirty hours of travel each way isn't going to be pretty, but I can make it happen."

Resting my hand on his chest, I pressed my lips against his. "Just when I didn't think I could love you any more..." I shook my head at the insane kind of fool I'd been. "You don't have to do that."

"I can't go two years without seeing you, not after what this week felt like."

"You don't have to travel to see me—because I'm going to be here."

"You found a job here?"

"Sort of. It's an internship. With all the money I saved this semester, I have enough to give myself a cushion—after you paid off my tuition, that is. I'm interning with an event planner." I ducked my head and swallowed against the blush brewing in my cheeks. "They work with a lot of charities and nonprofits, and I thought maybe I could help them get the word out and partner with bigger organizations."

He ran his fingers under my chin and lifted my head. Should I have run off to Burma to live in a hut for two years and help a local village? Probably. That's what a good person would do, but Jules had given me the idea and my wheels had started turning, the ones that had been thrown into turbo at Give on the Gridiron.

"That's the perfect fit for you. Think of how much more those groups can do with big names and even bigger money behind them. Doing good things doesn't mean you have to be Mother Teresa 24/7. Don't be afraid to do what makes you happy." He nuzzled his nose against mine. "And I know you'll put your whole heart into it. Anyone you work with will be lucky to have you at their side."

I blinked back those anxious tears and nodded.

"Speaking of doing what makes you happy...how much of how you felt about me had to do with me being a professional football player?" A glimmer of nervousness flickered in his gaze.

"About 0.001%. Why?"

"Funny you're changing the direction of your life, because I'm doing the same thing. This week was rough and made me realize a lot of things. Football isn't something I can do anymore. I've done it for my dad my entire life, and all it's going to do is grind me down. The paycheck isn't worth it when I can be here in the kitchen with Gramps. He needs to take it easy, and I'm the only one who can convince him to slow the hell down. So, I'll pay my dues and take it over from him soon."

"Wow."

"Right?" He laughed.

"You're sure about this?"

"As sure as I am about us." He dragged his thumb across my cheek. "This week was rough without you."

"I'm sorry I wasn't there, and I'll spend as much time making up for it as I can." I tightened my hold against his back, fisting his shirt between my fingers. "You've gotten under my skin since that first second."

"Are you sure you weren't just a bit awestruck by getting to see me buck-assed naked?"

"I won't say that wasn't part of the package." I let out a watery laugh.

"I knew it—you're just using me for my body."

"More like loving you for everything you are." I dragged my fingers through the hair at the nape of his neck, letting the soft strands run through my fingers.

"Including my ass."

"I'm more partial to this." I dragged my fingers along the indentation just below the waistband of his jeans.

"We'll have to make sure we get reacquainted soon." He stared at me like he was afraid I'd disappear right in front of his eyes.

I nodded. "And we have the rest of our lives to do that."

"The rest, huh?"

I swallowed past the thickness in my throat. Now wasn't the time for me to hold anything back. Every cell in my brain should've been screaming out for me not to make some crazy, rash declaration, but this time my brain and my heart were in perfect agreement. "Forever."

"I can deal with forever." He dragged his thumb across my bottom lip. The rough pads of his fingers sent shivers down my spine. "On one condition."

"Tell me."

The corner of his mouth lifted. "There is one thing you can do to make it up to me."

CHAPTER 38
NIX

"We're never giving up! We're never surrendering!" I slammed my back against the wall. A plastic cartridge filled with more darts slid into my hand. I rocked my head to the side and grinned at Elle, pulling her close to me and tasting her lips like I might never taste them again.

I wasn't taking another touch, another kiss, another night for granted when it came to her.

"This wasn't exactly what I had in mind when you said I could make it up to you." She licked her lips.

"We'll have plenty of time for *that* later." My gaze darted to her lips. "Right now, we need to kick some capture the flag ass." Two Fulton U flags were up for grabs; one was gold with a navy Trojan on it, and another was navy with a huge non-school-sanctioned FU in the center of it in gold lettering. The latter sat at the end of the upstairs hallway.

"Did you take me back for my phenomenal nerf battle skills?"

"One of many reasons." I pressed a quick kiss against her lips, unable to help myself.

Forty sweaty and victorious minutes later, we all kicked

back in some chairs in the backyard. Keyton and Berk, first out of the game again, had freshly made burgers ready to go.

"How many of these games do you play a year?" Keyton took a bite of his burger and took a swig from his beer.

"As many as we feel like." Berk crammed his burger into his mouth.

"Cool." Keyton grinned and had another drink.

"Although, I'd like to add boob shots to the no-nut, no-eye clause in the rules." Marisa raised her hand. "Taking a dart to the nip is no joke."

"Ris, seriously? We don't need to know about your nips." LJ covered each ear with half a hamburger bun.

"What's the matter, L? You don't like hearing about your bestie's breasts? My bosom? My sweater chickens?" She tugged at the edge of the bun, trying to pull it away from his ears.

"If you don't stop, I'm not going to dinner tomorrow."

She plopped down in her seat. "No need to overreact. Sheesh." She sullenly picked at her patty.

"What's the big deal about dinner?" Elle squirted some ketchup on her burger.

"It's dinner with my dad, the last one of the school year until I'm free."

"I guess you guys don't get along?"

"Hard to get along with someone who was never around and then lords his free tuition waiver over your head and makes you come to weekly dinners at his house, but other than that, we get along just fine. Peachy keen." Her brittle smile had everyone admiring the leaves and grass in the backyard.

A knock on the gate saved us all from the abject awkwardness that had settled over our group. Berk jumped up, nearly spilling his plate on the ground.

"Jules!" he announced to everyone in a three-block radius.

"Elle said you guys were grilling, and I know everyone is

leaving…I had a lot of brownies left over and didn't want them sitting in the freezer all summer. So, I wanted to drop them off." She shoved the container into Berk's chest.

"Drop them off—that's crazy. Stay for a bit. We've got more than enough food."

Jules edged toward the gate, but Berk wrapped his arm around her shoulders and tugged her over to everyone else.

Elle and Jules seemed to be having some kind of silent, eye-only communication, and Jules dropped into a seat looking like she expected to be offered up a turd sandwich.

With a plate settled on her lap, Jules took small, calculating bites like there was a game of mouth Tetris she needed to get right in order to eat. "How did your friend like the cake?"

Berk's head shot up with brownie crumbs on his cheek.

"What cake?" I snagged a brownie from the container he seemed perfectly fine with hoarding. "You're holding out on us and ordering cakes for yourself?"

"No…" His leg bounced up and down. "It was a birthday cake."

"How'd she like it?" Jules' fingers tightened on the edge of her plate.

"She said it was the best cake she's ever had." He said it quietly like it was a conversation just between the two of them.

Jules smiled at him, but it didn't reach her eyes. "I'm glad Alexis liked it."

She'd detonated the A-bomb. LJ whipped around, and Reece shook his head.

Elle, Jules, and Keyton all stared at us wide-eyed.

"No." LJ waved his finger in the air. "Nope. She's bad news, man."

"Do I need to remind you what happened the last time she came around?" Reece smacked the back of one hand into his palm.

"I got all the stuff back, plus, I didn't bring her here. I went to her."

Dragging my hands down my face, I shook my head. Berk's heart was way too damn big. She was a user, and every time she came around, Berk was left holding the bag and cleaning up her messes.

"You're going to be a pro football player—this is when you start thinking about the type of people you want around you and the type of people who'll be toxic to your success."

"I get it." He handed the container of brownies off to Seph, who squeezed his hand as he walked off. "I'll get more beers for everyone."

"Who's Alexis?" Elle looked to all of us.

"A friend of Berk's from before college. And she's...well, let's just say she's not good for him." LJ seemed to deflate back into his chair.

"He seems to care a lot about her. He got her a cake," Jules offered meekly.

"Sometimes he's his own worst enemy," Reece said as everyone looked through the wide kitchen windows at Berk shoving more bottles of beer into his arms. "I'll go help him before he drops an entire case of beer on the floor." Reece tapped Seph's leg and she stood, letting him save our beers. He tucked a strand of hair behind her ear. "So lucky."

Her cheeks burned brightly and she ducked her head as he rushed into the house.

These guys were the best friends I'd ever had, and in a matter of weeks, this house would no longer be one I called home. It wasn't like I'd be sad living in a place that didn't have the moniker the Brothel, but we'd gotten closer than friends there, more like brothers, and as an only child, that meant more to me than all the plays out on a field.

The backyard gate unlatched. Striding across the grass with his telltale limp, my dad had his gaze laser-focused on me. Jumping up from my seat, I rushed over to him.

"Dad, what are you doing here?" I led him back to the gate and stood at the side of the house with my arms over my chest.

He looked at me and took a breath, the kind he always took before laying into me about the thousand things I'd fucked up between waking up in the morning and the minute he saw me. Staring up at the sky, he shook his head.

"I fucked up."

My jaw dropped. I swear they heard the *thud* from a block away.

He stared at me with tears in his eyes. "You're—" He covered his mouth with his balled-up hand. "You're my son, Phoenix, and I love you. I love you more than anyone on this planet, and I've always wanted what was best for you. I wanted you to succeed and do even better than I ever could. I was a screw-up who still can't believe your mom decided I was the one for her." His voice cracked.

"Dad—"

"Let me finish. There's a lot I need to apologize for. When you were little—" He sucked in another breath. "When you were little, you looked so much like her it hurt. Every day was a reminder of what I'd lost and what you'd lost, and there wasn't anything I could do about it. All the money and all the fame and I'd have given it all away for another hour with her. So, I was a coward and I stayed away, letting Gramps take care of you while he was running the restaurant. Of course you learned to love it while spending time with him there."

He paced up and down the narrow walkway beside the house. "Then you got a little bit older and started taking an interest in football, and I latched onto that. That was how you were like me. I could fix all the football stuff, make you better, make you the best. I fixated on that and told myself your mom would've wanted it for you, but it was what I wanted.

Despite me, you've turned into the kind of man your mom would've been proud of."

Tears pooled in my eyes, and his blurry figure wavered in front of me.

"She'd have kicked my ass and been so proud of you for not letting me force you into a life you don't want." He pulled me close, wrapping his arms around me in a hug that belied his age and how much his body had been through. He buried his face in my neck as his shoulders shook.

We stood there with tears mending some of the cracks of a relationship I'd thought irreparable. He patted me on the back and broke his hold on me, wiping his nose. "I'm a freaking mess."

"Did you want to come and have some burgers?" I pointed my thumb toward the backyard, lifting my shirt to wipe my face.

"You've only got a few days left with these guys. Enjoy it. I'll see you at the restaurant."

My head jerked back. "The restaurant?"

"Yeah, Gramps'll need some help, and you can't do it all on your own."

"You cook?"

"You're not the only one who grew up there." The corner of his mouth lifted and he pulled me in for another hug. "I'll see you soon."

He waved and disappeared around the front of the house.

I stood in a daze, still not believing it had actually happened. Walking back into the yard, I caught Elle's gaze.

"You okay?" she mouthed.

Her worry shouldn't have sent a thrill through my body, her expression telling me she'd always be there and would always have my back. "I'll tell you later," I mouthed back before grabbing a beer.

Berk and Reece pushed back through our circle of chairs.

"When are you moving in, Keyton?" Berk rocked back in his chair.

"Whenever works for you guys. My lease is up at the end of the month, but I can find another place to stay if you need more time." Keyton tapped his fingers along the edge of his plate and looked at me.

"Nah, I'll get out of your hair and let you get settled before summer training camp starts. There's an apartment over Tavola that Gramps hasn't used in ages, so I'll move in and start fixing it up." I sat in my chair and pulled Elle onto my lap.

She sank into me, completely relaxed, and ran her fingers along the hair at the nape of my neck. This was a perfect moment, the kind you swear you'll remember forever until there's nothing but that glowing feeling of happiness, even when the details fade.

"*We'll* start fixing it up. It's not like we've got much else to do." Berk handed out the frosty bottles to everyone in our circle.

"And we'll make sure it has a comfy couch for when these two are driving me crazy." Berk jerked his finger toward LJ and Marisa.

"I vote we dump that couch. Anyone else in favor?" Marisa held up her hand like she was voting in a boardroom.

"I have a couch, if you guys need a replacement," Keyton offered.

"Have you sat on ours? We should ship it off to a torture museum to be added to their medieval punishment section. This is yet another reason I knew you'd make an awesome roommate." Berk clapped him on the shoulder.

"Happy to help."

"You know Berk's going to be at Tavola sniffing around for free meals." LJ kicked back in his chair.

"I still can't believe you're not going pro next year." Berk drained his beer before spitting it out and spraying it all over LJ and Marisa.

They both sat there holding their arms out to their sides like they'd just been hit in the face by a water balloon completely drenched.

"Sorry, there was a bee in it."

The two of them stood and waddled back into the house like they'd peed their pants.

"How much beer can you hold in your mouth? It looks like a firehose sprayed them both."

"Sorry, guys. I'll save a brownie for you." Berk opened a new beer, drank some of it, and set the brownie box in front of him. "You outdid yourself this time, Jules. These are insane."

"Thanks. I added espresso chocolate chips."

"Those are my favorite."

"I know." She said the words so low, I didn't know if anyone else other than me and Elle heard. I turned to Elle, and she shook her head, one quick move that told me not to touch that with a twenty-foot pole.

"These things are never easy, are they?" I whispered into her ear.

"Unfortunately not." She took my hand in hers. "But nothing great is ever easy, right?"

"You've got that right." I dropped a kiss on her shoulder and jumped back into the conversation with the guys. It was time to soak up as much of this as possible before the real world intruded and we all went our separate ways. I'd have Elle by my side, and that took the sting out of losing this place and these guys and made it a hell of a lot easier.

She was a part of me I hadn't even known was missing.

She was the first best decision I'd made in my life, and her love made every day worth it.

EPILOGUE

ELLE

Boxes lined the hallway of our two bedroom apartment over Tavola. We were still removing old wallpaper and re-painting the place, but over the past two months it was becoming ours. Between Nix's new role at the restaurant and my new position with one of the biggest event planning companies in the city, we were exhausted at the end of long days that sometimes stretched on until two am, but collapsing in bed each night beside him, I'd never been happier.

Folding back the flap to the box with 'Nix's stuff' scrawled across one side, I walked back out to the kitchen. The treasure trove inside deserved its own prized spot in the apartment.

He had every serving plate we'd unpacked so far piled high with food that made my mouth water. The sizzle and pop of the pan on the stove was a constant soundtrack in our apartment. While a lot of people always said chefs never liked to cook at home, Nix had years of pent up culinary expression ready for a delicious explosion and I was more than happy to be in the blast zone with my mouth open. Between him trying out new things and the quick and easy access to the restaurant, I was glad my job entailed a lot of racing across the city to get thing organized for the events I coordinated.

"You were holding out on me, Golden Boy." I looped my arms around Nix's neck, rocking from side to side.

He wrapped one arm around me and flipped the chicken in the pan beside him. "I've cooked for you before."

"I'm not talking about cooking."

He turned off the fire. "What exactly have I been holding out on you?" The charmer smile didn't just work on his football fans and customers at the restaurant. It still made my knees practically elastic.

When he was this close to me and smelled like yummy food and freshly folded laundry, it was hard to keep my train of thought.

"Your vinyl collection. You'd put most record stores to shame."

"Maybe I just didn't want to clue you into my secret stash, B + E." He rubbed his nose against mine.

"Maybe I'll look into it and see how much they sell for on eBay." I tapped my finger against my chin.

"I've got something for you to look into." He dipped his knees and lifted me, navigating our maze of boxes and dropping me onto our bed.

Pushing my hair back out of my face, I grinned up at him. "We have guests coming in about twenty minutes."

He looked down at me with a primal hunger that sent a sizzling flush throughout my body. "We'd better be fast, then."

I tugged my shirt up over my head. By the time my head was free from it, Nix was completely naked like a quick change magician. Laughing, I fought with the button of my jeans.

He leaned over, catching my foot against his chest and tickling my toes.

I bucked and twisted away from his grip. "You're supposed to be helping." Tears of laughter caught in my eyelashes.

Gripping the bottoms of my jeans, he tugged them down my legs. The feel of his hands on me never failed to drive the simmering ache into a full blown keening need in a matter of seconds.

"This is the first day off we've both had in over a month."

He fell down on top of me, bracing himself on his arms. "Are you sure you want to spend it with my pain in the ass friends?"

I hitched my leg over his hip and pushed my heel into his ass. "You missed them. And we haven't gotten a chance to show this place off yet."

Lifting his head, he looked at the wall behind our bed, covered in five different paint swatches. "Still a work in progress."

"Isn't everything?" I ran my fingers along the stubble on his jaw.

"Have I told you how much I love you?" He took my fingers and kissed the fingertips.

"Not today." I lifted my hips to meet the erection sandwiched between us. The head of his cock teased my entrance.

"Then I guess I should show you." He ducked his head and kissed me, pushing his tongue into my mouth and changing the angle of his hips and in an instant there was no tease to his touch. There was only hunger, power, and his love for me. A love I could return without reservation or hesitation.

My orgasm crashed into me, overwhelming all my senses. He knew my body so well it was like the playbook was seared into his mind. One second I could breathe and the next

I was floating, holding on as he tightened his hold on me and expanded inside me. Our collapse was short lived; a timer went off in the kitchen.

He rested his forehead against mine. "That's the bread." His breath came out in pants.

"You'd better go get it." I fell back onto the bed with my chest rising and falling in time to my heartbeat.

"Be right back. Hop in the shower and I'll wash your back." He jumped up and darted out of the room, giving me a very nice view of those still incredibly tight buns.

———

FRESH FROM OUR LIGHTNING QUICK SHOWER, I JOGGED TO THE door after the first knock.

Berk and LJ were back in town for training camp. Jules had thankfully stayed in our old place, now hers and Zoe's, so really hers alone. She'd have to go to an engagement party for her sister over the long weekend in a few weeks, so I was stocking up on booze and hugs. Marisa had worked on campus all summer.

"Where's Berk?" I peered down the short hallway.

"Said he had something to do." LJ shrugged.

"Probably to do with the new letter he got. I swear, he squirrels himself away for half a day whenever one of those shows up." Marisa handed over a container of god knows what, glowing like a radioactive isotope.

Jules chugged her entire drink and held it up even after she was done, inspecting the bottom of the glass and ignoring my gaze. No matter how many times I'd told her to come clean, she was adamant against it.

I got everyone a drink and we flicked through the movies on the screen.

"Guys." Berk threw the door open and nearly took a

chunk out of the wall behind it. He spun around with a letter gripped in his hand and slammed the door shut.

"What the hell, Berk?" Nix came out of the kitchen with a bowl of popcorn.

"She said she's done." His gaze was frantic.

"Who?"

He thrust the wrinkled piece of paper and envelope into the air.

"Your Letter Girl?" LJ pried them from Berk's hand.

"Yes." He sank into the arm chair by the door.

Jules became fascinated by the thread count of our Ikea rug, tugging at it and keeping her head down.

"What did you say to her?"

"Nothing outside of our normal letters. I got the next one and—" He gestured to the one in LJ's hand. He passed it over to Marisa, who tried to pass it to Jules. She shook her head and moved onto inspecting the wood grain of our coffee table.

"All it says is 'I don't think we should do this anymore.' Marisa flipped it over. "Why would she cut you off after months?"

Berk sank his head into his hands. "I don't know, but I put another note in the box when I went to pick this up and it's still there."

I tried to keep my gaze from boring a hole in the side of Jules' head.

"Maybe she's moving away and doesn't want a pen pal anymore." Nix set down another plate of food on the table.

Berk shook his head. "I'm not ready for this to be over."

Jules' gaze flicked to him. The corner of her mouth quirked up.

I caught her gaze and tilted my head toward them. 'Tell him' I mouthed.

I lifted my eyebrows and tilted my head toward Berk.

She gave me one hard shake of her head.

Marisa handed the note back to him. "Doesn't seem like you have a choice."

"What does Alexis think of all this?" LJ leaned against the fridge.

Jules' half step toward Berk froze and she recoiled like someone had dropped a rattlesnake in front of her.

"What about her?"

LJ crossed his arms over his chest and lifted an eyebrow.

"She's not someone I can just leave behind, get over it. But she doesn't have anything to do with Letter Girl.

"She can't just barge into my life with these notes and then peace out like it was nothing."

Jules throat worked up and down and she grabbed her beer off the table. Her gaze darted to floor.

"It seems like she can and just did."

"No, I don't accept that."

"What are you other options?"

"I'm going to find her." Berk's steely air of determination filled the room.

Jules's hacking cough drew everyone's attention. Foam bubbled out of the top of her beer and she grabbed a fistful of napkins to cover her mouth.

"Jules," Berk called out her name and dropped down to the floor beside her.

She stared back at him like her eyes were about to pop out of her head. A squeak that sounded a little like a 'yes' flew out of her mouth.

"You're in the same class as her. Well, we both are. She's a senior now too. Can you help me?"

"Maybe it's better to leave things like she said."

"It's not that easy. None of you understand." His panicked gaze swept over all of us. "Jules, you'll help me, right?"

Her mouth hung open and she stared into his eyes, nodding once.

Berk's big, wide smile could practically be seen from space

and he dove onto her, wrapping his arms around her, hugging her tight and shaking her from side to side.

She stared at me over my shoulder throughout the rag doll treatment and I shrugged giving her a helpless look.

He jumped up and paced in front of the tv, going over their Scooby Doo investigation options. Jules drummed her fingers on her leg like she was ready to bolt from the room at any second.

"We can narrow things down once classes start and everyone's back on campus. Maybe I can find a way to get handwriting samples." He tapped his chin.

Jules hid her hands behind her back like they'd give her away at any moment.

"I'm not stopping until I find her. We'll turn this place upside down. We'll be a great team, right Jules."

Her mouth opened and closed as her eyes widened straight past anime to trapped in the vacuum of space. The word was barely a squeak. "Sure."

There was no escape now. Berk was determined and it was only a matter of time before the pressure got to her. Let the fireworks begin.

———

For a look at Nix and Elle's life post-graduation, I've got a yummy bonus scene for you! You know you wanna! ;-) It's a move in day of another kind for these two. Grab it now!

———

Don't miss Berk and Jules' story, The Third Best Thing!

Grab your copy of The Third Best Thing or read it for FREE in KU!

———

The Fourth Time Charm - LJ + Marisa

My best friend. My new roommate. My coach's daughter.

———

The Fulton U Trilogy!

The Art of Falling For You

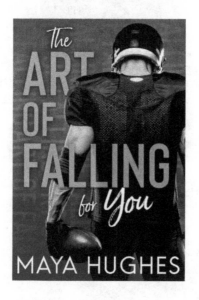

The Sin of Kissing You

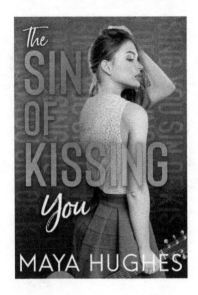

The Hate of Loving You

AUTHOR'S NOTE

Phew! That was a little tense :-) Those two are going to have so much fun in their book! But back to this book. Nix and Elle were another chance for me to dive deeper into the friendships and loves of the Fulton U guys. Their discovery of what's most important to them and finding that in their relationship as well as for what they want to do in their lives.

College is such a crazy time where there are so many things we're expected to do that it can be hard to focus on what we want to do. Even now, with college long past in the rearview mirror, I still find myself asking what I want to be when I grow up.

We're all on a path and sometimes it's hard to jump off that path, even when we know it's not right for us anymore. I've been there and feel free to shoot me a message if this book connected with you in the same way.

Thank you so much for reading and spending time with the guys! I can't tell you how much it means to me that you're on this journey with me. Every book hits home for me with the journeys my characters are going through and I love each one of them.

I have Berk and Jules' story on deck next. After which,

we'll be back to the Kings with Colm's book. I know you want it. I've gotten so many messages about his story and it's the beautiful one he deserves. While many of you have figured out who his heroine will be, I still want to leave that as a surprise until you dive into his story.

Thank you again for reading and feel free to leave a review letting other readers what you thought, if you have a moment.

Maya xx

EXCERPT FROM SHAMELESS KING

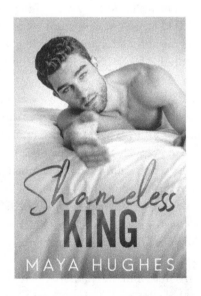

Declan - Prom

The Rittenhouse Prep prom committee had gone all out again this year. Limos and luxury cars lined the entrance to the building. Those cars cost more than my house was worth, but you couldn't tell that from the way people called out our names as we walked by. Me and the guys who'd had my back since our first practice together freshman year, The Kings, were State Champions—again.

I'd been to every prom since freshman year. It seemed even senior girls had no problem being seen on the arm of a freshman, as long as it was me. The thumping of the music guided us through the entrance of the building with a slightly fishy smell. Being right on the water, the building had a distinct salt-and-sea tinge to the air.

My rented tux fit well. Working my magic, I'd done a deal with the shop. Told people where I got mine from, and the shop rented it to me and had it altered for free. It was a pretty sweet deal. I figured if I was going to be uncomfortable in the thing, at least I'd look good.

And from the way heads turned as we walked in, I knew I did. Lots of guys walked in with their custom tuxes, but I didn't care because all eyes were on me and the rest of the Kings. Rittenhouse Prep Kings and state hockey champions in the flesh. People on the dance floor clapped and cheered when we came in through the double doors of the ballroom.

"Declan!" Someone whooped from a few tables away. A bunch of woo-hoos and Kings' chants later and we could finally leave our spot at the door. If Ford got any redder, he'd be ready to explode. He tugged at his collar. They'd had to special order his tux. But he had that strong silent thing chicks went wild for. Jet black hair, serious scowl that melted away in an instant. He hated the attention; that was fine. I could soak up more than enough for all of us.

The warm buzz from the pre-prom drinks we'd had at Emmett's meant I was feeling good. Nothing too crazy. We didn't want to get kicked out, but just enough to kick up the fun a notch.

"What did I tell you? We don't need dates." I grinned, and my eyes swept over a few of the more plunging necklines of some of the dresses our fellow students wore. We moved through the room, and people's heads turned as we walked past some classmates already seated. High fives were doled out for all of us as we strolled by.

"Declan, guys, this way, I'll show you to the table." One of the bubbly juniors rushed up to us and looped her arm around Heath's, tugging him forward. I rolled my eyes. Heath never had to bat an eyelash to get the women to fawn all over him. Blond hair worked for guys as well. He was easy to spot with the surfer look on the East Coast.

"We took the liberty of putting your tent cards on the table already. We didn't want you to have to find your names." She had a mountain of blonde hair piled up on top of her head. The curls were so tight it looked like she could bounce around on her head like Tigger.

Our spot was a prime location in the center of the ten-seater tables dotted around the dance floor.

"I have a feeling we're going to be dancing a lot," Ford grumbled, elbowing Colm as he took his seat. He looked as uncomfortable as I felt. The fabric of his tux was stretched to its limit on his shoulders—if he wasn't a gentle giant, who'd mastered the art of chilling the fuck out, I'd swear he was ready to Hulk out at any second.

"Don't worry, big guy; I'm happy to intercept any dance requests someone might throw your way." I lifted my glass of water to him as a toast.

Colm slid his flask across to my lap, and my eyes got wide. He was our resident mischief maker lately. Having your life thrown into chaos had a way of making people act not quite like themselves. Emmett by far got into the most trouble out of all of us, but with his parents' power and influence he never really had to worry about the consequences. Heath, Ford, and I were scholarship kids who knew how to toe the line. "Is this the older brother breaking all the rules?" I covered my mouth in fake outrage.

"Shut up. Olivia's not here, so what she doesn't know won't hurt her." Colm had become the guardian of his younger sister when their parents died earlier that year in a car accident. He'd always taken on the protector role, but that had gone into hyperdrive now that Olivia relied on him.

I drained the water and put my glass under the table, pouring some of the vodka into it.

"Declan, can I have a dance later?" A girl, Hannah—or was it Anna?—asked as she passed by on the arm of her date.

I winced and shrugged my shoulders at the guy. *Sorry, dude.* I'd convinced the guys to go solo. Well, except for Emmett. He'd of course brought, Avery. They'd been joined at the hip since sophomore year. But Heath, Ford, and Colm were by my side at our table. Blue light skated over the room from the massive fish tank that took up one entire wall.

Not many people got to say they had their prom at an aquarium. A group of other students crowded around one end of the tank where a fish that looked almost as big as Emmett hung near the glass. All it was missing was the giant bushy beard.

This was one of our last nights all together. The prom, the big pep rally, a final blow out at Emmett's, and then we were all off to college. Bittersweet in a way. Leaving most of the guys behind. Heath and I would be playing locally at the University of Philadelphia. Colm and Ford would be up in Boston, and Emmett was being cagey with his plans for next year.

A few hors d'oeuvres and a shot from the flask later, and the prom was really in full swing. Emmett arrived with Avery on his arm, beaming like he always was whenever she was near him. Dude had it so bad and he didn't even care. We didn't even give him shit about it anymore, that was just how it was. Avery meant everything to him, made sense when you had parents as shitty as his.

The room heated up, and I shrugged off my jacket, draping it over the back of my chair, ready to get back on the dance floor. While most people would have expected everyone to be uptight, it seemed that the dim lighting and fish as an audience meant everyone was ready to show off their moves.

"Holy shit!" someone behind me said, and my gaze darted all over the place to figure out what they were talking about.

I'd been hit in the chest with a puck before, but nothing quite compared to this feeling. Across the room, standing in front of the entrance, was a breathtaking sight. I don't remember what the hell color her dress was, all I knew was I couldn't take my eyes off her.

She stood there fidgeting with the small bag in her hands and glanced around the room.

"Wow, looks like the Ice Queen has finally thawed out a bit."

A slight murmur rippled through the people around me. My stomach dropped as my mind whirred trying to place her. And like a slow motion reveal, Makenna Halstead slid those horn-rimmed glasses she'd worn every second I'd ever seen her back on.

Avery spotted her and raced across the room, wrapping her arms around an incredibly uncomfortable-looking Makenna. It was like now that she knew all eyes were on her, she couldn't handle the pressure.

It wasn't just the glasses that were missing. It was also the telltale bun and the talk-to-me-and-I'll-kill-you stare. Normally, she walked with her shoulders square and a stomp that could shatter bone. I'd never seen her look so...nice.

She bit her bottom lip. It was the first time I'd ever seen

her look unsure. I'd have never thought her barely straw-berry-blonde hair was that long, since she always wore it up. She also swore up and down that dances and other stuff like this were a waste of time, so seeing her here had taken my brain at least a little while to piece it together.

Avery dragged her over to our table. We had a couple seats free. Mak gave the table a small wave.

"No, you're not wearing those tonight. You don't need them." Avery tugged the glasses off her face and shoved them back in her bag.

"Actually, I kind of do." Makenna reached for the bag as Avery smacked her hands away.

"Nope! I'm sure one of these strapping young men would be happy to lead you around like your very own seeing-eye stud if you do need to go anywhere."

The corners of her mouth turned down, but this time her lips were all soft and shiny. Deep pink brought out the full-ness I'd never seen before. I shook my head. This was Mak the Ice Queen we were talking about.

She sat on a seat beside Ford, who seemed completely content to be sitting beside someone who was also happy doing her best mute impersonation.

"If you don't dance to at least five songs tonight, I swear I'm tanking our final project on purpose."

Mak gasped, like a real-life hand-to-chest gasp in horror at Avery even suggesting it.

"They would never find your body, Avery." Mak grinned up at her with her arms crossed over her chest.

I laughed into my napkin, and Mak turned her glare on me.

"I'm sure Emmett would. He's like a bloodhound when it comes to me." Right on time Emmett slid his arms around her waist and planted his nose in her neck, letting out a sniff loud enough for everyone to hear.

"I smell someone who needs to get out there and dance." Emmett led Avery away from the table. Avery held out her hand, flashing a five at Mak over and over. I grabbed the flask from the spot Colm had stashed it and had another drink.

A long, slender hand slid its way down over my shoulder, stopping at my chest. "You promised me a dance." The smell from Anna's hot breath against my neck told me we weren't the only ones who'd snuck in a little booze tonight. It was not a good smell on her, and my skin crawled. Out of the corner of my eye, I caught the pissed-off face of her date. I did not want to have a fight tonight.

"Listen, I'm sorry. I would, but I already promised Mak a dance, and you know how she gets when she can't get what she wants, and it looks like tonight she wants me."

Mak's eyes got as wide as saucers, and her mouth hung open. Slipping out of the grasp of the date-ditcher, I rounded the table and held out my hand to Mak.

Glancing behind me at the very pissed-off Hannah or Anna and her even more pissed-off date, Mak perhaps sized up the situation and didn't want to be in the middle of a whirlwind of haymakers or thrown drinks, so she took my hand. A small jolt shot straight up my arm the second my skin touched hers. It was that same feeling you got standing in line for concessions at a movie you'd been waiting for forever. I shook my head. This was Mak we were talking about, and she didn't look one bit affected by my fingers wrapped around her.

"And tonight I want you?" She lifted an eyebrow at me as we walked out onto the dance floor with the corners of her mouth turned up the tiniest bit.

"I improvised. I know how people get when they don't get a piece of me." I grinned at her, but she just rolled her eyes.

"Probably for the best. Hannah can be a real bitch when she doesn't get what she wants, which probably means Edgar is in for a rough night. Poor guy." She glanced back over her shoulder to a very irate Hannah standing with her arms crossed over her chest.

People parted out of the way to give us some room. The moderately fast-paced song switched up to a slow one almost as soon as we found our spot.

We stood there staring at each other. I took a step forward, and Mak hesitated before looping her arms around my neck. The sensation was back now and worse than before. Staring down into Mak's eyes, I really saw them for the first time. They were the brightest blue I'd ever seen. Maybe it was the room or a trick of the lights, but I'd never seen so many blues in one spot.

It was the soft stroke of her fingers along the hair at the nape of my neck that made my hands tighten on her waist. The way she stared into my eyes, I don't even know if she realized she was doing it. Like her hands had a mind of their own, trying to soak up a little bit more of me. And I figured that was how she felt because my fingers had the same idea as I pulled her in tighter against me. Her lips parted, and her eyelashes fluttered.

The thud of my heart pounded as we moved to our own rhythm under the dim lights at the center of a sea of people. Electricity buzzed through my body, but I knew it wasn't just the vodka. It was all to do with the woman in my arms who usually drove me up a wall.

"I don't think I've ever seen you without your glasses before."

"I don't think I've ever seen you in a tux before." Her pink tongue darted out to lick her bottom lip. The wetness left behind drew my gaze to it, and I wanted to have my own sample of her lips.

"You've never been to prom before." My hands pressed into the small of her back, closing the tiniest of gaps that had been between us. *Why did she feel so good in my arms?* The blues and greens from the fish tank washed over us like a spell had been cast and we were living in our own little underwater bubble.

"Almost didn't come to this one."

"Why not?" I leaned my head back, savoring the trail her fingertip blazed along the base of my neck.

She never let herself have any fun. Normally, it also meant no one else could have any fun and it irked the shit out of me, but tonight I just wanted to hold her close on the dance floor all night.

"It's not really my thing, but I figured it's a rite of passage and all, so I decided to come." She shrugged her shoulders.

"I'm glad you did."

Even with the pretense of her helping me out of a dance with the devil—aka Hannah—gone, we stayed out there through a string of slow songs. At least I think they were slow songs; our tempo didn't change. It was the first time we'd probably had a civil conversation with each other in years. So weird that it would happen now. It was like one of those high school movies I swore I never watched, but I had at least a few times, where the big thing happened between the two nemeses.

My head dipped down slightly. It was like the warning sirens blaring on a submarine. My blood pounded in my veins, and I needed to taste her lips like I needed my next breath. It was an uncontrolled dive, and I didn't know exactly what I was doing, but she wasn't pulling back. She wasn't pushing her hands against me or cocking her hand back for a slap; if anything, she leaned in even more.

Her eyes almost fluttered closed as my lips parted, so close to hers. Her body went stiff, and her eyes snapped open wide. "Are you drunk?" She pushed back in my arms.

I let them drop. "No, I'm not drunk. I've had a couple

drinks, but that's it." I took a step toward her, and she took a step back.

Before I could say anything else, a booming voice came out over the squealing PA. "And now it's time to announce our prom king and queen." One of the prom committee girls grabbed me by the arm. "We need you up front, Declan."

With a strength I didn't think someone of her size could possess, she pushed me from the middle of the dance floor. I glanced behind me at a stone-faced Mak with her arms crossed over her chest. She was back at our table and had her glasses back on her face. Things were back just how they'd always been.

The bright lights hanging from the ceiling shined in my face as they went through whatever the hell they were doing up onstage. I kept my eyes on Mak with the corners of my mouth turned down as she slowly made her way toward the double doors.

"And this year's prom king is Declan McAvoy!" Someone placed a crown on my head, and everyone cheered. The doors closed behind Mak, and I couldn't help but feel like that was the end to something. The end of something that hadn't even really started. But I know one thing. If I'd known how long it would be until I got to hold her again, I'd have held on a bit longer.

———

If you'd love to know more about Declan and Mak's history it all starts in SHAMELESS KING!

Enemies to lovers has never felt so good!

Declan McAvoy. Voted Biggest Flirt. Highest goal scorer in Kings of Rittenhouse Prep history.

Everyone's impressed, well except one person…

I can't deny it. I want her. More than I ever thought I could want a woman. I've got one semester–only four months–to convince her everything she thought about me was wrong.

Will my queen let me prove to her I'm the King she can't live without?

Only one way to find out...

One-click SHAMELESS KING now!

ACKNOWLEDGMENTS

Where do I start?! Thank you for picking up this book and letting Nix and Elle into your heart.

I want to thank my editing team, Tamara Mayata, Caitlin Marie and Sarah. Without you all this wouldn't be just as amazing as the story that plays out in my head.

I wanted to thank every blogger, bookstagrammer, and reader for sharing all the news about these two as we lead up to the release. Your energy helped kick my butt when I needed it to get everything as perfect as possible.

It really means so much to me that you've taken the time to share and talk about how one of my books has brought all the feels, made you want to throw your kindle or needed a cold shower afterward.

And I can't wait for you to read it! <3

Maya xx

ALSO BY MAYA HUGHES

Fulton U

The Perfect First - First Time/Friends to Lovers Romance

The Third Best Thing

The Fourth Time Charm

The Fulton U Trilogy

The Art of Falling for You

The Sin of Kissing You

The Hate of Loving You

Kings of Rittenhouse

Kings of Rittenhouse - FREE

Shameless King - Enemies to Lovers

Reckless King - Off Limits Lover

Ruthless King - Second Chance Romance

Fearless King - Brother's Best Friend Romance

Heartless King - Accidental Pregnancy

CONNECT WITH MAYA

Sign up for my newsletter to get exclusive bonus content, ARC opportunities, sneak peeks, new release alerts and to find out just what I'm books are coming up next.

Join my reader group for teasers, giveaways and more!

Follow my Amazon author page for new release alerts!

Follow me on Instagram, where I try and fail to take pretty pictures!

Follow me on Twitter, just because :)

I'd love to hear from you! Drop me a line anytime :)
https://www.mayahughes.com/
maya@mayahughes.com